CONTENTS

WHAT'S BEST FOR HELENA	1
PROLOGUE	2
CHAPTER ONE	7
CHAPTER TWO	19
CHAPTER THREE	33
CHAPTER FOUR	70
CHAPTER FIVE	89
CHAPTER SIX	110
CHAPTER SEVEN	127
CHAPTER EIGHT	147
CHAPTER NINE	157
CHAPTER TEN	176
CHAPTER ELEVEN	198
CHAPTER TWELVE	218
CHAPTER THIRTEEN	241
CHAPTER FOURTEEN	257
CHAPTER FIFTEEN	274
CHAPTER SIXTEEN	303
CHAPTER SEVENTEEN	325
CHAPTER EIGHTEEN	360
CHAPTER NINETEEN	380

CHAPTER TWENTY	390
EPILOGUE	430

WHAT'S BEST FOR HELENA

Michelle J Nagy

PROLOGUE

Kelly Phillips glanced at her watch, the time showing almost 11.30. With her feet aching from dancing the best part of the night in her new stiletto shoes, had thoroughly enjoyed her close friend Sue's engagement party, only too aware that she would pay the price the next day with a few blisters to her toes which were already beginning to feel sore. Wearing her new purple sequined dress with the daringly low back bought in town earlier in the day especially for the occasion had been determined to look at her very best. The colour of her dress complimented her dark, naturally curly hair piled stylishly high on her head and also brought out the violet shades of her eyes.

Amazed at how quickly the evening had flown by, she helped herself to some of the remaining food from the buffet table, a few sausage rolls on a plate along with some crisps on offer, just waiting to be eaten. She knew it wasn't going to be doing any favours for her figure, but told herself this was a special occasion.

Kelly glanced over to Lee, who was standing in the far corner of the room, having a drink with her brother Bob.

Seeing her look towards him, he gave a wave and with that smile that always made her heart miss a beat, quickly turned away shyly, glad that the room was mostly in darkness and nobody would see her blushing. For most of the evening she would notice him glancing her way, but felt more than a little disappointed with all the excitement of the celebrations she never had much of a chance to spend time with him. How she would have loved him to come over and ask her to dance, but she was either mingling with the other guests or he was chatting with his mates.

With the music moving to a slower pace with Chris de Burgh's famous song, *The Lady in Red*, couples moved on to the dancefloor, slipping into each other's arms, dancing slowly to the timeless melody. Lost deeply in her thoughts, Kelly stirred as she felt a tap to her shoulder. Turning around, her heart skipped a beat as she looked into those dark twinkling eyes that never ceased to fascinate her.

'Well, someone has to stop you from finishing the rest of the food,' Lee said teasingly with a smile, as he took the paper plate gently from her hand, and placing it on a nearby table before leading her to the dance floor. She was certain he must have felt her heart racing wildly as he held her closely, suddenly feeling painfully shy, which was silly considering she had known him for just over three years.

'Have you enjoyed this evening?' Kelly asked trying to make conversation.

'Yes, it's been pretty good and always nice to see a few familiar faces all in one place.'

'Don't you think Sue and Barry make a great couple? I thought we'd have to wait until the end of the century for those two to finally think about tying the knot!'

'Hmm, yes, about time.' He looked deeply into her eyes appearing to be more interested in her than their conversation. 'You do realise you're wearing the wrong dress?'

She looked up to him with a confused frown creasing her forehead. *'Pardon?'* It was true the bold style wasn't one she would have normally gone for and although she chose it to mainly please herself, felt more than a little disappointed at his reaction as had so wanted to impress him.

Seeing that he'd hurt her unintentionally, Lee gently cupped her chin with his hand looking at her apologetically. 'Sorry, as usual I'm rubbish at making myself clear. What I *meant* to say was although you look sensationally hot in purple, you should be wearing *red* for this dance.'

Realising the feeble attempt of his joke, suddenly gave a peal of laughter, dissolving away any nervousness she'd felt earlier. 'Oh, Lee Fisher, you are such a tease!' As they continued to dance, looked to each other in amusement, when the next song to play was *Purple Rain*. Her body seemed to melt as she felt his arms gently enfolding her closer still as he whispered into her ear. 'Actually, you look absolutely stunning, that colour really does suit you.'

She relaxed in his arms as they continued to move in time to the music, so glad that she'd decided not to leave a bit earlier as had originally planned. Together they danced through the slower songs that followed in companionable silence until midnight with Lee holding her tenderly as she gently rested her face against his cheek. Kelly couldn't remember feeling this happy in such a long time, wishing this moment could last forever.

As the last song came to its end, Lee looked into her eyes with such an intensity she felt her heart couldn't possibly beat any faster. Gently, he held her chin as their lips touched. As the kiss intensified she responded by placing her arms around his neck, not caring who might be watching them. The moment ended abruptly as he released her.

'Sorry, I...I have to go,' he told her looking as equally flustered as she was feeling. 'My taxi will be waiting - I'll see you at work on Monday.'

She stood rooted to the dance floor, her body feeling as if it had turned to jelly with a great feeling of disappointment tearing through her, watching as he walked swiftly towards the exit without looking back, even forgetting to take his jacket with him.

CHAPTER ONE

Lee turned down the volume of the radio as he pulled up in his van by the small convenience store, in the village of Little Green. He was feeling tired, having spent most of the day delivering parcels around his home town of Old Church. With the time fast approaching 4.30, he still had one more delivery to complete, before returning to the Fast Link depot.

Having delivered around there for the best part of three years, he pretty much knew the area like the back of his hand, but was having difficulty in finding a property called The Woodlands. Why couldn't these people have house numbers like everybody else, he thought as he gave a deep sigh. Looking again, he could see it was a Next Day delivery, where the customer had paid extra money to receive their goods on time. Had it not been so urgent and were probably tracking their delivery every five minutes, would have gladly taken it back to the Depot to leave for the following day.

Helping himself to a sweet from his pocket, Lee thought back to Saturday night with Kelly. Why did he have to kiss her in that way and build her hopes up? He'd known for some time the way she felt about him, because her sister-in-law Carol had dropped enough hints. The truth was that he found her very attractive and happened to be one of the best friends he'd ever had. After all the things he'd gone through, she'd been so supportive and sympathetic, seeing him through some of the darkest moments of his life. With her cheerful and optimistic nature, had helped him to slowly pick up the pieces, making him see that life could still be good.

Kelly was a beautiful and loving woman, and Lee knew only too well she also had experienced more than her fair share of heartbreak. But the truth was he didn't want to have any commitments, not after Miranda, only to have his fingers burned again. Knowing she wasn't the kind of person to be content with just a casual no strings arrangement, had far too much respect for both herself and her brother Bob, who also worked for Fast Link as a delivery driver. It was through Bob providing him with some training when he began his employment with the company, that he was first introduced to Kelly who worked there as a senior customer services adviser. It was clear from the first day they met that there was a chemistry developing between them and within a short space of time they became close friends.

Feeling increasingly tired and thirsty, he looked towards the small convenience store that provided for the villagers of

Little Green. Of course, why hadn't he thought of this before, Madge the owner was sure to know?

'Hi my love, how's it going?' greeted the plump middle-aged woman as he came through the doorway.

'Hi Madge, not bad thanks,' he called as he helped himself to a bottle of cola from the refrigerator and a Kit Kat bar from the shelf.

'Are they keeping you busy?'

'Not half - I'll sleep well tonight, that's for sure!' Lee replied with that boyish grin she found so appealing. 'Everybody's decided to start ordering stuff for the summer holidays,' he added.

Madge shook her head in disbelief. 'It's only April, for goodness sake!'

'Customers tend to order early to make sure they have their stuff in good time.'

'Hmm, I see what you mean,' she said, running up Lee's purchases on the till.

'Actually, there's one thing I wanted to ask you,' he said thoughtfully, combing his fingers through his thick dark brown hair.' You don't happen to know where The Woodlands is situated? I've been driving around in circles for the past ten minutes and getting nowhere fast - even the Satnav's unable to work it out. I'm sure I've never come across it before, and I know this village like the back of my hand.'

She rubbed her small, plump hands together, a small frown creasing her forehead in concentration.

'The Woodlands...oh yes of course, The Woodlands! That's where Jess Cowlie cleans. Oh, no wonder you couldn't find it, it's not actually in Little Green, though the address probably comes under the village. It's a big posh house - you go down the main road, bear right, look to your left. The place is surrounded by trees and that's why you can't see it from the road. But if you look carefully you'll you see an unmarked driveway. It's just up there.'

Making a mental note of Madge's directions he walked towards the exit. 'Ah, yes, I think I know where you're on about. Great, now I can finally get that blasted parcel delivered and knock off home - I'm shattered!'

'Are you doing anything interesting tonight?'

'No,' he said with a twinge of regret, remembering this was meant to be his evening of badminton with Kelly. 'Just having my pizza delivery, putting my feet up and seeing what's on Netflix.'

Madge shook her head in disbelief. 'What's a handsome young man like you doing staying at home? I wouldn't have thought you'd have a shortage of young ladies waiting to be asked out on a date.'

"Fraid so,' he grinned sheepishly.

'Well, if I didn't have my Stan and I was thirty years younger, I would soon jump at the chance!' She laughed loudly, her small plump round face turning pink with pleasure. Indeed, she would have done; she was sure that this handsome young man, with his mop of brown-black hair and those twinkling eyes, had broken many hearts. Almost every day he would pop into the shop, wearing that navy uniform and hi viz jacket, over his tall well-toned body. Not only was he a looker, he had such a lovely way about him. Come along Madge, she thought to herself, you're more than old enough to be his mum.

'Thanks Madge,' he called as he left the shop. 'I'll probably see you tomorrow.'

With Madge's clear instructions, he was sure that he would have no problem at all in finding The Woodlands.

As he drove along he soon came to the unmarked drive. Seeing that the large black wrought iron security gate was open, Lee drove slowly along the long, winding cobblestone driveway, cutting through a neatly manicured lawn surrounded by a variety of fir trees and evergreen shrubs dotted on either side. He came to a large Georgian style house, which he had never been able to see from the road. He whistled to himself in admiration as it became obvious to him that this was a very exclusive kind of place, owned by people with some serious money. This would certainly be the sort of place he would buy if he ever came up on the lottery.

As he opened the back of the van to retrieve the parcel, he began to hear a dog barking and saw a Golden Retriever running over from a doorway at the side of the house.

Blast, he thought to himself, feeling his heart race with fear. It was hardly six months since a dog had bitten him on his delivery round, and it was an experience he would never forget. As he was making a delivery to a customer, an Alsatian dog came running out of the house and bit his leg. The wound he received was deep and needed a few stitches. The woman who owned the dog didn't even have the grace to apologise, explaining that the Alsatian thought he was the postman, and hated men in uniform.'

As he was about to jump into the van to protect himself, a voice suddenly shouted, 'Rupert!' The dog turned back and went running excitedly towards a young petite woman following close by. As it jumped up her excitedly, she suddenly lost her balance, falling on to the cobble driveway with her head making a sickening thud as she fell to the ground. Placing the parcel back in the van, Lee quickly rushed to her aid, as she lay there, looking dazed.

'Are you ok?' he asked anxiously. Slowly she sat up as he

put his arm around the back of her shoulders. Feeling the back of her head, she nodded, her eyes open wide in surprise.

'I...I just feel a little shaken, that's all,' she whispered softly, and smiling to reassure him that she was indeed unharmed. She spoke so nicely he thought, taking hold of her small hand that felt so soft and smooth as she slowly stood up from the ground.

He couldn't help but notice how beautiful she was, with her eyes a dark blue, fringed with long dark lashes that made a stark contrast to the long honey-blonde hair framed around her heart-shaped face.

'Thank you.' She whispered, before looking towards her dog reproachfully and patting him on the head. 'Rupert, you are such a naughty boy!' The retriever rewarded her with a lick to her hand as if to beg for his mistress's forgiveness.

'He won't hurt you, I promise,' she smiled, sensing Lee's nervousness.

Realising how foolish he must be appearing to this attractive young woman, he also stroked the dog.

He smiled apologetically. 'Oh, it's all right. It's just a few months since I'd got bitten by a dog and it's not something I'm likely to forget in a hurry.'

'Oh, I am sorry, but Rupert is such a big softy - he would only know how to lick you. See... he likes you.'

There was a moment's silence as they looked into each other's eyes. She was so incredibly beautiful, so young, and so innocent, especially when compared to...

'Helena!' A voice cried out in the distance. He looked back towards the house where stood a tall, slim elderly, rather distinguished looking man sporting a white beard.

'It's ok, Daddy,' she smiled reassuringly. Rupert knocked me over and this gentleman helped me up.'

Her father didn't seem impressed as he walked over.

'Are you sure you're all right, my dear?' He asked anxiously, examining his daughter's head, almost behaving as if Lee wasn't there.

'Daddy!' For goodness sake, don't make such a fuss! It was just a slight knock. I'm fine - honestly.'

He looked towards Lee as if noticing him for the first time. He peered over his spectacles, his expression looking rather disapproving. 'Can I be of help?'

'I have a package for a Professor Broadhurst that needs to be signed for.'

'I *am* Professor Broadhurst. Could I please have the parcel, I'm in rather a hurry.'

If you could please sign here, sir,' he asked handing the delivery scanner to the elderly man, thinking he seemed every bit the Professor with his cultured accent and short pointed beard on the end of his chin.

'It's quite a heavy package for its size. Would you like...'

'No that's quite all right,' the professor replied shortly, taking the parcel, which came from some Japanese company called *Matsushita*, from Lee's hands. 'I can manage. Hmm, I was expecting another item as well. The blasted thing will probably arrive tomorrow when we're out. Helena, your mother has made your tea - it'll be getting cold.'

'Thank you for rescuing me from Rupert,' she said with a broad smile.

Lee gave a mock salute. 'Anytime!'

As he drove off down the driveway, Helena continued to watch him until he disappeared from view, then turned to her father who reappeared from the back of the house.

'Daddy, was there really any need to be so rude? He was only being polite - what should he have done? Just leave my lying on the ground and thrown the parcel to me?'

The Professor's face softened. 'Now, now young lady, I'm only trying to take care of you, as a father should.' He looked closely at the back of her head where she had fallen then nodded his approval.

'No, I don't think there's any damage. Come along, shall we see what Uncle Ian's been doing in the lab?'

Back at Fast Link, Kelly had almost finished her work

for the day. She'd had such a busy Monday, with endless amounts of typing, from letters of apology to dealing with irate customers on the phone. The best part of the afternoon had been taken up by minute-taking taking during a disciplinary, where a driver had been suspended having been caught stealing parcels. Unsurprisingly the driver had been dismissed, as most delivery companies have zero tolerance of this offence. During the day she had found it hard to concentrate on her work after the events of the previous Saturday and still felt as if she was in a dream. Lee had finally kissed her. She'd felt for some time that he more than just liked her but wasn't sure why he would never take their relationship to the next level.

Of course, she knew just about everything there was to know about Miranda from their evenings out, and how she did the dirty on him. Kelly had broken up with Eric around the same time and finding that they had a common interest, would often go out for a drink together, sometimes a meal, and console each other. Over the time, she realised that she felt more than just friendship towards Lee, and was certain that something had changed for him too. She saw the look in his eyes, the way he laughed at her terrible jokes, but for some reason things had never happened. Sue, her colleague and best friend, could see the signs and often asked the same question.

Why didn't he take things further?

'Perhaps it's time for you to take charge of things,' her friend had suggested only days before the engagement party. 'He obviously likes you and enjoys your company. You two are practically a couple apart from the sex bit. Invite him over to your place for a romantic meal and take the initiative.

Kelly shook her head, closing her eyes with a frown. 'Sorry, but that's just not my style. I know a lot of the girls do ask the guys out these days, but I guess I'm just too old fashioned in that respect. I reckon if he was truly interested in me in that way then he would have done something by now. Maybe I'm just misreading the signs. He probably just looks on me as his mate's kid sister who's just there for a good laugh.'

'I think you're wrong there,' said Sue smiling knowingly as she checked over her spreadsheet on the PC monitor. 'Those looks and all the attention he gives you suggests to me more than just a platonic relationship.'

Kelly came back to the present with a smile on her face, realising her friend had been right after all. Remembering how he kissed her so longingly on her lips, still sent her heart racing, and the way she responded. But why did he suddenly leave the way he did, as if he'd made a terrible mistake? She hoped he might call her over the weekend to explain; after all they were meant to be playing badminton tonight. She guessed that was still on, but never got the chance to speak to him when she came to work as he'd already left for his delivery round. Earlier in the day she left him a voicemail to say she'd brought the jacket he'd left behind on Saturday to the office for him to collect.

Suddenly her thoughts were interrupted as the door to her office was opened and in came Lee, his brown eyes looking at her intently with a deeply troubled look etched on his handsome face.

She felt her face flush, knowing she had probably turned bright red as she thought back to the weekend. 'Hi. What… what sort of day did you have? I've had an absolutely manic Monday and…'

Ignoring her small talk, he got straight to the point. 'Sorry Kelly, I won't be able to make it tonight. I've had a really hectic day, so I need to have an early night. I'm sorry Kelly, but I think it's for the best.'

Feeling stunned, she watched as he quietly left the office, taking his jacket from the coat stand in the corner. He closed the door firmly behind him, closing the door on her and to what had happened between them, leaving her feeling cold, hurt and completely confused.

CHAPTER TWO

Kelly sat with Sue at the Adam & Eve pub that evening after giving her friend a call.

'Thanks for coming along, I know it's short notice, but I just didn't know what else to do.'

'You don't have to explain,' Sue assured her, taking a sip of her Bacardi and coke. 'Barry's having his judo lesson tonight and there's nothing worth watching on the box.' She shook her head in disbelief. 'I just can't understand what's got into Lee - this is so out of character.'

Kelly looked around the pub which was unsurprisingly quiet for a Monday. The dance music played from the jukebox whilst a young couple sat at the bar, the woman, probably in her early twenties, tapping her feet in time to the music. At one of the other tables an elderly couple sat, waiting for their meal to arrive.

Catching the smell of onions wafting through from the kitchen, Kelly knew it wouldn't be too long to wait for their meals to be served. She took a sip of her white wine, her expression uncharacteristically grim.

'I think it must have been the drink talking on Saturday.

What else could it be? He would have made a move on me long before now. Once he'd sobered up, he probably realised he'd made a terrible mistake.'

Her friend wasn't so convinced. 'I know I was wrapped up with things to do with the engagement and was all over the place speaking to everybody, but even I could see he wasn't that drunk. If I remember right, he probably only had about three pints. I saw those crafty looks he gave you when you were mingling with friends.

They stopped talking as Kay the landlady arrived with their meals. Sue's steak, with onion rings that still sizzled hot on the plate, her eyes wide in eager anticipation as she hadn't had a bite to eat since lunchtime. Although Kelly's only food since breakfast had been a packet of cheese and onion crisps, the large serving of scampi and chips, which lay before her, did nothing to whet her appetite.

Sue looked at her friend sympathetically. 'Come on get it down you - no man is worth wasting away over.'

Kelly smiled at her friend as she picked up her knife and fork. Despite the extra weight Sue gained since meeting Barry, she still looked as attractive as ever with her curvaceous body. With her light blonde hair styled into a fashionable bob which flattered her round face, and the most amazing almond-shaped brown eyes, definitely her best feature, was gifted with a smile that would melt the coldest of hearts.

Changing the subject, Kelly reluctantly poured a sachet of tartar source over her food and stabbed her fork into the scampi. 'So, next year in August, you'll be Mrs Susan Field.'

She nodded happily gazing at the solitaire engagement ring on her finger. 'I still can't believe after five years we're finally tying the knot! I know we took our time, but we've had some great moments along the way - taking some fantastic holidays, going just about everywhere and enjoying ourselves. But now we're on the property ladder, we felt the time was right to settle down and start a family.'

Something I will never have, thought Kelly grimly. Time wasn't exactly on her side as she approached her 36th birthday. Sue being two years her senior, had no such worry - she had got her man and after the wedding, they could soon get down to the pleasurable task of making babies!

'There's still time for you,' Sue grinned, reading her friend's thoughts as she studied her downbeat expression. 'A lot of women start families later these days, you know. Just look at Madonna, she's a shining example of a woman who knew how to juggle children with her career.'

'Guess it helps when you have millions stashed away in the bank,' Kelly responded with a wry smile. 'It's not having the children that bothers me, just a good decent man who knows how to treat me with respect.'

'That's what I thought you almost had until Mr Knight-In-Shining-Armour decided to throw a wobbly. Talking of such, Jason Hughes who delivers to Stevenage has really got it badly for you. Fancy turning him down for a dance! It might've made Lee jealous, given him that spur to have you.'

Kelly wiped her face with her paper napkin, trying to stifle a giggle. 'Some things just cannot be done in the name of love! I'm sure Jason's a lovely person really, but the thought of him smooching with that bad breath and greasy hair is just a bit more than I can bear. Lee would think I'm desperate!'

Sue nodded in agreement. 'I had to invite him along. Couldn't have him feeling left out, but I know what you mean. He's so patronising and he could so do with a good scrub-up - maybe then he might have a chance of meeting somebody.' Sue looked at Kelly thoughtfully as she cut into her tender steak. 'You'll find somebody one day too - I promise. I don't want to make your head swell but you're a downright attractive woman even though you don't believe it. I know a few of the drivers who would give a month's wages to take you out.' She looked at her friend intensely. 'Don't let what happened with that loser Eric put you off forever - they're not all made that way.

Kelly thought back to three years ago, just before Lee came to work at Fast Track. She had been with Eric for two years and he had not long moved into her flat. At the beginning they had been very happy together, even though he found it difficult to keep a job down; he revealed that he had issues dealing with authority. She was enchanted by his cheerful disposition and charisma, as well as well as his dark, good looks and the way people warmed to him. Even though her parents grew very fond of him over time, for some reason her older brother Bob could never take to him.

Maybe it's only when you live with somebody that you really get to know them, she reflected with sadness. Why didn't she see the signs? The way they stopped doing things together as a couple, going out for a drink, meeting up with mutual friends? More and more frequently he would go out during the evenings to meet his friend Andy and would find an excuse not to take her. Then things started to go wrong in the bedroom too when Eric said he was too tired after a busy day at work.

Things came to a head, when feeling completely fed up being stuck in the flat alone while her boyfriend was out enjoying his own social life, arranged an evening out with Bob's wife, Carol. Bob had agreed to look after the kids whilst the two women decided to go out for a meal at the new Italian restaurant which had just opened up in town.

Their desserts were just being served after a delicious main meal, washed down with a red wine when Andy came in with his girlfriend Julie whom Kelly had met on a few occasions. As soon as they saw her, Andy's face turned a deathly white with Julie staring at her boyfriend with a look of complete shock and horror.

She remembered as she walked over to the table, a red swirling mist appearing before her eyes. '*Where is he?*' she demanded. Andy and Julie looked at each other, not knowing what to say in this difficult situation. 'Hi Kelly,' Andy said sheepishly trying his best to keep the peace. 'Eric couldn't make it - said...said he wasn't feeling too good.'

Feeling completely uncomfortable with the situation, Julie looked down to her menu, nervously playing around with the breadstick on the plate before her.

Kelly felt her heart racing wildly, with her face burning with anger as she challenged Andy, who was unable to look her directly in her eyes. 'And you have *no* idea where he could be? Because he certainly isn't at home!'

He just shook his head, taking a gulp of the beer the waiter had just brought along. 'He...he probably stopped off at the chemist on the way home - he said something about a headache - he was probably going to get some painkillers.'

Kelly looked at him with disbelief. 'Surely you can come up with something better than this, Andy? Why would he need to stop off at a chemist when we keep plenty of pills at home?' Her anger getting the better of her she thumped her fist on the table firmly, startling both of her partner's friends who looked at her as if she was completely insane. 'Could you just try being honest with me and tell me where he really is. Who is *she*?'

'Kelly!' called a voice behind her. She turned slowly round to see Carol standing up from her chair, with an embarrassed look on her face, trying to beckon her over. In her anger she was aware that most of the diners were looking her way and realised that she was causing a scene, with the restaurant falling into silence apart from the music in the background playing *Amore*.

A waiter came over to her looking concerned. 'Is everything all right, *signorina*?' She looked at the middle-aged man, nodding apologetically. Probably the last thing they needed on their opening night was some slanging match taking place. Kelly slowly returned to her sister in law.

She sat back at her table, the customer's resuming their conversations. Carol studied her sister-in-law's troubled face, which was flushed red with anger. She noticed over the past few months that Kelly wasn't her usual happy self and felt that it must have been down to Eric who she didn't particularly care for and Bob had never trusted.

Kelly looked down at her ice cream that had almost melted and didn't have the appetite for anyway, swallowing some of the bitter red wine to steady her nerves.

'Why don't you give him a call? 'There might be some innocent explanation,' suggested Carol, but not feeling at all convinced.

Kelly dug her mobile from her handbag and tried calling a couple of times, but each time went straight on to voice mail. She didn't bother leaving a message. What was the point?

They sat in silence for a few minutes, Carol leaving her sister-in-law to her thoughts. She had suspected that he'd been cheating on Kelly, over the past few months at least. She'd lost count of the number of times Kelly had been left home alone while Eric was supposedly out with his mate Andy, going to the pub or to football matches, even staying away overnight on a job course. None of these stories rang true with neither herself or Bob who said he would deal with him if he found he was messing with his kid sister. But Carol insisted that they shouldn't interfere unless she specifically asked for their help.

Kelly grimaced as she put her phone back in to her handbag after trying in vain for a third time. 'He's cheating on me Carol, that's what he's doing. I've had my suspicions for a while. I've even confronted him with it, but he told me I was being paranoid and I was just being possessive.' She gave a wry smile as she shook her head in disbelief. 'And for a while he convinced me. Well, tonight has just confirmed what I've always suspected.'

Carol took a long sip of her wine. 'Have you any ideas of who he might be seeing? Anyone you might know?'

She shook her head. 'All I know is he spends a lot of time texting. Never says to who, or will never go anywhere without his phone. Even takes it to the bathroom! Sometimes when he received a text he would say that he would have to leave as Andy had some news about a possible job - strange how nothing ever materialised! How I would just love to throttle him!' Kelly added through gritted teeth.

Carol looked at her sister-in-law with pity. She was such a loving and generous person and deserved nothing in the way of what that jerk of a boyfriend had brought on to her.

'Well, I don't know about you, but I don't think I could manage any coffee - besides, I think we've caused enough excitement here on their big opening night. Do you fancy coming over to ours for a while? You know how the kids love having their favourite auntie spoiling them something rotten.'

Kelly shook her head. She wasn't in the mood for company, not even her nephew and niece who she loved so much.

'I've got to sort things out once and for all - I can't carry on like this anymore. When he gets home, he is so going to get it!'

Eric finally arrived back home around midnight which was way past Kelly's bedtime. But she was far too angry to be tired and he was quite surprised to find her sitting on the brown leather sofa watching TV.

She switched off the TV with the remote control, crossing her legs as she watched him intensely. 'Did you have a good night out with Andy?'

Looking cagey as he took off his jacket, which he flung on to the nearby armchair, the strong sickly scent of his aftershave wafting over. 'Yeah, not bad. You're still up? Thought you'd be long gone in the land of nod with your early nights. We went to that new Italian place in town that's just opened. He suddenly took note of the new skinny jeans she was wearing and the fancy red top she'd recently bought. 'So, you been out on the town too?'

She sat up straight, her heart racing and her body shaking with intense anger. 'Yes, actually I was at the new Italian place tonight too with Carol as I was sick to the teeth at the thought of another night in on my own! And you'll never guess who I bumped into? Andy and Julie, looking like they wished the ground would just swallow them up when they saw me!'

He looked up to the ceiling and had the grace to blush,

biting this bottom lip; just where he had a small scar from a fight with someone before they met. Giving out a long-drawn sigh he sat himself down on the armchair. Even at this moment she was aware of his handsome rugged looks. His dark, almost black hair which complemented his olive skin which he owed to his Turkish mother, making a stark contrast to his dark blue eyes. He rubbed the back of his neck. 'So, you felt you had to check up on me? Goodness, Kelly, anybody would think we're a married couple!'

That remark was like a knife being driven into her stomach. How she wished he would show some commitment and at some point, maybe at Christmas or on her birthday, he would surprise her with an engagement ring. But instead he gave her perfume or a music CD and she would try her best to hide her over whelming disappointment.

Kelly suddenly stood up from the sofa, flinging the remote control onto the nearby chair, glaring at him with such rage that it made him more than a little nervous. 'So, tell me who is she then? Someone I know? And don't you try to deny it, I've had my suspicions for ages.' Her eyes narrowed with spite. 'Was she some slag you picked up off the street? Is that what turns you on these days? Because it's quite obvious that I don't do it for you anymore!'

Eric sat back, folding his arms grinning, trying to look

braver than what he really felt. 'Well, where do we start? When I moved in here with you I didn't sign up for being put on 24/7 surveillance. I thought I was still entitled to have a life of my own without you constantly breathing down my neck every time I want to meet up with a mate of mine.' He looked at her with his eyes narrowing in disgust, causing a shiver to run down her spine. 'Have you taken a look in the mirror at yourself lately? Look at the weight you've piled on - you look disgusting! Not that sexy bird I first met with the pert pair of boobs and small bum. Heaven knows how you managed to squeeze your lardy backside into those pair of jeans!'

With her anger getting the better of her she slapped him hard across the face. 'You dare call me fat. I might not have the perfect figure but everyone thought I'd overdone the diet and said I looked gaunt. Just because your slapper might look like a super model doesn't mean we all want to starve ourselves!'

Suddenly he took hold of her neck with one hand squeezing it firmly as he pulled her away, looking at her with pure hatred. 'You try that again and I will be more than putting my hands around your throat. Well, as for my *slapper* she's an amazing woman, absolutely gorgeous with a fit body to die for. And yes, she's absolutely wicked between the sheets too!'

He suddenly felt uneasy as she rushed into the bedroom and edged his way towards the door wondering what she was up to. He wouldn't put anything passed her the mood she was in. She came out the room with bin liners, undoubtedly packed with his stuff, which she flung uncerimoniously towards him.

'Well, if she's as good as you say she is, you might as well join her! I didn't waste any time while you were out. She returned to the bedroom for some more bundles, which she chucked his way. 'Now get out of here before I call the police, and don't ever come back!'

Sue watched as her friend ate her last piece of scampi, leaving a few chips behind which she obligingly finished off for her. 'Well your Eric certainly got his just desserts in the end! Great karma when it turned out that his love interest was married and when her hubby found out where he was staying, gave him a good seeing to. Made bit of a mess of his nose if I can remember - shame! Wonder what he's doing now?'

Kelly waited as the barmaid took their plates away. 'Well, last I heard he upped sticks to heaven knows where and is probably penniless and between jobs. Couldn't happen to a nicer person!' Her expression suddenly became grim. 'I guess, though I really hoped on your engagement that would really be the start of things with Lee.'

Sue felt sorry for her best friend who seemed so unlucky when it came to love. 'Well, what goes around, certainly comes around where Eric's concerned! As for the gorgeous Mr Fisher, I think he's just feeling a bit confused at the moment. He's like you, been through all sorts of stuff and his head is probably all over the place - I'm pretty sure he'll come to his senses with time.'

'Yeah, I guess so, but within the next ten years would be nice!'

CHAPTER THREE

Lee had left the depot an hour later than usual to begin his delivery round. Roger Morgan, the General Manager had called him into his office just before he'd finished loading his van for the day's deliveries. He made his way up to the offices, relieved that it was too early for Kelly to be in yet; he needed to gather his thoughts together before he could face any conversation with her. At first, he wondered why Roger wanted to see him. In this industry he was only too aware that reason was usually when something was amiss. Well, he knew his work as a delivery driver couldn't be faulted and had never received any complaints as far as he was aware, from customers.

Unless… damn, he thought with a grimace, I hope that old bloke from yesterday, Professor Broadhurst, hadn't made some complaint. He didn't appear to like the idea of him helping his daughter when she fell. Yes, she was rather pleasing to the eye but that's all there had been to it. Yet you could never tell these days when everything had gone so PC. All he needed was an accusation of sexual harassment, after all that had happened in the not too distant past.

The door was already open to Roger's office and the man himself stood there waiting for Lee. 'Do come in, lad,' he beckoned as he gave him a firm handshake. 'Sit yourself down.'

Lee found Morgan to be a firm but friendly manager. His soft, plump middle-aged features, and the thick mop of silver hair, almost belied the fact that at times this jovial man with a seemingly good nature, could be one tough cookie that had sacked both managers and drivers that were not seen to be pulling their weight.

Although the weather wasn't particularly warm, Morgan sat in a blue short-sleeved shirt with a matching navy tie. Sounding slightly out of breath, he mopped his sweating forehead with his handkerchief. He waited a few moments for Lee to sit down on the chair opposite his desk, cluttered with framed photographs of family members as well as a thick pile of paperwork with a paperweight to hold it down, should a gust of wind come through the open window.

'I'm sure you must be wondering why I asked for you to see me,' he smiled kindly holding his pen as if ready to write on the empty page of notepaper before him. 'So, I'll put you out of your misery,' he added with a wink before his face took on a more serious expression and cleared his throat.

'You might've heard the rumours that I haven't been in the best of health lately. Problems with my sugar and bit of a dodgy ticker,' he explained putting a hand to his rather broad chest. 'As you'll know from our bulletins and newsletters, after some challenging times the business is now going from strength to strength and we're expanding fast as we take on more and more high-profile customers. Anyway, I digress.' He took a sip of water from a glass tumbler better suited to holding a generous shot of whiskey.

'Due to the current issues with my health and the business heating up, I've decided it's time to step down and take early retirement.'

Although Roger wasn't considered the fittest of people, Lee was rather taken aback that this manager, popular with his staff had decided to leave. He knew that he had been manager at Fast Link for well over twenty years and with him leaving would be considered the end of a huge era.

'Lad, I do appreciate it must have been difficult for you going back to being a delivery driver after being a senior manager for FPS, our main competitor. We're very aware and highly impressed with your achievements there and how you played a major part in helping to expand the business. If my memory serves me well, you took a great chunk of our business with signing up some of our major clients.' He referred to some notes in his hand, tapping his pen thoughtfully onto the desk. 'You created extra jobs with new depots opening all over the place. You certainly made the company one of the most competitive delivery services this country has seen for home delivery, even if you happened to give us a run for our money in the process,' he added with a wink.

He cleared his throat. 'It's plain to see that we need young blood and a fresh pair of eyes if we're to continue with our successes, and what I'm asking is this: Would you consider applying for the position of General Manager, with a view to taking over the reins from me?'

Taking in a deep breath, Lee's eyes widened in astonishment and it was a few seconds before he was able to reply. 'Well, I have to say Roger you've certainly taken me by surprise. Here was I, coming up to your office thinking I was to be torn off a strip for something I couldn't think I'd done wrong and…'

Morgan waved his hand dismissively. 'Lad, I know all about the business at FPS and why you were forced to resign out of a job that really took you places in your career. Nasty business, dirty politics if you ask me, and at least Porter-Stevens got his just desserts in the end. When you stepped down, they got too big for their boots and are now in big trouble and having to close depots. A big mistake on their part letting you go like that - and all on a whim over his precious daughter.'

The older man saw the look of pain cut across Lee's face as he thought back to all of the events of three years ago and decided to quickly change the subject. 'If you're interested, we need you to put your application in writing as soon as possible. As you know with vacancies, we are obliged to advertise internally throughout the network.' He looked towards the door making sure it was firmly shut before continuing. 'You probably realise Mike Stanton will have his sights set on my job.' He tapped his nose winking knowingly. 'Some might say he already believes he's in the job.'

Lee appeared deep in thought for a few seconds thinking of the opportunist deputy manager who ground on the nerves of most of the staff at the depot, before a grin spread across his face. 'All right, let's go for it.'

Morgan's face lit up with a huge smile and he clapped his hands in glee. 'Great stuff, that's what I like to hear! Feel free to use my PC now to put it in writing. Bring in your CV tomorrow or email it to me and I'll put your application through to HR.'

After a few minutes, Lee left the office with a broad smile on his face when he came face to face with Mike Stanton. The other man stood with a slight look of unease replacing the smug expression on his plump round face. Bereft of any hair gave him more than a passing resemblance to Humpty

Dumpty. Frowning, he looked at the chunky silver watch strapped to his wrist.

'And what time do you call this, Fisher? Can't have you going out late for your deliveries and letting down our customers! Just because you were once some high-flying manager doesn't mean you can stroll around here at your leisure as if you own the place!'

Lee gave him a look of mock surprise. 'As if I would have the time to strut around this place, doing nothing all day, getting fat - chance would be a fine thing!' As he walked by the pompous manager, who gave a snort of displeasure, he swiftly made a rude finger gesture behind his back.

He completed most of his delivery round by 3 o'clock and was ready to hit the rural areas. The weather had warmed, with the breeze considerably milder in contrast to the morning's chilly start. The sunshine added a golden hue to the ash and elm trees that were now coming into bloom.

Fortunately, despite his later start Lee didn't have quite so many deliveries to make as the previous day. He was interested to see another package from *Matsushita* had arrived for the Broadhursts in Little Green. Taking a look, he could see this one looked similar in size to the one he'd delivered yesterday and was surprisingly heavy despite being fairly compact. On a daily basis, he delivered parcels to people from all walks of life. Some were fairly affluent, as these people appeared to be, with the majority that could be described as more middle class and working class; but for some reason that incident with the young woman and her elderly father from yesterday had stayed at the front of his mind.

Judging by the large house, which at a guess had at least six bedrooms, wasn't so much struck by the property as the young woman who lived there. Now *what* was her name? Helena, he was sure her father called her? As soon as he met her, was struck by her natural beauty; those eyes were the most amazing blue with those thick dark lashes, the colour you would expect from a brunette like Kelly. But he would bet his last pound that the long honey blonde hair owed nothing to artificial colouring. At a guess he would have said she was in her mid-twenties but seemed to hold an innocence and vulnerability of somebody much younger.

'Come along, Fisher,' he chided himself as he stopped to let a bus pass by on the narrow country road. 'She's way too young for you and probably out of your league.' His thoughts turned back to Kelly. Maybe she wasn't beautiful in the classic sense, but she was a real cracker; she had a smashing figure since she'd put a bit of weight on from the time he'd first met her. After going on some diet, probably to please that loser she'd been living with, had looked much too gaunt. With her down-to-earth manner, Lee found he could talk to her just about anything. She was never afraid to give her honest opinions, whether you liked it or not. What would he have done without Kelly?

He closed his eyes, shaking his head as he thought what a spineless idiot he was to cancel their badminton game and not have the guts to call her. To be truthful, from the very first day he saw her, had always fancied her something rotten. But there was no way he could allow her be dragged into his problems.

Having arrived at the Broadhursts, had found the security gate to be open. He drove up the long winding driveway to The Woodlands as he did yesterday, wondering if he would receive a similar reception from Professor Broadhurst. This time there was nobody around in the garden as he pulled up and all he could hear was the sound of the trees rustling in the wind and the birds singing from the nearby woods.

As he rang the doorbell of the large Georgian house, Lee looked around at the well-kept lawn surrounded by a variety of rosebushes, fuchsias and plants his mother as a keen gardener would be more familiar with.

Within seconds he heard the dog barking from within the house but this time no longer felt the fear of being attacked. 'Rupert, shut up!' a voice shouted from inside the house. With that the dog immediately quietened down. A small plump woman with grey short curly hair opened the door. Lee would have guessed she was in her late 60's. Staring at him with a hint of suspicion in her small grey eyes, a frown creased the forehead of her round face, with its ruddy complexion. She held on to a can of *Mr Sheen* polish and a duster thoughtfully.

'Package for Professor Broadhurst,' Lee said hoping to put the woman's mind at rest in case she thought he came to do the house over.

She blinked, her features softening, gazed at the parcel and then in recognition at the handsome young man. 'Oh, you're that bloke I see coming around delivering stuff,' she told him in her gruff voice with that familiar country twang of the area. 'They've gone out I'm afraid - should be back soon.'

Lee felt surprisingly disappointed and this wasn't wasted on the woman. Suddenly he remembered what Madge had told him yesterday. 'Are you Jess who cleans here?'

The woman raised her eyebrows in surprise.

'Madge at the shop told me you work here,' Lee explained. 'I had something to deliver here yesterday and couldn't find the place and she remembered you worked here and gave me some directions.

Jess chuckled, giving a warm smile that immediately softened her stern features. 'Madge and a few of the locals often tell me about Lee the dishy van driver. I wouldn't be surprised if some of them order stuff just for you to pay them a visit!'

Smiling at the compliment, Lee looked down at the parcel, which was feeling heavier by the minute; heavens know what it might contain. All he knew about Matsushita was that it was a company in Tokyo, not one of the more familiar accounts that Fast Link delivered for. 'Well I guess it doesn't matter if you sign for it. It's a POD.

A puzzled expression crossed the cleaner's face.

'Proof of delivery,' he explained.

'I hate writing on these things,' she grimaced as she tried to write her signature on the hand-held scanner. 'Anyway, that's me nearly done for the day - Helena should be back soon, she popped to the shop.' She looked around before shaking her head in disapproval at Lee. 'I'm surprised she was even let out the house - the poor lass is practically kept under lock and key!'

'How do you mean?' he frowned as he took back hold of his delivery scanner.

Jess took a firm grip of her can of polish. 'Well, the Professor and his wife, they don't give her any kind of freedom. They seem to have their eyes on her constantly! Never seems to have any friends staying over either - no social life as far as I can see. A pretty young thing like her should be out and about enjoying herself. All she has for company apart from the dog and her parents is her Uncle Ian who lives here too. A very strange setup if you ask me.

Lee shrugged. 'Maybe she's just one of those people who prefers their own company - I guess the world would be a boring place if we were all the same.' But he had to admit that it did seem a pity that such an attractive young woman should be shutting herself away when she should be enjoying life more.

The older woman shook her head thoughtfully. 'You're probably right. Maybe that's just her way, but it does seem a shame, 'specially when her parents don't seem to be giving her much of a choice.'

After finishing the delivery, Lee headed towards the village and saw Helena leaving the convenience store, carrying a bag of groceries. He stopped his van and called her name. Startled for a moment, she then smiled in recognition.

He wound down the window to his van further. 'Your cleaner said you'd popped down to the shop.'

Her eyes widened in a moment of fear. 'Oh gosh, nothing's happened to Mummy and Daddy - or Uncle Ian?'

He smiled apologetically. 'I'm sorry, I didn't mean to worry you. It's just that I wanted to make sure you were ok after that fall yesterday and wondered, if you um, fancied a quick drink at the pub?'

She bit her bottom lip nervously. 'I'm not really sure. They'll be returning soon and ...'

He stopped and turned off the engine. 'I know that you don't really know me but I promise you I come in peace. Lee Fisher's my name,' he added with a grin as he shook her hand. He looked towards the nearby pub. 'We only have a few feet to walk - you don't even need a lift!'

Appearing reassured, she gave a smile. 'Ok, that would be nice - but I can't be too long!'

In a short space of time they were sitting at a table in The Three Ferrets Pub, which was fairly typical of most of the country pubs in the area. With thick oak beams running through the cream coloured walls, covered with a variety of pictures, many showing framed photographs of the building and village in much earlier times. As music played softly from the jukebox, the only other customers around were a couple of elderly men standing at the bar with their pints of beer.

Lee opted for a Diet Coke as he was still officially at work and Helena stuck to fruit juice. He looked over to the rather beautiful young woman who sat opposite to him, smiling as she shyly touched the rim of her glass. 'Tell me about yourself, I'm intrigued. What's a lovely young person like yourself doing living tucked away in the country?'

She smiled teasingly, her nervousness seeming to melt away. 'Are you saying that just because I don't live in a town or a city makes me boring?'

He shook his head apologetically. 'Of course not, I'm sure country girls go out and enjoy themselves as much as much as us townies do!' He took a sip of his Coke. 'Have you lived out here all your life?'

She sighed, gazing thoughtfully at her fruit juice. 'No. We moved here about three years ago - after, after my sister died...'

'I'm so sorry.'

Looking sadly, into his eyes, she continued. 'Her name was Sarah and she was about to get married.' She took a sip of her drink. 'One evening, about two weeks before the wedding was to take place, she was returning home from a party with her fiancé. As...as they were driving home a car was coming from the opposite direction and-and collided with them...'

Lee winced shaking his head in disbelief. 'Gosh, I'm so sorry.'

Helena was lost, deep in her own thoughts, oblivious to her companion's words. 'Her fiancé had been driving on that evening so she could drink - she liked the occasional glass of wine but didn't care too much for alcohol.' She wiped away a speck of dust from the table. 'It...it was just after midnight and they were driving along in the sports car that daddy had not long bought for her birthday. As they were driving along these bendy country lanes, a car approached them driving along from the opposite direction on the wrong side of the road at speed. She didn't stand a chance.'

Lee could see the look of distress cross the young woman's face. 'I'm so very sorry, Helena truly I am but I don't want you getting upset...'

Helena shook her head dismissively. 'It's ok -sometimes it helps to speak about it.' She took a long sip of her drink. 'Sarah took the full force of the collision and...and she was killed instantly along with the driver in the other car. After a post-mortem it was discovered he was four times over the legal limit of alcohol.'

Lee shook his head in disbelief. 'It's just incredible how some people can be so irresponsible by putting other people's lives in danger in the process.'

She nodded in agreement. 'My sister was such a beautiful and incredibly talented person. She studied art and graphic design for four years at university and took after Mummy in that respect. My mother Clarissa, used to help create a lot of the special effects in many of the movies you've probably seen at the cinema. University is where Sarah met her finance. Daddy used to lecture there in between working at a research establishment and he attended his lectures.'

Lee was suitably impressed but knew this wasn't the time to ask for details.

She smiled ruefully as she thought back to her elder sister who she had clearly loved so much. 'We have her paintings framed all around the house to celebrate her life. She had such a promising career ahead of her and a fiancée who loved her dearly. Then at just 25 years old that all came to an end, along with all her hopes and dreams.' She looked sadly into his eyes. 'I followed in her footsteps, studying art at university, but I will never be as talented as Sarah.'

'Are you working at the moment?' he enquired.

She shook her head. 'Unfortunately, I've had some health issues which have prevented me from working for some time. Hopefully with a little rest I'll be back to full health and continue pursuing my career as an illustrator.'

Lee didn't wish to press her further on that matter. Perhaps she might have suffered from a nervous breakdown after her sister's death. They had obviously been a close family, but there was just one more thing he needed to ask. 'What happened to your sister's fiancé? Did...did he die in the car crash as well?'

For some reason the question seemed to trouble her and she looked away quickly watching as one of the elderly gentlemen standing at the bar, left the pub. 'No. He...he was critically injured but fortunately pulled through.' She looked over to him, smiling softly. 'I'm sure you've heard quite enough about me for the moment. Tell me a little about yourself. If you don't mind me saying, you're not the kind of person I would imagine being a delivery driver. You have quite an air of authority about you!'

He couldn't help but chuckle. Helena might have led bit of a sheltered life, but seemed she didn't miss a thing. He smiled apologetically at her puzzled expression. 'Sorry, I'm not laughing at you it's just that you're a very astute person.' He offered to buy her another drink, which she declined.

He took a bite of one his cheese and onion crisps. 'It's true to say I've worked for about 15 years in the delivery business, though not always with the company I'm currently working for, nor always as a delivery driver. Some have remarked I had a very promising career as a senior manager with a delivery company you may or may not have heard of - FPS?'

The blank look on Helena's face confirmed that the name meant nothing to her.

'They were the competitors of Fast Link where I'm now working, Lee explained. 'I did start out in the business originally as a delivery driver, but I felt I could do more and did a Business Studies course in the evenings for two years as well as an NVQ. It was pretty hard going after a busy day delivering loads of parcels, but I was determined to see it through and follow my dreams.' He took a sip of his coke. 'Anyway, to cut a long story short, an opportunity came up where they needed someone to help take on new clients. After some competition with applicants from both inside and outside the company, I got the job!'

A look of admiration spread across Helena's face. 'And all that hard work you did at college for two years finally paid off!'

He gave a deep sigh as he thought back. 'But there were a few that would argue that I didn't get the job entirely on my own merits. The big boss, Frederick Porter-Stevens who the company is named after, offered me the position. It just so happens that his gorgeous daughter, Miranda also took a shine to me. She also worked for the company as a business development manager, helping to secure accounts from new clients.'

A far away expression appeared on his face as he thought back to the beautiful young woman with the thick long red hair, who would come over to him as he loaded his van in the morning before his delivery run. Wearing her designer black trouser suit, holding an equally expensive leather briefcase, she would walk over wiggling her pert bottom slightly, appearing tall in her six-inch stiletto heels. Along she would strut, the smell of her Chanel Perfume so strong would even overpower the diesel exhaust fumes as the vans set off on their journeys. 'I'd just come out of a brief relationship and wasn't looking elsewhere at the time,' he grimaced as he thought back. 'All the guys there fancied her, this rich gorgeous woman who was the Managing Director's daughter. We knew we were out of her league and didn't stand a chance - but for some reason she took a liking to me and made it very clear. I plucked up the courage and asked her out for a meal and she accepted.'

Helena gently brushed back her hair from her face. 'Did it take you long to realise you were in love with her?'

He looked up to the cream coloured ceiling smiling bitterly. 'I thought at the time I was head over heels in love with her. She really rocked my world. She was rich, beautiful and so incredibly sexy - her life was a world away from my own where I was brought up on a council estate. Her parents lived in a large ten-bedroomed house, set in its own grounds with a swimming pool and a tennis court. She had her own penthouse flat, which was bought for her by her father.' Lee smiled bitterly as he thought back to the woman who had stolen his heart. 'Miranda was very self-indulgent and enjoyed all the good things in life - she did like to get her own way with everything. She owned all the best designer clothes, dining in all the top London restaurants, not to mention about four holidays a year in the most exclusive locations - all paid for by Daddy, of course!'

Helena smiled sympathetically. 'How did that make you feel that you weren't able to afford to buy her all those luxuries?'

He sighed. 'To be honest, I began to feel overwhelmed. Oh, don't get me wrong, at the beginning it was very exciting, enjoying all the good things in life and experiences that I never thought in a million years I would have the chance to do. Even when I was promoted and earning good money I could only dream of maintaining that kind of lifestyle. Her father paid for almost everything and that I was truly not happy with. I felt her parents were running her life because they felt I wasn't good enough for her. She was happy to allow that to happen and it made me feel as if I was some gold-digger!' He took a swallow of his coke and sighed deeply. 'Within a year I popped the question and we got engaged and she asked me to move permanently into her flat. Before I knew it, arrangements were being made for a big church wedding, although I wasn't terribly keen on all the fuss.'

'It must have been rather overwhelming,' Helena agreed sympathetically.

'I would have sooner got married in a registry office or somewhere abroad. There was no big family to speak of on my side - my dad left home when I was nine years old and was brought up by my mum. But Miranda had always dreamed of the big white wedding as I guess a lot of women do. She'd been engaged three times before me and saw this as her chance of a lifetime. Who was I to get in the way of her big dream?'

A look of sadness shadowed Helena's face. 'My sister was going to have a church wedding. But it was something both she and her fiancé wanted. He didn't have much family to speak of, just an older sister but it was very much a joint decision. My parents adored him - he would have made the perfect husband for Sarah. They were so well suited...'

Lee smiled wryly. 'Ironic how life can kick you in the face and things don't turn out in the way you hoped. I know that only too well from first-hand experience. With us the rows started to kick in. My career was going places after I'd taken on several major clients for the company - parcels were flooding in and more drivers taken on and sadly Miranda took it personally that she hadn't achieved the same level of success. To be perfectly honest I don't think she was cut out to be a salesperson and she would take out her moods on the girls in the office who she accused me of flirting with. Although I would have a laugh and a joke with them, there was no truth in what she was trying to imply.

Helena looked at him sympathetically. 'It must have put a

great deal of pressure on you.'

Lee grimaced as he thought back to those difficult times. 'The tension didn't end there. The arguments started about taking off time for the umpteenth holiday of the year. I love going away as much as the next person, but for Miranda life was one big holiday.'

He took a look at his now empty glass. 'One day she came home and announced she was pregnant. At first, I was shocked as it wasn't amongst our plans with the wedding coming up the following year. But once the news sunk in, I was over the moon. I'd always loved kids and enjoyed time with my friend's niece and nephew, taking them on days out to the zoo and all that. The thought of having a child of my own felt like the most amazing thing on this earth!' He looked into Helen's large blue eyes as she listened intently. 'But sadly, Miranda didn't share this joy - felt it wasn't practical with the wedding coming up and all the dress fittings. In general, she wasn't too fond of children, as they didn't fit into her way of life. Because it was very early days only a few friends and close members of family knew. Her parents were absolutely delighted as this would have been their first grandchild. Her elder sister who'd been married some years was unable to have children even though she'd gone down the IVF route.'

He took hold of his beer mat, sighing deeply. 'I remember

that fateful day - it'll be etched on my mind for as long as I live. She was having the day off, said she was meeting up with her best friend Abigail, spending the day in London. I set off to work and went about my day as normal - even managed to sign up another successful client.' He fell silent for a moment as the barman came around, collecting empty glasses from some of the tables. 'I'd arrived home feeling dead chuffed that I'd managed to sign up one of the biggest retailers in the country. Seeing that Miranda had arrived home after her day out with Abigail, I was about to suggest us booking a table at one of her favourite restaurants to toast the occasion.' His expression became very grim. 'I found her sitting on that white leather sofa she loved so much - smoking a cigarette, when I thought she'd given up. She looked up at me, looking very pale despite her all-year-round tan, inhaling deeply and blowing out a cloud of smoke. "I'm so sorry, Lee," she said to me softly. "I had to do it. I was just not ready to be a mum."'

Tears came to his eyes as he thought back to that terrible moment. 'There was I, going to work as usual and my wife-to-be had conspired with her friend to go to a clinic and have an abortion.'

Helena shook her head in disbelief. 'That's so terrible! To just get rid of your baby, without even discussing things with you. Perhaps if she had spoken to you about her worries you might have been able to reassure her things would turn out ok and she would make a fantastic mother!'

Her companion laughed bitterly. 'I'm afraid with Miranda it wasn't just about her fears of motherhood. More about how it would spoil all her fun, not to mention the stretch marks it would cause and ruin her perfect figure! Instead she chose to go down what was the easy route for her. I was so ecstatic at the thought of becoming a dad and giving my child the life, I could have only dreamt of - but that had been torn away from me. Her parents were devastated when they found out what she'd done and her sister was so upset after all her own efforts in vain to get pregnant.'

Helena barely knew this young man that sat opposite to her, but she gently placed her hand over his. 'I'm so sorry you've had such a terrible experience. Life can be so cruel. Is this what caused you to break up?'

He shook his head. 'Oh, I forgave her, as crazy as that sounds now and we continued with our wedding plans. Though looking back, I could tell things weren't right. She became more distant and we more or less led our own separate social lives.' He let out a sigh. 'I was meant to be going to meet a potential client in Manchester and was actually on my way when I received the call from the guy telling me that it would have to be postponed because his son had been seriously injured in a cycle accident - got knocked down by a car.'

He looked to her as a bitter smile spread across his face. 'I was at a loose end but Miranda already had the day off and as far as I knew, apart from a trip to the shops she had nothing planned. Like a fool I thought I would return home and surprise her, thinking we could perhaps take a trip to the coast for the day and enjoy some quality time together before the big day.'

He looked her squarely in the eyes as he shook his head. 'Little did I know that I would be one to be surprised!' He screwed up the empty crisp packet into his fist. 'As I parked outside our apartment I saw this Jag that I'd seen before - a big black flash one with a personalised number plate which belonged to Ashley Palmer, one of directors who was a close friend of her father's. I was a bit puzzled as to why he'd dropped by knowing it was Miranda's day off and knew she wouldn't be pleased with anything that might come between her and her retail therapy. But I guessed it had to be something important.'

Helena looked intently at the troubled expression that spread across her Lee's face.

'I let myself into the apartment, expecting Palmer to be sitting on the sofa maybe having a shot of whisky, which he seemed so fond of. But when I entered the living room there was nobody to be seen. Then suddenly I heard laughter coming from Miranda in the bedroom. My heart raced, knowing what was to come, I rushed to our bedroom where I saw her and Palmer in our king-sized bed, completely naked with their clothes all over the floor. Her face looked as white as a ghost, as she started covering herself up with the sheet. "A bit late for modesty, isn't it, Miranda?" I asked sarcastically. I remembered she looked absolutely terrified but she couldn't help herself from saying, "You drove me to this, Lee - this is your fault for not paying me any attention. You were so wrapped up with yourself and your precious work that you couldn't see I was lonely!"'

"'Well," I replied. "I can see you found somebody to keep you company while I was out working my backside off trying to earn a living!"'

He placed the crumpled crisp packet back on the table as he turned his attention back to her. 'This red mist came over me as I saw Palmer getting out of our bed, trying to put on his boxer shorts. My anger getting the better of me, I took a swing at him and punched him firmly on the jaw and right on his nose, which poured with blood. I remember Miranda screaming and shouting for me to stop, trying to come between us. I have never hit a woman in my entire life, but on that day much to my shame was sorely tempted. I'd raised my hand to her in the heat of the moment, but had the good sense to hold back.

"Get out of my place, you bastard," I shouted to him, "before I kill you." He quickly put on his trousers and didn't waste any time buttoning up his shirt. He was out the door, before I had any chance of carrying out my threat.'

Helena visibly winced as the story unfolded. 'We were left alone in the bedroom and I just sat down on the bed, trying to take in what'd happened, feeling this was maybe just one big nightmare which I would soon wake up from. "Why, Miranda? *Why*?" I demanded. "How long has this been going on for?" I looked back at her as she was staring at me as if I was insane, afraid I might strike her. She had done wrong but would never have laid a finger on her. She quickly put on her cream silk dressing gown and lit a cigarette, blowing out a cloud of smoke.'

"Does it really matter, Lee? Well, if you must know it's been going on for the past year. I guess I just felt I wasn't ready for the marriage thing and having kids. I could see you were getting wrapped up with your work and I guess it just didn't feel fun with you anymore."

'I looked at her in what must have been utter disbelief. "I'm so sorry if life couldn't be just one big holiday with me Miranda, but we all have our responsibilities and we don't all have a rich daddy to pay for everything." It was at that moment that the realisation came to me. "You *weren't* going away on those weekend trips abroad with Abigail, were you? It was with that loser I just caught you in bed with!" 'She never bothered to deny it. It was going on right under my nose and I didn't see it. My heart raced as something else crossed my mind. "Was that baby mine, or did it belong to *him*?'

'She ground out her cigarette in the wine glass that was sitting on her bedside table and she broke down in tears, as she sat down on the bed.'

"I don't know, Lee. I *really* don't know - and that's the truth. All I know is that I wasn't ready to be a mother - I'm not sure I ever will be. And I'm afraid that I don't want to be your wife - I'm in love with Ashley. He says one day he would like to marry me."

'I laughed bitterly. "Oh, *very* good. And maybe it'll be fifth time lucky for him with wife number five. What the hell's the matter with you, Miranda? That bloke has a track record as long as my arm. All his marriages broke up for the same reason - he couldn't keep it in his trousers and he got caught out. What makes you feel that things would be any different with you?"

'She looked at me defiantly. "Well, I guess until I came along, Ashley simply hadn't met the right woman. I know with me he has remained faithful - I would know if he was playing around. The signs are always there."

"'Yeah and *don't* I know it now!" I laughed sarcastically.'

"Lee, if things had been that good between us, I would never have found a reason to look elsewhere. He was just a symptom of things not being right with us."

'I looked into those piercing green eyes that stared back at me with such hostility. "And now you believe with him it's all going to be happy ever after?"

'She shook her head smiling at me as if I was some stupid child. "That only happens in fairy tales, as we all know - real life tells a different story. I'm sure we'll have our ups and downs like everybody else. But really, once you get to know him, Ashley is a sweet guy, contrary to what others might believe. I'm sure that things will work out for us."'

'Slowly I rose from the bed, my initial anger having died down, but still in state of shock. I was resigned to the fact that things were over between us. "Well, seeing that this place was paid for by Daddy, I guess I'd best pack my things and go - no point staying where I clearly haven't been wanted for some time by the looks of things." I looked at her as she wrapped her arms around herself as if feeling the cold. Maybe it was down to the shock of having been caught out. But it wasn't until much later when I had time to think, that never once in our conversation had she said she was sorry for all of this.'

He looked back to Helena who stared intently. 'I'm sorry to go on like this, you barely know me and here I go, burdening you with all my hard luck.'

'Not at all,' she smiled reassuringly. 'Please continue, it often helps if you get these things out into the open. I'm sure you have more to say.'

'Well, a mate offered to put me up for a few nights until I found somewhere of my own. I went to work the following day -couldn't let my private life spill into my work even though we both worked for her father's company. Within five minutes having arrived, I received a call on my mobile from Miranda's father who was in the building, wanting to see me in his office. Didn't very often make appearances there as he had others to do the day to day running of the business while he went off to play golf and enjoy the good life.'

He smiled grimly. 'I pretty much knew what was coming - expected consequences and wasn't at all surprised to see that Miranda hadn't come to work.'

'I braced myself as I went to the office of the man who was meant to be my future father-in-law, but somebody who I'd never really taken to and the feeling I know was mutual. I knocked before I entered. Frederick Porter-Stevens sat firmly in the chair of his plush office. The rest of the offices where the staff worked, were badly in need of an upgrade with furniture and equipment that had seen better days. But when it came to our chairman, it seemed that no expense was spared, even if most of the time he wasn't there unless he cared to make a brief visit. He remained seated on his expensive leather executive chair dressed in one of his handmade suits, which I could see had got tighter on him. He peered at me from his half-moon reading glasses, his face a ruddy colour, probably from all the whiskey he liked to drink.

"Take a seat, Fisher," he ordered, his face set firmly staring at me squarely in the eyes. As I sat opposite him I peered at all the framed photographs on his desk showing his wife, an older version of Miranda and a photograph of a younger Miranda with her sister who had the more rounded features of her father. I looked as if for the first time, at the pictures on the wall of him competing at golfing tournaments, the trophy that proudly stood on a shelf under one of the framed pictures. I could see he was livid, heard his breathing was laboured and wheezy, probably from all those fat cigars he smoked. He took off his spectacles and breathed in deeply as he began. I could see his hands were shaking with sheer rage.'

"You've probably gathered that Miranda isn't in work today. She told me all about what happened yesterday evening and she was extremely upset. Couldn't stop crying when she called her mother who got straight on the phone and pulled me away from an extremely important meeting at the Conservative club."'

'I guessed it probably had more to do with an important drinking session but I wasn't about to argue,' he smiled wryly. 'He glared at me with such pure hatred as he began to lay into me. "When I arrived at her apartment, my poor daughter was in a terrible state. Told me how you had driven her into the arms of another man with all your flirting with the office staff whenever her head was turned - she was certain that you were having an affair with Sonia Lawrence. If she hadn't resigned she would have been dismissed."

'In anger and disbelief, I stood up from my chair, towering over the desk. "Oh, come off it, Frederick, I've never been near the woman. This is absurd - Sonia was having some problems in her relationship, which she discussed with me. But that's all there was to it. Miranda got the wrong idea and despite all my reassurances she made her life hell until she could take no more and resigned.'

'Porter-Stevens waved his hand dismissively. "Enough!" he barked. "Whether or not you were having an affair with the office girl cannot be proven - all I know is that it deeply upset my daughter who felt isolated and unloved. Enough for her to seek company elsewhere when she was about to get married."

He took a sip of the filtered coffee he had brought in just before I joined him. "To be perfectly frank I'm glad she saw you in your true colours before the wedding took place, because all along we felt she was making a terrible mistake - but you know how stubborn Miranda can be! Whether or not Ashley Palmer will be her future husband is of little relevance at this moment - I'm just glad she has seen sense and saw you for who you are."

'I felt my face burn with anger at the unfairness of what he was saying. "You never felt I was good enough for your precious daughter - just because I wasn't lucky enough to be born with a silver spoon in my mouth and go to a private school and have all the right connections. But at least I can say proudly that whatever I have achieved in life is all through my own hard work and not because of who I know, like some others I could mention!"

'At that remark I saw a nerve twitch in the side of his face. He slammed down his fine porcelain cup and stood up from his chair - his whole 5ft 6 inches looking up at me.'

"Miranda told me how you had the nerve to slap her face. How *dare* you lay a finger on my daughter! If...if I didn't have this heart problem I would beat you to pulp!"

Lee looked at Helena with such bitterness. 'As enraged as I was, there was no way I would have laid a hand on her, as much as I was livid about catching her in our bed with another man. What really hurt was how she could blatantly lie about me using physical abuse. I guess in many respects I can understand why her father chose to believe his daughter's version of events.'

Helena smiled at him sympathetically. 'Miranda had treated you very badly, but I suppose no matter how badly she behaved her father will always love her unconditionally.'

Lee nodded in agreement. 'I'm afraid that's not the end of it, as you can probably guess. Frederick had of course heard how I'd punched Palmer - told me how he wanted to get the law involved for what I'd done to that slime ball and his daughter. But I should consider myself very fortunate, he told me, as neither of them had wanted to press charges and just wanted to focus on their future.' Lee's eyes narrowed in disgust. 'He looked at me with such contempt and I saw a smug look spread across his face as he said the fact remained that I had put him into a difficult situation and was potentially spoiling the good reputation of the company with my wrongdoings. He also felt my work wasn't up to scratch. Never mind that I had introduced some key clients to the business, which would have ended if I hadn't managed to sign up these accounts. When I put this to him and he came up with the lame excuse that I was simply doing my job.'

He let out a deep sigh. 'Well, I knew what was coming.

For the first time in my working life I was given the push and informed I would never be given a reference and that my days of being in a senior position were over for good.'

Helena shook her head in disbelief. 'My goodness, the unfairness of all this! Couldn't you have gone to a tribunal and challenged this?'

Lee shook his head. 'I could have gone down that road, but it would have been a waste of time. The fact remained I *had* clouted Palmer and he believed I'd slapped his daughter, and an accusation of assault doesn't stand well in a case, no matter how I felt pushed into this. I'm afraid I just didn't have a leg to stand on.'

He found Helena to be such a good listener and before he knew it was telling her about how he started work at Fast Link and about Kelly who of course knew all about what had happened with his career and with Miranda.

'She sounds a very lucky person to have a friend like you,' smiled Helena. 'Would you say you are in love with her?'

Lee gave a sigh as he shrugged his shoulders. 'All I know is that Kelly is the best thing that's happened to me since Miranda and I can honestly say she's one of the best friends I've ever had. I know for sure she's interested. It…it's just that I don't want to do anything to spoil our friendship, especially after everything that's happened.

Just as his companion was about to speak, a call came on Helena's mobile. 'Oh, excuse me,' Helena apologised. She rummaged in her handbag for her phone, which she promptly answered.

'Daddy!' she cried smiling towards her new friend. Her smile disappeared, her expression looking grave. 'Oh dear, how long will you be? I see... yes, I'm fine. No, I wasn't at home. I just went down to the shops to get some soup and those crackers you so like.' Lee could hear her father's clipped voice on the phone. 'Honestly Daddy, you worry too much - I'm fine. Mrs Cowley will have finished for the day but I'll manage perfectly well on my own. And besides, I have Hugo and Rupert for company.' Although Lee couldn't hear what her father was saying he could sense by the sound of his voice that he was anxious. 'Really Daddy, I'll be absolutely fine. Just take your time. I'll be safely at home with Rupert and not to mention Hugo! Just send my love to Mummy and Uncle Ian.' With that she put her phone back into her small brown leather handbag. 'Daddy's such a worrywart!' she said, shaking her head apologetically.

'My parents were returning back from Cumbria when the Range Rover broke down,' she explained reading Lee's puzzled expression, then let out a long-drawn sigh. 'Actually, they had been to visit my sister's grave. Normally I would join them but

I wasn't feeling well and Daddy felt it was best if I stayed at home. It looks as if the road recovery won't be able to get to them for the next hour or two at least and they're still in the north at the moment, so it doesn't look as if they'll be back until later this evening.'

'It's a long way from here, especially if they were doing the trip all in one day, and not to mention the rush hour when everybody's heading home' agreed Lee. He had an idea. 'I know we haven't known each other long, but perhaps would you like to come out for a meal in town - I knock off work soon. All I need to do is to report back to the depot. You can come with me if you like - if you have nothing else planned.'

He noticed the way Helena was biting her lip anxiously. 'Look it's ok if you don't feel comfortable about the situation - I'll understand. I promise I mean you no harm. Just thought we could both do with a bit of cheering up, especially after the way I depressed you with my life story.'

At that Helena laughed, and she had such a beautiful smile, thought Lee with the cutest dimples each side of her face. 'Well, now that you put it that way, I think that sounds a very good idea and besides I'm rather hungry.' Her expression became serious, her almond shaped eyes widening. 'But first I'll need to drop these groceries at home and quickly see to Rupert.

Lee got up from his chair. 'Well, what are we waiting for? Let's hit the road!'

CHAPTER FOUR

As they pulled up outside of the Woodlands, a gentle breeze stirred through the evergreen trees as they descended from the van. Lee inhaled the sweet country air, so fragrant and so fresh compared to the fuel congested air in the town. For a moment he sensed Helena wasn't comfortable about him coming inside the house, but to his relief she beckoned him in. 'It's ok - no one is here. Mrs Cowley has left for the day and no Daddy or Uncle Ian to bite your head off!'

At that he smiled, as he thought back to her over-protective father. Maybe that would be him one day anxious about his own daughter or son. As she unlocked the large oak front door, she stepped inside quickly to deactivate the burglar alarm before following her inside. Maybe it was remembering her father who seemed quite elderly, was quite unprepared for the modern decor. As they entered the hallway, lights automatically came on from recessed lighting in the high ceiling above. Hearing their footsteps, Rupert came rushing from a door left open hurrying over excitedly to his mistress who rewarded him with a stroke to his ears, rubbing them affectionately. It seemed that the dog remembered Lee from yesterday, and panting, gave him a quick smell followed by a lick to his hand.

'I'm just going to let you out in the garden for a few minutes, my darling,' she informed Rupert, 'but I'm afraid I'll be leaving you after I have given you some dinner as this nice man is taking me out for a meal.' She quickly led him to the lounge whilst she saw to the golden retriever.

Again, he was amazed by the large spacious lounge with a large flat screen TV that must have been at least 50 inches, set on one of the high magnolia coloured walls. Adding to the contemporary style, the flooring a light glossy brown laminate, spread with cream coloured rugs, matched the colours of the large leather settee and armchairs. On the glass coffee table sat an array of square candles in colours of brown and white with their vanilla scent still wafting through the air from when they had been previously lit. He gazed towards some paintings showing watercolours of landscapes depicting the four seasons. He was no expert when it came to art, but could only be described as beautiful, showing great attention to detail.

'My sister Sarah.' He jumped with a start at the voice behind him. While he'd been busy looking around, Helena had quickly got changed into a silky blouse the colour of coral, complimenting her honey blonde hair.

'Sarah was so talented,' Helena explained with a faraway expression on her face. 'She just loved to paint and to express the world as she saw it. It's all she ever wanted to do.'

'It's such a waste,' Lee said grimly. 'For somebody to be so talented...'

Helena shrugged sadly. 'It is indeed. I too love to paint but I know I'll never be anywhere near as good as Sarah. Mummy and Daddy love my work but after Sarah had...I just find myself unable to paint anymore. No matter how I try.'

Lee gazed into her large blue eyes, so filled with sadness. 'Don't beat yourself up over this. You've been through a traumatic experience. Probably about the worst anybody could experience. All you need is time and it will all come back, I'm sure.'

'I do hope so,' she smiled. 'But after three years I wonder if it ever will.' As they walked around the corner to the large fireplace his attention was taken by a large oil painting hanging, depicting a young woman, possibly in her twenties. The subject standing, wearing a long sleeveless pink floral maxi dress, holding lovingly a fluffy white Persian cat in her arms. A large straw hat perhaps slightly too large was perched on her head, with that unmistakable long fair hair hanging down to her waste. That heart shaped face he would know from anywhere, with those blue almond shaped eyes fringed thick dark lashes and her smile that was almost shy.

'I know what you might be thinking, but that's not me!' she explained with a smile.

Lee was astonished. 'You're kidding me! Were...were you twins?'

Helena shook her head. 'Sarah was actually slightly older than me. Mummy painted this one - that's where Sarah got her talent for art from and why I love it so much.'

Lee was almost fixated to the painting. The likeness to Helena was uncanny. 'Well it's clear to see that Sarah was very beautiful - just like her sister.'

She smiled at the compliment. His attention focused to a portrait next to the painting, of a man, possibly in his mid to late twenties. With short dark curly hair and long sideburns, sporting a thick moustache, could see this was probably painted in the seventies. Wearing thick black-framed spectacles and a conservative blue shirt with a thick navy tie, reminded Lee of his maths teacher from back in the day.

'That's Uncle Ian,' she explained with a smile of affection. 'When he was much younger.' He was obviously somebody she was very fond of.

'Was that also painted by your mother?'

A trouble frown crossed across the forehead of the young

woman.

'No. No. I...I'm not sure who painted this one. But I know we've had this painting for a very long time. Anyway, I'm ready now. Shall we go?'

Within twenty minutes they pulled up outside of Fast Link building, displaying the famed large dark green company logo in deep green with its yellow arrow underling the name. With the brickwork encased with corrugated iron reflecting the reddish-orange sunset, Old Church depot was the second largest of the thirty depots within the Fast Link network.

Helena spotted a number of staff members glancing curiously their way as they drove inside of the building. 'Will they mind me being inside the van with you?'

He shook his head. 'It's against company policy for employed drivers to take unauthorised passengers, but because I'm self-employed I'm insured for this.'

He promptly climbed out of the van, leaving the engine running. Holding on to some paperwork, he walked briskly over to a young man possibly of West Indian origin, sitting at a desk busily working away on a PC. He checked methodically through the paperwork Lee handed to him, every now and then tapping away on the keyboard. As this was happening, a young woman walking by the van caught Helena's attention. With long dark curly hair, possibly in her thirties, dressed in a grey three-quarter-length coat, the sounds of her high heels echoing loudly against the concrete floor. As she walked closer to the vehicle, her attention turned to Helena, her face immediately draining of colour as if she had seen a ghost. Just as Lee finished his business at the desk he also noticed the woman, smiling as if he knew her quite well. But much to Helena's surprise, she walked on by without acknowledging him and rushed through the exit as if she was in rather a hurry.

As they drove off, Helena couldn't help noticing the look of disappointment on her new friend's face. 'Was that Kelly who you were telling me about?'

He nodded grimly in reply, as they passed some of the delivery vans that were now forming a queue, waiting to be booked in. 'Yes, and not very happy by the looks of things.'

She sighed. 'I believe she thinks I'm your new girlfriend. Oh Lee, I'm sorry, she looks *such* a nice person. You must explain to her that you don't really know me.'

Despite the heavy feeling in his heart, Lee couldn't help smiling at her suggestion. 'I think if I put it to her that way it would only make matters worse. Oh, I just don't know…Kelly is the most amazing person. I love her to pieces, but I just don't think I have anything to offer her but grief. Look, I'll need to pop home briefly to change. Have a think about what kind of food you fancy and we can then decide where to eat.'

Within a few minutes they pulled up outside his apartment in Osborne Grove that he'd rented since his breakup with Miranda. Thankfully he'd had the foresight to be careful with the generous salary earned from his position as a senior manager. With that and working some long and gruelling hours as a delivery driver, including most weekends had managed to rent a property in quite a decent area of the town. Set away from the busy traffic of the main road, the surrounding lawns and the trees added an almost rural atmosphere to the neighbourhood.

Lee invited Helena inside of the two-storey apartment, offering her the chance to stretch her legs whilst he freshened up and got changed out of his uniform. He opened the door, allowing Helena to enter first. She looked around the compact but smartly furnished living room, at the two-seater brown leather sofa that sat opposite a medium sized TV mounted on the wall. The cream-tiled floor was covered with a couple of brown cotton rugs, lending a distinctly masculine feel. Lee was clearly a person that liked to keep things tidy.

'Make yourself comfortable,' he beckoned, inviting her to take a seat on the sofa and switching on the TV with the remote control. 'I'll only be a few minutes.'

Helena sat down watching Sky News for a moment, but as soon as he left the room, stood up to take in her surroundings.

She glanced out of the large window where the cream vertical blinds had been drawn back. Taking a look down to the ground below saw a young boy was on his bike, riding along the pavement wearing a bright yellow cycle helmet. A black BMW drove slowly by in case the boy decided to swerve out onto the road. Turning back, she gazed at the living area, noticing how few pictures there were hanging on the walls and not a photograph to be seen, quickly deciding Lee clearly favoured the minimalistic look. He seemed such a nice person, she mused and had clearly been through his fair share of troubled times, and hoped things would soon work out for him.

'Ready when you are,' came a voice from behind, breaking her chain of thoughts. 'Sorry, I didn't mean to startle you,' he smiled apologetically, as she turned around with such an intensely serious expression etched on her face.

'It's OK, you didn't startle me,' she assured him, taking in his pale blue shirt and dark jeans, which complimented has dark brown hair, making him appear distinctly pleasing to the eye.

He picked up his denim jacket that was draped on the corner of the sofa. 'Hmm, did you need to pop to the bathroom before we set off?' He didn't remember her once having popped to the toilet in all the time they had spent together that afternoon.

She shook her head. 'Really, I'm fine.'

He smiled as he led the way. 'Ok, if you say so. Well, let's be on our way!'

After much deliberation and Helena's insistence that she didn't mind where they ate, Lee opted for a pizza restaurant he knew well and was one of his favourite go-to places after a busy day. He smiled as Helena studied the menu intently. 'I know, there's so much choice - it's hard deciding what to settle for! Are you vegetarian?'

She shook her head as she continued to study the menu.

He took a sip of the mineral water that the waitress had brought along earlier. Being situated conveniently in the town centre, the restaurant was fairly busy, as most people had finished work for the day

'My ex was a vegetarian,' he revealed. 'Nothing wrong with being one I guess, but in my own case could be bit of a pain at Christmas. She always looked at me as some kind of villain when I tucked into my Turkey as if I was murdering it on my plate.'

Helena smiled. 'I guess there are arguments for and against eating meat but I've got to say that for me, there is nothing better I love than a Sunday roast with beef and all the trimmings with lashings of gravy!'

'It's the same with Kelly, only she loves roast pork but

dollops it all over with ketchup and...,' he shook his head. 'Oh, I'm sorry Helena. Here's me meant to be taking you out for a meal to cheer us both up and here I go harping on about my failed love life.'

She gently placed her hand on top of his, so surprisingly cold considering the milder weather, but so soft. 'Really, I don't mind. You have every right to feel sad. You've been through such an ordeal and I know you're missing Kelly as she's been such a rock for you.'

He smiled appreciatively and studied the menu again. 'Well I think I have decided on what I fancy - how about you?'

Within about half an hour they were tucking into their starters, Helena opting for toasted Pagnotta bread and Lee some dough balls.

Helena sipped her large glass of Pinot Grigio appreciatively as she studied her companion sipping his glass of sparkling mineral water. 'Oh, I do feel a bit guilty drinking alcohol.'

He gave a chuckle. 'Don't you worry about me. I can't afford to drink and drive when my job is based on delivering parcels, but I promise you once I get home I'll be cracking open a bottle of Budweiser! Do you drive?'

She took another sip of her wine thoughtfully. 'Well, yes I do, but I don't anymore if that makes any sense.' A troubled frown creased her forehead.

'It's ok,' Lee reassured softly. 'There's nothing that you have to explain to me.' He regarded her with pity. That accident and losing her sister had obviously made a huge impact on her life, which was hardly surprising, but he hoped it wouldn't be too long before she would get her life back on track.

She sighed deeply. 'I do sometimes drive around the grounds in Daddy's Range Rover and sometimes Uncle Ian will sit next to me, but he looks at me as if he's worried out of his mind. They both make *such* a fuss!'

Lee couldn't help thinking that perhaps instead of wrapping her up in cotton wool and holding her back, maybe they should be working together on helping her regain her independence. But he guessed it wasn't his place to say anything without knowing all the facts.

After a while the waitress came with their main courses. Lee looked appreciatively at his pizza with hot spicy beef with pepperoni and red onions. Helena had opted for chicken, green peppers with red onions, looking equally as delicious.

'I think I was just about ready for this,' Lee remarked licking his lips appreciatively. 'When you're busy delivering and on the road all day you barely get time to eat.'

The young Polish waitress kept smiling at Lee knowingly

as she served their food. This was a place that he would often come to with Kelly after going to the cinema. How was she to know there was really nothing happening between him and Helena? They were just acquaintances. Weren't they?

The time passed quickly as they worked through their main course, chatting about their school days. During her earlier years, because her parents work involved a great deal of travelling to different counties, had for a time attended a boarding school in Canada. Her mother's career as a special effect's artist would also mean working in different locations across the globe, on various high-profile movies including Hollywood. On her return her mother would share news about some of the famous big screen legends she had met along the way.

Fascinated, Lee cut into his thick pizza. 'With all that travelling, did you find it a bit difficult to form friendships?'

'Hmm, it could be a challenge at times, but on the whole found it fairly easy to adapt. When I returned to England I attended the same boarding school in Derbyshire as my close friend, Katherine Jolley. Actually, we lived in the same village and our parents were also close friends.' She speared a small piece of chicken with her fork as she thought back. 'Often, during half terms we would stay at each other's houses having sleepovers. Her father, I remember worked very high up in defence. Couldn't talk about it much as all top-secret stuff, so knew better than to ask any questions.' She took a sip of her third large glass of wine, which to Lee's amazement didn't seem to have any effect on her.

She smiled fondly as she reminisced. 'Katherine had an older brother Michael who used to fancy me something rotten, but at the time I found him a bit too plump and boring for my liking. He kept on asking me for a date and I had to think of endless excuses why I couldn't until he finally gave up.'

'That's one of the perils of being so pretty,' Lee smiled, looking deeply into her eyes.

Helena laughed. 'It might have been one of my biggest regrets as he slimmed down a few years later and looked very handsome. Katherine and me actually attended University together, studying Art and I went to stay at her house and I saw him there, tall, dark and very, very handsome. With his fiancé!'

Lee joined in with the laugher. 'The one that got away - tell me about it! Has there been anybody special in your life?'

The smile suddenly left her face. 'When I was at University there were one or two friendships, but nothing serious. Apart…apart from one.'

Seeing she looked clearly distressed, Lee took hold of her hand, which again felt so cold to the touch. 'Hey, it's ok, you don't have to discuss anything that makes you feel uncomfortable. We're here to have a pleasant time and to forget our troubles for a while.'

She smiled appreciatively. 'Thank you, you're so very kind and perceptive. I for one believe Miranda was absolutely crazy to let you go.'

Helena dabbed her mouth gently with her napkin as she finished eating her tiramisu and Lee patting his stomach after enjoying a generous serving of chocolate fudge cake with ice cream.

He glanced at her with a grin. 'Well, I don't know about you, but I'm absolutely stuffed. I've just no idea where you put it - we must have eaten tons and you look so dainty!'

'Thank you,' she replied shyly. 'And thank you for such a marvellous time.'

'My pleasure. I've enjoyed myself too. Perhaps we can do this again some other time.'

There was just a slight moment of hesitation before she agreed and soon they were exchanging phone numbers.

Suddenly Helena's mobile sprang into life as she finished adding Lee to her contacts.

'Daddy!' she greeted as she answered the call. She peered towards him, her expression suddenly became very grave as he could hear her father speaking loudly.

'Daddy, I'm fine - honestly. I'm out to dinner. With Lee... the man who delivered the batteries to our house yesterday.'

He could hear her father sounded livid. 'Daddy there's no need for you to worry. I'm glad you arrived home safely with Mummy and Uncle Ian. And I did see to Rupert before I went out.'

She glanced over to Lee as she spoke to the professor, her eyelids looking suddenly very heavy. He'd noticed she'd looked quite tired for the past hour so maybe it was getting towards her bedtime. Or maybe she was just getting bored with his company.

Helena looked at her watch. 'I promise I'll be on my way shortly. *Please* don't worry -I'm fine!'

She hung up giving a long sigh. 'I'm so sorry about this. My parents are not used to me being out especially at this time.'

Lee also glanced at this watch and to his surprise was almost 10 O'clock. Apart from another couple, the restaurant was almost empty. Having so much to say to each other, the time had simply flown by.

'It's me that should be apologising,' he assured her. 'Your parents must be going frantic. They know nothing about me, for all they know I could by some psycho. After a stressful day with their vehicle breaking down they come home to an empty house. I know in their position I would feel the same.'

As Lee called the waitress to settle the bill, Helena took hold of her handbag. 'I'm the one being thoughtless – I should have made sure I was back in good time. And besides, I'm sure you'll have an early start tomorrow and will need your sleep.'

After settling the bill, Lee glanced at her coyly. 'I just need to pop to the Gents. Do you um, want to powder your nose?'

Helena couldn't help giggling at the old-fashioned term, shaking her head. 'It's ok, I'll wait here until you're back.'

Soon they were heading back to The Woodlands, Helena appearing increasingly tired and a couple of times it looked as if she'd fallen asleep as her head rolled forward.

'Hey are you ok there?' Lee asked, briefly taking his attention from the road as he glanced at her.'

'I'm fine, just a little tired.'

'Do you think you might have perhaps overdone it a little with the wine?' he suggested with a wry smile.

'Maybe,' she replied rubbing her eyes, smudging her mascara slightly. 'But if I'm being honest I'm usually in bed by now. When it comes to this time, I suddenly come over very, very tired.'

She smiled. 'I remember once I was watching TV with Uncle Ian. We were watching that film *Ghost* with Patrick Swayze. I've seen that film so many times but I love it so much and wanted to watch again even though it was well past my bedtime. I remember Uncle Ian smiling and warned me what happens by midnight. But I didn't take any notice. The next thing I knew, it was morning and I had woken up in my bed with the clothes I had on the day before!'

Lee chuckled. 'It sounds like you'd fall into a deep sleep while the world was ending.'

Helena gave a small shiver. 'I do hope so. I wouldn't like to be awake to experience that!'

As they pulled into the drive of the Woodlands a security light automatically lit up the large property. The Broadhursts' black Range Rover was pulled up outside the large double garage to the left of the house. Lee stopped the engine of his van and was about to thank Helena for a very pleasant evening, but to his alarm, her head was back on the seat and her eyes firmly shut with her mouth slightly open.

'Helena, are you ok? Helena?'

His heart racing with fear, he touched her shoulder gently but she didn't respond.

Within a few seconds the large brown door opened to the front of the house and saw two men making their way over to the van. One was Professor Broadhurst trying in vain to keep up with the younger man in who he didn't recognise. The unknown man opened the van door on the passenger side looking earnestly at Helena before glaring at Lee accusingly.

Suddenly Lee recognised the short curly grey hair and the thick lensed spectacles, from that painting earlier; only now the hair was almost completely grey. Unlike the painting he'd seen earlier, Uncle Ian's face sported a short grey beard that was barely covering a jagged scar that ran across his face.

'Helena, are you ok,' he cried out and again stared at Lee accusingly, when there came no response. Professor Broadhurst came close behind, his attention focused on Lee with a mixture of both anger and fear.

'Young man, I blame this on you entirely. How *dare* you take out my daughter who you barely know and put her life in danger?'

Lee suddenly felt very angry. 'I do apologise sir, but I was under the impression that your daughter was old enough to make her own decisions about her social life and who she can go out with. And I can assure you I meant her no harm. I assumed she was just feeling tired. I can promise you I wasn't aware that she might have some illness.' He watched her as she lied back almost peacefully seemingly unaware of what was going on around her. Suddenly he felt very anxious.

The two men looked at him almost apologetically before Broadhurst gruffly replied. 'It's best never to make assumptions on matters you know nothing about.' He glanced towards Ian who gently lifted Helena out of the van and held her tenderly in his arms. It looked as if he was struggling.

'Can…can I help?' Lee offered, not exactly sure what was going on but nonetheless feeling terrible about the situation.

Broadhurst waved his hand dismissively. 'I think you've done more than enough this evening, don't you?'

He watched as they entered the house, with Helena lying limp in Ian's arms and it was only then that he noticed the silhouette of a woman with a short bob standing in the doorway, appearing very concerned. With that the door firmly closed as they went inside. Lee sat there for a minute or two, stunned by what he'd just encountered before reluctantly driving off.

CHAPTER FIVE

The following morning Lee finished loading his van with the day's parcels to deliver. With a grimace etched on his face, he walked carefully towards the works canteen for a quick coffee. Despite all the manual handling training he'd been given, had still managed to strain his back after lifting a box of wine. Noticing Bob sitting in the corner texting on his mobile, took a seat next to him, letting out a deep sigh. Bob peered at his friend with a grin, having a similar round shaped face to his sister Kelly, only with fuller plumper features and the same curly dark hair, only shorter and peppered with grey.

'Well, looks like someone's feeling full of the joys of a Thursday morning,' he teased, placing his mobile gently on the table. 'You're looking about as happy as my kid sister. When I asked her to check to see if my wages were correct, she had a face on her like thunder - nearly got my head chewed off!'

Noticing his friend seemed unusually quiet and solemn as he checked the figures he'd written on the log sheet, raised his eyebrows in question. Taking a sip of his coffee, Lee ran his hand through his hair, letting out a deep sigh. 'I'm sorry mate, just had bit of a rough night. Didn't get to sleep until three this morning and just as I was really getting into a deep sleep, the alarm clock went off! Could've cheerfully chucked it out of the window!'

Bob gave a chuckle. 'Did you have a late night out on the town? That'll teach you for being a dirty stop-out!' His banter didn't receive the response he was expecting. 'Oh, don't mind me I'm only jealous 'cos I'm a married man and miss out on all that fun now!'

'Oh, it's nothing like that. Yes, I did go out and now I wish I hadn't.' Seeing Bob was looking more intrigued by the second, explained all about the events of the night before, including the dramatic ending to the evening.

Bob rubbed his bristled chin, not bothering to have a shave that morning. He was going to wait until the evening when he'd take Carol and the kids out to see some Disney film that they'd been going on about for ages. His eyes so similar to Kelly's, widened with astonishment after Lee had finished. 'Well, I really don't know what to say about all this, my friend - it really doesn't sound good. Are you sure it wasn't down to the drink?'

'I'm pretty sure it wasn't. I've got to admit, she did drink three large glasses of white but strangely she didn't seem one bit affected. Maybe she's used to drinking that amount, I don't know. But you should've seen her father and that guy, Ian. They seemed to know this would happen to her but they behaved as if I'd abducted her. And she must be about 24 or 25 for goodness sake!'

Bob chewed the top of his pen thoughtfully. 'It's possible that she's got some condition she's not yet told you about or maybe it's to do with the grief with the sister you mentioned. Though you would've thought, after three years she might have begun to come to terms with things.'

'Hmm. I know a death in a family is a terrible thing, especially when that person was young and didn't have the chance to live their life. But terrible as it is, I would have thought the family had worked things through by now. I've tried calling her but it went straight onto voicemail. I've left a couple of messages to see if she's OK but not had a response so far.' Lee took another sip of the bitter vending coffee, which gave its usual half-cup. 'It's Kelly I feel bad about,' he admitted guiltily. 'When I came back to the depot yesterday evening, she spotted Helena in the van and looked daggers at me and completely blanked me out. I guess she got the wrong idea. I think I will need to see her to explain.'

'I wish you luck on that one mate, the mood she's in,' Bob added with a chuckle as his friend stood up from his chair and walked wearily out of the canteen. *Had* his sister got the wrong idea, he wondered. He knew from Carol how clearly Kelly was besotted with Lee and by all accounts it seemed he felt the same way about her. Always going everywhere together and from what he'd heard on the grapevine they'd had a snog at Barry and Sue's engagement do. As much as he liked and respected Lee, he wouldn't allow him to hurt his kid sister whom he loved to pieces.

Lee went up to the office where Kelly was tapping away on her keyboard, frowning in concentration as she worked on some spreadsheet on her monitor, with a barely drank mug of coffee on the desk beside her. Sue sat at the desk opposite, engrossed in a telephone conversation. From the looks of things, it wasn't going too well with her face reddening as she tried conversing with the person at the other end, not giving her the chance to speak. She took the receiver away from her ear as she looked at Lee in exasperation, shrugging as a voice at the other end was shouting. She continued with the conversation. 'Sir, if you insist on using another swear word, I'm afraid I will have no choice but to terminate this call!'

As Kelly grinned at her friend, giving an encouraging thumbs-up, she suddenly became aware of the other person in the room with them. Her face paled as if she'd suddenly seen a ghost, and then was immediately replaced with a frown and a look of contempt.

Judging by her mood, Lee found himself wondering if coming to see her was such a good idea. 'Can I just have a quick word with you, Kelly?'

She looked for a moment at her monitor. 'I'm rather busy at the moment. I've got to get this report finished by 10.30 and I can't miss the deadline.'

With a frown, her attention was now focused entirely on him, looking him squarely in the face with her arms folded, waiting for him to speak. Although engrossed in her telephone conversation, Sue was also looking on with interest to see what was happening.

'It'll only take a couple of minutes,' he promised. 'I've got things to do too. Um, can we go somewhere in private?'

Kelly sighed as she got up from her chair. Really, she wasn't so pushed with that report; most of what she needed to do was done, but why should she have to come running to him just when it suited him? Leading him out to the kitchen area nearby, he took in the smell of burnt toast and the sound of the dripping tap at the sink as if trying to provide some background noise to compensate for the silent treatment that he was clearly being given.

With her arms folded squarely across her chest she stared at him without blinking, waiting for him to speak. Her heart stirred as she was reminded of that night only days ago at Sue and Barry's engagement party when he'd taken her in his arms. Coming to her senses, she forced herself away from gazing into those smouldering brown eyes, now appearing to be clouded with sadness.

'Lee, *what* is it? I haven't got all day. I've got...' He shook his head apologetically. 'It's ok. This won't take long - I promise.' She looked so angry and could see she was more upset than she would care to admit. Trying to place a hand to her face, she suddenly backed away. 'I...I just wanted to say I'm sorry for everything. For the way I treated you the other night - and since.'

Suddenly she laughed but there wasn't any sign of humour on her face. 'Well, I guess it wasn't meant to be. Things would have happened by now otherwise. Anyway, it looks like you've found yourself some company since.'

He shook his head trying his best to reassure this woman he cared so much for. 'I know this sounds so cliché, but it really isn't how it looked. And I mean it. Helena's somebody I met very recently and I couldn't even say she's a friend.' He went on to explain the events of the past few days, how he met Helena when making that delivery and how the evening ended so badly the previous evening.

After he finished, Kelly looked at him and shrugged. 'I really don't know what to say, Lee. It could well be down to the drink. I know when I've been on a night out and had a drink or two when I feel it hasn't had much of an effect on me, I will suddenly come over tired. Maybe this girl has a drinking problem. Sounds like her father knew what was to come when you brought her home.'

'I guess, it's possible. But she doesn't look the sort to go out boozing.'

Kelly went over to the sink and filled the kettle with water.

'What do you *know*, Lee? You've only just met this woman so you know nothing about her or her life. Like you said, she might have some illness or condition you don't know about, or she might be a chronic alcoholic. It's not any of my business but I would try and stay out of things. Sounds like there are issues going on and you might end up regretting that you got yourself involved.' She switched on the kettle, which sprang into action. 'Anyway, I can't stand here chatting to you all day. I've got stuff to do here and I'm sure you've got customers waiting for their deliveries. If it makes you feel better, then try calling her again just to see if she's ok.'

'Ok Kelly, I won't take any more of your time. I've got a lot to get through today as you can imagine. There are a few sales going on and I've got more parcels on than usual. Look, thanks for listening and if you feel up to it one evening, perhaps we can go out for a drink?'

Suddenly feeling angry but trying her best not to show it, said the first thing that came into her head. 'Actually, I've got a lot on at the moment. Sue…Sue has invited me out and I've got other stuff going on.'

'Ok, but when you're free, just give me a call - or send a text.'

As she heard him walking down the stairs, with the door closing firmly, she returned to the office where Sue had just finished her telephone conversation.

Her curiosity getting the better of her, was eager for some answers. 'Well, what went on in the kitchen while I was dealing with the customer from Hell?'

Kelly sat herself down angrily onto her office chair, wincing as she took a sip of her mug of coffee made earlier, which was now stone cold. 'He claims that woman I told you about is just an acquaintance, not even a friend. Just one big coincidence that she happens to be so amazingly pretty.'

Sue regarded her with pity. Why was Lee acting like such a complete heel? Until now she thought he was so perfect for Kelly who was completely crazy over him. For some time, she felt that something would finally happen between them until he threw this wobbly at her engagement, and now this other woman had come onto the scene. Maybe it *was* all completely innocent. Well, at least for the moment. So why did he go and have to spoil things just as it looked like they were finally getting their act together?

She grinned, taking the black and white striped mug that Kelly was still holding. 'I'll do those drinks you started to make before your conversation with Lover Boy. Let's go out at lunchtime and we can have a good chat about things. Ok?'

Kelly smiled weakly as she thought back to her bad morning with Head Office's system messing with the drivers' pay. She would need to apologise to her poor brother who did nothing to deserve the sharp end of her tongue earlier. At least with Sue she had one good friend to share her misery with.

After having finished loading his van, Lee tried one more time without success to contact Helena. As with all the other calls, it rang a few times then went straight onto voice mile. With a sigh, he hung up. No point leaving another message. Perhaps she'd decided to have nothing more to do with him. Or more to the point, her father had decided. But just as he was about to leave the exit of the depot, his mobile rang. Parking to the side he took the call.

'Lee?' came a woman's voice sounding distorted but just about audible. 'Lee, is that you?'

'Helena! Hi!' he replied trying not to sound as relieved as he felt. 'Sounds like I've got bit of bad reception - I've got to admit at the moment you sound like one of Doctor Who's Daleks!'

There were a few seconds of silence before Helena suddenly laughed. 'I'm sorry about that, but the problem must be at your end because you sound perfectly clear to me!'

'Yeah, it probably is - it's not unusual round here to be having a phone conversation and to suddenly get cut off, but there you go. How's everything with you? Are...are you ok after last night? I was getting seriously worried about you.'

'I'm so sorry I missed your calls,' she said apologetically. 'It's just that I'd left my phone in my handbag and didn't see your dozens of missed calls and messages you'd left.'

'But are you ok?'

'Yes,' she replied reassuringly. 'Really I am. I think I mentioned to you last night that I have to go to sleep by 11.30 because otherwise by midnight, I will just fall into a deep sleep and nothing, no matter what I do will stop that. I will always sleep right through without waking up, until the morning.'

Lee chuckled. 'I wish I knew your secret. Quite often I'll wake up at least a couple of times and not always get back off straight away.'

There were a few moments of silence apart from the line made a continuous buzzing sound, which he found slightly irritating.

'I'm so sorry I frightened you last night. I guess the wine didn't help, but I promise you I'm not a drunk. But I would like to apologise for the way Daddy and Uncle Ian reacted.'

'Really, it's not a problem. They were simply worried about you. I know I would be in their shoes if a daughter of mine returned home, in a state of collapse, with a man I knew nothing about.'

She laughed softly. 'But I would like to thank you for a wonderful evening. I really did enjoy myself. Maybe we could do it again some time.'

Taken a little by surprise, Lee wasn't sure what to say. 'Yes...yes. That would be nice, though I'm quite busy with things at the moment. Maybe when things have quietened down at my end, I'll give you a call.'

'That would be nice.'

After Lee hung up, he watched as one of his fellow van drivers passed, giving him a friendly toot with his horn. Waving back, Lee felt it was very unlikely that he would meet her again. Kelly was right, he thought. Best to stay out of things.

Helena hung up on her mobile and was still smiling as she returned to the large dining room, where her parents sat along with Uncle Ian at the long black glass table, the centrepiece of the room. They stared at the young woman, watching her in earnest as she returned to her chair. Her mother resembled an older version of her daughter, the same high cheekbones giving her an almost youthful look, only her eyes a paler shade of blue. Age had meant that she no longer had quite the same thick eyelashes as her daughter and the short, bobbed honey blonde hair these days owed its colour to regular visits to her stylist.

'Well?' demanded her mother. Helena swallowed a spoonful of her cornflakes before she replied. 'Lee was fine. He apologised, although he had no need.'

Her mother finished spreading the marmalade on her toast and gently placed the knife down bedside the plate before her. A small, almost sad smile appeared across her face. 'Darling, you know you cannot continue to see that young man. You realise, don't you?'

Helena turned her attention away from Rupert who was sitting under the table waiting for his usual morning treat of some grilled bacon from Uncle Ian.

'But why not, Mummy? Why shouldn't I see him again?'

Her parents and Uncle Ian stopped eating, looking at each other in what was in obvious surprise. Her father almost poured his tea from the pot onto the white linen tablecloth. Only Rupert seemed unaffected and lied back down in resignation as there didn't appear to be any further treats forthcoming today.

The silence was almost deafening and was only broken by the large clock ticking on the wall. Looking again to her husband and then to Ian, her mother gently placed her hand over her daughter's. 'Darling, it simply isn't possible.'

Professor Broadhurst dabbed his mouth gently with his white napkin, his breathing sounding slightly laboured. 'My angel, you've never before asked to have friends. We've always believed you to be quite content just to be at home with your Uncle Ian and us - not forgetting Hugo and Rupert of course!' he added with a wink gazing down to the golden retriever. 'Haven't we given you a happy life? Not to mention a privileged one? There are lots of girls who would've given anything to travel around the world and go to the best private schools, as you have done. Both your mother and I have done everything possible to give you a good life. Haven't we, Clarissa?'

Clarissa focussed her attention back to her daughter, gently stroking her long fair hair affectionately. 'Your father's right, darling. I know I did a lot of travelling with my film work, and you didn't get to see me very often. My job took me away a lot of the time, working on all those special effects. But despite that, I know that made you very proud, didn't it? I clearly remember how you and Katherine would boast to your school friends about the big films I worked on and the

Hollywood stars I would meet!'

Helen smiled as she thought back to those days. 'Yes, it gave me a such a buzz when I went to the cinema with my classmates and could say that those weird alien creatures in those Sci-Fi's were mostly down to Mummy!'

'There you go,' said her mother smiling warmly. 'You've had a very fortunate life. And of course, we mustn't forget Daddy and Uncle Ian!' The attention of both women now focused on the men sitting opposite.

'I'm very pleased to hear we also get a mention!' Professor Broadhurst remarked smiling affectionately at his wife. His attention turned back to his daughter. 'Yes, my sweet child, there are not many that can boast about the special work that Uncle Ian and I have done! As you well know, we've done some pretty spectacular stuff... not to mention extremely important. But I've always told you that you're never to mention the nature of the work we've been involved with to anyone outside of this family. I'm sure you still realise this.' He watched Helena expectantly.

She nodded and looked to each in the room sitting close by. 'I love you all dearly. But...But I just feel the need to meet other people. Spending time with Lee seemed such fun - I had such a nice time.'

This time Uncle Ian spoke. 'But you know it's not possible,

Helena, don't you? Remember what happened last night?'

Helena watched him with a wide-eyed expression.

'Maybe you don't,' he suggested gently. 'But you know it's not possible for you to stay out late. And we know if you stay up late, what happens to you?'

Helena looked around in turn to her parents and then to Uncle Ian, suddenly feeling angry. 'But now I've decided that I *do* want other friends, to go out and do all the things I used to do before…before. Oh, what's the use!' With that she got up from her chair storming out of the room, slamming the door firmly behind her and rushing up the stairs to her bedroom.

In stunned silence the three people remaining around the dining room table, turned to each other in complete shock. Clarissa was the first to speak out. 'Helena has never, ever expressed any desire to meet with other people before.'

Both Broadhurst and Ian turned to each other with equal surprise. 'We didn't think Helena had it in her,' Professor Broadhurst remarked, shaking his head.

'This is a new side to her we've never seen before,' agreed Ian. 'What do we do?' Clarissa took a sip of tea from her cup. 'I think we all want what's best for Helena, and that's for her to be happy.'

All three nodded in mutual agreement. Helena's mother started gathering up the breakfast plates from around the table. 'But I think it's in our best interests if we keep an eye on the situation and make sure that matters don't get too much out of hand.'

'I think we're all with you on that one,' nodded Broadhurst. 'As you know, there are ways and means of dealing with this, but I would prefer things to stay as they are for the time being. The alternative should only be used as a final resort.'

A key turning in the front door distracted their attention.

'Mrs Cowley,' confirmed Clarissa. Let's keep quiet about this for the moment - the last thing we need is for news to spread. Let's just see how things develop. It may all turn out to be just a storm in a teacup.'

That afternoon, Kelly and Sue walked along the pavement, trying their best to avoid the large puddles. A few people walked around with their umbrellas at the ready in case the heavens decided to open again.

'Well, I'm glad that rain stopped before lunch break,' remarked Sue, as they headed towards the most popular coffee house in town.

Kelly gazed up to the sky, now mainly blue, but a large dark angry looking rain cloud loomed from the horizon. 'I wouldn't hold my breath,' she said with a frown. 'I think there's more to come by the looks of things.'

They entered the building where the aroma of freshly ground coffee greeted them. It looked as if others had the same idea and popped in to avoid another rain shower. Kelly quickly spotted a spare table while Sue bought the drinks.

After a few minutes, Sue came with a tray laden with two Caffe Mocha lattes and two helpings of triple chocolate cookies. 'What's all this?' Kelly cried out in exasperation.

'Just what the doctor ordered,' Sue grinned. 'Loaded with a million calories but very effective at getting rid of the blues.'

Unconvinced, Kelly picked up her fork, looking at the generous helping on her plate. 'It might be delicious, but not so effective at getting rid of those inches around my hips. But boy, this looks good!'

'Go, girl, get it down you and enjoy!' Sue took a sip of her chocolaty coffee. 'Sheer bliss!' she sighed. Despite her chocolate indulgence, her friend seemed lost in her own small world. 'So, what are you going to do about lover boy?'

Kelly shrugged. 'What's there to do? Just when I'm starting to feel that things are beginning to happen, he gives me the brush-off and now he's hanging around with a woman he says is "just an acquaintance!" Well, as far as I'm concerned she's welcome to him!'

Sue slowly stirred her spoon into her hot drink. 'But he *did* explain there was nothing more. Somehow, I don't think Lee's the kind of guy who would lie to you. He's a very straight down the middle kind of person. Are you going to take him up on his offer of a drink?'

Kelly thoughtfully chewed a mouthful of the delicious chocolate cookie. 'I really don't know. At the moment I feel I'm getting mixed signals. The last thing I need after all that aggro with Eric is to get hurt yet again.'

Sue dabbed her mouth gently with her paper napkin. 'What I think is that you're in serious need of a night out. You've been a complete nightmare today. Not that I'm blaming you, with that major gaff at head office with their blessed payroll system, and all this business with Lee. What you need is an infusion of fun!'

Kelly laughed. 'I'm not one for anything too wild these days - you know what I'm like when I've had too much to drink. And I never want a hangover like the one I had a few years ago at the Christmas do. That's one I'll never forget in a hurry!'

'That makes two of us! I think we're both a bit older and wiser for that kind of "fun" now. Actually, I have something else in mind.'

'Why do I think that I'm not going to like the sound of this?' Kelly frowned, feeling more than slightly nervous about the mysterious look on her friend's face.

'It's nothing sinister, I promise. Do you remember me telling you about Barry's mate Carl, who couldn't make it to the engagement because he came down with the flu?'

'*Yes?*' The sound of suspicion was unmistakable in Kelly's voice.

'Well, he's over it now and will be coming over to see us soon. Well, I've just had an idea and want to bounce it off you. Barry and me have been planning to go to the Chinese in town, and I thought maybe we could make it a foursome, with you and Carl.

Kelly wasn't sure. 'Oh, I don't know Sue. I don't think it's a good idea..."

Sue looked at her friend firmly in the eyes. 'I'm not saying there has to be anything in it. Just that I think you could both do with a night out. I'll tell you a few things about him. He's just come out of a long-term relationship - his other half left him for somebody else and he took it badly. I think that's why he came down with the flu because he's normally a pretty healthy guy and does judo with Barry. I promise you, he's really nice and I wouldn't put you in a situation I wouldn't think you'd be uncomfortable with.

She knew Sue only meant well, and to be honest a night out might just help shift this dark cloud which seemed to be constantly following her. 'Maybe I'll give it some thought.

Could you tell me what he looks like?'

Sue felt happier at her friend's sudden change of heart and grinned. 'Well, I can do better than tell you what he looks like. I've got a picture of him on my phone.' She took her Android out of her handbag and showed her a picture of the man, sitting with Barry on the sofa grinning like a pair of Cheshire cats.

'Excuse the stupid faces these two were pulling,' Sue smiled affectionately. 'They were both completely over the moon because Spurs beat Arsenal.'

It was difficult to gauge too much by the photo. Carl's hair appeared to be a strawberry blonde and receding slightly at the temples. At a guess, she would have said he was a similar age to herself and Sue. His face she would have described as oval and seemed to have piercing blue eyes. Although she wouldn't have considered him handsome, he had what appeared to be a kind face with a warm smile, which appeared to be his best feature. But really, it was difficult to tell much from just one picture, and Sue said she didn't have any more of him on the phone.

'Ok,' she relented. 'But as long as you make it clear to him this isn't a date. Just a few friends getting together.'

'I promise. I'll speak to Barry about it tonight and see when Carl's free as well, and get back to you.' Sue patted her stomach. 'I don't know about you, but I'm feeling completely stuffed.'

Kelly winced, thinking of all those extra calories that would take forever to shift. A pity she couldn't go to badminton with Lee anymore and didn't know of anyone else who was interested in the game. Sue was the first to admit that she didn't care for the fitness thing. Glancing at her watch, she gathered up her handbag from the crumb covered floor. 'Guess we'd better make tracks, it looks like we're have to make a dash for it!'

Sue's eyes followed Kelly's gaze to the window where huge raindrops fell down. 'Hmm, looks like we were destined for a soaking today!'

CHAPTER SIX

The week had passed uneventfully for Lee. Maybe a little too much, he thought grimly as he finished his last delivery for the day. Kelly was still giving him the silent treatment, despite his best efforts to put things right. He'd tried calling her a couple of times but on each occasion his call was diverted to voicemail. She would never call back or reply to the texts he'd sent her. In the end he gave up. What was the point when she was in this mood?

He wasn't sure whether or not he was imaging things, but when he went out with Bob for a drink a couple of nights back, he felt sure that Bob had wanted to tell him something but was holding back. Maybe it was just all in his mind and was reading into things too much. As for Helena, thankfully he didn't hear any more from her, so it looked like things had died a natural death in that area. Although he always had regular deliveries in Little Green, much to his relief hadn't received any more for the Broadhursts with those small but heavy parcels from that Japanese company.

Just as Lee finished his final delivery in Bishop Street and was about to climb back into the van, his mobile vibrated into life in his pocket and saw the call was from Roger Morgan.

'Hi lad,' greeted the manager. 'Hope you've had a nice busy day!'

Lee chuckled. 'You could say that! Since the launch of that new Notebook that everyone's been raving on about, it feels like the whole population of Old Church has placed an order for one!'

'Tell me about it! We've had loads of customers coming to collect from the depot ready to use at the weekend.' There was a moment of silence before he continued. 'We did have a couple of embarrassing moments when the customers came to collect from the depot and the Notebooks were nowhere to be found.'

Lee shook his head in disbelief, although he knew his boss wouldn't have been able to see. 'But surely all those Notebooks should be secured in the high value cage. As far as I'm aware they all require a signature on delivery?'

'Precisely! And as you know those customers' goods are noted in the high value register. So, there's obviously a thief at large, possibly more than one, and it looks as if we'll have to step up on our security checks. Anyway, that isn't the reason why I called you, as bad as things are. The interviews for General Manager are now being organised and I'd like you to pop up and see me when you get back to the depot.'

Lee looked briefly at his watch. 'I've just finished my last drop for the day, so I should be with you in the next ten minutes or so.'

Not long after he returned to the depot and booked in, he received another call on his phone and grimaced when he saw Helena's name on the display. He quickly put the phone onto silent. The last thing he needed at this moment was any unwelcome distractions. Hopefully, when he didn't answer the call, she would take the hint.

He went through the office to see Kelly engrossed in a phone conversation as she tapped away on her keyboard. Only Sue looked up to nod in acknowledgement before looking towards her friend. The door was open to Roger Morgan's office and the man was there ready to shake his hand.

He gave Lee the details about the interview, which was to take place a week from today in the conference room where he was to give a presentation to Roger himself and the Regional Manager, James Close. He also learned he was up against five other candidates which included Mike Stanton, who believed the job was as good as his. Three other candidates who were to attend were already in management roles at other depots within the network. But more worryingly, one of the interviewees was a general manager for a smaller but up and coming delivery company, and had secured some impressive clients.

Having done a number of presentations in his previous role as a senior manager, felt that the one he was soon to make was probably the most important one of his life. This time he was fighting back for the career he had lost. There was no shame in being a delivery driver, in fact that's how he started out in the business and because of that, he could appreciate all aspects of work within a delivery company. But Lee knew his heart was truly in the operations side and felt a great sense of achievement at how he played a major part in the success of FPS until everything had gone so badly wrong. In no time at all, his dreams along with the life he become accustomed to, all turned to dust.

Lee walked out from Roger's office, watching Kelly who was still on her call, with her back to him. Sue gave him a smile, waving to him as he walked by. As he closed the door behind him, Kelly placed the receiver down and breathed a sigh of relief.

Sue couldn't help but smile. 'I'm sure you had him convinced that you were on the phone all that time, but he must think that receiver's glued to your ear!'

Kelly peered over to the door, worried in case he would come bursting into the room again. 'I know I'm being dead childish, but I just don't feel I want to talk to him at the moment. After ignoring all his texts, I hope he's finally got the message that as far as I'm concerned he's history.'

Her colleague and friend raised her eyebrows, not at all convinced she was being truthful to herself. Who was she trying to kid? It was clear to see she was still smitten with him.

Kelly looked at her watch then began switching down her PC, with Sue's look of disbelief seemingly lost on her. 'Well, another day over with and our night out to look forward to one day closer. So, tomorrow I finally get to meet this Carl you've been raving on so much about.'

Sue briefly checked her mobile. 'I'm sure you won't be disappointed. He's a really nice guy and he's been asking lots about you.'

Kelly felt her cheeks burning. 'Well, let's hope he's not in for a disappointment!'

Later, after Lee returned home to his flat, having showered and eaten his ready-meal heated up in the microwave, sat down at the laptop in his bedroom. The room was of a reasonably good size where his double bed with the black quilt and matching sheets took centre stage. The fitted wardrobe along the opposite wall gave ample room to hold most of his clothes. The room was clean and tidy with plain painted grey walls, where hung a couple of pictures of racing cars and a shelf of books, with autobiographies being his favourite read. He sat at the small black desk, putting together a presentation. Thankfully he still kept his Power Point software, probably not the most up to date, he mused, but did the job.

Sighing, he rubbed his eyes, the fatigue now setting in as he relaxed after a busy day. For about the tenth time he looked at his mobile then listened to the message that Helena had left earlier in the day.

'Lee, hi, it's Helena. Hope you're ok and that all that business with Daddy didn't put you off. He really is a sweetie once you get to know him. I...I was wondering if you could give me a call once you've received this message. Anyway, I hope to hear from you soon. Bye.'

Frowning, he placed the smartphone back on his desk. That reception from Little Green was pants and made her voice sound so distorted. It was hard work trying to understand what she was saying.

He gave a deep sigh, rubbing his hand through his hair giving it a slightly ruffled look. Against his better judgement, he called Helena's number.

'Lee!' cried Helena, answering almost immediately. 'Thank you for calling back.' Despite the poor signal, he could detect a note of desperation in her voice. He might live to regret doing this, but believed he would have felt worse if he decided otherwise. There was a pause. Lee wasn't sure what to say, but she continued. 'I hope you're well and had a good week.'

He put the call on hands-free as he continued tapping away at the keyboard, wincing at the crackly line. 'Can't complain. Hectic as always at work, but hey, it pays the bills! How about you?'

'Good. Good, but nothing special. Took Rupert out for his walks. I helped Mummy with cooking her signature chicken curry recipe. Watched Daddy and Uncle Ian in the lab working on one of their latest projects.'

That girl really didn't have a life he thought. 'No catching up with friends?'

There was a moment's silence, before she sighed. 'No, I'm afraid not. I guess as we grow older, our lives change and we simply drift apart.'

'That's true,' he agreed. 'I guess our friends come and go as we move on in different directions. What happened to your friend from uni?'

'You mean Katherine?' Again, there was silence, apart from this hissing sound that broke through the reception. 'I'm really not sure what happened to Katherine. We had such a fab time at university. But I guess as you say, our lives simply change.'

A pity you don't seem to have made any other friends, he thought to himself. 'Have you done any more painting?' he asked, deciding to change the subject.

She laughed lightly. 'Actually, I tried painting Rupert, but it turned out to be a complete disaster. Normally he loves nothing better than to snooze on the floor next to the fire, but when I decide to immortalise him on canvas, he decides to walk off!'

Lee pressed the Save button on the laptop. 'That's pets for you! But you keep practicing and I'm sure it'll all come back. I remember how brilliant those paintings were when I came to your house. Don't waste your talent!'

'Actually, there's something I wanted to ask you. I was wondering if you would like to come over for dinner on Sunday? That's if you have nothing else planned.'

Lee immediately sat up. An invitation to dinner at the Broadhursts was the last thing he expected. 'Helena, I really don't think that would be a good idea - especially after what happened last time. I was made to feel as if I was being accused of your abduction and attempted murder!'

'Really Lee, Mummy and Daddy realise it wasn't your fault. They were just worried. Actually, they know I'm inviting you and they're fine about it. It's their way of a peace-offering.'

Lee was unconvinced. 'Are you sure? Your father and um,

Uncle Ian looked livid.'

'Really, there isn't a problem. Nobody's blaming you, everybody was just worried about the situation at the time.'

He tapped his fingers lightly on the desk in thought. 'I really don't know, Helena. I've got this presentation to sort out for an interview and I really need to get this right.'

The crackly silence was almost deafening. 'I see. I do understand. I appreciate you must have a busy life with your work, and your friends. It's just that I had such a really nice time when we went for that pizza, that I simply wanted to thank you.'

Lee couldn't help but feel a bit mean. His life might not have turned out the way he'd hoped, but here was poor Helena who had lost her sister and the whole business had obviously turned her entire life upside down. It wasn't as if he had anything better to do. Kelly didn't want to know him, and Bob was spending time with his family.

'OK, then. I'm sure it'll do me good to take a break from making slide shows. What time's best for you?'

A few minutes later he hung up. Sunday at one o'clock it was. He hoped he'd made the right decision.

After their phone conversation, Helena returned to the living room. Her mother was sitting in front of an easel near the window, working on her latest watercolour. Professor

Broadhurst sat on the leather sofa nearby with a clipboard perched on his lap, working on some calculation to do with his work; beside him sat Uncle Ian tapping away at his laptop resting on the coffee table. The large TV screen was showing some old black and white film, with background music booming away on the sound system. But nobody was paying attention to the screen. All eyes were focused on the young woman, looking happy as she sat down in the armchair, stroking Rupert who was lying down on the floor next to her.

Her father sighed, slamming down the clipboard on to the glass table, startling the others around him. 'I take it you contacted Lee, judging by the pleased look on your face?'

She nodded, her expression becoming serious, her eyes widening with anxiety. 'Mummy said it was ok. Didn't you, Mummy?'

Clarissa momentarily turned to her latest masterpiece on the easel and before muting the sound on the TV with the control. 'Yes, I know I did darling, but it doesn't mean that I'm approving of all this.' She looked at Helena, feeling troubled at the sudden look sadness on her face, turning towards her husband and Ian for support.

Broadhurst got up from the settee and walked slowly over to Helena and stroked her long hair affectionately. His finger joints showing arthritic swelling, which often comes with age.

'My dear, please try not to take this all so badly, but we're only trying to do what's best for you.'

Frustrated, Helena covered her hands over her eyes, sighing deeply before looking up to her father with an angry expression that clearly took him by surprise.

'But how can it be the *best* for me to be here all by myself, with nobody else to speak to? To have a nice time with?'

Professor Broadhurst removed his spectacles before wearily rubbing his eyes, his face looking clearly fatigued. 'My dear, until lately you were more than content with our company. And we mustn't forget Hugo!'

Both father and daughter turned their attention to Uncle Ian who had long forgotten about the work on his laptop, listening intently to the whole conversation. Helena could swear there were tears in his eyes. Although he wasn't a blood relation, she adored this man who had always been around in her life as far back as she could remember. In fact, she could say hand on heart that she loved him every bit as much as Mummy and Daddy.

She stood up from her chair and walked over to Ian, giving him a hug. 'I'm so sorry. I really didn't mean to hurt you. Nobody could *ever* take your place. You have all been so wonderful to me. Nobody could be any more special. Uncle Ian, there's nothing that makes me happier than spending time with you and Daddy in the lab and seeing all the amazing work you both do. And as for Hugo, he's simply amazing!'

Ian smiled sadly, taking hold of Helena's soft hand, giving it a gentle kiss. 'My sweet, talking of Hugo, when your new friend comes to dinner on Sunday, you mustn't breath a word about him. He must stay our secret. Is that understood?'

Helena turned her attention to her parents who watched her expectantly before her father added, 'Do we have your word?'

Smiling gently, her attention turned to Rupert, stroking him on the chin. 'Don't worry. I won't mention a thing about him. Come along on Rupert, let's take a walk in the garden.'

As she left the room with the dog following close behind, Broadhurst returned to the sofa. He gave a deep sigh, his shoulders stooped as if they carried all the troubles of the world on them. 'I really don't know what we might have started here Clarissa, and I can't say I'm at all happy with you agreeing to all these arrangements. Why is Helena suddenly expressing a desire for different company? Until now she seemed quite content to simply be with us. I cannot understand why she suddenly feels the need to socialise. What on earth is happening?' He looked over to Ian as if he might hold all the answers.

But the other man just shrugged his shoulders. 'I really

have no idea. I'm equally as baffled. Helena has never shown these traits before. Why they should suddenly manifest themselves, since the day that delivery driver made his debut is a mystery. But this certainly was never meant to happen.' He looked to each of his companions in turn. 'As we all know, there are ways we can deal with this matter, but not without consequences.'

His wife placed one of the paint bushes in the glass of water on the small table beside her. 'I think it would be for the best if we simply go along with what Helena wants for the time being. Whatever the reasons, she has shown a desire for other company and I believe that as long as we keep a tight rein on matters so they don't get too much out of hand, no harm can come to her. All I can see is that Helena's feeling unhappy. She tries so hard to paint those landscapes and feels frustrated that they're not as good as the ones she had done in happier times. She doesn't understand.' She turned her attention back to the watercolour on her easel. 'I'm sure we're all in agreement that we want what is best for Helena. And that's to give her as normal life as possible.'

On Saturday evening, Kelly finished getting herself ready for her night out with Sue and Barry, not forgetting Carl. It wasn't officially meant to be a date but she felt more than a little nervous. Since breaking up with Eric, she hadn't allowed herself to become close to any other guy, apart from Lee. But now it was time to put him firmly out of her mind, she thought as she studied herself in the mirror after having put on some lipstick.

Instead of doing her usual cleaning up around the flat, which she tended to do on Saturdays, she popped into town to treat herself to something to wear for the evening. She had to admit she was more than a little pleased with the result as she studied herself in the full-length mirror, wearing the pale blue shift dress which flattered her narrow waste, with the shorter length making her legs appear longer. For a change she decided to wear her long dark curly hair loose, making a striking contrast to the colour of her dress.

Slipping into her shoes with the very high heels she brought as well, realised she'd been a little extravagant, but the blue was such a perfect match to the dress that she couldn't resist. Having applied a couple of squirts of her favourite light floral perfume, she heard the sound of a car pulling up and tooting. Taking a quick look out of the window, confirmed her taxi had finally arrived. It wasn't a date, she reminded herself. Just a night out with two of her good friends who happened to be bringing one of their own friends to make an even number. Before leaving, she quickly texted Sue to let her know she was on her way.

In less than ten minutes she had arrived outside Mr Wok's Chinese restaurant where Sue was waiting just outside the door, her arms folded, feeling slightly cold in the evening air.

Seeing Kelly, her face lit up with a warm smile. 'Hey, look at you! You look amazing. That dress looks beautiful. I don't think I will ever get into your dress size. I had a struggle to get into these trousers.'

'You look fab as well,' Kelly kindly remarked but could see her friend was looking more curvaceous.

Sue laughed as she gently patted her rounded stomach. 'I think we both know I'm not getting any slimmer.' Her expression turned more serious. 'Just thought I'd tell you that I'll be a little later coming into work Monday. Not long after I got home yesterday, I had a call from the surgery wanting to see me about my cholesterol test I had the other day.'

Kelly was very concerned. 'I guess they wouldn't give you a clue as what it could be about? I hope everything's OK and whatever it is I'm sure will be addressed quickly.'

'That makes two of us. But let's not worry about it this evening - not much we can do until next week. I intend getting you introduced to Carl and start tucking in!'

They went inside and unsurprisingly being a Saturday, the place was very busy, being one of the most popular restaurants in town. The smell of cooked food was inviting as they weaved their way through the tables until they came to the far corner where she recognised Barry with his shaved head and dark goatee beard. Sitting next to him another man she recognised from the picture on Sue's Android. As they noticed them approaching, both smiled and stood up. Barry greeted her as usual with a big hug and a kiss on the cheek and soon she was introduced to Carl, who was surprisingly tall and well built at well over 6ft. He towered over her as he gave her hand a firm shake. His smile was warm and clearly liked what he saw as he regarded her appreciatively.

Having ordered drinks, they studied their menus as they chatted about their day. Kelly took a sneaky glance at Barry's friend, noticing there was a little grey peppered around his temples of his hair and as with most redheads had very pale, freckly skin.

Like Barry, Carl was dressed casually but smart in a green rugby shirt with jeans. The food was pleasant and a lot of the time was spent discussing Barry and Sue's wedding, which was to take place the following year with Kelly being Maid of Honour.

Sitting directly opposite Carl, often caught him glancing her way with his pale blue eyes, which seemed to look straight into her soul. She knew, had she not drunk a glass or two of wine, would be blushing like a beetroot at all the attention.

He revealed to her that he worked as a manager for a large insurance company for over ten years and had recently broken up from a long-term relationship. Although she did mention about her relationship with Eric, didn't have the inclination to go into any further details. Like Barry, he loved all kinds of sports, from rugby to football and was even a Black Belt at judo.

The evening passed quickly, with Kelly and Carl exchanging phone numbers before going outside to their taxis. It was just as they were leaving the restaurant, with Kelly standing close to Carl, chatting and laughing, that Lee drove by in his van after getting a takeaway, watching the scene before him, feeling numbed with shock.

CHAPTER SEVEN

Lee made his way to The Woodlands, with a mixture of apprehension and a heavy feeling gripping his heart. Reluctantly, he'd accepted Helena's invitation but was looking forward to this even less after what he'd witnessed the night before, and consequently had a lousy night's sleep. Why hadn't it occurred to him that Kelly might be seeing someone else? From what he could see, she looked absolutely stunning in that dress and hadn't seen her looking so happy for some time. More fool him, he thought grimly. Kelly had made it clear from day one that she was interested and all along he'd felt the same.

But thanks to his messed-up head with Miranda, decided not to act upon those feelings, and now it was too late. No wonder she hadn't returned his calls when she was hanging around with some tall muscly guy!

Well, now he was on his way to have Sunday dinner with a pretty, but strange young woman he'd only recently met, along with her parents. That Uncle Ian, he could swear, had taken an instant disliking to him. Why on earth had he agreed to all this? he thought with regret as he drove into the grounds of

The Woodlands, along the windy cobbled drive.

As he pulled up in his white van outside the large house, the door opened with Helena coming out and Rupert following not far behind. He wasn't quite sure how he should dress for the occasion but decided on casual, with a thick blue checked shirt and jeans. Much to his relief, Helena was dressed in her tight jeans and a long pale pink tee shirt, with her long hair tied back into a ponytail. A warm smile spread across her heart shaped face as he climbed down from the van, peering at the bottle of wine he was holding.

'Wasn't sure what was for dinner, but I've brought along a bottle of Red.

'Wow, that's brilliant! We're having roast beef so that should go down pretty well.' As they entered the house, the unmistakable aroma of meat and vegetables came wafting through from the kitchen. Her parents stood together; along with Uncle Ian in the lounge all dressed in fairly casual attire. All three stared at him firmly and Lee felt an involuntary shiver run down his spine from the frosty reception he was clearly receiving.

'I guess I should introduce you all formally after having so rudely fallen asleep before,' she smiled apologetically. 'Lee, these are my parents, Clarissa and Sebastian.' Both reluctantly shook his hand in turn. 'And this is Ian Peterson, who I've always known as Uncle Ian. He's not a true relative, but I couldn't love him any more even if he was,' she added fondly, pointing to the man standing at some distance behind her parents. After a moment's hesitation he gave Lee a rather limp handshake. The hostility he displayed was unmistakable with his skin visibly paling, emphasising the angry, jagged scar that ran across his face. This didn't look set to be a fun-packed Sunday afternoon, he thought grimly.

The one thing that struck him instantly and took him by surprise was Helena's mother. Judging by her appearance she must have been well into her seventies. He was already aware that Professor Broadhurst was of around a similar age, but wrongly assumed he probably had a younger wife. There was no question of Helena having been adopted as the resemblance to her mother was so striking. He guessed the couple had decided to have their children later on in life. If he didn't know better, would have assumed they were her grandparents. Maybe they simply appeared older than their age.

'I don't think I've mentioned to you before that I love cooking!' Helena revealed trying to make conversation to bridge the awkward silence. Mummy and I have been working hard all morning, preparing everything.'

'No, I don't think you've made any mention of your culinary skills. Well, it certainly smells very appetising.'

'Well, the waiting is nearly over, so why don't you gentleman make yourselves comfortable in the dining room as dinner is about to be served,' suggested Helena.

Lee knew that Helena was doing her best to break the ice between them but it would take more than a sledgehammer to do that, he thought ruefully.

The men sat around the large glass dining room table, in uneasy silence as Helena and her mother got down to serving the food. Despite the atmosphere, Lee felt his appetite returning at the sight of the large joint of cooked beef on the serving plate. Peterson offered to carve, but Helena insisted that was her job. After the meat was served on his plate, Helena smiled, watching with pride as Lee helped himself to carrots, broccoli and roast potatoes. The silence was suddenly broken as her mother cried out in horror as the knife slipped, cutting deep into her Helena's hand. Quickly, he stood up as blood oozed onto the white tablecloth.

'It's ok,' Peterson reassured him. 'I'll see to her.'

Lee felt deeply concerned. 'That looks like one deep cut, perhaps I should drive her to the hospital. It looks like she might need some stiches.'

'I said it's ok!' barked Peterson. 'It's just superficial – nothing more. Come along Helena, let's get you to the kitchen!'

To Lee's surprise, Helena gave a small reassuring smile

but Lee knew that in her shoes, he would probably have fainted. He helped to lift the plates as her mother quickly took away the blood-stained tablecloth. Despite all the shock with the turnaround of events, Lee couldn't help but notice that her blood looked much paler than the deeper red he would expect from such a deep cut. Professor Broadhurst sat there staring accusingly at him, as if Lee himself was to blame for the accident. Within a few minutes, a sense of normality returned, as Helena came back to the room with her left hand bandaged up, looking apparently none the worse for her ordeal. After her mother replaced the tablecloth, Helena put down the crockery with her uninjured hand and Peterson busily carved away at the joint of beef.

'Are...are you feeling ok? That looked a really nasty cut.' Lee couldn't help but feel concerned.

'Honestly, I'm absolutely fine,' she replied with a smile. 'It wasn't as bad as it appeared.'

Lee wasn't at all convinced, even though she'd been surprisingly brave and didn't show any visible signs of shock or pain.

Professor Broadhurst walked over to examine her hand. 'Is it bandaged tight enough?' he asked Peterson.

'Yes, though I've asked Helena to keep her hand as still as possible for the time being until things are sorted out later.'

Clarissa passed around the gravy to those who wanted it. 'Helena's a strong girl - she'll be fine. Now, let's have our dinner before it goes completely cold. Ian, be a love and uncork the wine that Lee so kindly brought along.'

Reluctantly he uncorked the bottle as if he found the whole process a wasted effort. He graciously poured wine first for the ladies and then Professor Broadhurst. As he served a measure for himself, looked over to Lee with a scowl. 'I trust you won't be having any seeing that you're driving,'

He shook his head. 'Of course not, I would never drink and drive - that would be crazy when driving is my livelihood.'

Everybody in the room looked reassured and realised that the memories of their daughter being killed as a result of a drunk driver was something that would never leave them.

Peterson took a sip of his wine. 'So, tell us more about your fascinating life as a delivery driver.'

All attention was focused on Lee, who felt he could have cheerfully punched this man who seemed to have taken an instant disliking to him for no apparent reason.

'Well, it might not be some highflying job and nothing in comparison with brain surgery, but it's a living.'

'Have you ever strived for more?' Professor Broadhurst asked politely. 'As you say, there's no shame in being a delivery driver. A man has to do what he can to put bread on the table, but have you ever wanted to do more?'

Lee went on to explain about his previous life as a senior manager at FPS, without going into the business of Miranda and her father. Hoping not to tempt fate, told the professor about the opportunity of promotion that had come his way, and how he would try as hard as possible to succeed.

Peterson shook his head cynically. 'But surely you've been out of touch for too long to resume a senior position? Your chances must be pretty slim compared to candidates who are still leading and not being led.'

Lee took a long sip of his water then held his breath for a few seconds to remain calm. This man was irritating beyond belief.

'Well, I guess the fact that I was approached by the General Manger himself to apply for the job, must count for something. He was aware of my previous track record for turning around the fortunes of FPS.' He looked thoughtfully at his glass of water. 'I'm unable to predict the outcome but will try my hardest to be a success.'

Trying to steer the conversation away from himself and Peterson's sarcastic remarks, Lee changed the subject. 'Helena was telling me that you have a lab here where you work from.'

Her parents and Peterson shot Helena an accusing glance as if she had committed the ultimate sin by revealing this secret.

Her father's laugh seemed a little nervous. 'That daughter of mine has such a vivid imagination. Really, it's just a small workshop that Ian and I use to play around with small ideas. Nothing fancy, I can assure you.'

Helena cut into one of her roast potatoes, which she dipped into the gravy on her plate. 'Daddy, you're being far too modest.' She peered over to Lee. 'Daddy and Ian are both very clever people. 'I don't think I've mentioned to you before that Daddy is one of the leading people in the world with his work on Telemetry.'

Lee frowned in puzzlement. 'Telemetry? Ah, yes isn't that something to do with wireless data transfer?'

Both Broadhurst and Peterson looked suitably impressed as if they didn't expect him to know anything beyond driving a van and delivering parcels.

Helena looked proudly towards her father. 'He's such a clever person. And of course, so's Uncle Ian. You would be amazed at the projects they've worked together on and what they specialise in.'

'Enough Helena!' ordered her father firmly. Your friend didn't come here to be bored, listening to what us boring old fogies get up to in our workshop.'

A hurt expression shadowed her face. 'I'm sorry Daddy,

but it's just that I'm so excited about Hugo. Can't we introduce him to Lee?'

Her mother raised her eyebrows in warning to her daughter. 'Helena! Will you *please* just keep quiet! What's got into you?'

Helena placed down her knife and fork on the plate without finishing her food. 'I'm sorry.'

Her mother's face softened. 'I think it's all the shock with cutting your hand on that knife. I tell you what, before we serve dessert, why don't you take a walk with Lee? Perhaps on the same route that you take Rupert for his walks?'

Her face lit up. 'Yes, that sounds a great idea, but I don't think I'll take Rupert as he tends to get a bit lazy at this time of the day.'

Broadhurst looked concerned. 'I'm not sure it's a good idea them going out, Clarissa. They've given out possible thunderstorms for this afternoon on the weather forecast.'

There were just a few seconds of hesitation on Clarissa's face, before shaking her head as she gathered up the plates. 'Oh, stop worrying, Sebastian! It's April and highly unlikely to come too much. Besides, the storms are forecast further north. They'll be fine and I'm sure she will be in safe hands.'

Lee noticed a nerve twitch at the side of Peterson's jaw at the remark. But he was too relieved just to leave the house and the peculiar atmosphere to care. 'Um, would you like a hand with the washing-up?' he asked politely.

A small smile appeared on Clarissa's face as she continued clearing the table. 'No need, that's what dishwashers are for. Now get yourselves out of here and enjoy some fresh air.'

As they left the house, Lee began to believe that Professor Broadhurst was right about the storms. The sky was beginning to appear overcast with ominous dark clouds floating by with a muggy feel to the air. Although he didn't relish the idea of getting soaked in the rain, just about anything was preferable to the tense atmosphere of that house. Why these people were being so over-protective towards Helena, was a mystery. It was understandable that there should be some concern after what happened to their elder daughter. To lose a child was every parent's worst nightmare. But in the process of their grief, they were not allowing Helena to live her life and move on in the way she deserved to.

Together, they walked down the steep road on the route Lee would take to Little Green and the other surrounding villages. But now walking instead, he could appreciate the scenery, the scent of the grass and the sounds of birds singing. Simple pleasures he couldn't appreciate inside his van, where all he had for company was the sound of the radio and being in a constant rush. Helena led him to a footpath that ran through the woods. The shade of the trees provided little relief from the unseasonably humid atmosphere. Lee gave an exasperated sigh as he mopped the perspiration from his forehead with a handkerchief. Helena, however, seemed undeterred and as radiant as ever as she smiled in appreciation as she peered up towards a blackbird singing merrily high up on the branch of an elm tree.

'This is such a beautiful place,' she remarked dreamily. 'I come this way with Rupert twice a day and I never tire of all its hidden treasures. There's always something different to see. Would you believe, I've even seen the odd fox or two scurrying, and both grey and black squirrels climbing fast up these branches?' She paused for a moment, absorbing everything in around her as if seeing it all for the first time. 'The changes of the seasons never cease to amaze me. After winter, there's the spring to look forward to, where everything is so new and fresh with all the cherry trees in bloom. That's the time for new beginnings. And then comes the summer, where everything's alive and fragrant.' She closed her eyes for a moment as she smiled. 'But most of all I love the autumn with all the leaves changing to red and gold, falling to make a beautiful carpet on the ground. That's a time to reflect on everything.'

'It really is a lovely area,' agreed Lee. 'I was brought up in the town and I guess I've got used to the noise and the bustle of traffic and people constantly coming and going. But I think I could easily get used to a place like this. Trouble is properties in the country don't come cheap unless you buy a place to renovate, and that's just not something I know a lot about. Guess I will have to wait until I win my millions on the Lotto.'

Helena laughed. 'Never say never. Sometimes you never know what might be around the corner. Opportunities come along when you least expect them to. When is your job interview?'

'Towards the end of next week, and it's by no means certain I'll get the job. I'm up against some pretty stiff competition.'

'Well, I know I have only known you for a very short time, but if there's one thing I have learned about you, is that you strike me as a very determined person.'

Lee couldn't help but smile at that remark. Seeing an old fallen tree log he sat down on it, patting the side next to him inviting her to do the same.

'You're not tired already?' she asked teasingly. 'Our walk has only just begun.'

'I guess I am. I had a terrible night's sleep and when I did get to sleep I had some really strange dreams.'

'I never dream,' she admitted, tugging at some grass.

'You must do sometimes. You probably just don't remember them.'

'I definitely don't have dreams,' she looked at him with defiance. 'Every night when I go to bed, I go straight to sleep without waking once during the night. I always wake up at 8 o'clock on the dot every single day.'

He laughed. 'I wish I knew your secret to a good night's sleep. If I did, I would write a book about it and I'm sure it would become a best seller.' He studied her expression, which looked so happy and contented.

'I'm surprised you don't feel hot,' he added with a smile, feeling more than a little envious of her looking so cool in the warm and balmy weather. 'I think your dad's right, there's going to be a storm.'

Helena sat up straight, her large blue eyes, widening in alarm.

'You're afraid of thunderstorms,' he stated.

But she shook her head.

'There isn't any shame in being afraid. My mum has a real phobia of them - I've known her to hide under the table when there's so much as a flash of lightening!'

She gave a peel of laughter. 'Honestly, I'm really not scared. It's just that my parents go into a complete panic if they see me go out in a storm. It's not as if they're particularly afraid of storms - I believe they think I'm going to vaporise or go up in a puff of smoke.'

'That's parents for you. They never stop worrying, no matter how old we are.'

Suddenly a bright flash of lightning startled them both, followed by a loud clap of thunder.

Lee peered towards the tops of the trees to what he could see of the sky. 'I think we should start heading back soon. It's definitely heading this way.'

'I told you...'

'I know you're not scared but I'm more afraid we're going to get a soaking any time soon.'

Helena looked into his eyes, her face serious. 'Kelly is a very lucky lady.'

Lee started to get up from the log, wiping his jeans as he did so. 'Try saying that to Kelly. Now she doesn't want to know me, and now it looks like she's seeing someone else.'

She gazed into his troubled face, his dark eyes looking so sad without their usual sparkle. Suddenly, without warning, she stood up; holding his face as she slowly kissed his lips.

'Helena!' He was completely taken by surprise as hadn't seen this coming. For a brief moment to his shame, found himself responding before gently pulling her away.

Another bright flash of lightning lit the darkening woods, along with a deafening clap of thunder, only much louder than before. Helena's eyes widened in what he first had taken to be surprise, until her body appeared to go rigid as she fell to the ground backwards, with a sickening thud.

'Helena! Oh my God!'

As the rain suddenly poured down, the young woman lay on the ground, her body convulsing from head to toe as if she was having some kind of fit. Her eyes were wide open and unblinking, appeared to be completely unaware of Lee or her surroundings. At first, he tried to hold her but realised his efforts were no match to the strength she was displaying at that moment. He remembered reading somewhere that when people were having fits it was best to let it take its course, making sure they didn't bang into objects and harm themselves further.

Oblivious to the rain that soaked them both, he rummaged in his pocket for his mobile in the hope that Helena had left her phone where her parents would hear it if he called the number. He tried to call and after a few rings went straight onto voice mail. Damn it, he thought angrily, shoving the phone back into his pocket.

Normally, Lee prided in himself in staying calm in a difficult situation, but had to admit he was really more than just a little afraid as he stood helpless as Helena's body shook and convulsed in a way he had never seen with anybody before. Then just as he was about to try and call the emergency services her body suddenly went limp and very still, with her eyes firmly shut.

'Helena? Helena?' Beginning to fear the worst, he was about to check her heartbeat when her eyes suddenly opened wide but appearing not to recognise him. 'Helena, speak to me. Speak to me!'

Her mouth opened. 'Begin…begin.' It was said clearly and coherently as if she was giving him an instruction.'

Her body soaked with rain, her hair sticking to her face, with her eyes blinking, she repeated herself. 'Begin…begin.'

Her mind was obviously affected by whatever had happened and she didn't appear to be aware of him or where she was. Slowly and carefully he picked her up and started to carry her, knowing this was the only way to get her home.

For her height and build, she was surprisingly heavy. Fortunately, they hadn't gone too far into their walk which was just as well as the hill leading back to the house was quite steep. Just as he felt he would need to put her down for a moment as his back was beginning to ache, Ian Peterson met him, dressed in a blue waterproof mac with a hood. They both held her, with Lee carrying her from the shoulders and Peterson from her legs. The rain slowed down as they approached the house, with her parents waiting at the bottom of the drive, frantic with worry but appearing unsurprised by what had happened. As they entered the house, Broadhurst glared at his wife in anger.

'See woman, I told you there would be a storm. But would you listen to me? Now you see what's happened!'

Clarissa watched on, biting her lip nervously as they carried Helena into the lounge, and to Lee's surprise, placed her onto the floor, making a large wet patch on the laminate. Helena's eyes still wide open, without blinking, looking up to the ceiling appearing oblivious to those around her. 'Begin... Begin,' she repeated with a clear voice giving no indication that she had suffered some kind of seizure.

Puzzled by their reactions, Lee looked to each in the room, as Rupert came along to investigate. 'Shouldn't we call for an ambulance? She appears to be in a very bad way.'

'No!' they all chorused taking Lee by surprise.

Seeing that he was worried, Clarissa tried to explain. 'This has happened to Helena before. When she suffers from waves of anxiety that can be triggered by thunderstorms, she sometimes experiences these random convulsions.'

Lee was unconvinced. 'But she told me that she's not afraid of thunderstorms and you are the ones that are more afraid of her going out in one.'

Her mother laughed mirthlessly, with the smile not quite reaching her eyes. 'She might tell you she's not afraid, but we know our own daughter. It appears that she simply didn't want to look foolish in your eyes.'

Peterson kneeled down, examining Helena who remained staring at the ceiling vacantly. 'I think we'd better take Helena away and get her seen to.' He glared at Lee as if telling him this was his cue to leave. But he wasn't going to have any of it.

'I'll wait here until I know she's ok,' he insisted firmly.

Helena's parents and Broadhurst all turned to each other, not quite sure what to say to that remark.

'Very well,' Clarissa finally agreed. We'll just get Helena seen to. It might take an hour or so.' She looked at him firmly with her frosty blue eyes. 'However, we would very much appreciate if you didn't spread word of this to anyone in the village. And that extends to Mrs Cowley - you know how gossip can spread.'

'You have my word,' he assured her.

Her smile was more of a grimace as she watched Peterson carry Helena out, with Sebastian Broadhurst following closely behind. 'I think I'd better get you some towels to dry off and I'm sure Helena would like you to get started on the strawberry cheesecake she made earlier.'

Lee didn't have the appetite for strawberry cheesecake, but didn't want to tread on anybody's toes after the events of today.

It was a good hour and ten minutes before Peterson and Broadhurst returned, with Helena walking in front. Apart from a change of clothes now dressed in pale blue top and beige trousers, Helena looked non-the worse for her ordeal and looked towards Lee, smiling happily.

'Are…are you ok?' he asked astounded at the transformation from what he witnessed an hour or so ago.'

'I'm absolutely fine, I promise you,' she informed him, looking down to the plate of cheesecake that stood on the table. She sat down and poured some cream over her dessert, before turning her attention to Lee. 'Would you like some more? There's plenty to go around.'

He shook his head, turning his attention to Clarissa who was sitting in the armchair busily solving a crossword. She peered over her reading glasses, giving a brief nod to him, affirming that all was well with Helena and that he had nothing to worry about.

After an hour, feeling satisfied that everything was in order with Helena, he left in his van, with the Broadhursts waving him off and Peterson staring back with his usual look of hostility. He knew these people were hiding something about Helena and was certain he wasn't being given the complete truth. Somehow, he believed her when she told him that she had no fear of thunderstorms. But the main thing to take was that she seemed in good spirits and didn't seem to have suffered any lasting damage from her ordeal. It was just as he was approaching Old Church, that something dawned on him. When Helena had returned to the living room fully recovered, he realised she hadn't been wearing that bandage on her injured hand. And come to think it there was no sign of any wound either!

CHAPTER EIGHT

Monday morning was a hectic one for Kelly, with having to process all the information for payroll. This proved to be a challenge, with a deadline of 9.30 to meet, and Sue having gone to her doctor's appointment. Why was it on a day like this that the calls had to be extra busy and the customers from Hell to contend with, she mused, letting out a deep sigh.

With the last piece of work finally submitted, she took the opportunity to read the text message she didn't have time to read earlier. As she suspected it was from Carl, thanking her for a pleasant evening and asking if she fancied coming out for a drink later on in the week. Biting her lip nervously as she studied the message, Sue walked into the office.

'How did everything go at the doctor's?' she enquired. But the expression on her friend's grim face, realised the news wasn't good.

Sue took off her grey jacket, which she draped around her chair, before sitting down firmly with a sigh. 'Not good, I'm afraid - it's my sugar. The reading was way too high. Apparently, a normal reading should be below 5.4 millimoles ideally, but not higher than 6.2 and Yours Truly has a whopping 6.8!'

Seeing the tears welling up in her eyes, Kelly went over to comfort her friend. 'I'm so sorry hun, I really didn't see this coming. What's the next step?'

Sue dabbed her eyes with a creased-up tissue from her handbag. 'Well I've got to go back tomorrow for another blood test. A fasting one this time, where I have to stop eating for twelve hours beforehand - that should be great fun. At least it's an early appointment.' She tried to force a smile.

Kelly sat back down on her chair. 'Try not to get too worried at this stage. I know sometimes these readings can get a bit erratic - it might be better news next time.'

'I hope so - but I don't think I've done myself any favours by piling on all this extra weight. And the doctor wasn't shy in telling me so. I'll just let Roger know I'm going to be in late *again* tomorrow.'

Kelly smiled at her friend sympathetically. 'Roger will understand that your health has to come first. Guess who I had a text from earlier?'

'Carl? He told Barry he really enjoyed Saturday night and said he thought you were really lovely. Said he hadn't felt this happy since finishing with Fiona. That's his ex. What are you going to do? Say yes?'

Kelly shrugged. 'Oh, I don't know. At the moment I just feel I can't be bothered about dating and all that stuff.'

Sue chuckled. 'Listen to you. You're still in the prime of your life and sounding like a proper spinster. Go for it, girl! Just because Lee can't see sense doesn't mean that you can't be out there having a good time!'

Kelly let out a big sigh as she got up from her chair. 'Guess I'll give it some thought. Not like I have anything better to do. I'll get the kettle on for a tea and then have a think.'

❖ ❖ ❖

Helena woke up from her deep sleep at 8 o'clock on the dot as she always did, with Uncle Ian watching over her, smiling with affection.

'Did you have a good sleep, dear?' he asked. She returned the smile. 'You know I always sleep well, Uncle Ian - when have you ever known me to have a bad night? I sleep so soundly that I don't even have dreams.'

He stood back as she climbed out of bed. 'I wish the same could be said of me.'

'You drink far too much coffee you know, and all that caffeine is bad for you!' A frown crossed her forehead as she studied him. 'Have you got a cold? Your throat does sound a little husky this morning.

He gave a nod. 'I'm afraid so, and your mother and father are the same. Is everything ok after that storm yesterday?'

She gave a yawn and smiled. 'You and daddy do fuss so much - I'm feeling very well. I did enjoy Lee coming over yesterday. It would be nice if he could come over again some time.' Helena noticed how her uncle's face paled at the mention of Lee's name. 'I...I don't think that would be a very good idea. There's something about that man I just don't like. - much too sure of himself for his own good.'

'Nonsense. He's a very nice person who's been through a rather bad time.'

Peterson's face reddened. 'I would think very carefully - whenever he's around bad things tend to happen.'

'But Uncle Ian, none of this was Lee's fault. He didn't cause me to fall asleep on the way home from that meal the other day, and he certainly didn't start the thunderstorm!'

She looked at him, her expression filled with sadness. 'It really is nice to have friends around. I can't remember the last time I spoke with Katherine - it would be nice to see her again.'

Peterson nodded, a gentle smile softening his hard features. 'Yes of course - one day you can catch up with Katherine and talk about old times.'

He glanced at his watch. 'Well, I'll leave you to get changed - I'm sure Rupert's eager to go for his walk.'

'Ok, and then I must see Hugo. It's been a while since I've seen him and I do so miss him.'

She smiled as he left her room. Uncle Ian really was the most fabulous uncle in the world, she thought. Every morning he was there as she woke up, making sure she'd had a good night's sleep. Always ready with a smile, although sometimes she could swear there were tears in his eyes. Considering some of the bad things that had happened in his life, he had every reason to feel that way. Had it not been for that ugly scar across his face, he would have been quite handsome. Clearly, he was feeling poorly with this cold that Mummy and Daddy had too by the sound of things. Luckily, she'd never had a cold and was unlikely to catch one this time.

Opening the door of her wardrobe, she tried to decide which pair of jeans to wear, and opted for the paler blue and her white Laura Ashley jumper. Looking at her reflection in the full-length mirror of the wardrobe, Helena carefully brushed her long hair. Looking over to the wall she touched the framed photograph Mummy took of her and Katherine on graduation day. Both of them were giggling and trying their best to look serious so as not to spoil their parents' proudest moment. Katherine was so slim and beautiful and never seemed to put on any weight. She could eat just about anything whereas Helena had to only look at chocolate cake and would put on pounds. Fortunately, she didn't seem to have that problem anymore she noticed as she studied her slim waist in the mirror. She could eat and drink just about anything without having to worry about her weight. Yes, she would love to meet up with Katherine soon and catch up with all that's been happening in their lives since university.

◆ ◆ ◆

During the evening, Kelly sat down on the sofa with a mug of coffee after having finished her spaghetti bolognaise and seeing to the dishes. Sighing, she picked up the remote control and tried to see if there was anything worth watching on TV. She grimaced as she flicked from channel to channel. Most of the mainstream channels consisted of repeats or a drama series half way through, which she'd never began watching. Just as she was considering a movie on *Netflix*, her thoughts were stirred as the phone rang. Probably Mum, she mused as she picked the cordless phone from the coffee table having switched off her mobile earlier.

'Kelly?'

'Lee?' Feeling her heart missing a beat, she sat upright on the sofa.'

He paused for a moment. 'How's things at your end?'

'Good. Good. And you?' Surely, he hadn't called to ask

about her wellbeing!

'Can't complain. I guess you heard about my interview?'

She took a sip of her coffee, feeling slightly more relaxed, though she could hear from the tone of his voice that he was feeling slightly nervous. 'Yes. I had to make hotel bookings for a couple of the candidates that live bit of a distance away. Some of the interviews are quite early, so they wanted to come down the night before. Are...are you all prepared?'

He gave a chuckle. 'As prepared as I'll ever be! I've got some pretty stiff competition - one of the guys is already a manager for another delivery company and apparently he's turned their place around.'

'You'll be fine,' promised Kelly. 'What you achieved at FPS was pretty amazing. Roger Morgan knows this and the others would be crazy to overlook that fact.'

'Thanks for the vote of confidence Kelly, just wish you were on the interview panel!'

They both laughed and for a moment it felt just like times not so long ago, when they were close and looked as if things might go to the next level.

'Actually, there was another purpose to me calling you, other than updating you on my interview.'

Kelly felt a pang of anxiety. What did he want?

'You've probably seen the posters plastered all around the

depot about the dance in aid of the Old Church Hospice.'

'Yes, I know all about it - I'm the one who put up those posters up.' She knew what was coming.

'The Novettos are appearing. Remember when we went to see them at The Anchor last year? Sounds like it's going to be a really fab night.'

'How can I forget?' she smiled, fondly remembering back. 'I love their music - remember how we danced through every song and you got doubled up doing The Twist?'

'That was *definitely* unforgettable,' agreed Lee with a chuckle. 'Anyway, I was just calling to see if you'd made any plans to go. If so, would you fancy coming along with me?'

Kelly nervously bit her lip. A thousand thoughts were racing through her head at that moment and causing a cocktail of confusion. Not so long ago she would have jumped at the chance. 'Well actually I will be going, but somebody else is taking me.'

There was a painfully long silence as if he wasn't expecting this. 'Oh, I see - guess it was that guy I saw you with the other night when I was getting a takeaway. Ok, it was just a thought.'

Kelly felt herself getting angry. 'Never mind. Perhaps this Helena would like to come along - or maybe *she* couldn't make it.'

'To be perfectly honest I didn't ask Helena. Never mind, I'll leave you to it - I need to prepare for that interview.'

After she hung up, Kelly flung the phone onto the nearby armchair, holding her hands to her face, sighing in exasperation. What was she supposed to do? He said there was nothing going on with this Helena, but she had to get on with her life. Until now things had well and truly cooled off between them, and then he decides to have a change of heart. And when he sees her with another guy, just doesn't like the thought of anybody else having her. The cheek of the man! she thought angrily. The truth was she hadn't intended going to the dance, even though Sue had kept nagging her to go along and have some fun. Picking up the phone, she dialled Carl's number and hoped that he hadn't made other plans.

Lee was lying back on the sofa, gazing blankly at the ceiling. Well, it certainly looked like he'd goofed things up. Didn't know when he was onto a good thing with Kelly. Didn't realise how much he was in love with her. And now she was seeing some other guy because he was foolish enough to let her slip through his fingers!

Helena, well she was a very beautiful young woman, with the most amazing figure and the sexiest eyes. That day in the woods, just for one moment he did begin to respond to her kiss. But there was something that just wasn't quite right. He wasn't sure what it was. She was so nice and sweet, but perhaps a little *too* nice, if that made any sense. Kelly had spirit and passion, and had been such a rock when he was going through all that stuff with Miranda. That Eric was a fool to let her go, but he guessed that made two of them, as he was no better. Sighing, he got up from the sofa to get back to working on the presentation on his laptop. Maybe his lifelong friend Stuart would be up for a night out.

CHAPTER NINE

Fortunately, Carl was free to come to the Old Church Hospice fundraising dance. Kelly knew she would have felt a proper idiot if he couldn't make it. She slammed down the lid of the photocopier she'd been using, startling Sue.

'Hey, steady!'

Kelly sat down at her desk, gently placing down all the pages of the documents. 'I'm sorry - it's just that I can't get over the cheek of it. He sees me with Carl and has the nerve to ask me to the dance!'

Sue grinned as she glanced towards the spreadsheet she was working on. 'Must be nice to be so popular with the opposite sex and having to fight them off!' But the joke didn't amuse Kelly.

'I'm sorry. But why does he have to decide now that I'm seeing somebody, that he's made a mistake? For ages I've fancied him like crazy, wishing something more would happen and when it does, he suddenly gives me the cold shoulder and goes off with some other woman!' She looked at Sue, her face glum. 'Doesn't help much that this other one is so damned pretty.'

Sue turned her attention away from her PC monitor. 'Now stop putting yourself down. Not that I'm trying to make that head of yours swell but you're a pretty attractive woman and I know of a few drivers that would give anything to take you out.'

Kelly smiled apologetically. She had to admit, there had been one or two of the guys from work that had asked her out for a drink, but she just hadn't been interested. But it was nice to know that she was considered attractive by the opposite sex. 'It's just that his timing is lousy.

'I'm sure Lee is telling you the truth if he says there's nothing going on with this Helena. If I'm being perfectly frank with you, I think he's realised he made a big mistake in giving you the brush-off. It sounds like his head's all over the place and he's feeling confused.'

Kelly collected some of the pages she had just copied and stapled them together. 'Well I'm going to this dance with Carl, and if he decides to go with or without Helena I'll show him that life still goes on without him.'

Sue raised her eyebrows. 'Just be careful and make sure you're not going out with Carl just to score points with Lee - the last thing Carl needs is to get hurt. He took things very badly when Fiona broke up with him.' She looked at her watch.

'I'd best pop to *Sainsbury's* and get the tea and coffee in ready for those interviews - you know what our lovely Regional Manager Mr Close is like if he's lacking caffeine!'

As Sue went down the stairs, Kelly concentrated on the task of stapling her documents. No, she definitely wasn't using Carl to get back at Lee; no way, that would be cruel, but if Lee happened to be jealous that was just too bad.

Her thoughts were interrupted as Sue came back into to the office, probably having forgotten to take her car keys.

'There's some woman just came to the door and wants to speak to somebody,' Sue informed her. 'You wouldn't mind seeing to her? Just that I'm in a bit of a rush to get this stuff before it gets busy in Sainsbury's. I've got to warn you, she doesn't look too happy, and looked at me as if I was something she'd just scraped off the bottom of her shoe.'

Kelly got up from her chair. 'It's ok you go on ahead. Probably some customer who's came unannounced to collect her parcel because she keeps missing the driver. All the usual fun of life in Delivery World!'

She allowed Sue to rush on ahead as she followed behind. At least she was good at dealing with angry customers and normally had a solution for a difficult situation. As Kelly reached the door she composed herself in preparation for a load of verbal abuse. She looked at the woman with long red hair, who stood there holding a briefcase. Dressed in a black power suit with trousers covering long slender legs that Kelly would have given anything to have; she knew without a doubt this was Lee's ex, Miranda.

Miranda stared at Kelly with those piercing green eyes that she had become so familiar with. Feeling she knew every inch of this woman, having studied her Facebook page countless times to check for possible updates on her movements. Not that there was much to see, as Miranda had set her privacy settings so only her profile was accessible to her friends. Apart from a few photos of her many holidays that she took each year, there wasn't much else to see. Lee who wasn't into social network sites couldn't have cared less about what Miranda might be up to and as far as he was concerned she was history.

The other woman glared at Kelly indignantly. 'Well, are you going to ask me what I've come about, or are you just going to stand there all day with your mouth open, waiting to catch flies?'

Kelly felt her face turn hot with anger and knew she must have gone as red as a beetroot. That woman's voice sounded every bit as irritatingly high and shrill as she imagined. She took a sharp intake of breath and counted to three. 'How can I help you?'

'Well, you can help me by telling Lee Fisher I would like to speak to him.'

'I'm afraid it's not possible to speak to Lee - he's out on the road driving at the moment.'

Miranda sighed and looked up to the sky in exasperation as if she was trying to explain to some stupid child. 'Yes, I *know* Lee is out driving. I *do* have *some* knowledge of the delivery business, you know - my father happens to own FPS, which I'm sure you're aware, is your fierce competitor.' She sniffed, daintily dabbing her nose with a tissue. 'I would like his telephone number, please.'

Kelly frowned looking at the woman squarely in the face. 'I'm afraid I can't do that.'

'*Excuse me?*'

'I said I can't do that,' she repeated. 'It's against company policy. We're not allowed to give personal information about our staff without their consent - as you should be well aware.'

Miranda gave a sarcastic laugh looking at Kelly as if she was completely stupid. 'My dear, I'm not just any member of the public - I happen to be Frederick Porter-Stevens' daughter as well as Lee's ex fiancée.

Kelly tried to compose herself and stop saying something she might later regret. 'I'm afraid it's irrelevant whether your father owns a business and certainly doesn't hold any weight as to whether or not you're an ex-fiancée - these rules still apply regardless.'

Miranda's haughty composure dropped and her face reddened. 'It is of the utmost importance that I speak to him. Please could you call him and get a message to him as soon as possible.'

Kelly was annoyed at the arrogance of this woman but knew she wouldn't leave without getting what she wanted. 'Very well, if you could just follow me to the office and I will see that he is made aware.'

Miranda climbed up the stairs behind her, her high heels stomping loudly as she followed. The scent of her expensive perfume filled the air with an overpowering smell.

The woman sat herself down on Sue's chair without being invited. Putting down her briefcase and crossing her legs, she watched as Kelly called Lee's mobile number. It rang a few times before going on to voice mail.

'I guess he can't answer his phone,' explained Kelly. 'As you should know, it's illegal to speak on a mobile whilst driving.'

Miranda gave another of those irritating laughs. 'Thank goodness for Blue Tooth - couldn't do my job without it, I would be forever stopping at a service station otherwise. We always *insist* our drivers use this - makes the business run *so* much more efficiently. *Please* try him again.'

Feeling increasingly annoyed at Miranda's arrogance, Kelly did as she was asked. The sooner she got this obnoxious woman off her back, the better. Fortunately, after three rings, Lee answered the call.

'*What?*' cried out Lee in disbelief when Kelly explained in a polite voice that Miranda was sitting right next to her, and wanted his phone number. For all these years he felt he was well rid of her, having changed his number shortly after they broke up. What could she want after all this time? What was there left to discuss that couldn't have been said back then?

Kelly heard him sigh. 'What *does* she want? Look, go ahead and give her my number and I'll take full responsibility if she creates hell.' He paused for a moment, letting out another big sigh. 'I'm so sorry Kelly that you've been put in this position - the last thing I want is for you to get caught up in something that has nothing to do with you.

She smiled. 'Look, it's ok. If you're sure about me passing on your number?'

Reluctantly, she jotted down Lee's mobile number and passed it to the woman who was barely older than her, but behaved as if she owned the world.

'*Thank you,*' she said in a sarcastic tone, snatching the piece of paper from Kelly. 'I have got to say I'm most unimpressed with your attitude - had you been one of my members of staff, you would have been seriously admonished. I will make sure your superior is made aware of the treatment I received today.'

Just as Miranda finished saying her piece, Roger Morgan came walking from his office. 'Does there appear to be a problem, Madam?' he asked the woman as she stood up from her chair.

'I think your staff could do with a little more training on their customer service techniques.'

Roger raised his eyebrows in surprise. 'Really? Now you do surprise me, as Kelly is an excellent member of staff and I've never had anybody make complaints about her before.'

Miranda picked up her briefcase and smiled at him sweetly. 'Well I guess that's the difference between your company and FPS - we train our customer service staff to the highest standards and do away with the dead wood.' With that she made her way out of the office and slammed the door firmly behind her.

Kelly cried out, holding her fists in the air. 'Ooh that woman. What a cow!'

Roger chuckled. 'I'm sorry I couldn't come out sooner - I got stuck on a call with James Close about the interviews. But you handled things really well - I don't know what I would have said to that bitch of a woman in your position. I know I wouldn't have been quite so polite.'

Lee pulled up into a parking space in Sycamore Avenue as his mobile rang. Knowing it would be Miranda, he realised if he didn't answer this call he would never get any peace from her. What could she possibly want after all this time?

'Lee! Hi!' she greeted in a loud and happy voice as if she was greeting some long-lost friend.'

He grimaced. 'Miranda.'

'It's been a long time - I hope everything's going well for you.'

'Actually, all things considered, yes things are going pretty well.'

There was a moment of silence. 'Oh, *please* don't be like that.'

Lee took a sharp intake of breath to try to overcome the anger he was suddenly feeling. 'What do you expect me to say, Miranda? What is it exactly you want?'

'I need to speak to you - something I need to ask you.'

'Well ask!'

'This is something I need to discuss with you in person.'

This just gets better thought, Lee grimly.

'I thought we could perhaps meet up for dinner this evening at *La Dolce Vita*? Remember that was always our favourite Italian in town?'

'Yes, I remember well.' Trust Miranda to pick out the most expensive restaurant. He remembered how the owner Lorenzo had a thing for his ex-fiancé. 'Miranda, do we really need to…?'

'This is important,' she stressed. 'And don't worry I appreciate you're now on a driver's salary and this place might be a bit too pricey for you these days - I'll be picking up the tab by courtesy of Expenses!'

Patronising as always, thought Lee. Some things never changed. He guessed it was better to go along and see what she had to say and to see what was so important that she couldn't discuss now over the phone.

'Very well, then tonight it is.' No point in putting this off; he knew what Miranda could be like and wouldn't let go until she got what she wanted.

'Fantastic! I promise you won't regret this.' She sounded so happy that he could just picture Miranda smiling triumphantly at getting her own way yet again.

He sighed after hanging up. The cheek of the woman! Wanting to pick him up from his place; no way was he going to have her coming over and try to worm her way back. It had taken him a long time to rebuild his life, which had literally fallen to pieces. Thank goodness for Kelly who came into his world, bringing such happiness he couldn't have imaged, and proving that not all women should be tarred with the same brush. What a fool he'd been. All along he'd been in love with Kelly, the best thing that had ever happened to him and was too blind and stupid to do anything about it. And now it seemed it was too late and she'd got herself hooked up with some other guy.

He was startled as his phone rang again. A part of him hoped it was Kelly ringing to see if everything was ok; but he looked at the display and saw Helena's name. In frustration he flung his mobile on the passenger seat next to him. Damn! Why did it seem that just about every woman around wanted him, but not the one who was always in his head, and in his heart?

The evening turned out a little different to what Kelly expected. Carl asked if she fancied going out for a drink that evening seeing that they were now going to the works dance on Saturday. Kelly agreed it would be good way for them of getting to each other a little better; something a little more one to one.

Carl was the perfect gentleman, leaving it to her to make the choice of venue, and not assuming that she would be available at such short notice. Kelly opted for the Adam And Eve, deciding to keep to more familiar territory.

Her date was considerate, wanting to make sure they sat

at a table to her liking. But much to Kelly's disappointment, for most of the evening he spoke about his job and most irritatingly. his ex. Fiona came up quite a lot in the conversation. She understood that he'd only recently finished with his girlfriend after being in a long-term relationship and things were still raw, but she didn't need to keep hearing how wonderful his ex was and how she broke his heart after running off with her swimming instructor. Kelly had told him a few brief facts about Eric but didn't feel any need to go into details, as it was all history. As for Lee, what could she say when he'd never even been an ex? Not that Carl appeared interested in anything she had to say, with the subject quickly reverting back to himself.

Kelly looked at her watch. Was the time really going slowly or was her watch due for a new battery? During the evening, she found herself wondering why Miranda wanted to speak to Lee so urgently, and more importantly, would he find that the spark might still be there after all this time?

◆ ◆ ◆

Lee met Miranda outside the *Dolce Vita* at 8 o'clock as arranged. She was certainly dressed to impress, in a short cream dress that accentuated those long legs. Clutching, in a matching colour another of the designer handbags she was always so fond of collecting. Seeing Lee, she rushed over, embracing him as she gave air kisses each side of his face. The scent that overpowering French perfume she favoured instantly brought back memories of times best forgotten.

She looked deeply into his eyes, as if searching for his soul. 'It's been such a long time.'

Lee raised his eyebrows. 'Yes, Miranda it has - and a lot of water has passed under the bridge in that time.' The nerve of that woman, he thought angrily. After the way she'd treated him and now behaving as if he was some long-lost friend. He took a look at his watch. 'I guess we'd best get inside. I can't stay too late, I need to be up early first thing.'

In the restaurant he found the staff to be so patronising and pretentious. He could see no sign of Lorenzo the proprietor, ready to lay dish out the charm to the ladies.

'Lorenzo no longer owns the place,' informed Miranda as if reading his thoughts. 'The restaurant changed hands a couple of years ago. The food is still as good as it's ever been but I guess the ambiance of the place has changed.'

More likely the new owner didn't show her any interest thought Lee, as he studied his menu, glancing over to Miranda briefly. In three years, he guessed she hadn't changed that much. The red hair was still the same, but maybe longer than he remembered. He swore there were a few more lines around her face, particularly around her eyes and around her forehead; probably damage from all the sunshine on her many holidays abroad every year, had finally taken their toll. No fake or spray-on tans for Miranda, only the real deal would do. His eyes wondered to her ample cleavage that also seemed to have increased in size despite looking thinner than she did before and suspected that was probably down to some boob job, maybe something that Ashley or *Daddy* had treated her to.

The waiter having taken their orders earlier, Miranda smiled, laughing lightly at Lee as she took a sip of her Merlot.

Lee shrugged, finding the woman as every bit as irritating as he had years ago. 'What?'

She pouted her lips. 'Nothing. Just that you are so good not drinking wine and sticking to your trusted Diet Coke. Can't you just be a little naughty for once and have just one glass of red?'

He shook his head. 'No Miranda, I can't afford to be a *little naughty* and risk losing my licence - you know as well as I do at the moment my livelihood depends on being able to drive.'

They stopped speaking as the waiter came along with their food. Lee opted for his filet steak, which he liked, well done and no doubt Miranda would have something to say about that too. Not everybody liked meat raw as if it was about to jump off the plate.

After the waiter had finished topping up Miranda's wine glass, she took another sip sighing in appreciation. 'Speaking of your work, the attitude of your office staff leaves a lot to be desired - that woman I was dealing with was so rude and unhelpful.'

'You mean Kelly? No way - she's a lovely person and very professional with her work.'

Miranda gave a snort of disagreement. 'You could have fooled me. In fact, to be perfectly frank, I believe she has bit of a crush on you. As if you would fall for somebody like *her*!'

He was beginning to feel more than just a little bit angry as well as impatient. 'Could you tell me exactly what the point was of inviting me out for this meal, because I'm sure it has nothing to with a trip down Memory Lane or to speak about my work?'

She cut into her aubergine covered in baked cheese. 'Well, that's where you might be wrong. Actually, I invited you here to make an offer.'

Lee found his annoyance being overtaken by curiosity.

'You may or may not have heard through the grapevine that Ashley has left the company - he thought the grass was greener on the other side. And it seems he thought the same of our relationship and hooked up with somebody else,' she smiled bitterly. 'All I can say is it's *his* loss. Ok, I will cut to the chase. What I'm asking is, would you like your job back?'

Lee looked at her in total disbelief and laughed so loudly, causing a few of the diners to look his way. This was the last thing he expected. 'Are you kidding me?'

Amanda blinked, her expression serious. 'Do I look as if I'm joking? Daddy realises he was perhaps a little hasty in letting you go. Ashley has made a few operational decisions that have had disastrous consequences and has meant us having to close five depots mainly in the north.'

'So why isn't your father having this conversation with me?'

'You know Daddy and his pride. Lee, just think about it. The chance to be back in the game and not just be a delivery driver. You'll be there, back in the driving seat along with Daddy, and making the kind of decisions you're so good at - and he will make an offer you can't refuse.'

When Miranda told him the exceptionally high salary on offer, he laughed.

'Do you take me for a fool, Miranda? You had an affair right under my nose and I catch you in bed with some guy, to boot one I couldn't stand the sight of. Because I happened to get mad at the hurt and humiliation, you go crying to Daddy. I end up losing everything mostly importantly the chance of becoming a father when you got rid of what was very likely *our* baby without first discussing with me. And now that things have gone downhill you expect me to come running back.'

Miranda daintily dabbed her face with her napkin. 'I also remember you came that close to slapping my face.'

He sighed deeply. 'Not my proudest moment I agree, but I did see red when I came home and saw that scene in front of me - but to lie to your father that I had *actually* slapped you.'

The frown disappeared from her face and her expression softened. 'If you must know, I deeply regret it now. I mean with choosing Ashley. To begin with, he was all sweetness and light, but as soon as he moved in, things changed. He would go out most nights without me and then I found he was seeing Charlotte - his ex. The next thing I knew he was packing his stuff and going back to her.'

Lee shrugged. 'Well, what can I say? Just goes to show that nothing in life comes with a guarantee. No doubt you'll have some other guy waltzing into your life.'

She looked at him seriously. 'I really did make one huge mistake in letting you go. And I believe, by the look in your eyes, that you too miss the happy times we had together.' Smiling softly, she licked her lips. 'I'm sure you remember very well that this is also a hotel as well as a restaurant. If you fancy, I can order a bottle of the best champagne and book a room. Do you remember when we stayed here when we first consummated our relationship? If I clearly recall, we didn't get much in the way of sleep!'

Lee put down his knife and fork, not having the appetite to swallow another mouthful of food. 'Yes, Miranda I do recall, but as you're aware, things change. A lot has changed in three years, including any love that I might have once had for you. So, if you thought you saw a twinkle in my eyes you are seriously mistaken.'

He wiped his face with his napkin. 'Furthermore, I would rather stick pins in my eyes than come and work for your crumbling empire from where I was so unceremoniously booted out from, because you preferred to get screwed by someone else. And for your information, despite being demoted to delivery driver, I have a much greater appreciation of what is involved in the delivery industry. Remember that's how I began in the business years ago? And that's why I've applied for position of Depot Manager at Fast Link.

Miranda laughed spitefully. 'My dear, I get to hear everything that goes on within the delivery world, including what goes on in that shambles of a depot. And I just can't imagine why you believe you stand a chance against people who are already managing well-established delivery companies! Especially when you were sacked as Senior Manager!'

'Well, I'm prepared to take my chances, especially as I was advised by the current depot manager to apply for the position. I may or may not be successful, but hey, nothing ventured, nothing gained as they say. Whatever happens it will be so much more preferable to working for your business which is falling apart all around you and getting offers of sexual favours from the company mattress.'

With that he got up from the chair, opening his wallet, placing three £20 notes on the table. 'Here, take this I'm off - I would hate to be accused of not paying my way. As you well know Miranda, there's no such thing as a free lunch.'

Walking out of the restaurant, he left her sitting there, her mouth open in amazement at the fact that for once she wasn't going to get her own way.

CHAPTER TEN

The day for the interview for Depot Manager had finally arrived and Lee was in work at the later time of 10 o'clock. He tried to kid himself he wasn't too nervous and to trust in fate, but found himself going over his presentation in his mind, trying to anticipate the questions he might be asked. He guessed all that business with Miranda hadn't helped matters, as she brought the reality home to him loud and clear, that he was up against some very stiff competition. But no way would he ever consider going back to FPS, not after everything that had happened and he knew there would be strings firmly attached to the offer. What he needed was a fresh start; as much as he loved working for Fast Link and the way the company was progressing, if he wasn't to be successful with this position then he would look around for other possibilities.

Before leaving home that morning, his heart felt warmed by the number of messages he received from friends and colleagues sending their best wishes. He couldn't help but smile earlier, when his mum called to make sure he was wearing the nice dark grey suit which suited his colour and made him look very professional. But most importantly, apart from Mum wishing him all the best, a text came through from Kelly hoping that the interview went well and that if anybody deserved a second chance, it was him.

He popped briefly into the canteen for a coffee, to be greeted to the sound of cheers from the other drivers, including Bob as he came in dressed up in his suit and holding the black leather briefcase he used during his management days at FPS.

'Good luck mate,' Bob said, patting his friend on the back. 'I know you have a few other people to compete against, but you've definitely got what it takes. You've done it before and would've continued if all that other stuff didn't happen, none of which was your fault. We all have your back, so don't you forget that.'

Lee swallowed the lump forming in his throat, feeling genuinely moved by all the support. 'Cheers, mate - I might not get the job, but I'm going to have a bloody good try now I have been given this opportunity. I'm the first interviewee of the day. Not sure whether or not that's a good thing, but at least I'll get it over with.'

'You'll swim it.'

'Let's hope. If I'm a serious contender, I'll be asked along for a second interview - but let's see how this one goes first.'

Sue popped down into the canteen, looking straight towards Lee in admiration. 'My, you're looking dapper! If I wasn't about to be getting married, I'd snap you up myself!' Her expression became serious. 'Anyway, I've just come to tell you that Roger and James are ready for you.'

He swallowed the remainder of his coffee, throwing the cup into the bin on his way out, giving a wave to everyone as they cried out "Good Luck!"

◆ ◆ ◆

Helena had been taking Rupert out for his morning walk. The weather had been glorious, with wall-to-wall sunshine, until some clouds had begun to gather. She walked through the part of the woods where she had walked with Lee not so long ago. Sitting on that fallen log, she tried to call his number for the umpteenth time that morning, but again the call went straight on to voicemail. In frustration she stamped her feet, covering her hands over her eyes. She felt so empty. Why was it that she could never cry in the way Mummy did whenever she spoke about Sarah? No matter how down she might feel, the tears would never come. How she envied those women in movies or documentaries, where the tears would just roll down their faces. Maybe if she could do the same, she might not have this empty feeling inside of her.

She'd hoped that Lee would call her again to arrange to meet, but that had all been in vain. She appreciated he was very busy with his work and knew he was to have an interview which could mean promotion; but it would have been nice to receive a call or a text from him to see how she was. Maybe things had worked out with Kelly and they were friends again. But that shouldn't mean he couldn't have time for her anymore! She retrieved her mobile from the pocket of her jacket and this time left a voicemail asking if he could call her back.

Clarissa Broadhurst was in the garden, watering some of her plants with the watering can. No longer having the agility to tend to the large garden, they employed gardener who came over once every fortnight to cut the grass and to see to the plants. In her younger days she had a great passion for all plants and knew all their botanical names by heart; in fact, had her career not been so successful would definitely have taken up horticulture. Rupert came running down the driveway to greet her and watched as with a heavy heart Helena slowly trailed far behind looking deeply unhappy.

'What on earth's the matter darling?' she asked as Helena fell into her arms.

'Mummy, I'm feeling so lonely.'

Clarissa looked over to Professor Broadhurst with surprise

as he came to see what was happening.

She stroked her daughter's hair affectionately. 'But darling, you have us, Uncle Ian - Rupert. And how could we possibly forget Hugo?'

Helena loosened herself from her mother's embrace, wiping her eyes for the tears that never came. 'Mummy. Daddy. I love you all very much. But it's just not enough. Hugo is funny and amusing, but Hugo is Hugo. I need more. I tried to call Lee but he never comes back to me.'

Her parents turned each other, both with grim expressions. Her father gently took hold of her hand. 'My dear, it really isn't a good idea to get involved with that young man. Oh yes, he seems very decent but I don't think he's a person you should become too involved with, and you know that Uncle Ian isn't too happy when he's around.'

'I really can't understand what Uncle Ian has against him. I believe he's just jealous because he thinks I pay him more attention!'

Again, her parents looked at each other, her mother frowning and shaking her head in disagreement.

'I'm sure he's just concerned about you - like we all are.'

Helena bit her lip. 'All I'm asking is to have some company. I see all these people on TV having a nice time with their friends - just the way I used to with Katherine. I must catch up with her - it's been so long. But I can't find her telephone number anywhere and I don't have her email address. Mummy, Daddy, one of you must have Katherine's contact details.'

'I'm sure Katherine's very busy at the moment,' Professor Broadhurst chided gently. 'Remember she lives in Dorset and that's not very close by. She must be very busy with her work too.'

Helena turned to each of her parents with a look of desperation, which surprised took them by surprise.

'But I would like to speak to her - just to see her again and to speak about our times at school and university. We were such close friends and I'm sure she misses me too.' A look of fear suddenly crossed her face. 'Is there something you're not telling me? Has something happened to Katherine that you don't want me to know about?'

Her father chuckled, trying to reassure her. 'Of course not. Nothing's happened, my dear - we would soon tell you if we knew something was amiss.'

Clarissa briefly glanced briefly to her husband then turned back to her daughter with a fixed smile. 'I'm sure we have her number somewhere, darling. When I'm not quite so busy I will try to find it and then perhaps you can give her a call.' Quickly changing the subject, looked up to the sky. 'Just take a look, I spent all this time watering the plants and it decides to rain. Let's get indoors quickly - I'm sure Hugo could do with a bit of company!'

Lee came out of the interview breathing a huge sigh of relief. Roger and James Close, who was notoriously known for being tough on interviewees, certainly gave him a run for his money with all the tough questioning. He went to the canteen, which was now empty of drivers, and bought a vending coffee.

'How did it go?' asked a familiar voice coming from behind.

'I think as well as can be expected, Kelly.' He offered to buy her a drink from the machine, which she accepted and both sat at a table. He took a sip of the bitter coffee and winced. 'Tastes disgusting as always, but boy, did I need this!'

Kelly smiled. 'I could have made one for you upstairs - those vending drinks are rubbish and they're getting so expensive.'

He returned the smile. 'Thanks, but I'm sure you've got better things to do than wait on me.'

'So how did it go?'

He sighed. 'Well, I got asked all the usual kind of stuff that I expected and prepared for, such as how, if necessary, I would deal with a disciplinary with somebody I'd worked with for years.'

'You mean if say, Bob did something out of line and you had to deal with the matter?'

He nodded. 'Not that I think Bob would, but you get the drift. I was asked loads of stuff about how I would deal with certain situations and what my aspirations were. How I would move the depot to the next level to take on more clients.

Kelly's eyes widened with astonishment. 'Gosh, it sounds like you were given the third degree! I'm sure in a similar situation I would have just fallen to pieces after the first five minutes. I hate being interviewed, full stop.'

'That makes two of us,' Lee said with a grin. 'But I feel I owe it to myself to give it a go. I should hear within a week whether or not the interview was a success. If it went ok, I'd be invited along for a second interview. Or I could get a *Dear John* letter.' He looked at her, his expression becoming serious. 'How's everything?'

She shrugged. 'Guess I can't complain - work hasn't been too bad. Sue had a bit of a health scare with her sugar. Was afraid at one point she might be diabetic, but it looks like she's borderline and the doctor's put her on a diet to try and manage things.'

Lee raised an eyebrow. 'Wow, poor Sue - must have given her some worry. My gran was a Type Two Diabetic and had to take a load of tablets. Would be good if she can avoid all that.

How's Josh and Amy?'

She gave a chuckle. 'Still the best nephew and niece anybody could ever wish for and as always getting spoilt rotten by Mum and Dad.'

'That's what grandparents are for. Is everything else going ok?'

Kelly knew what he was hinting at. 'Do you mean with Carl? Well, it's still early days, but he seems very nice and considerate - he certainly has plenty to talk about, especially when it comes to Fiona, his ex.'

Lee's eyes narrowed with suspicion. 'Hmm.'

'Yes, I know what you're thinking but the break-up only happened recently, and I guess he needs to have a vent. Are you still going to the charity event?'

He nodded. 'I'm taking Stuart along. He was at a loose end as his other half is going out on a hen night.'

'So, what was so urgent that Miranda needed to see you straight away?'

He went on to explain how she invited him for a meal and the job offer to return to the sinking empire of FPS and the fact that she even offered herself to him.

Kelly laughed. 'Well that woman certainly has some nerve. Was there just the *tiniest* spark?'

'Not on my part there wasn't. I guess three years isn't that long ago, but I swear she's aged - probably overdone it with the sun or losing weight. Her hair's a bit longer than it was before.'

'Hair extensions,' she confirmed. 'Trust me - us women know of these things.'

'Wouldn't have a clue.'

'How's Helena?' She just had to ask.

He shrugged his shoulders. 'I'm not so sure. I've lost count of the number of times she's called or text me to see how I am, but I've just not had the heart to get back to her, and I know that's really bad of me.'

Kelly looked at him sympathetically. 'It sounds like she's lonely. Maybe she doesn't have anyone close to her.'

'I'm not really surprised. She has some friend she's spoken about from her uni days but her parents don't seem to allow her to have a life of her own - there's something odd going on there. I have to admit to you now, I was invited over the other week for Sunday dinner.'

'Oh. Sounds very cosy.' Kelly didn't mean to sound jealous, but Lee went on to explain about the turn of events when Helena had that fit. But felt it was best left unsaid how she went to kiss him.

She bit her lip thoughtfully. 'I've got to say it does all sound very strange. Perhaps she's got some serious illness she's either in denial of or doesn't wish to discuss with you yet. Maybe this is the reason why her parents are so protective of her.'

He drank the remainder of his coffee. 'I don't know Kelly. It's all a bit strange and now wish I hadn't got so involved. I was only there in the first place to deliver some parcel. And now all this! If she turns out to be ill, I would have thought her parents would be happy for her to enjoy her life, especially if it turns out she doesn't have much of one left.

'So incredibly sad losing their first daughter in a car crash.' Kelly remarked shaking her head sadly. 'That's something that will stay with them forever.'

'Every parent's worst nightmare,' he agreed.

Lee gave a yawn as he loosened his tie. 'Well, I guess I'd best get home and change. I've got some parcels to deliver even though I'm not doing a full day.'

Kelly stifled a yawn. 'Well, I've got some health and safety minutes to type up too and I don't want to give Stanton a good excuse to come down on me like a ton of bricks.'

The following day, Kelly arrived with Carl to the Old Church Hospice fund raising dance being held at the local Conservative Club. Judging by the look of things, the turnout was good as she waved to a number of drivers she recognised. Roger Morgan was chatting away with his wife Barbara and a couple of suited men she didn't recognise. Noticing Kelly, he gave her a friendly wave. Looking around the room she spotted Sue and Barry and weaved her way through the crowd of people.

Sue studied Kelly in admiration. 'Girl, you're looking really fab tonight - red is definitely your colour!' Kelly had pushed the boat out and bought a dress, the colour bringing out the darkness of her hair, and being just above the knee made her legs appear longer.

'Hey, you're not looking so bad yourself.' Sue gave a little twirl proudly showing off her black dress.

'Thanks. And you'll never guess - I've lost four pounds in weight! This dress has never felt this loose on me before.'

'Keep up the good work - you're doing brilliantly.' She had a quick look around the room. 'Is Lee about?'

Sue gave her meaningful look. 'Haven't seen him yet but it's still early.' She moved closer to her friend. 'How's everything going with Carl?'

They both looked over to the man in question, who was some distance away, chatting with Barry.

'To be honest he seems a little preoccupied this evening. Seems a bit quiet and checking his mobile every five minutes.' She didn't mention that she felt more than a little disappointed at not paying her the slightest compliment on her appearance.

'Hmm,' Sue pondered with a thoughtful expression. 'Perhaps he's got something on his mind.'

Kelly frowned at her friend's remark. 'Is there something I should know about?'

Sue smiled brightly. 'No, of course not. Come on, let's get the drinks in - looks like those pair of jokers over there are bigger gossips than us women!'

The music suddenly came to a stop, with just the sound of people chatting and laughing in the background. Mike Stanton went onto the stage holding a microphone. Gazing at his white jacket with matching trousers and a white open shirt revealing some of his dark hairy chest, Kelly and Sue broke out into fits of giggles. 'John Travolta, eat your heart out,' whispered Kelly, making Sue burst out in fits of laughter. Stanton peered down indignantly as somebody jeered. Seeing that some hostility was developing, Roger quickly joined him on the stage and saved the day as everybody cheered and gave a huge burst of applause. He thanked everybody for coming and remarked how it was hoped they would raise loads of money towards the Old Church Hospice.

'I do hope so,' gushed Sue. 'They were marvellous with Barry's gran towards the end - couldn't do enough to make sure her remaining weeks were as pain-free and as happy as possible.'

'I can't think of a more deserving cause,' agreed Kelly. 'I think it's a great idea the company giving our spare flower deliveries to the hospice. I used to love it when we could take the unwanted bouquets home, but it's nice to know they're going somewhere where they'll be appreciated.'

'Looks like Roger's stolen Stanton's thunder,' chuckled Barry. They peered at the man in question who wore a broad smile which didn't quite reach his eyes. 'That twat will do anything to get brownie points for the manager's job.'

Kelly's eyes narrowed. 'You're telling me. I didn't say anything to Lee, but when he came out of his interview, he walked back to the office strutting about like a peacock, telling us all how well the interview went and how Roger and James were so clearly impressed.'

Sue shuddered. 'Let's just hope he's wrong - heaven help us all if he gets the job. Our lives would be hell and I don't think Lee and a few other people will want to stay around.'

Just as the band was being announced by Roger, Kelly spotted Lee out of the corner of her eye, coming through the door with another guy with fair hair who she recognised as Stuart. Yes, she knew she was on a date with Carl, but she had to admit she could feel these ripples of excitement running through her body at just the very sight of him. She turned to Carl who was sitting beside her and seemed to be immersed in his own bubble. To be honest he hadn't said that much to her so far this evening and had to admit that just after having a couple of dates with him, had already begun to realise he was a total bore. No wonder this Fiona had gone off and left him for someone else!

Her thoughts were broken as the crowed clapped and cheered as the Novettos walked onto the stage. The music then burst into life as they performed their rendition of *La Bamba*.

Kelly and Sue tapped their feet in time to the music before succumbing to join some of the others that had already stepped onto the dance floor.

'This is the best workout ever,' Sue said loudly. 'Beats going to the gym anytime.'

'And not to mention a good bit cheaper!' chipped in Kelly with a wink.

Through the crowds, she glimpsed Lee moving over to their table and striking up a conversation with Barry. Noticing her, he gave her one of his heart-melting smiles and waved. Carl sat there looking vacantly ahead, seeming oblivious to everything going on around him. She couldn't help wondering why he'd bothered to come.

After a few dances and feeling thirsty, the women sat down while Barry went to get some much-needed drinks at the bar. Kelly peered over to the empty chair beside her. 'Where's

Carl?' Sue shrugged. 'Maybe he's popped to the Gents.' But when Barry came back to the table with their drinks, the mystery was solved. 'I'm afraid he had to leave - said some emergency cropped up.'

'That's charming!' piped up Sue. 'He didn't even have the decency to let Kelly know, then just ups and leaves!'

Although Kelly had never really made any bond with Carl, she couldn't help but feel humiliated at his total lack of respect towards her. She could see from the start that his heart wasn't really into this and wondered if it might have something to do with the wonderful Fiona who until she'd run off with someone else, could do no wrong, in his eyes.

'Oh Kelly, I'm so sorry about this,' apologised Sue.

'It's really not your fault - I guess something came up as we were bopping about on the dance floor.'

Sue shook her head defiantly. 'Well I'm afraid I feel responsible for this because I was the one who set you both up. Whatever his reasons, you don't deserve to be treated like this - you're far too lovely.'

Kelly smiled. 'It was done with good intentions. You had no way of knowing what the outcome would be and I really don't blame you at all.' She took a swallow of her Bacardi and coke. 'I certainly don't have any intention of letting this spoil my night. When we've had a breather, it's back onto that dance floor!'

But before they had a chance, the music came to a stop, as the raffle draw was to take place.

'Feeling lucky?' came a voice behind her. Lee came and sat down beside her.

'Well, I've bought a few tickets but I'm not holding my breath.'

'So, what happened to your companion?'

When she told him, he was unable to hide his disgust.

'What a loser!'

'I guess if he had an emergency, he had to go,' she remarked lamely in his defence.

'But there are ways of doing it and should have had the decency to let you know. Still, I guess in a way I got stood up as well - Stuart had to go home, he was really sick earlier. Didn't look too good before he got here and told him he should have stayed at home. But you know Stu, didn't want to let me down and felt at bit at a loose end, with his other half out on a hen night.' He looked at her with concern. 'How will you be getting home?'

Kelly shrugged. 'Well, Carl drove us here but Sue and Barry came here by taxi - I guess I'll be doing the same.' She was determined she wasn't going to let this incident spoil her night, and now that Lee had come over to join them, she knew somehow that everything would be just fine.

The raffle was called and to her delight Kelly won a microwave. 'This is amazing!' she beamed. 'My current one's on the blink, so couldn't have come at a better time. I never win at anything so I'm well chuffed.'

'I wish the same could be said for me,' grinned Lee screwing up his tickets. 'Bought ten and not so much as a box of chocolates.'

'At least the money's gone to a good cause,' Sue said, trying to console him. Nobody could disagree with that.

As always, the Novettos gave a good performance, with their diverse repertoire of songs, ranging from the sixties to the current. Most people at some point got up on the dance floor, including Roger, and his wife Barbara. Lee and Barry took off their jackets and danced along with Kelly and Sue.

The band began to play more slow songs as the evening began to draw to a close and Lee took Kelly onto the dance floor again, holding her gently in his arms.

'You know that's a really lovely dress,' he remarked. 'Red's definitely your colour.' Kelly smiled to herself and felt as if her heart was melting. She never imagined she could feel this happy after having been stood up. At that moment nothing else mattered. She was with the man she truly loved. As far as she was concerned the evening couldn't have been any better. The subject of Helena didn't come into the conversation and Kelly was satisfied that there was no chemistry going on. At least there wasn't on Lee's part.

'I think she may well have a crush on you,' she remarked.

Knowing who she was referring to, gave a shrug not having the heart to tell her about that moment in the woods when she kissed him. 'All I know is she's very lonely. A young woman living right out in the middle of nowhere with two elderly parents, and a guy she calls her uncle, but isn't really related and for some unknown reason happens to hate my guts.'

Kelly gazed into his dark eyes, by far his best feature and even after all this time still made her heart skip a beat. 'I think it's quite likely that this uncle or whoever he may be to her, is jealous of you. No, I don't mean in that way because from what you've told me before he's old enough to be her father. Probably until you came on the scene he had her undivided attention.'

'I suppose you could be right, but what really bothers me is that the one friend that she keeps talking about, Katherine I think her name is - her parents seem to go out of their way to prevent Helena from meeting up with her.'

'Very strange,' Kelly agreed. 'But maybe there's something

about this friend we don't know about. Maybe she was into drugs or a bad influence in some other way.'

'Who knows? But whatever the reason, surely Helena is adult enough to make her own decisions?'

Kelly's eyes widened. 'Lee you've just given me a brilliant idea. The girl definitely needs some female company and the chance to meet up with her best friend as well.'

He looked at her, smiling with a puzzled expression. 'Now what have you got in mind?'

'Just hear me out because I think I have the answer which could help to change Helena's life for the better.'

After Kelly told him of her plan, he chuckled holding her closely to him. 'Phillips, you're a genius - don't know why I didn't think of that.'

She gave him a teasing smile. 'It takes a woman to know how another woman is thinking. Now a little less conversation and a bit more dancing!'

The remainder of the night went well and Roger Morgan announced the large sum of money that had been raised so far that evening. Everybody clapped and cheered in appreciation. Kelly glanced behind her to Sue who winked, giving Kelly the thumps-up sign to confirm things with Lee seemed to be back on track.

He glanced at his watch. 'Think it's time for me to call for a taxi. Tell you what, if you didn't make any arrangements after that idiot went off, why don't we share a taxi?'

Kelly shrugged. 'Don't see any reason why not. The journey is on the same route, so it makes sense.'

About ten minutes later, after saying their goodbyes to everyone, they went out to meet the taxi, with Lee carrying her newly won microwave. As they pulled up outside her flat, he carried it for her even though it was relatively light, and she was just on the third floor.

Suddenly, feeling a little shy and nervous, she fumbled in her handbag for her keys.

'Hope it didn't turn out to be such a bad night with that Carl going off the way he did. Maybe he'll call you tomorrow with some explanation.'

'If I'm being completely honest I really don't care if he doesn't. I only went out on two dates with him and nothing happened - all he would talk about was the wonderful Fiona who broke his heart.'

He chuckled. 'She probably got fed up of him being with a complete bore. If you don't hear from him, it's his loss.'

She smiled softly. 'Well, the evening didn't turn out so bad, thanks to my amazing dance partner!'

His expression became more serious. 'The pleasure was all mine.' With that he kissed her softly on the lips.

Kelly felt her heart race as she began to respond to his kiss.

Slowly he pulled away. 'I guess I'd best make a move with the taxi waiting for me. Can you manage this?'

She took the microwave from him. 'Of course, thanks.'

As he was leaving, he turned back. 'I'll give you a call.'

She let herself inside her flat, closing the door firmly behind. Placing the box on the coffee table, she cheered loudly. 'Yes!'

CHAPTER ELEVEN

Kelly had spent a pleasant Sunday at her parents, along with Bob, Carol and the children. She loved her mum's Sunday roasts with the Yorkshire puddings that always turned out so much bigger and better than her own.

While Mum and Dad took a well-earned rest in the living room watching a movie, and Josh and Amy playing out in the garden, Kelly and Carol got down to the task of washing the dishes. Despite her best efforts she was never able to convince Mum to buy a dishwasher. Her argument had always been that she didn't believe they were any less labour saving, besides you always had to rinse the dishes beforehand.

That morning, before leaving for her parents, Sue had called her mobile, admitting of learning that Carl had got back together with Fiona.

'He called about an hour before we left the house,' Sue explained apologetically. 'Said that Fiona had been in touch and she'd left the other guy, realising she'd made a terrible mistake.'

Kelly shook her head in disbelief. 'I really don't know why

he bothered coming along – I could tell his heart wasn't into it. It would just have been best if he'd pretended he was unwell or something.'

'Barry advised him not to come along and that we'd take you instead, but I think he just felt bad about letting you down. I know you said on your couple of dates that Fiona was the only thing he could talk about. But between me, you and the garden gate I don't think they're going to last five minutes. And if he approaches you when it all ends in tears again, just tell him to get lost - I feel bad enough as it is that I tried to set you up with him.'

But she was quick to reassure her friend that she wasn't blaming her in any way and appreciated that things had been done with the best of intentions.

Kelly passed a washed plate for Carol to wipe up. 'Carl did have the grace to send me a text this morning and apologise for leaving without speaking to me first - said he hoped we could remain friends.'

Carol's eyes narrowed. 'And do you want to remain friends with a creep that treats you that way?'

'Well I wouldn't go as far as to have him on my Christmas card list, but he'll very likely be invited to Sue and Barry's wedding - it's best to stay adult about these things.'

'So, do you reckon things are back on track with Lee?'

asked her sister-in-law as she put away a stack of plates in the cupboard.

Kelly immersed a saucepan in the hot, soapy water. 'Well, after Carl did his disappearing act and Stu went home ill, he did spend the rest of the evening with us. It was a great night - you would have loved it.'

'Maybe we'll come another time - but you know what Bob's like, he'll never get up and dance and I've got two left feet!'

Kelly chuckled. 'Well, I'll never make it to the finals in *Strictly Come Dancing*, but I'm determined when I go out to have a good time - even if I happen make an idiot of myself in the process.' Her expression became more serious. 'To be honest I don't know what the future holds with Lee, if anything. 'We shared a taxi home and he gave me a goodbye kiss - he's supposed to be calling me some time later today.'

Carol raised her eyebrows in surprise. 'Hmm, sounds interesting - I just hope that guy will come to his senses and realise you're both made for each other. You're a lovely and funny person but in a nice way and you deserve so much better than what you've received of late.'

With that, her young niece and nephew came bursting through the kitchen door, both screaming.

'Mummy, Josh has taken Chloe and won't give her back!' Amy cried out in protest as her older brother held her doll high, out of her reach!'

Carol folded her arms crossly. 'Josh, give her back Chloe else there's no chocolate mint ice cream for you later!'

Pouting his lips sulkily he reluctantly returned the doll to his sister who came to her Auntie Kelly for a cuddle.

'What a couple of monsters I've raised!' exclaimed their mother in exasperation.

Maybe, thought Kelly with a smile. But how she would love one day, to have children of her own. She appreciated they could be very hard work at times, and certainly kept Carol on the go and keeping her slender figure in shape in the process. But despite her harsh words, Kelly knew her sister-in-law and Bob loved their children unconditionally and would lay their lives on the line for them if necessary.

◆ ◆ ◆

Helena ventured into the garden to join her mother who was sitting out on the patio drinking some homemade lemonade with ice, concentrating on the crossword in the latest edition of *The Daily Telegraph*.

She peered over the top of her reading glasses, giving a smile as Helena joined her. 'Are you ok, darling?'

Her daughter slowly sat down on the chair opposite. 'I suppose so. I just beat Hugo at a game of chess - it's the first time in *ages* that he's lost a match!'

Clarissa laughed lightly as she poured Helena some lemonade out of the clear glass jug. 'Hmm, I can quite imagine that Hugo was none too pleased about that!'

'He certainly wasn't - got very sulky and refused another game. Uncle Ian said I must leave him alone and let him rest.'

Her mother picked up her newspaper. 'I think he's right. You know what Hugo can be like when he's challenged and doesn't have his own way.'

Helena took a long sip of her drink before slowly putting her glass on the round table before her. 'I'm bored.'

'Your bedroom could to with a tidy-up. Mrs Cowley doesn't have the time to sort through your wardrobe and drawers and I wouldn't expect her to.'

Helena rubbed her hands across her face with frustration. 'There must be something *more* interesting to do.'

Her mother sighed, taking off her reading glasses. 'Helena, there's always plenty of things to do if you put your mind to it. You know your wardrobe is long overdue for a tidy-up and to get rid of all those unwanted clothes - or you could always have a practice at your painting.'

Helena's face appeared glum. 'I don't think I'll ever be able to paint that way again. No matter how I try.'

A look of sadness spread across her mother's face. 'Such

beautiful paintings too - I will cherish those forever.' Rousing herself from her thoughts, she looked at Helena with a frown. 'I'm sure Hugo will enjoy your company later, once he gets out of his sulk.'

'Did you manage to find Katherine's telephone number?'

Clarissa shook her head. 'I mislaid it somewhere and can't for the life of me remember where I put it. I'm afraid memory loss is one of the perils of getting older - besides you know how occupied Katherine must be trying to get her business together.'

But Helena remained defiant. 'She might be busy, but I know she would want to see me - we've always been so close and did everything together. Do you remember when you took us both to Oxford Street where we both bought our very first bra?'

Her mother laughed as she reminisced. 'I certainly do and remember you both making a such mess of the displays and giving the assistant nightmares!'

'I'm going to give Lee another call,' she announced.

Her mother looked at her in exasperation. 'Why, for goodness sake? Your father and Uncle Ian are right - Lee might be a nice young man but really, he isn't somebody you should get involved with. Besides it's totally off-putting for a man to have a woman chasing after him, particularly if the attention is unwelcome - which appears to be so in this case!'

Despite Clarissa's best efforts to deter Helena, her daughter pulled out her mobile from her pocket and made a call.

'Lee! Hi, it's me!'

Seeing the look of excitement on her face, Clarissa gave a snort of displeasure and continued with her crossword.

Kelly sat back on her sofa later that evening, catching up with the latest episode of *Loose Women* that she'd recorded a couple of days ago. Feeling weary, she gave a yawn and stretched herself. Josh and Amy gave her no end of pleasure, but they could be very tiring, wanting her undivided attention; playing computer games and taking them to the park where they played along with their friends. She had, over time, got to know some of the parents quite well and today a few of them were asking after Lee, who they assumed to be her partner.

Gazing at her watch let out a deep sigh. She'd hoped that she would have heard from him, calling her as promised or at least send a text. It seemed she'd heard from just about everybody today, including the spineless Carl and his farewell text! Just as she began to watch some talent show and almost falling asleep, her mobile startled her as it rang loudly.

A wave of excitement coursed through her at the sound of Lee's voice. He apologised for not calling her sooner. When he went to visit his mum, he explained the neighbour was having problems with their car. Not that he was an expert himself with mechanics, but managed to get it started after some trial and error. He asked about her day, and she filled him in on the antics of her young niece and nephew who he had to admit missed a great deal. Kelly revealed that the children were asking after him.

'Well, I was originally going to ask you if you fancied coming out for a drink tomorrow night, but this morning while I was at mum's, I received another phone call from Helena. I felt I had to answer because I knew she'd keep calling otherwise.'

Kelly couldn't help feeling that Helena was doing her best to come in between them. 'Well she's certainly persistent, I'll give her that!'

He sighed apologetically. 'Kelly, I know it's a big ask, but do you think maybe tomorrow night, we could go through with Plan B as you suggested?'

Well, she had been the one to come up with the idea. She felt fairly sure there wasn't any chemistry on Lee's part and had to admit she felt more than a little intrigued about this mysterious Helena and all the things that Lee had mentioned about her.

'Ok, you're on.'

'Thanks Kelly, you're a star. I promise when we've seen this through we'll have some quality time together again - it's been too long.'

Kelly kept her thoughts to herself but she had to agree. Her life seemed empty without the one person who meant so much to her.

The following evening, they were travelling to The Woodlands in Kelly's Astra. 'This place is certainly right out in the sticks,' she remarked as she negotiated the narrow country roads, having to pull in as a car in the opposite direction came speeding by and cursing at the driver's negligence.

Lee chuckled. 'Now you're just getting a small taste of what I have to put up with on a daily basis - maniac drivers are all in a day's work.'

'Rather you than me, but I hope you won't have to be doing this for much longer.'

He sighed deeply. 'That makes two of us. I should be hearing back one way or another sometime next week, whether or not I'm in the running. According to Stanton and his digging remarks that I don't stand a chance, it takes all I've got to hold back on saying something I just might regret.'

Kelly gave a smile. 'I've got to say he's strutting around and already behaving like he's the big boss. But if he does get the job I know more than a few people who would think about leaving.'

Lee turned his attention back to the road ahead. 'Just a few more yards and we're there. It's not very easy to spot, so I'll tell you when.'

Within a few moments Kelly was moving along the long windy driveway to the Broadhurst's residence. She blew out a long whistle between her teeth. 'You weren't kidding when you said this was big house. Must be worth a quid or two being in a rural area.'

As they pulled up outside the large Georgian style house, the big wooden door opened and Kelly watched as a woman of slender appearance and fair hair styled into a bob, stepped outside. Despite her best efforts to stay calm she felt more than a little apprehensive, wondering if she had made the right decision to get more involved in something that really had nothing to do with her. But she realised now it was too late to be having second thoughts.

As they emerged from the car, a slim elderly man with a white beard also appeared from the house. The woman poked her head through the open door and called back into the house. 'Helena, come along, your friends have arrived!' Within a few seconds the young woman in question came outside. At first, she turned towards Lee, smiling and then to Kelly in recognition, remembering her from the day she pulled up into the delivery depot.

Even dressed in faded jeans, Helena looked radiant. The cream cotton top she wore complemented the honey blonde hair. With sparkling blue eyes, fringed with thick dark lashes, Kelly thought she was one of the most beautiful women she had ever seen.

Lee broke the silence. 'Helena, hi. This is Kelly who I've told you all about.'

'All good, I hope,' giggled Kelly nervously. Helena's parents looked sternly in disapproval. The young woman politely shook her hand. Kelly immediately noticed that although her hand was very soft, felt surprisingly cold, causing a shiver run down her spine.

'Lovely to finally meet you,' remarked Helena still smiling brightly. Kelly wouldn't have blamed Lee for feeling some kind of attraction to her even though she must have been at least ten years younger than herself. Helena's expression became more serious. 'I'm very sorry for being so rude! Let me introduce you to my parents. My mother, Clarissa.'

Clarissa Broadhurst appeared how Helena might look in forty years' time. Kelly shook the older woman's hand, which she immediately noticed was peppered with age spots. Although at first glance her shorter hairstyle had similar colour to her daughter's, realised that the shade couldn't have been natural; judging by her appearance the woman seemed considerably old to have a daughter of Helena's age.

'This is Daddy,' she smiled affectionately towards her father. 'Sebastian Broadhurst.'

'*Professor* Broadhurst,' he corrected as he shook Kelly's hand. Again, she noticed that Helena's father was also elderly and looked more like her grandfather. Like his wife, he was quite tall and upright. Both had voices that were clear and cultured. His handshake was surprisingly firm, also with those tell-tale age spots.'

'Uncle Ian!' Helena cried as another man emerged from the house. Kelly studied him with a frown that creased her forehead. So, this was the much-loved uncle who wasn't related but a close family friend, and worked with her father. Her attention was immediately drawn to the large, deep jagged scar that ran across his face. Judging by the faded appearance, the cause must have happened some time ago. In many ways Ian Peterson, who was possibly in his early sixties, appeared to be a younger version of Helena's father. His thick hair almost completely grey, along with a short beard, and spectacles perched on his nose, added to the boffin image. Only he was shorter in height and unlike Helena's parents, bore the tell-tale signs of middle-aged spread around his waist.

He gave Kelly a rather limp handshake and scowled at both

herself and Lee as if they had no right to be there.

Having probably sensed the hostility, Helena spoke. 'Ok, I'd best be on my way, mustn't hold up Lee and Kelly.'

She gave a kiss on the cheek to her parents and finally to Peterson. 'Remember not to be back late,' warned her father sternly.

'You have nothing to worry about, sir,' assured Kelly. 'Neither of us can afford to be out too late as we both have an early start at work tomorrow.'

With Helena choosing to sit in the back of the car, Lee climbed into the passenger seat beside Kelly, before they set off to the town of Old Church.

'Are you sure you're happy to go bowling?' asked Lee.

'Absolutely fine,' Helena confirmed. 'I mentioned I've not done it for some time, but I'm looking forward to the challenge!'

After a couple of hours at the bowling alley, Kelly wondered who'd had the biggest challenge. For somebody who hadn't played for some years, Helena was amazingly good and for most of the time had hit all the pins in one strike.

'You're an incredibly good player,' Kelly told her. 'I come here quite often - sometimes with Lee and my niece and nephew who enjoy playing. To be honest I thought I wasn't that bad, but I'm afraid you've put me to shame.'

'But you're a very skilful player,' Helena remarked modestly. 'You certainly gave me a few challenges!'

In between games, Helena revealed a little about her life and her parents' careers, which meant a lot of the time, staying at boarding schools both in the UK and Canada.

'The work your mother did in films must have been amazing, helping out with all the special effects. Did she do stuff with computer graphics?' Kelly asked.

Helena took a sip of her Diet Coke, shaking her head. 'She was more into creating the heads of beasts and aliens from latex and all varieties of monsters which looked very realistic. The way she can recreate the likeness of humans is totally awesome, and you'd barely be able to tell one from the real thing. Mummy is so clever!' Kelly's eyes widened in amazement as she told her about a few of the films her mother had been involved with and some of the many stars she'd met along the way.

◆ ◆ ◆

Ian Peterson sat in his bedroom not long after Helena had departed with her new friends. Sebastian and Clarissa were sitting downstairs watching a documentary he didn't much care for; he knew they were worried about Helena being out with people they knew next to nothing about, and were feeling equally as anxious as he was feeling at this moment.

Moving to the stereo, standing in the corner of the bedroom, he took The Carpenters CD from the shelf and selected the track, *Close to You*. Slowly he lay back on his single bed, listening to the beautiful voice of Karen Carpenter and was instantly transported back to a much happier time and place.

From the very first day he saw her, knew she was the person he wanted to spend the rest of his life with. Almost every day he would see her between lectures walking down the corridor with her fellow students and she was the most beautiful female he had ever seen. Every day, he would see her walking by and she would look his way, making his heart completely melt. In the canteen, their eyes would meet and she would smile shyly before continuing to speak with her best friend, but he could never find the courage to speak to her. Never having been one to mix easily with others, let alone the opposite sex, the words he wanted to say to her eluded him completely.

Then came the day of that students dance. It took a lot of persuading from his friends to come along, as jazz and classical music had been more his forte. He remembered that day so clearly as if it was only yesterday. Through all the crowds of people dancing, drinking with some smoking something not strictly legal, there she was standing with some friends, and for a moment it was as if there was nobody else in the room but the two of them. Wearing one of the long flowing maxi dresses of the time, and that beautiful long hair tied back with a large pink ribbon, she was one of the most beautiful women he had ever seen. He could tell, from the conversation she was having with her friend that they were talking about him and hoped it was something good.

The music suddenly became slow, and saw the guys asking the girls to dance. He'd never asked a girl to dance before but knew he had to ask her. It was now or never. The worst she could say was no.

But to his delight, she smiled and allowed him to walk her on to the dance floor. They moved slowly along as he held her in his arms, listening to the beautiful lyrics of *Close to You*. He had no idea how to dance, but somehow that no longer mattered as they swayed closely together. From that day onwards, they were inseparable. *Close to You* had become *their song* and a few weeks later she bought him that single for his birthday. Later, she admitted to him she had a secret crush on David Cassidy, but despite that, The Carpenters famous melody became their special song.

Ian came back to the present and stared at the very same

vinyl record she'd given him for his birthday, and now took centre place in a glass frame on his bedroom wall. He turned to his bedside table, lifting up the framed photograph that had been taken of the two of them in much happier times. They both looked so happy and carefree, and the love shining from her eyes was unmistakable. But then she had to leave him. Forever. His heart was completely broken and the tears would never stop. When she went away, he knew his life was over. They had made so many plans, with so much hope for the future. But then it was all taken away. Everybody told him he should move on and learn to love again. But he knew there could never be anybody else. No other woman would fill the huge void in his heart that she left behind.

Slowly he placed the photograph back on to the bedside table, and lay back on the bed as the song came to an end. A tear trickled slowly down his cheek.

◆ ◆ ◆

Later, they drove towards Little Green with Kelly and Helena chatting away happily. Things had gone better than Lee anticipated. Initially he'd been worried that there might be some hostility on Helena's part, but the girls seemed to get along very well. They finished their bowling a little later than planned, and they decided on a pizza to round off the evening.

Kelly looked in the rear-view mirror to Helena who leaned back sleepily on the back seat.

'Are you all right there?'

'Mm,' she nodded. 'Just feeling a little tired.'

'Did you have a good time?'

'Fantastic!'

Kelly glanced briefly towards Lee then back to Helena. 'Do you fancy a girls' night out?'

Helena sat up, her tiredness forgotten for just one moment. 'Do you mean without Lee?'

'Yes, that's if you'd like to,' she grinned. 'Just a night out for us girls, nothing too wild. Maybe we could go out for a meal or perhaps the cinema?'

Helena thought for a moment. 'Well, yes that would be very nice and I must admit it's been ages since I last went to the cinema. I was just concerned that Lee might object to being excluded.'

Lee shook his head. 'Not at all, please go ahead - I've got tons of stuff to get through and I can't really focus on anything until I hear one way or other, whether I get a second interview. I think it'll be a nice way of you getting to know each other better.'

As they pulled up the driveway of the Woodlands, the girls swapped phone numbers. As the security light came on automatically, her parents appeared from the house. 'I'll give you a call during the week once I know what my plans are,' Kelly promised.

Lee looked briefly at Kelly as they drove off. 'So, what are your thoughts on Helena?'

She smiled. 'Well, she's a proper *Cinderella*, needing to get back home before the clock strikes 12. I could see her getting more tired as the night wore on.'

'So, what was really behind your idea with this girls' night out?'

Kelly looked ahead thoughtfully. 'Well, my first impressions of Helena are that she's a very nice girl and obviously she's very pretty - but I can tell she leads a very sheltered life. I know I'm not exactly one for being a wild party animal, but she just doesn't seem to be leading a normal life.'

Lee rubbed his chin. 'Who's to say what's defined as a normal life?'

Kelly shrugged, helping herself to a sweet. 'Maybe she's happy with how things are - I know it's not everyone's scene to be out on the town every night and dating loads of guys. From what you've told me about her, there's a chance she might have some illness. I remember when I shook her hand earlier it felt *so* cold.'

He grinned. 'So, you've decided to do a little more

research?'

'Well, I have to admit to you now, that when you asked me to meet her this evening I felt very apprehensive and asked myself if I'd made the right decision. But now having met her, I feel I need to know more. I don't know what it is about Helena, but I feel there's something very strange about her - something not quite right.'

Lee took one of the sweets from the bag Kelly offered. 'I know you with your hunches, but I know nine times out of ten you're always right.'

She laughed, deciding to take this as a compliment. 'Call it a woman's intuition, but I think I just need to dig a little deeper to see if I can find out more about her. And if I can't make a friend of her, I'm going to find a way of reuniting her with this Katherine Jolley. No matter what may be going on in our lives, it's always important to have at least one special friend.'

CHAPTER TWELVE

As Helena woke up in her bed, she found her mother watching over, looking intently as she stirred from her sleep. She smiled in surprise as Clarissa handed her a mug of tea. Rubbing her eyes, she took the drink and sipped appreciatively. 'Mm, that's a nice treat - tea in bed! For what do I deserve this honour?'

Clarissa chuckled as she undrew the deep pink velvet curtains. 'Well, don't get too used to it - this is just a one-off. So, did you have a good night's sleep?'

'As always.' She looked at the clock on the bedside table, the time just passed 8 o'clock.

'Did you have a nice time with your new friends?'

Helena smiled. 'Yes Mummy, I told you last night - we had a great time. Kelly is so lovely and interesting. She's promised to give me a call this week and we're going to have a night out on our own.'

Clarissa looked concerned. 'Are you sure that's such a good idea?'

'Mummy, Kelly's a nice person and I'm sure she's not going to try and lead me astray!'

Just as Clarissa was about to reply, her father and Uncle Ian entered the room, watching Helena curiously. A small frown creased her forehead and she laughed.

'For what do I owe all this attention? I promised that not a drop of alcohol was consumed last night - I'm completely sober!'

'I've no doubt,' her father said with a wry smile. 'Just wanted to see how well my daughter had slept.'

Helena took another sip of her tea. 'Daddy, you know as well as I do that I sleep as sound as a log!' She looked around at the three most important people in her life who were all watching her intently. 'Is there something the matter? Something that I should know about?' They peered at each other in turn, shaking their heads and smiled at her reassuringly. She put down her mug on the bedside table. 'Well I have to say you're all making me feel a little uneasy. Are you sure I didn't have one of my fainting fits?'

'No, my dear, there hasn't been any fainting.' Her father touched her forehead, smiling softly. 'There certainly aren't any signs of a high temperature, so I'm sure you're fit and well and ready to tackle the day ahead!'

Clarissa briefly glanced at Professor Broadhurst and then to her daughter. 'I think it would be a good day for you to try out some of your painting. It's gloriously sunny outside this morning and would be the perfect inspiration for you. I have a very good feeling you'll make some big improvements today!'

'I do hope so,' Helena replied with a faraway expression. 'I look back on all the work I used to do and I feel I will never be back up to that standard again - I'm sure a five-year old will have more chance of creating a masterpiece than I ever will again!'

Her mother smiled sadly. 'I know this is all very frustrating for you darling - it is for all of us. But I'm going to be painting today and I will be there on hand to guide you.'

Helena smiled brightly. 'You're right, Mummy - I'm not about to give up.' She looked over to her Uncle Ian who stood at the doorway, appearing to be lost in his own thoughts.

'Perhaps we can do some driving, Uncle Ian?'

'As long as I'm there sitting in the passenger seat,' he reminded her a little more sternly than he intended.

'It would be nice one day if we could venture further out of the grounds. I'm sure I wouldn't have any difficulty in driving into Old Church.'

Her parents and Peterson looked to each other with concern before her mother spoke. 'I don't think that would be a good idea for the moment, Helena. You need to learn to walk before you can run. All in good time.'

Helena felt more than a little disappointed. 'If you say so, but I would like at least to have a drive around in the grounds, if nobody has any objections.' Everybody turned to each other, shaking their heads.

Professor Broadhurst glanced at his watch, and then to Peterson. 'Well, I think it's time for us to dash back to the Lab - there's plenty to do as always.' He turned to his daughter, smiling affectionately. 'I'm sure Hugo would enjoy your company at some point today. Maybe once you've finished driving the car, the two of you could give it a good wash. You know how mucky it can get around these country lanes.'

She gave her father a mock frown. 'Daddy, you can be such a slave driver at times! Well, if you don't mind, I would like to get up now and have some breakfast - it looks like I'll have a busy day ahead of me!'

After everybody finally left the room, she took out her mobile from her bedside table and noticed she'd had several missed calls from Kelly. Once she had got dressed, she would return her call.

◆ ◆ ◆

Kelly was busily working at her PC processing the daily report for the delivery figures from the previous day and had just about managed to meet the deadline, despite being interrupted by an unusually high number of phone calls.

Sue's face appeared livid after dealing with a particularly irate customer on the phone.

'What do these people expect?' she demanded in disbelief. 'This woman has ordered goods on next day delivery service - knows exactly when she's going to receive them, and what does she do? She goes down to the gym and misses the driver! Then she has the cheek to ask me what I can do about it!'

Kelly smiled. 'They will never change, Sue - they order their stuff online and don't give any thought as to how they're meant to receive it. If they're too busy to wait in for a parcel, they should give us a break and go down to the shops and buy it at a time when it does suit them.'

'Well, if it wasn't for the fact that good old Wayne is able to return back to the address in the next few minutes to redeliver, I think I would have said something that might well have got me the sack!'

Seeing her friend appearing distracted and knowing the reason why, Sue looked towards the door to their manager's office. 'Lee's been in with Roger for some time now and I've been on that for call at least ten minutes.'

Kelly nervously bit her lip. 'Well I know that decisions have been made about who's getting a second interview for Roger's job. I just hope that the fact he's been in there for some time is a good sign and not to console him. The way Stanton slammed the door earlier, with his face looking like thunder doesn't sound like he's made it to the second round.'

As the door opened, they quickly got back down to their work. It was just Lee that left the office and he closed the door firmly behind him, looking firstly to Sue and then Kelly.

Seeing that they were both eager to know how things went, he quickly put them out of their misery. 'I've been asked to come along for a second interview.'

Both Kelly and Sue cheered and clapped their hands and an impish smile spread across his handsome face. 'Steady girls, I haven't been offered the job yet - don't want to count my chickens and all that stuff yet.' His face became serious. 'Have you got five minutes you could spare, Kelly?'

She peered over to Sue raising her eyebrows. 'I'm fine,' Sue reassured her friend. 'Take as long as you need - you never take a proper tea break, even though we're entitled to one, and there's nothing urgent here at the moment.'

Kelly and Lee made their way to the canteen, supplied with mugs of tea that Sue had quickly made.

'Beats that vending machine rubbish,' remarked Kelly, sipping her tea appreciatively.

Lee chuckled. 'Actually, I don't think we had much choice because it's completely packed up. I managed to get a drink earlier, but no vending cup to contain it!'

She rolled her eyes up to the ceiling. 'Looks like that'll be the third call I've made to the company this week. I just don't know why head office don't just change suppliers.'

'Guess they were the cheapest but definitely not the best!'

She took another sip of her tea. 'So, what's now happening about the second interview?'

Lee gave out a long drawn out sigh. 'Well, unfortunately James Close is on his holidays next week, so the interviews are taking place the week after. Apparently, the short list's been narrowed down to two.'

Kelly gave a knowing smile. 'Between you and me I don't think that other person is Mike Stanton - he came out of Roger's office, and if looks could kill, we would've all been dead. He really laid into one of the drivers who phoned in sick, which was totally out of order as the poor guy hardly ever has time off with illness.'

Just as Lee was about to speak, Kelly's mobile rang. She raised her eyebrows in surprise. 'Hmm, it's Helena!'

Kelly frowned as she tried to listen to the call. 'Helena, you'll need to repeat that the signal isn't great. Your voice is coming out very strange, you're sounding a bit like an alien!' She tried walking around the canteen to see if the signal improved but only made a slight difference. 'Yes, I can just about hear you.'

Lee noticed a puzzled expression on her face.

'Ok. Ok. Are you free this evening? We can see what's on at the cinema then maybe we could go for a pizza or a burger. Good, I'll pick you up at seven.'

After hanging up, Kelly joined Lee and slowly sat down.

'Well, that looks like your evening's sorted out. I was going to ask if you fancied coming out for a drink, but I think I need to start preparing for that second interview. I know it's a couple of weeks away, but I can't afford to get this wrong.'

But Kelly was lost in her own thoughts. 'Oh sorry, it's just that I'm a bit confused. I know the signal was bad when I spoke to Helena but I'm sure I didn't misunderstand.'

Seeing the puzzled look on Lee's face, she tried to explain. 'It's just the way Helena was speaking about our night out at the bowling as if it was last night and she doesn't seem to realise that it all happened three days ago. I did try calling her a few times a couple of days ago, but her phone went straight onto voicemail and I didn't bother leaving a message.'

They sat, staring into each other's eyes, not knowing what to think.

Later that evening as Kelly went to collect Helena from The Woodlands, she received the same frosty reception from the family, as they all came to watch their daughter leaving. It was almost as if they were worrying she might not return, thought Kelly feeling slightly offended. She was sure it had everything to do with their other daughter they had so sadly lost in that car crash, but it wasn't really fair on Helena to wrap her up in cotton wall and not allow her to live her life.

As they drove along the country lanes, Kelly looked briefly to her companion. 'You're looking very happy today.'

'Well I have to say I'm feeling pretty chuffed at the moment. I mentioned to Lee once before, that after everything that happened to Sarah, one of the things that seemed to deteriorate was my ability to draw and paint - art had always been my one big talent. I was never particularly good at maths and physics, like Daddy. I took after Mummy, with the art and literature and always came top of the class and won various competitions.'

Kelly smiled. 'I used to love English and was never too bad at maths, but when it came to drawing I've always been pretty useless. Was it always something that you had a passion for?'

'Yes - painting was something I've always loved and a way I felt I could express myself. Mummy is a brilliant painter too and when I was about four or five years of age, I would sit with her as she painted a landscape. I would watch with total fascination as the watercolours she used, transferred the blank canvas to an autumn woodland or a winter landscape. She wasn't only good at scenery - people would pay her good money to have their portraits painted.

Kelly looked briefly across to Helena. 'I hear your sister Sarah also shared your talent.'

She smiled with a faraway look in her eyes. 'Indeed, she did, and was so much better than I ever will be. She may no longer be with us but she will live on through her work, which will always be cherished. Her one wish apart from marrying her fiancé, was to become a graphic designer. I know for sure had she lived, that's what she would be doing right now.'

Kelly was feeling curious and felt she had to ask, 'Do you still keep in contact with Sarah's fiancé? Lee told me he was injured in the accident but survived.'

But Helena didn't reply and Kelly turned to her seeing that her face appeared to be filled with confusion.'

'Hey, it's OK. You don't have to tell me anything you don't feel comfortable discussing. Never mind my inquisitive nature.' She felt a wave of relief as her companion smiled reassuringly, giving a nod. 'I guess I'd best get a move-on - there's nothing worse than missing the beginning of a film!'

◆ ◆ ◆

Lee sat back on the sofa after having put some figures together on spreadsheets, along with some ideas on how he felt he could take the depot forward to the next level. He also believed there were some possible clients where he could offer some attractive rates and services, which he knew with certainty that FPS wasn't providing. Speaking of FPS, he looked as a text message came through on his mobile and sighed heavily. This must have been the fiftieth text message that he'd received from Miranda in the past few weeks. At first, the texts had seemed innocent enough, thanking him for a pleasant evening. At the beginning, he replied out of politeness, that it was good to see her again and wished her all the best for the future.

In hindsight, Lee wished that he hadn't replied, because having wished Miranda well for the future, she clearly took this for the brush-off it was intended. After having tried to lure him to bed that evening, he felt the kindest thing was not to give her false hope so she knew exactly where she stood. But then, the texts took on a much less pleasant tone, making unkind remarks aimed at Kelly. The messages would state that she could see that "tart" in the office, clearly had her eyes set on Lee and he was obviously sleeping with her, probably along with most of the drivers at Fast Link. That was really the red rag to the bull for Lee, and was the reason he hadn't mentioned any of this to Kelly. He called Miranda, who clearly didn't have the nerve to answer her phone, and left a message defending Kelly and to leave her out of things, otherwise he would take matters further. But the texts persisted, hoping in vain that if he ignored these; she would get fed up at not getting a reaction out of him. He looked at the latest message and his face went white with rage.

ARE YOU OUT WITH THE OFFICE MATTRESS TONIGHT? OR HAS SHE FOUND SOMEONE ELSE TO KEEP HER WARM IN BED TONIGHT?

Without thinking, he dialled Miranda's number, shaking with anger. He didn't care what names she called him; he was big and ugly enough to take it. But as for Kelly, she deserved none of this. Miranda had always been a jealous and insecure person, but even she had sunk to a new, all-time low.

He didn't expect her to answer, but she did. 'So, the bitch isn't seeing you tonight?' she asked nastily. 'You never know, she might be in bed with your friend Stu - doesn't seem as if your little friend is very choosy!'

'Miranda, will you please cut out all this crap! You are seriously beginning to grate on my nerves, not to mention the fact that all these calls and texts, constitutes harassment and defamation of character.'

She laughed. 'Oh, cut it out sweetie, I know you would never dream of reporting me for *anything*. We go way too far back for all that, you know you would never find anybody else like me, ever again! I can't possibly begin to understand why you have set your sights on some brainless little tart who's not even particularly attractive.'

'Miranda I'm not going to tell you again. WILL YOU CUT THIS OUT! Firstly, I am not your sweetie and I would be happy for the rest of my life if I don't find somebody like you ever again, because why would I want to spend my days with some hedonistic bimbo who sees life is one big adventure at the expense of others?' His hands shook with anger with his heart racing. 'Furthermore, I would like to point out that Kelly's a lovely person with a big heart and is certainly no mattress as you so eloquently put it. There was only one matress I knew of, but thankfully I broke up with her three years ago. So please Miranda, no more texts or phone calls. Yes, I could block your number, but nothing would give me greater pleasure than reporting you to the police. I have stored all your texts and messages as evidence, and if I should hear so much as another word out of you or you try to do anything to harm Kelly, I will make sure your career is over for good. Wouldn't go down to well if Daddy knew his precious daughter was harassing old flames and giving FPS an even worse reputation than they already have.'

Miranda laughed nastily. 'Oh, don't you worry. I will have nothing more to do with you. If you want that trollop, that's up to you, but I know you'll never get that manager's job and you will look back on all this and wish you had taken us up on our very generous offer. Nothing will give me greater pleasure than see you ruining your already miserable life!' With that she hung up and Lee slammed the phone down on the seat next to him, rubbing his eyes wearily.

Whatever had he seen in that woman? Yes, she seemed very sexy and attractive at the time; he would have been blind not to see that. But just scratching beneath the surface revealed a very ugly-minded woman; he didn't realise it at the time but Ashley had done him a huge favour. Hopefully Miranda wouldn't bother him again; he didn't particularly want to change his phone number as had had it for years. But if it came down to it he would block her number and make good of his threat to report her to the police.

◆ ◆ ◆

Kelly and Helena came out of the cinema after watching a chick flick, starring Sandra Bullock that was every bit as good as some of the others at work had promised it would be, making their way to the nearest McDonald's.

'Did you enjoy the film?' Kelly asked noticing how Helena appeared totally absorbed with the film but didn't laugh along with the comedy parts that everybody else seemed to find amusing.'

'Yes, it was very good and very funny - Sandra Bullock is such a great actress,' Helena gushed.

'I have to agree with you there, I love her films - Johnny Depp was looking pretty hot too! I don't know about you, but that buttered popcorn didn't do much to fill me up. What do you fancy?'

Helena bit her lip. 'I really don't know. What would you suggest?

'Well do you have any particular favourites? Maybe something that was part of your regular diet as a student?'

She smiled. 'Well it was *some* time ago, and the menu's changed a bit since then, I would imagine!'

Kelly looked at her wide-eyed in amazement. 'You mean you haven't had a McDonald's since you graduated? Oh, you are good. No wonder you have such a fabulous figure - I wish I had your willpower. Almost every time I've been to the cinema with Lee or some other friend, we usually end up coming here, and I normally have a Big Mac and a large portion of fries - no wonder I look like a truck!'

Helena looked at her with disapproval. 'Kelly you mustn't put yourself down in this way - you have a beautiful figure, and I can see why Lee is so completely smitten with you.'

Kelly felt her face flame with embarrassment and couldn't help but smile. 'I'm not so sure he's smitten, but I do enjoy his company. Shall we take a quick look at the menu and decide the best way to fatten ourselves up?'

Within a few minutes they sat at a table with trays laden with McChicken sandwiches and Potato wedges. Helena grinned as she dipped her straw into her large banana milkshake. 'I bet there are a few calories packed into this drink.'

'Maybe, but we have gone fairly healthy with the rest of the food - so, enjoy!' She took a bite of her sandwich and sighed with ecstasy. 'Pure Heaven!

They sat in silence for a few minutes as they savoured their meals, oblivious to the noise from the other diners around them. Kelly sighed, patting her stomach. 'Boy, was that good, but I'm completely stuffed.'

Helena dabbed her face with a paper napkin. 'Same here, so no supper for me tonight, I think!'

Kelly smiled at the young woman sitting opposite her. 'Tell me how you normally spend your time, when you're not with me watching cheesy chick flick movies?'

She crumpled up her paper napkin onto the tray. 'When I'm not on a night out with you or Lee? Well, I will take Rupert our golden retriever out for his daily walks regardless of whether it's rain or sunshine - a dog has to be taken out no matter what. I enjoy painting, even though I'm pretty useless at the moment. But I've suddenly started to improve again so I have every faith I may create something worthy of hanging on the living room wall once again! There's one thing that doesn't seem to let me down and, that's cooking. I haven't poisoned anybody yet and Lee can vouch for that!'

Kelly frowned slightly. 'What about friends other than Lee or me? Do you have any contact with friends from school or uni?'

Helena shook her head. 'I had a few good friends, but I guess over the time, we tend to lose touch as our lives head in different directions. I also travelled abroad a great deal of the time, and on some occasions, it meant going to different boarding schools. But there was one lifelong friend who remained constant, and that was Katherine Jolley.

'Do you keep in contact with Katherine?'

She shook her head glumly. 'Not for some time, I'm afraid. Once upon a time we did practically everything together. Actually, we have known each other since we were both five years old. Our parents were also very close because at one time we were neighbours. Although we moved on, Katherine and me remained close. The last time we were in touch she was in the process of setting up a stained-glass company.' A faraway smile spread across her face as she reminisced. 'We went to the same boarding school and because we were both interested in following similar career paths. We were both lucky enough to get into Oxford University and continue our friendship. How amazing is that! Even more so, as that's where Daddy lectured for many years!'

Kelly smiled warmly as she finished off her banana milkshake. 'I've got to say, that's pretty awesome. Did your father teach you?'

Helena laughed lightly. 'Heavens no! I don't think I could have put up with that! I love Daddy to pieces, but imagine how the other students would have reacted, having Professor Broadhurst teaching his daughter - besides, daddy is pretty useless with a paintbrush. Give him numbers and various mathematical formulas to resolve and he's more than happy!'

Kelly was feeling very curious. 'What field of work did your father specialise in?'

Helena smiled with fondness as she spoke about her father, whom she clearly loved dearly. 'Daddy specialises in computer science and subjects such as telemetry, and has worked on many special projects with scientists from other countries around the world - that's how he got to know Uncle Ian. They have worked together for many years on projects of a sensitive nature, often matters that can't always be discussed with neither Mummy or me!'

'Hmm, that sounds pretty mysterious. Have you known

Uncle Ian a long time? I remember you saying that he's not related.'

Helena looked thoughtfully at the carton of potato wedges that she didn't quite manage to finish. 'Oh, he's been with us ever since I can remember.'

Kelly was eager for more information, but didn't want to appear as if she was prying. 'I can see clearly that he cares about you very much. Has he ever married, or has there been a special somebody in his life?'

'Uncle Ian doesn't talk much about the life he had before he came to live with us. I know that originally, he came from Newcastle, though you wouldn't guess from the way he speaks now. But I know he came from quite a humble background; his father was a shopkeeper and his mother a school assistant. He also has an older sister who is a retired schoolteacher. He told me his parents encouraged him and Sylvia, his sister to do well at school. I guess he didn't disappoint them as he excelled in most subjects, especially in physics and chemistry and went on to university where he eventually met Daddy.'

She looked apologetically at Kelly. 'Excuse me for digressing away from the subject. Mummy did mention to me in confidence, that there was once a special lady in his life. Apparently, they were hopelessly in love with one another, until one day she left him and never came back.'

Kelly blinked in surprise. 'Oh, my goodness, how sad - to be so in love with somebody and for them to just up and go like that is so cruel. Somebody once did something similar to me, so I have some idea how that feels.'

Helena looked at her with sympathy. 'I'm so sorry, but I just can't understand that - you're such a lovely person.'

She smiled at the compliment. 'But I guess, in the end things got so bad that I'm glad they ended between us, even if it did leave a bitter taste for some time after. Did Ian ever meet anybody else, after his relationship ended?'

'Not that I'm aware of, certainly not while he's been with us. I guess she was the love of his life and he never got over her. Mummy always told me not to talk about her to him because she knew how upset this would make him. His sister Sylvia, who I mentioned, is very ill with cancer. I don't think she has much longer to live.'

They both sat in silence for a few moments, with Kelly contemplating how she would feel in Peterson's position. He must have loved that woman a great deal, but probably he was so absorbed with his work, that he didn't allow himself time to form other relationships. Now, it appeared he was about to lose his sister too.

Kelly tried to move the subject onto a lighter note. 'Does your father and uncle still work, or are they retired?'

'I guess you could say they are semi-retired, but even though neither are so young now, they do still keep a finger in different pies so to speak and still have some contacts with various institutes in Canada.'

'Hmm. I suppose when you have an interesting career it becomes such a part of your life that absorbs you.'

Helena nodded. 'I feel you're very understanding of this. Mummy was also very career-minded in her heyday, and although their jobs were very different, somehow things worked well between them.

Kelly tried to divert the conversation back to her friend from her uni days. 'So, has it been quite some time since you last heard from Katherine?'

She gave a sigh. 'Sadly, it's been some time - I do miss her. Katherine was always such a laugh and somebody I could share all my girlie secrets with. I do enjoy your company Kelly, but as you can imagine, Katherine and I go back a long way, and have a lifetime of experiences and memories that we share.'

Kelly waved her hand dismissively. 'Oh, don't mind me, you've barely known me five minutes. But have you tried contacting your friend? You know, she's probably just been occupied with stuff. Give her a call, I bet she would be thrilled to hear from you again!'

Helena shook her head sadly. 'I'm afraid I've lost her

phone number. I keep asking Mummy, who never gets around to giving me it, but I think she's lost it too and doesn't like to say. I've tried my best to locate her, and the only clue I have is that she lives somewhere in Dorset, but I'm afraid that's as far as it goes.'

'That's very sad,' Kelly remarked with a troubled frown. 'With all the information on the Internet I would've thought it would make things easier to track her down. So, I guess apart from your parents and Ian, you spend pretty much of the time on your own.'

'Not exactly,' she answered with a knowing smile that added to Kelly's curiosity. 'I do kind of have a special friend called Hugo.'

'Hugo? Hmm that sounds mysterious. Is this Hugo a boyfriend?'

Helena looked at her as if she'd said the most amusing thing in the world, and burst out laughing. 'Heavens, no! I would definitely not consider Hugo a boyfriend!'

Kelly noticed a few people on other tables glance as her new friend laughed, holding her hand across her mouth, and she felt her face heat with embarrassment. What could she have said that caused this reaction? Helena looked at her apologetically.

'I'm so sorry Kelly, please forgive me. I don't mean to

be so rude, but you have no idea about Hugo so you're not to know. Let's just say that Hugo is a good companion, who likes to spend time with me. He's pretty clever and likes to be competitive when it comes to games such as chess and Scrabble. But he's such a sore loser if I beat him. But I can forgive him for his bad moods, as he will often help me wash the cars or give me a hand with household chores - not to mention the fact that that his efforts at painting are even worse than mine! When he gets over losing to me, he really is quite a sweetie and is a font of all knowledge!'

Kelly raised her eyebrows. 'Well, this Hugo sounds like a very interesting person.' And sounds like a match made in heaven, she thought to herself. 'One day, I would love you to introduce me to him.'

'Perhaps one day,' she agreed cryptically. 'At the moment, you could say he's a well-kept secret, but an opportunity might come along for you to meet him.'

'I look forward it,' Kelly said, rubbing her chin thoughtfully. 'I guess I'd best take you home. It's almost 10 o'clock and I can see you're looking tired.' And woe betide me, if I should leave it too close to midnight, she thought to herself.

CHAPTER THIRTEEN

After finally finishing work the following day, Kelly made a dash home to freshen up. Earlier, she had received a phone call from Bob's wife Carol asking if she fancied coming over for dinner. It was all a bit last-minute, but knew the chicken fillets she'd taken out the freezer would keep for another day; besides she always looked forward to seeing Amy and Josh, even if they could be bit of a handful at times!

Having made herself a mug of coffee, she took a quick shower and dressed into her comfortable jeans and cream sweatshirt. After applying some eye shadow and mascara, tied her long wavy hair back into a ponytail. As she put away her washed up breakfast crockery left over from the morning, she thought back with regret that she didn't get the chance to contact Lee and update him on her night out with Helena. She was aware he barely had a minute to spare, with the extra number of parcels he had to deliver at the moment, and because of some minutes she needed to get typed up earlier, missed out on her full hour lunch break. But Roger being a fair boss had allowed Kelly to leave an extra hour early. If she left

Bob and Carol's in good time, maybe then she would give him a call.

Most of the rush-hour traffic had died down and she arrived at her brother's house in reasonably quick time. As usual, Carol was busy in the kitchen preparing the evening meal.

'It's unusually quiet,' remarked Kelly, listening to the sound of silence, apart from the sound of the well-used hob fan rattling away in the background.'

'We've got a few minutes of peace, so let's make the most of it. Bob's just picking up Amy and Josh from the Perkins' house. I don't think I've mentioned to you that Amy's got a huge crush on their eldest son Martin who's ten! Looks like she's got a thing for the older ones!'

Kelly peeled with laughter, placing five plates into the top oven to warm up while her sister-in-law busily set the table.

'Be a love and put an extra plate, we have a guest.'

Kelly raised her eyebrows with curiosity. 'You mean apart from me?'

'Yes, one of Bob's friends is popping round. He was a bit at a loose end, so thought we might as well invite him over.' Carol put the final touches to the kitchen table, adding the salt and pepper mills.'

'Oh, I see.' Kelly suddenly thought, I hope I'm not being set up on another blind date. She knew although that if that was the case it was being done with the best of intentions, but what a disaster it turned out to be with Carl!

'Sounds like our peace is about to be broken' sighed Carol,

peeping out of the Kitchen window. 'They're back!'

Hearing the car doors slamming loudly, followed by the front door opening, her niece and nephew came rushing through hugging her, demanding their usual kiss on the cheek. 'Auntie Kelly!' they both cried. 'You got some sweets?' asked Josh, getting straight to the point, but looking as if butter wouldn't melt in his mouth.

'Yes Josh, I have but not until later. Dinner's almost ready and I don't think Mummy will be too pleased if you gobble all your sweets now and spoil your appetite!'

Carol looked at her son sternly. 'Yes, Mummy will be well annoyed if you leave half your food on the plate - money doesn't grow on trees, you know!' She clapped her hands. 'Sit down you two, I think our remaining guest has just arrived.'

Bob went to answer the front door. 'Get yourself in mate!' he beckoned.

Kelly turned around in surprise as the children cried out in a chorus, 'Uncle Lee!'

Dressed in slim fitting jeans and a white t-shirt, Lee looked directly at Kelly, looking equally as surprised to see her. Neither of them could stop the grins from spreading across their faces, realising they had been set up. First, he hugged Carol's slim frame, giving her a gentle kiss on the cheek, causing her face to flush. 'Oh, what are you like? You'll do just about anything you can to get a taste of my spicy chicken with rice! And what's this?' She asked taking hold of the bottle of Pinot Grigio he offered to her. 'Wow, thanks! That'll go down a treat with the meal.'

Finally, he turned to Kelly, his brown eyes sparkling as his expression became a little more serious. Her body appeared to turn to jelly as he gently placed his hands on her shoulders, brushing his lips gently with hers. Smiling, he gently cupped her chin. 'Fancy bumping into you again like this, people will start to talk!' Bob and Carol looked at each other with a knowing smile.

Kelly helped Carol serve up the meal and poured out a small measure of wine to each along with glasses of orange squash for the children. Everybody sat together happily enjoying each other's company, just like old times. Kelly caught Lee glancing her way frequently but she guessed it was rather difficult for him to do otherwise with him sitting directly opposite; but it was the *way* he in which he looked at her that completely melted her heart.

Later, despite her best efforts, Carol wouldn't allow Kelly to help with the washing-up. She studied her sister-in-law with a mock frown. 'You've both had a hard day at work - you deserve a rest.'

Kelly shook her head despairingly. 'And *you* don't? A part-time job at TESCO, two kids and that lazy brother of mine to care for and you feel you don't deserve to put up your feet?'

Carol shook her head. 'The dishwasher will do all the hard work and I will get this lazy lump of a husband to help me load it up and help me clean up the rest of the mess. The kids are upstairs with a couple of DVDs' so let's make the most of a bit of peace and quiet.' She pointed towards the living room door. 'In there, both of you. Now!'

Lee grinned from ear to ear. 'She's a bossy one, that sister-in-law of yours. I guess we'd better do as we're told because I don't think she's going to take no for an answer!'

They sat back together on the comfortable sofa, for a while sitting in companionable silence watching the latest episode of Coronation Street on TV, one of Kelly's favourite programmes. But really this evening she wasn't in the mood to watch, would never have been able to concentrate that now she was with one of the most important people in her life sitting so close to her. As he placed his arm around her shoulder, it felt the most natural thing in the world to cuddle up to him, and couldn't remember when she had last felt as happy and relaxed as she was feeling now.

'Bliss,' sighed Lee mirroring her thoughts. 'No work, just to be happy and spend quality time with friends.' He looked intensely into her eyes which appeared to sparkle in the semi-darkness of the room. 'Especially you Kelly, I've really missed you.'

She swallowed hard, suddenly feeling overcome with emotion. 'Me too.'

'Sorry I didn't get time to call you today and ask about last night. I barely got a chance to stop today and only that was when I had to deliver a parcel! So, how did everything go with Helena last night?'

Kelly looked up to the ceiling thoughtfully. 'Interesting - even more than I had anticipated.'

Lee was feeling curious. 'Tell me more.'

'Well, to begin with, I feel there is something very unique about Helena, and I think I only got to realise that a bit more last night after spending some time with her alone. She comes across as a really nice person and kind-hearted, but she does seem to lack the sense of humour gene. That movie we went to see, I guess one you wouldn't take much interest in because I know action films are more your scene. Well, it did have some hilarious moments, but while practically everyone else nearly fell off their seats laughing, Helena just sat there intently taking everything in but not seeing the joke. She might as well have been watching some real-life crimes documentary!'

Lee chuckled. 'I guess the movie just wasn't her scene. Maybe she's into more serious stuff, and being Helena, was just too polite to admit that.'

She rubbed her chin thoughtfully. 'Maybe. But what amazed me even more was how she remembered everything in the finest detail. She's got the most incredible memory and that's what makes the fact that she's lost the ability to draw or paint, even more disturbing. She also told me some pretty amazing stuff about her father and this Uncle Ian. Sounds like they were doing some pretty interesting work at Oxford University and places in Canada, when they were doing computer science and Tele-something.'

'Telemetry,' Lee corrected.

Kelly frowned. 'Never heard of it. What does it mean?'

'Well I'm no mathematician, but I've been known to watch the odd science programme. What I 've learned about telemetry is that it's a technology to allow data measurements to be made at a distance. What I do know about it that the data is transferred through a wireless, like radio link or perhaps a telephone or a computer network.'

Kelly's looked astonished. 'Wow, that sounds like something completely beyond my comprehension. What on earth would that kind of technology be used for?'

Lee shrugged. 'I guess that's the big question, and maybe why the work has been so hush-hush. I'm not sure for what purposes these people would be working with this, I'm really not that clued up on the subject. But now you've got me really curious, I'll have to look up some more info about this on the Net.'

Kelly took a sip of her coffee, which had cooled considerably. 'I'm really concerned that her parents seem to be doing their best to stop her having contact with her friend, this Katherine Jolley.'

'Maybe there's something bad about her that we're not aware of. Perhaps she's been in some kind of trouble or there's some other reason why her parents don't want her hanging out with this friend.'

'I guess that's a possibility, but knowing what I know about Helena, I can't imagine she's the sort of person who would be friendly with a girl of dubious character. Besides, surely, she's old enough to be able to make her own decisions on the choice of her friends. I mean, she barely knows us, yet her parents allow her to spend time with us, even if it's begrudgingly.'

Lee rubbed his face thoughtfully. 'I've got to admit there's something a bit strange about all this. Do you know whether this Katherine lives locally? If she does, I suppose I could take a look when I'm out driving.'

Kelly shrugged her shoulders with a sigh. 'I found out roughly where she lives, I'm afraid it's somewhere in Dorset, not exactly just down the road and it's quite a large county. Helena claims she's tried to locate her through the Internet without any luck.'

'It makes me wonder how hard she's really tried to find her,' Lee remarked, frowning in thought. 'Because with the Internet just about anything's possible.'

'Hmm, that that was my same thought, and Jolley's not a particularly common name, as is Smith or Jones. Provided her friend hasn't moved out of the area, she should be fairly easy to track down.'

Lee looked at her with a knowing grin. 'Now why is it I get the feeling that you've got something up your sleeve, like you want us to step in and try to contact that woman?'

Kelly sighed, shaking her head. 'Lee, you should have seen her the other night. She's missing her best friend like crazy and for some reason she's lost contact with her. Maybe they'd fallen out at some point or just drifted apart. Did she mention to you about some guy called Hugo who she's close to?'

Lee rubbed his chin thoughtfully. 'Actually, she did mention him when I went over for that Sunday dinner. Said she wanted to introduce me to somebody called Hugo, but for some reason her parents were dead against it.'

'Well, apparently they appear to be quite close, but just as friends and nothing else. She told me they like playing chess and washing cars together and practice drawing. It sounds as if he lives with the Broadhursts, but I've never seen anybody else around, apart from their dog, and obviously nor have you on your visits. But I do have my own theory on this one.'

'And what's that, Miss Marple?' asked Lee with a grin.

'Well, it does seem that maybe she's suffered from an illness, whether it's physical or otherwise. I remember you saying how she reacted with that thunderstorm when she was having some kind of a fit, not to mention the time she was practically in a coma when you took her home. I can't get my head around the fact that she seems to have lost three days after we'd gone bowling.'

'I've got to say it's all pretty strange,' admitted Lee. 'There's definitely something which isn't right.'

Kelly could only come up with one conclusion. 'I believe this friend is imaginary, you know, the kind of imaginary friends you have when you're a kid. I guess she's so lonely with only her parents and that miserable uncle for company, that's the only way she gets by. She told me he was bit of a secret, but would introduce me to him, when she got the chance.'

Lee drank the remainder of his coffee. 'Well let's see if you get introduced, she might surprise us all. I've got to say I'm really impressed how much you've learned about Helena. Just shows she needed a bit of female company!'

Kelly sat upright, easing herself gently from Lee's shoulder. She didn't want to come across as clingy but there was something she needed to know, something that had bugged her for the past few weeks. 'Has there been any word from Miranda?' She tried to make it sound as casual as possible.

Sighing deeply, Lee sat forward, rubbing his hands wearily across his face. 'I was in two minds whether or not to tell you, but I wasn't sure how you'd react and didn't want you getting upset.'

She looked at him, her eyes widening as her face turned pale. Surely, he's not started seeing her again, she wondered. Not after all the hurt she put him through? But seeing the look of horror on her face, he was quick to put her mind at rest.

'No, don't worry love, I'm not crazy enough to go back to that bitch. I wasn't going to tell you, because I was so angry about her behaviour which involved you, and I didn't want you getting upset especially as you've done nothing to deserve this.' Carefully he explained to her about the texts and the voicemails he'd been receiving from Miranda when he turned down her offers of a job and a night at the hotel.

Afterwards Kelly shook her head in disbelief, her arms tightly folded, annoyed that she'd been branded a whore. 'I just can't believe that woman, calling me names like that when she knows nothing about me. How I'd love to knock her lights out!'

Lee looked at her grimly. 'Now you can see why I kept this from you. She could obviously see there's chemistry between us, and she latched onto that straight away. Remember I told you she was a very jealous and insecure person, when she had no reason, but it looks like it's still continuing even though we've had nothing to do with each other for years. The woman is a lunatic!'

Kelly turned to him looking apologetic. 'Oh, don't mind me, I'm not about to turn into the psycho that she obviously is. But I'm just so mad at being called such disgusting names. I might not be everyone's favourite person, but I'm just not used to people showing such hatred towards me.'

'And why should they? You're such a lovely person, Kelly. You are kind and sweet and downright beautiful and that's what she can't stand.'

She laughed lightly as her eyes sparkled. 'If you carry on with those compliments, you're really going to make my head swell!'

He gently took hold of her hand, kissing it lightly. 'Well, I'm not saying anything that's untrue. I'm hoping now I've threatened her with the law, she'll see sense and back off.'

Kelly nodded in agreement, savouring the kiss, which sent small shivers of delight down her spine. 'If she's willing to risk her career, not to mention her reputation, then she's even more crazy than we realised.'

Lee watched her intently, appearing to gaze deeply into her soul, causing her heart race. Gently, he cupped her chin as his face moved closer to hers. Just as their lips brushed, the living room door opened widely with Amy and Josh bursting through. Amy's eyes widened with astonishment.

'Wow, you're both kissing! Are you going to get married?'

Judging how her face was burning at that moment, Kelly was in no doubt it must have turned such a deep shade of red as if she was about to self-combust! Lee simply chuckled and ruffled Amy's hair affectionately. 'Well that's for us to know and for you to guess!'

'I've got a secret to tell you,' announced Josh. 'Amy loves Martin Perkins!'

Pouting her lips crossly, Amy ran over to her brother trying her best to hit him. 'No, I don't!'

Josh ducked down missing Amy's hand. 'Yes, you do. You want to kiss him, and he's ten years old!"

Amy blinked crossly looking as if she was about to burst into tears, now that her secret was uncovered. 'Just because you love Chelsea Cunningham.'

'I don't, she's so ugly!'

At that point Carol and Bob entered the room, with Carol

carrying a tray, with mugs of coffee and Bob holding two large glasses of orange squash.

'Hey, what's going on here with all this shouting? Carol demanded crossly, putting down the tray on the small table. Give Kelly and Lee some peace, please. I'm sure they don't want their eardrums to burst with all your screaming!' Smiling, she changed the subject. 'Well I've put this hubby of mine to good use and he got the kitchen sink sparkling - think I could get use to this!' Whilst Lee and Bob discussed work, Carol silently whispered sorry to Kelly for spoiling their moment.

Kelly would have loved the evening to go on forever, but by 10'clock Amy and Josh had been long asleep after both she and Lee had read them their favourite bedtime stories. There were a couple to times that she had drifted off to sleep on the sofa and woke up to see the others smiling at her.

'I promise not to take it personally, and presume you're just dead tired after a busy day, and not bored with our company,' grinned Carol.

Bob looked over to her. 'She's always been the same. When we were kids she would always fall fast asleep on the settee by 8 o'clock and nothing would wake her up, apart from when I would spray her with my water pistol!'

Kelly looked at him with a scowl. 'And don't think I've forgiven you yet, Bob Phillips for wetting my whole face, not to mention my PJ's which mum had to change!'

'Well you would have to snore like a demented pig while I watched Star Trek.'

She looked at her brother with surprise. '*Me* snore? Never! There might have been one person who could snore for England and keep the entire household awake, and that person wasn't me!'

Carol looked at her husband with a wry smile. 'You don't need to convince me Kelly, I could tell you a story or two about how his snoring was so bad, that I've had to kip in Amy's room!'

There were peals of laughter all round and eventually realising that their hosts also needed to sleep, departed before they outstayed their welcome.

Later when Kelly arrived home to her flat, she switched on the light, which dazzled her for a few seconds. She would have loved to invite Lee in for a coffee, but knew like her that he was very tired and had to be up in a few hours. Knowing what the consequences might have been, had she invited him in, wasn't sure if she was ready for the next level in their relationship. Having changed into her comfortable silk pyjamas, she climbed into her bed reading her current crime novel. Just as she was about to settle down to sleep, a text came through on her mobile.

THANKS FOR A LOVELY EVENING KELLY. WAS GREAT TO SPEND SOME TIME WITH YOU - HOPEFULLY SOON IT CAN BE JUST THE TWO OF US XXX

Smiling, she sent him a reply.

LOOK FORWARD TO IT - WAS LOVELY TO BE WITH YOU TOO. SWEET DREAMS XXX

Within seconds another text came through: *XXXX*

To Kelly, the evening couldn't have ended more perfectly. With a smile, she turned off her bedside lamp. Within a few minutes she was fast asleep.

CHAPTER FOURTEEN

Helena sat down on the patio, in front of her easel working on her watercolour of Hugo standing by the pond, with Rupert at his side. She looked proudly at her work of art and called her mother, who was working on a painting of her own in the opposite corner.

'Mummy, take a look, I'm definitely making improvements.' Clarissa carefully placed down her paintbrush on the small table beside her and walked over to take a look.

She put on her reading glasses and studied the painting carefully, with a grimace. 'Well, I must say you have certainly improved - you've certainly captured Hugo very well.'

Helena smiled proudly. 'Thanks Mummy, but it's a pity that Hugo decided to return to the lab with Daddy and Uncle Ian. I was getting on so well, and he had to be such a spoilsport. Thankfully, I have a good memory for details!'

'Now, now,' chided her mother. 'You know as well as I do that there were good reasons why Hugo had to return to the lab!'

'I know, but I'm just so pleased that my talent hasn't

completely eluded me.'

Clarissa smiled gently. 'Darling you are doing very well and I'm so proud of you. I have every confidence that you'll continue to improve, over the next few weeks.'

Helena looked at her latest painting with a frown. 'I guess I can continue with this when Daddy and Uncle Ian have finished with Hugo.' Smiling all of a sudden, she looked up to her mother. 'I must show Kelly my new paintings some time - I told her I've been pretty rubbish lately and I know she'll be so pleased that things are improving.'

Her mother looked mortified but tried not to show it. 'Darling, you haven't mentioned about Hugo to Kelly, have you? Because we did agree that he should remain our secret.'

She looked at her mother in astonishment. 'No, of course I haven't Mummy. I'm very much aware Hugo is our special friend and nobody else is to know about him.'

Clarissa smiled, feeling more reassured. 'Good girl, I didn't think you would mention anything. I know our daughter would never be capable of telling lies - you just don't have it in you.'

Helena smiled at her mother sweetly. 'Of course not, Mummy.'

◆ ◆ ◆

At lunchtime, Kelly and Sue sat in the canteen. Instead of her usual ready-meal that she would normally heat up in the microwave, Sue was now opting for a healthy salad garnished with a low-calorie dressing.

Kelly looked at her friend in admiration. 'Well, the salads are certainly working for you. I see you every day, and even I can see you've lost weight - ou're looking amazing.'

Sue smiled, flushing slightly at the compliment. 'I weighed myself on the bathroom scales yesterday and I've lost almost seven pounds!'

'Good on you! I think I might start packing a salad now and again - I do get a bit fed up of sandwiches. There are only so many fillings you can choose from, and I always end up with the same old.'

Sue dug her fork into a slice of tomato. 'I know what you mean. But I guess the same can be said for salads, but I make sure I do something nice and substantial for the evening meal. It's amazing how you can have the same things, but grill instead of fry - boil the potatoes instead of roast, and as many vegetables as you like.'

'I bet Barry must be so proud of how well you're doing.'

'He's very supportive bless him. When we met, I was pretty slim as you know, but somehow over time, with eating out and getting a bit complacent, the pounds started piling on.

He's never complained or told me I was fat. When I would moan and say my jeans were getting tight, always said the most important thing was how I felt. Said if I started feeling uncomfortable about my weight, then it was up to me, if I felt something needed to be done.'

Kelly finished off the last bite of her sandwich. 'That's love for you.'

'I guess it is, but in the end, it was my health at stake. I know I want to look the best I can for the wedding next year, but I would rather try and avoid becoming a Type Two Diabetic. Because the doctor made it very clear there can be other consequences, such as possible heart and kidney problems and a whole host of other things. Anyway, enough about me and my eating habits, do you feel that things are finally heading in the right direction with Mr Fisher?'

'They seem to be, but there's so much going on at the moment, with the second interview coming up this week. Things were really beginning to get interesting until Amy and Josh came bursting through the door!'

Sue laughed. 'That's kids for you! I can't wait until me and Barry start a family. I know it's going to be the end of our peace and quiet, and decisions made around just the two of us for at least the next 18 years or so, but that's all the part of parenthood. So, what do you make of this Helena and her strange family?'

Kelly updated her friend on their night out at the cinema and all the things that Helena had told her about her family, and what she told her of the work that Professor Broadhurst and Ian Peterson did together.

Sue sat back on her chair, with a grimace. 'It all sounds a bit weird to me. Do you think this Helena could be a bit mentally unstable? How can anybody just forget three days of their life, the way she did when you went bowling? It sounds like she's unwell.'

'That's what I'm suspecting, Sue. I think the death of her sister affected her badly. All I know is that she's not allowed to have a life like the rest of us. For some reason, her parents are hell-bent on stopping her from having an independent life, and from seeing her best friend Katherine Jolley. And I'm going to do everything I can, to track her friend down and try to find out what's going on.

'Are you sure that's a good idea?' Sue was beginning to feel concerned about how things were developing. 'Her parents might have their reasons for stopping her from having the life that most of us take for granted. It could well be for her own protection.'

'It's possible. Look, I know you're worried because you care, but I promise I won't do anything that can cause any harm - I'm just going to find out what I can on the Net.'

Sue sealed down the lid on her lunchbox firmly. 'Good, because I know Lee wouldn't want you to get yourself into anything too deep. Come on, let's get back to work and deal with our wonderful customers!'

◆ ◆ ◆

Helena had enjoyed her day so far; the weather couldn't have been more perfect on her morning walk with Rupert. The woods had looked spectacular with the sun shining down on the leaves, bathing them with a golden hue as they stirred gently in the cool breeze. She felt as if she was the only person on this earth and this was her special moment. With a new wave of inspiration flooding through her, knew that she would have to get this vision of beauty down on canvas. Only too aware her family wouldn't hear of her spending time here by herself with her easel and watercolours, thankfully had the gift of a photographic memory for detail and could wait until later to begin her work of art.

Later she began painting in the garden, after Eddie the gardener, who came once a fortnight to cut the grass and tend to the plants, had finished his work. He was such a nice man, probably a little older than Uncle Ian, but with white hair and a ruddy complexion and slightly more rounded. Often, she would chat to the gardener about her day, and he would update her on news in the village and people she'd never met. If she had a real uncle, she would definitely have loved somebody just like Eddie. The only villagers she really knew, apart from Mrs Cowley, were the gardener and Madge at the shop. He looked at her painting efforts and praised her work and said she was doing very well.

Just as Eddie left in his old jeep, her mother called her from the house. Her expression looked solemn as she stood with her father.

Feeling concerned, she gently placed her arms around Clarissa's shoulders. 'What's up Mummy?' She could see the tears welling up in her mother's eyes, which was so uncharacteristic as her mother was normally a very strong woman emotionally. The only times she would come close to tears was when talking of Sarah.

'I'm afraid we've had some rather sad news,' her father informed her sadly. 'It's Uncle Ian's sister Sylvia - her condition has taken a turn for the worse with her cancer and she's not expected to make it through the night.'

Helena was mortified. 'Oh, that's so awful. Poor Auntie Sylvia - she has suffered for so long but I guess it's not totally unexpected. Where's Uncle Ian?'

'He's in his room,' informed Professor Broadhurst. 'He

needs some time to digest the news - it's been very much on the cards that Sylvia was going to die. Every time Ian went to the hospice, he could see that she was deteriorating, but it doesn't make the sadness any less.'

Clarissa dabbed her eyes with her handkerchief. 'It's devastating to lose somebody you care for deeply even though it's expected and this isn't going upset him any less than...'

Helena couldn't remember seeing her mother cry in this way for a very long time. She gently held her in her arms.

'A very sad time for us all,' said her father. 'Helena, this does mean that your mother and I will have to drive with Uncle Ian to Newcastle, to see Sylvia before, well, you know.'

'You mean you'll be travelling there today? It's an awful long way from here.'

'I know, but it's important that we go today as tomorrow it'll probably be too late, and Uncle Ian would never forgive himself.'

'Couldn't I drive us there?'

Clarissa smiled gently, stroking her daughter's hair. 'It's a very kind gesture. I know you're desperate to get behind the wheel and drive, but you know it's not possible.'

Helena sighed. 'Yes, Mummy, nothing would please me more than to be able to drive again, but it's not purely for selfish reasons. I do realise Uncle Ian won't be in the right frame of mind to drive. But don't you think that a journey of that distance will be a little too much for you and Daddy?'

Professor Broadhurst looked to his daughter, chuckling. 'Are you saying that your mother and I are too old to get behind the wheel and drive for miles? I will have you know, in our younger days we were driving up and down the country in our MG sports car with not a care in the world!'

'Oh Daddy, it's just that I worry about you both. The traffic is so much busier now, with everybody in such a hurry.'

His expression softened. 'It's ok, my dear, I'm only jesting and I know you mean well. I promise we'll take things easy and we'll take it in turns to drive.'

Clarissa glanced at her watch. 'Well I suppose we'd better start preparing - I'll make a booking at that hotel near the hospice.'

Helena felt very sorry for Uncle Ian that he was about to lose somebody special from his life again. She was sure that he'd never got over the girlfriend that had left him, and even though she hadn't known him then, knew the episode had broken his heart. But at least he still had Mummy and Daddy and Helena felt that he loved her in his own quiet way. But now she realised that for the first time in a very long time, she would have the entire house to herself, apart from Hugo and Rupert, and she smiled as an idea suddenly came to her.

❖ ❖ ❖

After a busy day at work and having finished a plate of Spaghetti Bolognese, with some wildlife documentary playing on *Amazon Prime Video,* Kelly sat down on the sofa with her laptop on her knees, tapping into the Google search engine the name Katherine Jolley. She wasn't sure if Helena's friend's name was spelt with a C or a K or whether Jolley was with or without an e. She remembered Helena once telling her that Katherine was interested in doing designs for stained glass windows. To her surprise there were quite a few people with that name, spelt in various ways, in the Dorset area. Then she tapped in Katherine Jolley stained glass window designs in Dorset. To her surprise, the Google search engine came up with *The Glass Palace, Katherine Jolley-Herbert Stained Glass Window Designs,* in Christchurch, Dorset. Kelly frowned thoughtfully. She couldn't remember Helena referring to her as Jolley-Herbert. Perhaps she normally preferred to abbreviate her name just to Jolley. Perhaps this was all just a big coincidence; maybe this wasn't Helena's friend.

She jumped with a start from her thoughts as her mobile rang. 'Hi Lee,' she greeted warmly. 'How's everything going? Are you prepared for tomorrow's interview?'

He chuckled. 'Prepared as I'll ever be, with receiving the

third degree from Roger and Close. And what have *you* been up to? Watching *Loose Women* or some wildlife documentary while you're having your dinner if my memory serves me well!'

Kelly smiled. 'You know me well. Actually, I've also been doing some research on the Net about Helena's friend Katherine.'

'Have you managed to find anything out, Miss Marple?'

She stared at the screen in front of her. 'I believe I might have found something, but not really had a chance to read through in detail. I've just come across a Katherine Jolley-Herbert in Christchurch, Dorset. But as far as I can remember from what Helena says, she always refers to her just as Katherine Jolley.'

Lee paused for a few seconds as he thought things through. 'I guess it's possible that her friend just didn't bother with the double-barrelled bit, or could it be that she's got married and uses both her own and her husband's surname?'

'I guess that's possible, about her getting married. But I would've thought that Helena would have mentioned something about it.'

'Check out the site about the business.'

Kelly clicked onto the About Us page link. 'Now, this is strange if that's Helena's friend - says here this is a long-established family business that's been going since 1980. If she were around the same age as Helena she wouldn't have even been born then. There are some beautiful photos of the stained-glass windows and doors, which they do for both private homes and establishments - looks like they manufacture and make repairs too. But I guess it can't be the same Katherine Jolley we're looking for.'

'I wouldn't completely rule it out at this stage,' Lee suggested. 'It could be that maybe the business was started up by either one of their families and now they're running it.'

'I suppose that's possible. The annoying thing about a lot of these kinds of sites is that they don't have any pictures of the people running the business, only what they produce.'

'Ok, what I'd suggest is to bookmark it and when I've got this interview over and done with tomorrow, I'll take a look and see what we should do about it, if anything.'

Just as he finished speaking, Kelly could see another call coming through. 'It's Helena. I wonder what she could want?'

'I'll hang up then and sort my interview suit out for the morning - if there's anything interesting, let me know.'

She quickly answered the call. 'Hi Helena.'

She listened intently as Helena told her the news of Ian Peterson's cousin Sylvia dying from cancer at a Hospice in Newcastle. 'I'm so very sorry.' Kelly murmured sympathetically. It looked like both the Broadhursts and the

Petersons had received more than their fair share of tragedy.

'It's very sad,' agreed Helena. 'But I guess it will be a happy release as Auntie Sylvia has suffered for so long. It does mean that Mummy and Daddy will be away for a few days and I will actually have the house to myself.'

Kelly raised her eyebrows in surprise. So, the Broadhursts were actually going to allow their daughter to have some breathing space?

'I was wondering if you'd like to come around this evening when Mummy and Daddy have gone?'

Kelly really wasn't in the mood for going out this evening, as curious as she was to ask further details about her friend. 'Unfortunately, I can't make tonight. I've already made plans to go over to Sue's - that's my friend who I work with in the office.'

There was a moment's silence. 'It's ok, really it is. It was just a thought, and I'm sure you have a million and one other things to do!'

She could tell Helena was bitterly disappointed. 'Look, I tell you what, I'm free tomorrow evening. Actually, I could come straight from work and we could catch up then. That is if it's ok with you?'

'That would be super! I could cook us some dinner and that will save you having to cook for just one and the same goes for me. Do you have any preferences, any foods you don't like?'

Kelly laughed lightly, Helena was so eager to have some company. 'Cook whatever you feel - I have no particular dislikes or food allergies or anything like that. Would about 5.30 be ok for you?'

'5.30 would be great. I'll have a think about what to cook in the meantime. Maybe this will also give you the chance to finally meet Hugo!'

Kelly felt intrigued. 'Well I'm certainly looking forward to meeting your friend! See you tomorrow.'

As she hung up, she looked to the screen on her laptop. She would leave it until another day to decide whether or not to look further into the Katherine Jolley mystery. It looked as if meeting Helena tomorrow would turn out to be more interesting than she anticipated, now that she would get to meet the mysterious Hugo.

Helena watched on, as her parents and Uncle Ian came down the stairs with their overnight bags, all looking very solemn.

'Are you sure you don't want me to cook you something before you drive off?'

Clarissa closed her eyes for a few seconds, shaking her head. 'It's ok dear - I don't think any of us have the appetite for food at the moment. We can always stop off somewhere along the way.'

'That's true. I'll probably make myself an omelette and some salad, when you've gone. It will seem so strange without you all here but I'm sure when Mrs Cowley comes tomorrow, she will fill me in on all the gossip in the village.'

Her parents both looked at each other gravely before her mother spoke. 'Mrs Cowley won't be coming tomorrow, dear. We decided to give her the day off as there would only be you here and not much to clear up.'

As Rupert came along to sniff everybody, seeming to sense that something was afoot, Professor Broadhurst attached a dog lead to Rupert's collar.

'Are you taking Rupert?' asked Helena in surprise.

'Yes, Rupert's coming along with us,' confirmed her father.

'But why? I'm perfectly capable of looking after him.'

Professor Broadhurst turned to his wife and then to Ian before gently smiling at her. 'My dear, we're all very sad that Auntie Sylvia is dying and having Rupert with us would be a great source of comfort, especially for your mother. Fortunately, the hotel we're staying is dog friendly - you know how much she adores him. Probably more than she does me,' he added with a wry smile.

'Ok.' Suddenly Helena was feeling more than a little disappointed at the prospect of her newfound freedom. As much as she was looking forward to having some time on her own and to seeing Kelly, that wasn't to be until the following evening. With no Mrs Cowley dropping in and no Rupert to walk, it looked as if she would be in for a lonely time.

Professor Broadhurst, seeing her look of complete disappointment tried his best to reassure her. 'It's only for a day or so. I'm sure you'll find plenty of things to do around the house and it'll be a good opportunity for you to make headway with your painting. I'm hoping that on our return you'll have a masterpiece to show us!' He looked at his watch. 'Well I think it's time we were making a move.'

Helena looked on as the others picked up their overnight cases, first giving Uncle Ian a hug, wishing him well. It was difficult knowing what to say in these kinds of circumstances.

She turned to her father who took her in his arms, placing an affectionate kiss on the top of her head. 'Drive safely Daddy and if you get tired, promise me you'll stop off along the way for a bite to eat and a rest.'

'I promise,' he replied gruffly, giving her a final hug.

Finally, she turned to Clarissa, who looked as if she was about to break down in tears. Helena took her gently in her arms. 'It's going to be OK, Mummy - soon Auntie Sylvia will be in a much happier place.

As Clarissa held Helena closely in her arms, she watched

intently as Peterson suddenly placed his hands around the back of Helena's neck, squeezing firmly for a brief moment. Helena lifted her head up, her large blue eyes widening with surprise before collapsing limply on the laminate flooring.

The Broadhursts watched on as Peterson gently picked her up from the floor, carrying her up the stairs, with her long honey blonde hair cascading down from her head, her eyes staring lifelessly towards the high ceiling.

After just a few minutes, Peterson came down the stairs alone as her parents watched on with concern.

'Is she ok?' asked her mother anxiously.

Peterson nodded his head. 'She'll be fine and won't come to any harm while we're away.'

Feeling reassured, Clarissa looked to her husband and then to Rupert who sat patiently. 'Well, let's be on our way, we've got a long journey ahead of us!'

CHAPTER FIFTEEN

Kelly was just finishing off at work and for once, her day hadn't been too bad. The phone calls were less frequent and she managed to complete her reports without the system either slowing down or crashing. She wondered how Lee had fared in his second interview, having no indication of what was taking place in the conference room across the road. Not wishing to disturb him last night while he was busy preparing for the second interview, she had sent a text wishing him good luck.

As she was lost deep in her thoughts, locking the windows to the office, she was startled as a hand gently touched her shoulder. Turning around, Lee was standing there in his charcoal grey interview suit, looking extremely handsome. He grinned at her roguishly.

'A penny for them! You were miles away - I bet you can't wait to get off home and chill out!'

She shut the window firmly, her heart racing, not sure if it was because he had taken her by surprise or just because he was so devastatingly gorgeous.

'I wish! After I'd spoke to you last night, Helena called.'

'Yes, I remember she rang just as we were finishing our conversation.'

'Well, it turns out her parents are travelling up to Newcastle with Uncle Ian whose sister is dying of cancer at a hospice, and Helena's actually been allowed to stay home alone.'

Lee grimaced. 'But all the same, a sad reason for having some of her own space. Maybe some of your influence has rubbed off on her parents.'

Kelly smiled. 'I guess that's possible. Well, to cut a long story short, I've had an invite for dinner after work. Helena was so chuffed, bless her, I just didn't have the heart to turn her down. She actually wanted me to go around there last night but I was just too tired.'

Lee was impressed. 'Well, that's pretty good going'

Kelly's looked at him apologetically. 'Oh Lee, here's me going on about my social life and I've not even asked how you got on at the interview!'

He chuckled and looked at her with a mock frown. 'Oh, it's ok - I can take the hint when someone doesn't care about me! Actually, it did seem to go very well, and I think I managed to put things across well on outlining my ideas of how the company can move forward to gain more high-profile accounts.'

Kelly felt secretly optimistic. 'Well, the guy from that other delivery company didn't spend as long as you at his interview. To be honest he didn't look terribly happy - certainly didn't come across as somebody I would like to see running this place.'

Lee grinned. 'But then you're biased. Hey, I'm only kidding it's not yet set in stone who's going to be successful, but I should have some idea by the beginning of next week.'

Kelly switched off her PC. 'Hmm, I bet the time's going to drag for you between now and then.'

He had a thought. 'Do you think Helena would mind if I invited myself along to dinner this evening?'

She shrugged. 'I'm sure she wouldn't. I know she enjoys some company, but I'll check it with her first.' She took out the mobile from her handbag. After dialling the number, Kelly frowned. 'That's strange. She's not picking up the call - I know she definitely arranged our get-together for this evening.'

'Perhaps she's popped out in the garden or something.'

Kelly put away her phone. 'That's probably what it is, or in the bathroom. Oh, I forgot to mention, she said that she was going to introduce me to Hugo. I'm intrigued who this guy is to her because she firmly denies that he's a boyfriend.'

Lee looked at his watch. 'Well I guess all will be revealed soon. I suppose we'd best be on our way - we might as well travel together. Shall we go in my van? Can always drive back to the car park later.'

After thirty minutes slightly late, having got stuck in the rush hour traffic, they arrived at The Woodlands. Noticing that the large wrought iron gate to the driveway was closed, they turned to each other with puzzled expressions.

Kelly gave a shrug. 'I'm pretty certain we did arrange this for today and I'm sure if there had been a change of plan then Helena would have given me a call. Lee turned off the vehicle engine and both climbed out of the vehicle. Kelly gave a small shiver, as despite the sunshine there was a chill to the air.

Lee ran his hands through his hair in thought, giving it a slightly ruffled look. Having taken off his jacket and tie earlier, and opening the top buttons to his shirt, Kelly had never found him so devastatingly attractive as she did right now. He walked up to the gate, giving it a slight nudge and opened with ease.

'Well, they haven't locked up so maybe she's still at home.'

'Let's just hope that and she's not had a change of plan and decided to go with her parents,' she added with a wry smile. 'I would be so gutted as I was looking forward to someone else doing the cooking for a change.'

Having driven up the long winding driveway, Kelly rang the doorbell. Frowning, she looked towards Lee. 'It doesn't look like anybody's there - I can't see any windows open.'

They decided to walk around to the back of the house, to investigate further. Lee peered through the kitchen window and saw some mugs on the draining board. 'It's possible she might have popped out somewhere - heaven knows where as there's not much to do around here, and I don't think there's much of a bus service to get out and about too often.'

Kelly took out her mobile from her handbag. 'I'll give her a quick call. If she decided to go along with her parents to Newcastle she could have at least had the decency to let us know and save us a wasted journey!'

She pressed the number in her contacts list and it rang a few times before going on to voice mail. But not one to be defeated, she called the number once again. After several rings, Helena finally answered.

'Hello…hello.'

Kelly frowned feeling concerned, as Helena sounded confused.

'Helena, where are you? I'm at your house - remember you invited me round for dinner? But you don't seem to be here - did you decide to go along to Newcastle?'

A few seconds passed before Helena replied. 'I'm at home. Mummy and daddy went with Uncle Ian to Newcastle and - oh gosh, I must have fallen asleep! Could you bear with me - I'll be with you in just a moment.'

Lee turned to Kelly searching for answers.

She gave a shrug. 'I don't know what's wrong, but she sounds completely confused - said she'd been asleep. I hope she's ok.'

They both jumped with a start as all of a sudden, the burglar alarm loudly burst into life, almost deafening them in the process.

'What the heck's going on?' demanded Lee. 'Anybody passing by will think we're doing the place over!'

They hurried back to the main entrance of the house, watching in eager anticipation as the door to the house opened, with Helena peering through briefly before retreating back inside the house. The alarm came to a stop abruptly.

As she returned to the door, Kelly and Lee almost stepped back in shock; instead of her normally casual but smart appearance, was now looking decidedly dishevelled with her usually smooth long blonde hair hanging loose and tangled. To add to the look, the mascara from one of her eyes was smudged down her face, with her blue tee-shirt slipping slightly down from one of her shoulders, exposing a white bra strap.

Kelly was beginning to feel extremely worried about her new friend.

'Helena, are you ok? Has something happened?'

She pulled back the tee-shirt over her shoulder. 'No...no, I'm fine. Mummy and daddy took Uncle Ian to Newcastle and I must have fallen asleep.'

Kelly's face paled. 'But that was yesterday, wasn't it? You called me after they left.'

Running her hands through her hair, Helena looked thoroughly confused. 'Yes. Yes of course - I'm so sorry. I must have fallen into a deep sleep - I'm just feeling a little disorientated.'

Lee studied her feeling equally as concerned. 'Are you *really* ok, Helena? I hope you don't mind, but I invited myself along as well as I was at a bit at a loose end after the job interview. But if you're not feeling up to having guests right now, we can always make it another time.'

Helena waved her hand dismissively. 'I've been looking forward to your company very much and I'm not about to turn you away.' She looked at them apologetically. 'Here's me being very rude and keeping you waiting - please follow me inside!'

They both turned briefly towards each other, feeling more than a little worried as Helena led the way, walking slowly and on a couple of occasions almost losing her balance with both taking it in turns to steady her to prevent her from falling. As they entered the lounge Lee insisted that she sat herself down on one of the large leather armchairs.

He studied her with a frown marking his forehead as she sat there with her large blue eyes open wide with confusion. 'Helena, I don't mean to alarm you but I'm truly worried about you - I'm sure I'm speaking for Kelly as well. I think we should call the doctor and get you checked out.'

Helena looked completely horrified. 'No, *please*, I'm absolutely fine - really! It's just that it's been rather a stressful, time with Auntie Sylvia dying and I guess none of us have been sleeping very well.'

Lee shrugged. 'Ok, if you insist, but just say the word if you change your mind. I'll get you a glass of water.'

'I'll get it.' Kelly insisted as she made her way to the kitchen. 'Actually, I think we could all do with a coffee.'

As Kelly brought in the water for Helena, then returned to the kitchen, busying herself with putting on the kettle and preparing mugs, Lee watched as the young woman took a sip of water, her hand trembling, almost spilling the contents on the floor.

Kelly returned to the living room appearing rather grim. 'We seem to be completely out of milk - does anyone mind taking their coffee black?'

'I'll drive up to the shop before it closes,' Lee offered, taking the van keys from his pocket.

Helena looked at her friends apologetically. 'I'm so sorry everybody, but I don't think I've prepared anything for our meal.'

Kelly turned to Lee, shaking her head in disbelief. 'How about us having an Indian or Chinese delivered? I can order something from one of the local restaurants on the *Just Eat* app - a few things that should suit everybody.'

Within an hour after unanimously opting for Indian, their order arrived. While Lee had popped out to buy the milk just getting to the shop in the nick of time, Kelly took the opportunity to help Helena tidy herself up, giving her hair a brushing and tied back neatly into a ponytail, giving her an almost schoolgirl appearance. Kelly looked at her feeling more than a little envious, wishing she could have smooth glossy hair instead of those wild out-of-control curls.

Much to their relief, Helena seemed to revert back more to her usual self and had laid out the dining room table with placemats and cutlery, lighting up vanilla scented candles in the middle of the table to add to the ambiance.

Having heated some plates, the women served up the variety of dishes, including onion bhaji, chicken korma, Rogan Josh, special fried rice and naan bread. Lee poured out the glasses of Diet Coke.

Kelly inhaled appreciatively the fragrant aroma of the

spicy dishes. 'I think I'm just about ready for this.'

Helena took a sip of her drink, looking apologetically at her guests. 'Hey, I'm so sorry about all this. I invited you here to entertain you and now I've let you both down - the least I can do is pay towards the meal.'

Lee firmly shook his head. 'My treat, and that's final.'

Kelly grinned. 'Well, I guess he's not going to take no for an answer and I'm definitely not going to turn down a freebie!'

Unlike Helena taking her time eating every morsel, Kelly and Lee finished their meals quickly, neither having eaten anything substantial since lunchtime.

Kelly took a drink of her Diet Coke. 'That was awesome,' she sighed, gently patting her stomach. Lee took out the plates and dishes to load into the dishwasher, dismissing Helena's objections.'

Impressed, she turned to Kelly. 'Wow, he's very domesticated - it's not very often that Uncle Ian will offer to help us around in the kitchen. And well, as far as Daddy is concerned, I'm afraid he's a lost cause.'

'I guess, it's a generational thing where it was expected that women saw to all the chores around the house while the men brought home the bacon.' Kelly felt with Lee now out in the kitchen busily seeing to the dishes, this was the perfect opportunity to broach the subject. 'Have you managed to get in touch with your pal Katherine?'

She shook her head ruefully. 'Unfortunately, I've not had much luck tracing her.'

'That's a pity. I remember you telling me she was living around the Dorset area. I'm sure I recall you mentioning that she was in the process of setting up a stained-glass windows business?'

Helena smiled brightly. 'Yes - her big ambition was to have her own stained-glass business and carrying out restorations. Katherine was always amazing at everything she applied herself to and I'm sure if that's what she's decided to do then she will make a huge success of it.'

Kelly refilled their glasses with more Coke. 'Was she seeing anybody when you last saw her?'

'You mean as in boyfriends? Oh yes, Katherine had loads of boyfriends whilst we were at university - unlike me. I can understand why all the boys were attracted to her. She was so beautiful with loads of charisma and I'm afraid I was always the shy one who followed in her shadow.' She gazed thoughtfully into the glass she held. 'But that was until one special person who came into her life, and that was Robert Herbert.'

Kelly felt the blood drain away from her face as she recalled the name from the Internet site. The Katherine Jolley-

Herbert on The Glass Palace site had a partner called Robert. This just had to be more than a coincidence. Her heart was racing at the prospect and it took all her willpower not to call Lee and tell him right there and then.

'Was it serious - do you think he was The One? Oh, I'm sorry, don't mind me I'm just plain nosey and a hopeless romantic!'

Helena laughed lightly, waving her hand dismissively. 'It's ok, no offence taken - I mean it. To answer your question, yes things got pretty serious between them - in fact so much so that they were discussing their engagement."

Kelly raised her eyebrows. 'Can I ask you something Helena, and feel free to tell me to mind my own business, but was there any reason why you lost contact with your best friend? Did you fall out over something?'

The smile slipped away from Helena's face and she appeared to be lost in her thoughts, appearing confused again. 'No, no, Katherine and me always got along very well. I'm not saying we didn't have the odd tiff and differences of opinion but... but...' She held her hand to her head as if trying her best to remember something but having difficulty in recalling some event.

Feeling concerned that Helena might suffer another bad turn, she tried to put her mind at rest. 'Hey, it's ok - I'm not trying to pry, just trying to make conversation, that's all. I promise to keep my big mouth shut in future.'

Lee returned from the kitchen holding a tray laden with mugs of hot steaming coffee. 'Well, that's the women's work done - don't know what all the fuss is about?'

Kelly looked at him with a scowl. 'Which one of us is going to stuff the dish cloth in his mouth?'

Helena laughed, her mood now much happier than a few moments before. 'Why don't you both take the coffees into the living room and make yourselves comfortable - I want to show you a few of my paintings which I've been working on over the past few weeks, and show you how much I've improved.'

'We're looking forward to it,' Kelly said with a smile.

As Helena made her way up the stairs, Kelly quickly put her drink on the small glass table in front of her and told Lee what she'd learned about Katherine Jolley.

'It has to be the same Katherine as Helena's friend - there's too much there for this to be just one big coincidence.'

Lee raised his eyebrows thoughtfully. 'Well, I've got to admit it does seem very likely, but we'll delve into things a bit later or maybe tomorrow - I will check out Facebook and Instagram to see if she has any social media accounts.'

Kelly bit her bottom lip. 'I think the sooner the better, because I'm really getting to become intrigued by the whole thing - I did search for Helena on Facebook but couldn't come up with anything.'

She took a walk around the living room admiring the paintings, some which had been done by Clarissa Broadhurst and others by Helena herself. 'Well, there's certainly plenty of talent between Helena and her mother - these are simply amazing.'

Lee stood up and stood close behind her, gently placing his hands around her hips causing her heart race wildly; surely, he could hear the sound of her heart beating like crazy. 'Well there *was* plenty of talent, but at the moment it seems to have eluded Helena.'

'It's such a pity - she really is a lovely person and I realise I barely know her, but I'm worried. She seems to be in some bad place at the moment and I'm not sure whether that's due to something physical or emotional - or perhaps a bit of both. Hey look at this!'

She studied the large painting that first caught Lee's attention just a few weeks ago, of the beautiful women with the long flowing blonde hair, wearing a large straw hat and long maxi dress.'

Lee gently placed a gentle kiss on her shoulder. 'I know what you're thinking - but I've been firmly assured that the lady in the painting isn't Helena but her sister Sarah.'

Kelly shook her head. 'No way is that her sister! I know we can never get to meet this Sarah, but I tell you this is Helena and I'll explain why - take a look at her right cheek, she has that small brown mole under the cheekbone the way Helena has.'

'Hmm, I think you may well be right.'

'I *know* I'm right even though this painting hasn't been signed. If this was her sister, she would be an identical twin, and from what I understand this Sarah was meant to be a few years older.' Her face screwed up for a moment in confusion. 'The mystery is, *why* all the lies? There's something here that's not quite adding up.'

They abruptly stopped speaking as soon as Helena entered the room, holding some fairly large canvases in her hands. 'Well I don't pretend to be some Rembrandt and I do realise I'm nowhere near as good as I used to be.'

Kelly turned around wishing the moment Lee kissing her shoulder could have lasted just a little longer. 'Well let's take a look at your masterpieces.'

Helena proudly showed them in turn each painting that she had worked so hard on, appearing to be oblivious to the puzzled expressions on their faces, which quickly turned to ones of pity.

'I guess I don't need to tell you this is one of Rupert. He does love to laze about in the garden - but on that day for some reason he did decide to have a walk around.'

Kelly looked thoughtfully at the paintings, nervously biting her lip before turning briefly towards Lee. 'Yes, these are very nice - you obviously enjoy painting very much. By the way where's Rupert? I haven't seen him around since we got here.'

The look of unease hadn't gone unnoticed by Helena. 'Oh, you don't really like them, do you?'

Lee quickly stood to Helena's defence. 'Kelly, from what I saw a few weeks ago Helena has improved tremendously. Good work Helena, and I know in a few weeks' time you'll be even better.'

She smiled at the compliment. 'I haven't shown you the one of Hugo as it's not quite finished - but I can go one better and introduce you to him. If you just give me a few minutes, then you can become acquainted with him. Oh, by the way, Mummy and Daddy took Rupert along with them.'

As she left the room they both looked to each other, completely intrigued now that they were both about to get to meet this mysterious Hugo.

As Lee placed his arm around her, it felt the most natural thing in the world just to relax and rest her head upon his shoulder.

Kelly's face was grim. 'Lee, I'm so worried about Helena.

Heaven knows how long she'd been sleeping for before we arrived - how had she been managing with eating when there didn't seem to be anything in the house left to eat?'

Gently, he stroked her hair before lightly kissing her on the head. 'Well, while you were both chatting away earlier, I did check the cupboards and there were a few things left such as cans of soup and baked beans - saw a few eggs in the fridge which she might have had for breakfast.'

She gave a sigh of relieve. 'I guess she's been feeding herself and all that but when she showed me those paintings, I've got to tell you that tears came to my eyes. She was so proud of what she'd done but the truth is, I was painting and drawing better than that when I was eight years old.'

Lee grimaced. 'Yes, those paintings showed none of the talent she displayed in her earlier pieces before her sister died. But compared to the stuff I saw a few weeks ago she has improved - but nowhere near enough to have her stuff exhibited at the Tate Gallery!'

'Hmm. To begin with I was all for her parents giving her a little independence, but having witnessed what I've seen this evening, I'm not so sure it was such a good idea - she seems barely capable of looking after herself. Knowing what they must know of her condition, whatever that may be, I'm surprised they left her behind.'

Kelly gave a big yawn after taking a long sip of her coffee. 'Oh, excuse me - it's just that I've had a really tiring day as I'm sure you've had too.'

'Yes, it's been a hectic day and a bit frustrating, now I'm waiting to hear whether or not I've got the job - but I know that neither you nor Sue has it easy in the office since Laura left. If I'd been Roger, I would have replaced her, even if it were with a part-timer to begin with. I know budgets were tight for a while but I've been doing my sums - just between me and you, if I am successful that's one of the first things I'm going to see to.'

She smiled wryly. 'Well it would certainly be a big help when one of takes our holidays or is off sick - because things can be a real nightmare as you well know.'

His expression became serious, making his brown eyes appear darker. 'Kelly, I have missed you so much - you just can't begin to know how sorry I am that I messed up for a while. Hope you can find it in your heart to forgive me for being such a numpty?'

She couldn't help but smile. 'Oh, you might be a complete numpty and make my life hell at times - but I know you've been through some tough times.'

'Doesn't excuse me for treating you the way I did.'

She gently put her finger to his lips. 'Hush - the past is in the past and enough said.'

Suddenly, to his surprise and great delight, she put her fingers through his hair as her lips caressed his and he responded to her gentle kiss. But as suddenly as her kiss begun, she quickly pulled back, staring ahead; her face turning as white as a sheet as if she had just seen a ghost. 'Oh, my goodness!' came the words slowly and softly.

As Lee turned around, his mouth opened wide in amazement, not believing what he could see in front of him. Helena then spoke, with a beaming smile on her face, startling the pair of them as if from a hypnotic trance.

'Kelly, Lee, I would like to introduce you to Hugo!'

Standing beside Helena stood a tall white figure with broad shoulders. Towering over Lee who was almost six feet, reminded Kelly a little of a white version of the Cyber Men in *Doctor Who*. Both of them stood up, staring in disbelief at what they were seeing in front of them.

Helena smiled kindly, seeing the look shock on their faces. 'Hugo, I would like to introduce you to my two new friends, Kelly and Lee.'

Hugo turned his head to study them, his movements a little slow as he offered to shake their hands. Reluctantly Lee gave his hand.

'It's Ok,' Helena reassured him. 'He won't hurt you - he's such a big softie!'

Then it was Kelly's turn to be greeted; although his hand was large and metallic, felt surprisingly warm as he gently took hold of her own. Hugo gazed at her from two small round eyes appearing hollow, from his large rectangular head, giving him an appearance of astonishment. A round black circle painted on the top of his head, took the place of hair, with large round sockets on each side where there should have been ears, adding to his almost comical appearance.

Kelly almost jumped as he said, 'Pleased to meet you Kelly. Please to meet you Lee.' His voice was coming from a slit in the place where there should have been a mouth, surprisingly clear and very well spoken and had the sound of a ten-year-old boy.

Lee looked almost slightly embarrassed as he looked up to the tall figure. 'Um, pleased to meet you Hugo.' He looked to Helena, not believing he was asking this question. 'Is he, is he a robot?'

She nodded. 'This is the work of Daddy and Uncle Ian, along with the help of some engineers from Oxford University.'

Lee couldn't shift his eyes from Hugo. 'This is amazing. I know there's work being done on robotics, but I've never seen anything at all like this before - only in sci-fi movies!' He looked at Helena suspiciously. 'This is some serious piece of equipment here - shouldn't he be locked away in some lab? He must be worth a fortune!'

Helena placed her arm around Hugo's narrow waist affectionately. 'Actually, Daddy and Uncle Ian have a lab which is adjoined to the house. I'm sorry I can't show you around because that's one place that is strictly out of bounds for everyone, with the exception of Mummy and me.'

Lee and Kelly stared on totally awestruck, as this was nothing like they had ever seen before.

Helena's voice took them away from their thoughts. 'Hey, I must show you some of the things that Hugo can do - he's amazingly clever. 'Come Hugo, let's do the Tango!'

Within seconds Hugo held one hand gently around the small of Helena's back, gently holding her hand with the other, and together they moved around the living room. Helena herself was a very accomplished dancer, and although Hugo had large clumsy looking feet, was surprisingly agile. Kelly thought Hugo could give many of the contestants on *Strictly Come Dancing* a run for their money. She couldn't stop herself from staring at this strange looking being and thinking if this was all a huge joke and this was somebody dressed up in a fancy-dress costume; but deep down she knew that this wasn't the case. Taking out her mobile phone to record the event on the video, she couldn't help but smile as Hugo mimicked Helena's dramatic head movements. After the performance ended, Kelly and Lee gave a round of applause, as Helena gave a small curtsy and Hugo gave a bow.

As everybody returned to their seats, Helena ordered Hugo to make her guests some coffee, instructing him that Lee preferred his drink strong with two sugars and Kelly medium with no sugar. In next to no time he returned from the Kitchen with a tray of beverages and even a plate of biscuits. Lee chuckled, not believing what he was witnessing. 'A pity he wasn't around a little earlier when I was doing the washing-up.'

Helena took one of the biscuits that she daintily bit into. 'Oh, he's very useful to have around - he can even do some basic cooking, though we do tend to keep an eye on him, as on a few occasions he has allowed the vegetables to boil over, which Mummy wasn't too pleased about! But he's incredibly handy at Christmas when we're putting up the decorations - being so tall, he can get to those hard to reach places such as putting up the trimmings on the ceiling. But he doesn't have such flair for decorating the tree.' She looked at them with a wry smile. 'He's actually even worse than me at the moment in the artistic field - Daddy and Uncle Ian have tried their best to upgrade him, but although he does make small bursts of improvements, there's nothing to enable him to set the art world on fire with his efforts!'

Kelly took a sip of her coffee and to her surprise, found that Hugo had made it to perfection. 'I guess he can't be good at everything - it must be very challenging to programme up a robot to do such complicated tasks. But he definitely gets my vote in domesticity!'

Helena brushed some biscuit crumbs from her lap. 'He's an absolute treasure, especially when it comes to cleaning the vehicle, which quite often get muddy along these country lanes. But there's so much more to Hugo - he's such a brainbox too.' She gave him a series of numbers to add up, multiply and divide and came up with answers instantly, which were one hundred per cent accurate. Not only was he good at figures, but also had an amazing wealth of general knowledge. Kelly and Lee asked Hugo a number of questions from early to modern history, and answered those accurately and in detail.

Lee shook his head in disbelief and couldn't help but smile. 'My, he is a person, sorry, a robot of many talents - he would certainly come in handy on a pub quiz night!'

Kelly desperately needed to go to the toilet. 'Helena could you tell me where I could go to powder my nose?'

For a moment Helena looked at her blankly. 'Oh, of course! If you just go through the door over there and it's the second along.'

Kelly gave a yawn as she walked down the corridor. What

an incredible night it had been. When she agreed to meet Helena for dinner, there was no way she could have predicted how the evening would turn out. After a difficult start, not knowing if her friend was even there, and worried about her wellbeing, who could have predicted that she would have spent the evening, being entertained by a giant robot? Nobody in their wildest dreams would believe her and felt it would be better for her and Lee to keep this just between them; people would either think they were making the whole think up, or were just plain crackers!

As she opened the door to what she thought was the toilet, she fumbled in the darkness and clicked on the light switch and realised by mistake she had entered the wrong room. What she could now see was a small sitting room, much less formally furnished than the modern lounge. Instead of the leather sofa and chairs, were a soft beige settee and two armchairs with a smaller TV on a stand instead of the wall-mounted flat screen, in the main room. But her attention was instantly drawn to a large, framed black and white photograph on the wall. On the picture was a strikingly attractive woman who sported a short stylish geometric Vidal Sassoon haircut. Although the picture was not in colour she could guess that her hair was that familiar honey blonde, realising this must have been a much younger Clarissa Broadhurst. She smiled to the camera; her pale eyes fringed with thick lashes, which Kelly guessed must have been false ones. At her side stood a much younger Sebastian Broadhurst, still with the beard and spectacles, but with much darker hair. Although by no stretch of the imagination could he be described as handsome, his face wore a smile, which gave him an almost youthful appearance. Sitting in the middle of the couple was a girl in her teens, with fair, shoulder length hair smiling brightly to the camera. She took a closer look and realised it was Helena as she had that tell-tale mole on her cheek.

Frowning, and biting her lip in concentration, knew this wasn't making any sense; judging by the age of Clarissa and Sebastian this appeared to have been taken many years ago, but knew this couldn't be the case, as Helena wouldn't have even been around in the sixties. But then she realised that Helena's mother was an artist and also had a career working on special effects in the film industry. It was most likely that what she was looking at what must have been Photo Shopped to make a nice family photo. The black and white, gave it a very retro feel, and seemed to capture a moment of much happier times of a bygone era.

She looked around and saw other photos mounted on the wall, noticing one of a small baby in a large white cot, possibly either Sarah or Helena. Another showed a later photo of Clarissa and Sebastian at some party. Helena's mother was toasting with a glass of champagne and the Professor doing likewise, holding a cigar in the other. All the photos seemed to be taken in happier days before their daughter Sarah was taken from them. Kelly noticed that there didn't seem to be a single photo of their late daughter, unless she was the one as a baby. Maybe it was be just too painful for the family to have her photos hanging around the place. Her thoughts were suddenly disturbed by the sound of Helena's laughter in the background; she quickly switched off the light, closing the door firmly behind her.

After she returned to the lounge she found Hugo sitting at the table with Lee, playing a game of chess. Lee peered over to Kelly with a grin. 'Must admit I'm a bit rusty at chess - haven't played it since I left school and Hugo's beating me shamelessly!'

Helena laughed from the armchair, eating another biscuit. 'Hugo is extraordinarily clever at most things, but I have beaten him at chess sometimes and he doesn't like it one bit.'

Kelly gave a wry smile. 'What happens when he doesn't win? Does he swipe the chessboard on to the floor and have a tantrum like a typical man?'

Lee looked at her with mock frown. 'Steady!'

'Actually, he just stops playing and freezes on the spot, and that's when Daddy and Uncle Ian have to take him back to the lab to be reset.'

Lee looked thoughtfully at the chessboard. 'Don't think there's much chance of him getting into a strop with me this evening - he's beating me hands down!' He peered at Helena, the smile slipping from his face. 'Joking aside, it might be a good idea if we stop our game now just in case something goes wrong with Hugo and your dad and uncle won't be here to sort him out - don't want him to get out of control while everybody's away!'

'You're right - Hugo, it's time for you to go back to the lab. I'm sure Kelly and Lee enjoyed meeting you, and you can see them another time.'

Kelly raised her eyebrows. 'It's certainly been very interesting and surprising, and good to finally meet Hugo!'

As the robot obediently followed Helena to the back door stomping with his over-sized feet, he suddenly turned around and gave a wave. 'Goodbye Lee, goodbye Kelly, it was very nice to meet you - see you both again very soon!'

Once finally alone, Kelly stared at Lee in total disbelief at what they had witnessed that evening. 'Tell me this is all a dream and I'm about to wake up very soon.'

'Tell me about it - how on earth did that robot get to be here? Surely it must be worth millions and should be at some lab or some organisation - what's this all about? No wonder her family wanted Hugo kept a secret. And what on earth made her tell us about him? It's not as if we're very close friends.'

Kelly looked at him grimly. 'But anybody can see she's very lonely and probably we are the closest she has for friends. I strongly believe, that woman I found on the Net is *the* Katherine Jolley.'

'Ok. We'd best keep quiet for the moment, I think that's Helena coming back now. I tell you what, if we say our goodbyes shortly, you can tell me about it on the way home and we'll delve into it a bit more deeply.'

After Kelly and Lee departed, Helena finished clearing up, making sure that all the foil trays from the takeaway meal were thrown into the dustbin and all the chess pieces put back away in the cupboard. She smiled to herself, thinking what a fabulous evening this had turned out to be. Heaven knows how she'd fallen asleep and forgotten about Kelly coming over; Mummy and Daddy had always stressed to her that Hugo had to be just their secret, but it was great to introduce him to her two special friends, who she was sure loved him as much as she did. Wearily, she blinked her eyes. It had been an amazing evening, but now she felt she was totally lacking energy. Glancing at the time on her watch, saw that it was 10 o'clock and was getting passed her bedtime. After switching off all the lights, she made her way up the stairs to her bedroom.

As she walked towards the window to look at the moonlit sky she almost lost her balance. The evening had taken it out of her completely and simply didn't have the energy to change into her nightwear. Smiling contentedly, she untied the band from her hair, allowing it to fall loosely over her shoulders. She climbed into her bed, covering herself with the duvet, before switching off her bedside lamp. As soon as her head touched the pillow she was dead to the world.

CHAPTER SIXTEEN

The following morning Kelly was sat at her PC in the office, having just completed one of her daily reports, yawning deeply as Sue brought her a freshly made mug of coffee. 'Looks as if you're in need of this,' she grinned.

Kelly gratefully took a sip of her drink. 'Tell me about it. We stayed out a little later than intended and it was ages before I managed to get off to sleep - Lee's the lucky one because he's on a day's holiday.'

Sue sat opposite her friend, holding her mug thoughtfully. 'So how did your evening with Helena turn out, with the unexpected pleasure of Mr Fisher tagging along as well?'

'Well apart from a bumpy start, where we thought Helena had decided to go away with her parents, it was pretty interesting to say the least.'

As Sue raised her eyebrow quizzically, she explained what happened when they first arrived at the Broadhursts and the confused state Helena appeared to be in.

Sue shrugged her shoulders. 'Hmm. It all seems very strange - maybe, with hindsight, she would have been better off going along with her parents. To be perfectly honest it sounds like the girl is suffering from some mental illness.'

'It's quite possible. There's something that's not quite right - especially the fact that until her sister died, she was a budding Rembrandt. You should have seen the paintings she did, they were amazing! She obviously takes after her mother who made a whole career out of special effects in films. That's what made it so sad - when she proudly showed me her latest efforts that were no better than those of the average child still at primary school.'

Sue shook her head in disbelief. 'That's pretty sad. Poor kid - I hope she gets back whatever it was she lost, because it must be really frustrating for her as well. So how did everything else go? Did you get to meet the mysterious Hugo?'

Kelly looked at her friend nervously biting her bottom lip. There was no way Sue would believe her if she told her that Hugo was a sophisticated robot. Even she herself was having difficulty getting her head around this. 'No. No, Hugo wasn't around and I didn't ask.'

'Hmm. Probably only exists in her imagination - I guess it's how some people cope with loneliness.'

'Yeah, I guess so.'

Sue took sip of her coffee. 'So how did everything go with Lee? Did he go back to yours afterwards?'

'No, it was pretty late by the time we left - Helena was beginning to look pretty jaded and I was feeling the same. He just dropped me off at the car park, but we're meeting again this evening.'

Sue took one last look at Kelly, before resuming with the letter she'd been working on. She couldn't help but feel that her friend was holding back on something, but she wouldn't press her.

◆ ◆ ◆

Lee let himself inside his flat, rubbing his eyes wearily having just returned from his mum's after doing a few DIY jobs for her. He could have thought of more exciting ways to spend his day off, but there were other things to see to, such as the faulty light switch to the living-room and a leaky pipe to the washing-machine that could no longer be put off.

Sitting down on the sofa, he switched on the TV with the remote control. He gave a big yawn as he watched the remaining part of some science documentary. With having the luxury of not working, he'd hoped to have a longer sleep; but no matter how much he tried, his efforts were in vain, spending most of the night tossing and turning as he thought back to the evening's events. Who would have guessed that his time would be spent being entertained by a robot? The whole notion was surreal.

Leaning his head back on the sofa with his thoughts filled with Kelly who'd looked so tired when they parted company. With a look of sheer fatigue on her pretty face as he dropped her off outside the delivery depot where she'd parked her car, he gently kissed her on those soft rosebud lips. How he would love to have taken her home! Still, they were meeting up this evening, with the promise to cook her dinner. So, who knows what could happen from there? He thought back to what she'd mentioned about Helena's friend, and had to admit that the woman she'd found on that website sounded like she could be the Katherine Jolley that they were looking for.

At this moment in time, Lee felt his whole life was in a limbo, not knowing if he would be successful with the manager's position. To add to his frustration, James Close, the very person who had the final say was absent with flu. Feeling too agitated to sleep, he switched on his laptop and tapped in the link that Kelly located for The Glass Palace. As she mentioned, the business had been going for well over thirty years, and appeared to have been a family run business, probably handed down from parents. The company had specialised in the design and manufacture of stained glassed windows for both the home and business market, boasting of work on glass restorations in churches. Although he wasn't a huge fan of stained-glass windows, Lee had to admit that the designs were pretty impressive.

The proprietors, Robert and Katherine Jolley-Herbert, also offered some courses on the art of stained-glass design. A pity they didn't have photos of these people on the site, he mused, because even though he wouldn't know them from Adam, would perhaps give some idea of the woman's age and some indication whether or not they had found the right person. Clicking on the page with the contact details, which gave both an email address and telephone number, Lee made a note of both. Thoughtfully, he placed the laptop on the coffee table as his mind raced with some possible ideas on how to follow things up. His first priority was to prepare the meal ready for when Kelly came over. He needed to make a good impression and to make this a night which neither of them was likely to forget.

◆ ◆ ◆

Jess Cowley unlocked the door to the house at The Woodlands with a frown, gathering up a few letters that had been posted through the letterbox. She was surprised to see that the gate hadn't been locked to the driveway before the Broadhursts left for Newcastle, and even more concerned that the security alarm hadn't been set. Shaking her head in despair, she closed the door firmly behind her. She mustn't be too hard on them she thought; they did have a lot on their minds before leaving the house. That Ian Peterson wasn't a man she had particularly taken to, she mused and could be dead grumpy at the best of times. Maybe he didn't have much cause to be happy with that terrible scar on his face, which he tried in vain to hide with that beard; but he didn't deserve to lose his sister in the way he did. Just a couple of days ago, Mrs Broadhurst called to inform her that Sylvia Peterson had passed away peacefully at the hospice.

She gazed at her reflection in the mirror hanging on the wall in the hallway and tried to smooth her short grey hair that got ruffled in the strong wind outside. But it was a happy release, she thought to herself - it was an awful time when her sister Maggie's husband, Bert, was taken away with cancer. He was such a fit healthy man in his time, and to see him waste away like that, well she wouldn't wish that on her worst enemy.

Walking through to the large modern living room that she cleaned out three times a week, Jess looked around as if seeing the place for the very first time. Somehow it felt different without the Broadhursts around. Not that she saw much of the Professor and Mr Peterson, locked away in that big lab, adjoined to the back of the house. That was one place that was out of bounds to her. Heaven knows what went on in there; anybody would think it was something top secret. Mrs Broadhurst was getting on in years, as was the Professor, and it was a surprise to her to find that they had a daughter as young as Helena. When she first went to work for them a couple of years ago, when they moved to the village, Jess assumed that she was their granddaughter. Well, young Helena must be in her early to mid-twenties but suspected her parents must be well into their seventies. She learned there had been an elder sister that got killed in a car crash, but the family never spoke of her, and only gleaned pieces of information when Helena would do those awful paintings and tell her how good she once was before this Sarah had died.

A shiver ran involuntarily down her spine as her feet echoed loudly on the laminated floor, breaking up the almost deafening silence. It did seem strange without Helena greeting her as she always did on her cleaning days here. The poor lass never had any company and it seemed the only excitement she got was when either herself or Eddie who came to do the garden. A pretty young thing like her should have been out and about enjoying herself, perhaps with a nice young man, not with three old-timers like them. Perhaps going to that funeral as sad as it was, might give her a chance to meet people closer to her own age. Looking down to the floor she found a chess piece that she picked up. Not sure where the box was kept with the board, she placed this on the large marble mantel piece, where to her great delight found her reading spectacles neatly folded.

Thank goodness, she thought with a smile. Wasn't sure why, but had a feeling that's where she'd left them. Oh, she had a spare pair at home, but her prescription had changed since then and was giving her a headache straining her eyes to read that newspaper print. Picking them up she placed them into her handbag. Happy that her trip hadn't been a wasted one, she took a walk into the kitchen to make sure everything was in order. Everything looked neat and tidy with all the cups away, but shook her head in disapproval at seeing an empty cola bottle standing by the sink. Picking this up, she took a final look around to make sure the windows were all safely closed.

Just as she was about to leave, she wondered whether she should take a look upstairs, but thought otherwise. Jess took pride in her work, and didn't want to be seen as somebody who pried; besides she didn't see the need, as thankfully the house hadn't been burgled. A small wonder with the gate being left unlocked and the security alarm switched off. Before leaving, Jess made sure this was activated. About to throw away the drinks bottle into the dustbin, she was surprised to see foil trays from a takeaway. She raised her eyebrows in question, as the Broadhursts were never ones for eating junk food, opting instead for traditional home-cooked meals. But there again, they were going through some difficult times, and probably a ready-made meal seemed the best option before that long drive. Thankfully she knew the combination number to the gate and made sure this was locked securely. Satisfied that everything was now in order, didn't see the need to come back until the Broadhursts returned from the funeral in a few days' time.

Upstairs in her bedroom with just the clock on the bedside table ticking loudly to break the silence, Helen laid in her bed her eyes firmly closed, completely oblivious to Mrs Cowley's visit.

◆ ◆ ◆

Kelly arrived in a taxi at Lee's flat later that evening, after having left work and quickly getting herself ready. Carrying a bottle of red wine, Lee whistled in appreciation at Kelly's appearance. Wearing a cream silk blouse with her skinny jeans she looked absolutely stunning, noticing she was wearing that subtle scented perfume he always found so erotic. 'My, you're looking very tasty this evening, Miss Phillips, even tastier than my filet steak with peppercorn sauce!'

'Flattery will get you everywhere, Mr Fisher, but I think you're just trying to get around me because as I know you so well, you're just trying to butter me up to see to the piles of washing- up after.'

Lee looked at her sheepishly. 'There's no fooling you. How did your day go? Hope it was more exciting than mine, doing DIY at Mum's!'

Kelly sat herself down in one of the armchairs. 'Oh, nothing terribly exciting going on at my end. Gary Pritchard was covering your area today but I'm afraid he brought back a load of the parcels, saying a lot of the customers weren't in.'

Lee grimaced. 'That's a load of rubbish. Yeah, a lot of them are out working, but there's always a neighbour to leave it with, or a safe place if a signature isn't required. Oh, I can see tomorrow I'm going to have a ball catching up with the backlog.'

He poured her a glass of wine which Kelly sipped appreciatively as she leaned her head back, relaxing. 'Not sure what's up with Sue, but she doesn't seem herself - was well grumpy which is so unlike her.'

'Maybe she's had a domestic with Barry.'

'Yeah, maybe, but I guess there must be a lot of stress with organising the wedding.' She looked up to Lee, who remained standing, peering at her with only what she could describe as concern.

'Did you sleep ok last night?' he asked topping up her wine glass.

'Not too much for me until dinner's served, thanks - you know how it goes to my head on an empty stomach.' She sighed shaking her head, the knowing smile that he gave appearing to be lost on her. 'Actually, I slept badly - I couldn't stop thinking about what we'd seen last night. There's no way in my wildest dreams would I have guessed that the mysterious Hugo is a robot.'

He nodded in agreement. 'I must admit, I spent the best part of the night, trying to get my head around everything. After I came back from Mum's, I did a bit of digging on the internet about the work of Sebastian Broadhurst. It did give some mention about his work on a project called Devotion, which they worked on in various universities during the seventies and eighties in Ontario, Canada and Oxford University - apparently, Ian Peterson played a major part in this. It gives a mention about research into robotics and artificial intelligence, but no matter how hard I tried, couldn't find any specific details on what this involved. It sounds to me like something that's being kept under wraps.'

'Sounds pretty heavy stuff,' Kelly remarked, her eyes widening in astonishment. 'I guess Hugo must have been a part of that project. How on earth did the Broadhursts manage to keep him, because one thing's for sure, that a lot of money must have been invested into a robot of that kind.'

Lee shrugged, taking a sip of his wine. 'It's something we may never know for sure.' He looked at his watch. 'Anyway, I'd best press on with the meal before we completely starve. If there's nothing on TV, feel free to surf the Net and see if you can find out any more than I did.'

'Are you sure you don't need a hand out in the kitchen?'

'No. For once, enjoy an evening of being wined, dined and being taken care of.'

Kelly sat back and smiled as she heard the sound of the radio coming from the kitchen as Lee got to work. She could certainly get used to this! Flicking the remote control around and seeing there wasn't anything worth watching on TV, she decided to take Lee's advice and to see if she could find out any more about the Broadhursts.

Later, seeing that Kelly was totally engrossed with searching on the internet, Lee placed his hands on her shoulder gently kissing the top of her head, causing her jump with a start.

'Sorry, but I was totally wrapped up with this.' She took a sniff. 'Mm, I can smell something very appetising coming from the kitchen and making me feel very hungry.'

'Well, you won't have to wait any longer as dinner's about to be served. So, have you found anything interesting out about our friends?'

She gave a wry smile. 'I wouldn't go as far as to call them friends, maybe apart from Helena, but I found out a few interesting facts about Ian Peterson - a pretty brainy guy who was awarded a scholarship from the Vale Fund to undertake his DPhil. As we already learned, he spent a lot of his time at Oxford and that's where he completed his undergraduate degree in computer science - also received a university medal for outstanding academic achievement.'

Lee whistled through his teeth. 'Don't understand what half of this means, but it sounds pretty impressive.'

Kelly shrugged her shoulders. 'Me neither, and do you know anything about algorithms? Because Peterson was involved in some kind of research into that subject and apparently has something to do with the visual world as seen through a camera.'

'Hmm, not really sure about that, but it does sound like it could have some connection to the robotics and artificial intelligence - might well explain how Hugo is able to see. Anyway, shall we get dinner served? I don't know about you, but I'm starved!'

After Kelly set the table up in the lounge, with a lit candle set in the middle and the lights dimmed low, the couple enjoyed their dinner in blissful silence.

'This is so delicious,' sighed Kelly, taking a sip of her red wine. 'That steak is to die for - it's so tender.'

'Mm. It's pretty good. Got it from Morrison's at a pretty decent price too!'

She watched him thoughtfully. 'This waiting to see whether or not you've got the job, must be killing you. Of all the times, for James Close to come down with flu, when it's unknown for him to be off sick.'

'Tell me about it - I was hoping to know one way or another this week. But what can I do? I guess I will just have to hold out 'til next week. So, did you find out any other interesting facts about the Broadhursts while I was slaving away in the kitchen?'

Kelly cut into her steak, which she dipped into the peppercorn sauce. 'Well I did find out a few more facts about Clarissa Broadhurst and all the films she's been involved with. You'd be amazed at some of the horror and sci-fi films she's worked on, especially during the seventies and the eighties - she was also quite a name in the art world too. There was also mention about her marriage to Sebastian Broadhurst and how they met at a birthday bash of some big film director of the time - it went on to say, how they lost their daughter in a car crash, just weeks before she was due to marry. It didn't go into too much detail, no dates, or stating whether the fiancé survived the crash. In fact, it was so vague and sad that not even Helena and her sister's names got a mention!'

Lee poured some more wine into their glasses. 'Hmm, that's a bit frustrating. From what I read Professor Broadhurst has done some pretty amazing stuff, and as I mentioned before, he worked on this project named Devotion and carried out a lot of work on the controlling of articulated objects which Peterson played a big part in developing. I can only assume that must have everything to do with Hugo, and how he was designed. I guess these universities in Ontario must have been involved, and it's bit of a mystery why the Broadhursts had the privilege of taking him home and use him as a playmate for Helena!'

Kelly dabbed her mouth with her napkin. 'I guess the only person that might be able to give us a few answers about Helena and just exactly why she's being wrapped up in cotton wool, is her old friend Katherine Jolley.'

Lee gave her a knowing smile. 'And why is it that I think you have something in mind and I think I know what's coming up?'

'I think we should meet her,' she confirmed. I know she lives miles away, but I think this is the only way we'll get answers to all these questions. I know you think we should leave it well alone, because we hardly know them and...'

'Hush! I know what you're thinking and you thought wrong because on this I agree with you entirely - until we knew of Hugo, I would've just said leave things well alone. But the more we learn, the deeper this mystery seems to get. Shall I try to give her friend a call and see if we can meet up with her in Dorset, say on Friday? If we both try and book half a day's holiday, we should be able to beat the rush hour traffic on the M25.'

Kelly bit her bottom lip. 'It's a bit short notice, but as far as I know Sue's not booked any time off and I'm sure you'll be able to get one of the drivers to deliver some of your parcels. But I think we should give this Katherine a call first, as she might have other plans.'

Lee pressed the numbers from the site on his phone and after about four rings a woman answered.

'Is that Mrs Jolley-Herbert?'

Lee gave Kelly a thumbs-up sign. 'Excellent. It's just that me and my partner are looking for some stained-glass windows for our new home and were very impressed with the designs we saw on your website.'

'Thank you, that's very kind of you.'

'I was wondering if it would be possible, if my partner and

me could meet with you, to discuss things further. By the way, my name is Lee Fisher and my partner is Kelly.'

There was a moment's hesitation. 'Well, yes I suppose we could meet, though if you would prefer I would be happy if you send me an email to begin with and perhaps some photo attachments.'

Lee looked at Kelly, who was feeling more than a little curious about whether or not this was the Katherine they had been looking for. 'Actually, we were planning to head over to Dorset this weekend to Christchurch, as it's one of our favourite places, and wondered if we could meet you there. If possible, could we meet you Friday afternoon, say about three o'clock?'

'Well yes, I suppose we could, and I'm sure the family could manage without me for an hour or so. I'll give you my phone number, just in case you get delayed.'

Lee wrote it down before giving Katherine his mobile number. 'The Half Moon Pub in Gable Street is fine - thank you for meeting us at such short notice. I have to be honest, that it wasn't just through the internet we learned of you. I believe you are friends of the Broadhursts and of course Helena.'

There were a few seconds of silence, and at first Lee thought the woman had hung up. 'Oh, my goodness yes. Oh, you have taken me by surprise. It's been such a long time and they are such wonderful people - the best. But you know how time seems to just slip away. Anyway, I have to go now as I have an urgent job to finish. Please say hello to Clarissa and Sebastian for me and I'll see you on Friday.'

Lee looked at Kelly intently when he hung up. 'Well your hunch was spot on - this *is* the Katherine Jolley we've been looking for.'

Kelly saw the troubled frown that creased his forehead. 'What's bugging you?'

'Well, there are a few things. It was Katherine herself - she didn't have the voice of somebody of Helena's age. If I didn't know any different, I would have said she sounded as old as my mum.'

Kelly took a sip of her wine. 'But a lot of people look completely different from how you expect when listening to their voice on the phone - I should know that from customers, when speaking to them on the phone and when they come to the depot to collect a parcel.'

'Yes, I take your point, but she was really shocked when I mentioned the Broadhursts and I could swear I could hear the emotion welling up in her voice. But what really puzzled me, was that she asked me to say hello to Clarissa and Sebastian but gave no mention of Helena.'

Kelly rubbed her chin thoughtfully. 'That's a bit strange,

especially when they're supposed to be the best of friends - maybe this rift went deeper than we realised. Now I'm really intrigued.'

Lee looked to her thoughtfully. 'I've got to admit, it all sounds a bit strange, but we haven't got long to wait. As you heard, I managed to make an appointment for us to meet in Christchurch, now all we have to do is get the time off work and go down there.'

'I really can't wait, because all this is really beginning to bug me.' She started collecting the plates. 'Now let's get this washing up done - if I know you well, the kitchen will be declared a disaster zone!'

Just as Kelly put away the last of the plates, Lee finished preparing the coffee. She looked at him with a mischievous grin. 'Well, you did seem to use every single kitchen utensil available, but I've got to say that meal was absolutely delicious.'

They returned to the living room where they relaxed on the sofa. Lee gently placed his arm around her, and it seemed the most natural thing in the world, to rest her head on his shoulder. He switched off the TV with the remote control.

'This is bliss,' she sighed.

Lee closed his eyes. 'Mm, it's good just to relax to the sound of silence. I hear it's pretty good in Christchurch, very pretty with The New Forest Close by and Bournemouth just around the corner. I was wondering if you fancy making a weekend of it?'

He felt Kelly's shoulders tense. 'Sadly, I can't because I've promised to take Josh and Amy to Legoland on Saturday.'

'Never mind, it was just a thought.'

She could see the look of disappointment on his face. 'I'm really sorry because it sounds a lovely idea.'

He gave her a reassuring smile. 'Hey, it's ok - I'm the one who should be saying sorry for not giving you enough notice, and I know how much those two mean to you and how you hate to let them down.'

She cuddled up to him again, feeling terrible for turning down a weekend away with him. The truth was she could easily have changed her plans with her niece and nephew, but she wasn't quite sure if she was ready to take the next step. She knew without a doubt that she was in love with him, and had waited so long to get to this stage, but at the same time wanted to make sure she wasn't rushing into anything she might later regret.

Looking up to him, she could see the disappointment etched on his face. 'I'm really looking forward to this Friday, and I don't just mean to see this Katherine.'

Without any warning, she suddenly kissed him on the lips, taking Lee completely by surprise as he responded to her urgent kisses, lowering her down further onto the sofa. They both jumped with a start as the silence was broken by the sound of Kelly's mobile ringing.

'Ignore it,' he begged her as the ringtone finally came to a stop. Just as he held her in his arms and caressing her hair, the phone began to ring again.

'I'd best see who this is, it might be something urgent,' she said apologetically. 'It's Sue.' And it must be something pretty serious for her to be calling, she thought; because she was aware she was spending the evening with Lee.

'Hi Sue.' Lee saw the look of anguish spread across her face. 'Hey, what's the matter? Look, it's ok I'll come over. No, it doesn't matter - really. I should be there within the next 15-20 minutes.'

Kelly looked grim after she hung up. 'I'll have to go, Lee. I'm so sorry but Sue is crying her eyes out - Barry's out and she's got something she needs to tell me. I can't leave her in that state.'

He rubbed his face. 'No, it's ok. You must go and see to her. I'll run you there.'

'I'll call a taxi, I won't have you driving when you've had too much to drink.' She pressed the number of the local taxi firm from her contacts.

Within ten minutes, Kelly was gone. So much for their

night of passion and the promise of an interesting weekend to follow, but he saw the look of surprise on her face that made him totally unprepared for the way she suddenly kissed him. He guessed it was his fault for giving her mixed signals for so long and knew it was going to take some time to win her over. But she was worth it, and he would do whatever it took to do this. Giving a long yawn he decided to head straight to bed.

CHAPTER SEVENTEEN

Helena opened her eyes, seeing the daylight shine through a small gap in the closed curtains. Immediately sitting upright as she heard somebody walking up the stairs, felt concerned and alarmed that somebody might have broken into the house. Pulling up the sheet as the door opened, a look of relief immediately spread across her face as her mother came into the room with a mug of tea.

'Mummy! You're back already!'

Clarissa gave her a cheerful smile. 'Yes darling, we're back. Actually, we returned a few hours ago, but seemed such a shame to disturb you when you were fast asleep.'

Helena looked over to her alarm clock on the bedside table, and saw the time was 11.30! Never had she remembered waking as late as this in her entire life. She pulled back the bedclothes ready to get dressed.

'There's no hurry dear, just relax and drink your tea first.'

Sinking back onto her bed, Helena realised she was wearing her blue nightie when she could have sworn she went to bed in her day clothes. But she had to admit she was very tired then, and not quite with it.

Taking a sip of her tea, she gazed at her mother who appeared a little dark under her eyes and the strain on her face was clear to see. 'Has Auntie Sylvia passed away?'

Clarissa sat on the edge of the bed. 'Yes darling, she went peacefully. I think she was holding on until we arrived. I know it was expected, but Uncle Ian was absolutely devastated.'

Helena looked on with pity. 'Poor Uncle Ian, he does seem to have had a lot of sadness in his life - but it's a happy release, because she had been ill and suffering for such a long time.'

Her mother grimaced. 'Yes darling, and now Auntie Sylvia is in a better place. Did…did you pop out to the shops while we were away? I see there was a new container of milk in the fridge that's been started on.'

Helena swallowed nervously as her instincts warned her that her mother wouldn't have been pleased knowing that Kelly and Lee had visited and been introduced to Hugo. 'No, Mummy, I spent my time in the house tidying up.'

Clarissa's eyes narrowed suspiciously, appearing unconvinced. 'Perhaps Mrs Cowley dropped by and left it and made herself a drink. And do you know what I saw in the recycle bin? Some foil dishes from one of those hideous takeaways! I just hope that nobody has been taking any liberties while we were away.'

'Mummy, I can assure you that I've been here by myself and not had any takeaways, and I'm sure Mrs Cowley isn't a person to take advantage.'

Her mother gave a long drawn out sigh. 'I suppose you're right. We knew it couldn't have been you, but I did mention to your father as we left, that I was sure we'd left the gate unlocked.' Shrugging her shoulders wearily, she gave a loud sigh. 'I suppose it's not out of the realms of possibilities that a passer-by could have stopped off and left their rubbish. But why they would have chosen to use our bin is totally beyond me!'

Helena peered at her mother sheepishly, knowing that she made a terrible liar. 'So, when is the funeral to take place? I think for that, I should come along and pay my last respects.'

Clarissa quickly got up from bed to open the curtains, seemingly to avoid eye contact. 'Actually, the funeral took place yesterday. We managed to organise matters amazingly fast. I'm sorry we couldn't have waited until next week, but we felt it was a long way to travel, and thought we might as well arrange it sooner rather than later.'

Helena looked on, eyes open wide with astonishment as her mother left the room gently closing the door behind her. How on earth had her parents managed to arrange Sylvia's funeral so quickly? As much as she tried, had no recollection of having changed into her nightwear, nor did she remember removing her make-up before going to sleep.

She climbed out of the bed and changed into clothes that were folded neatly on the chair. It wasn't that she'd been drinking the night before, at least nothing more potent than coffee; nothing to explain why she had difficulty in remembering things. Slowly Helena got changed, feeling disturbed when she recalled Kelly frantically calling her on the mobile and hadn't even prepared any food for her visit. What was the matter with her? It was nothing short of a miracle she had received the call as the battery was about to die on her phone.

Combing her long hair, which she tied it back with a band, checked her reflection in the mirror. As far as she could see she didn't look unwell; but perhaps Lee was right and she needed to see a doctor. There had to be something seriously wrong, firstly losing her ability to paint and now these lapses in her memory. Perhaps her parents knew more than they were revealing; after all, that could be the only explanation why she wasn't allowed to drive a car anymore.

Grimly, she checked her mobile to see if there were any messages from Kelly or Lee, before realising that the battery was completely flat and quickly putting it onto charge. Perhaps she would skip breakfast, as it was so late and go and see Uncle Ian who must be feeling sad and lonely at losing his only living family member.

Kelly and Lee set off early Friday morning as they headed for Dorset, hoping to beat the rush hour traffic, but it seemed all their efforts had been in vain.

'Good old M25 never fails to disappoint,' Lee remarked with a grimace. You would've thought with an early start, it would have been a doddle - and then something happens to hold you up.'

Kelly tried to look as far ahead as possible but all she could see were all the lanes blocked with endless queues of traffic. 'Just hope it's not an accident, some poor person injured or worse on their way to work! Well, at least once we get moving we've got the Satnav to help us on our way.'

'Yeah. I've been to Bournemouth and Weymouth, but that was a few years ago.' He looked across to Kelly. 'What was all that business about with Sue so rudely interrupting our evening?'

She looked at him apologetically; although they had spoken a few times at work and sent each other silly texts, Kelly didn't get the chance to mention the reason why Sue called her at the very time they were just about to get intimate. 'You remember me telling you that Sue didn't seem her usual cheery self? Well, it turns out, for a few days, she thought she was pregnant and even did a test that was positive.'

Lee gave a whistle through his teeth. 'I take it with her crying it wasn't planned.'

'You're right, it did take her by surprise and she was worried with being a borderline diabetic and all the implications that could have. But it turns out that it was a false alarm. She did the first test before Barry came home from work and didn't mention anything to him. But she um, got her period the following day and did the second test in the morning and it was negative. I do know for a fact that you're meant to do these tests in the morning, when they're more accurate.'

Lee took the sweet that Kelly offered him. 'Poor Sue. I guess she must have had mixed feelings, because I know from what you've told me in the past, they want to start a family, so maybe she wasn't happy with the timing with her health and the wedding coming up next year.'

'That was pretty much her words and I think she would rather wait until the wedding is over with, because there's enough stuff there to worry about. She did confess to Barry, but he was really sweet about it and devastated that she'd kept her worries to herself.'

◆ ◆ ◆

Dinner was a solemn affair at the Broadhursts, as the family ate in awkward silence. Helena tried her best to pass her condolences on to Peterson, which he accepted graciously, but she could see, by the bitter, almost angry expression on his face that he wasn't in the frame of mind to make conversation. Her mother had always believed that it was better to speak of those that had passed away and often they would speak about Sarah and remember with fondness her positive and cheerful nature.

Peterson watched Helena with a puzzled expression as she looked at his wrist. 'That watch, isn't the one that Auntie Sylvia bought you one Christmas?'

Her parents looked towards each other wondering if it was such a good idea to broach the subject.'

He wiped his mouth with his napkin. 'Yes Helena, this is the very watch Sylvia bought me about five years ago.'

'It's a very good brand,' remarked her mother, trying to make light of the conversation. 'I gave Sebastian the same make for his birthday twenty years ago and is still going strong.'

Broadhurst looked at his watch with a smile. 'Indeed. Very reliable and even the batteries seem to last at least eighteen months - very good.'

Helena sprinkled some more pepper on her roast dinner.

'Auntie Sylvia was such a lovely person and always had a kind word for everyone - wasn't she just amazing at knitting?'

Peterson took a sip of his glass of water. 'Yes, Helena, she was truly incredible and she knitted very well.' The fact that his face had turned an angry shade of red, unlike Helena, wasn't lost on her parents.

'Helena, why don't you give Hugo a hand in the kitchen to clean the pots and pans?' suggested Clarissa, concerned that the scene was about to become unpleasant.

She looked towards her mother indignantly. 'Mummy, surely you can see I'm in the middle of eating my dinner - as you are.' Again, she turned to Peterson.

'Uncle Ian, don't you agree it's very important to hold on to the memories of our loved ones who've passed away and to cherish all the happier times we shared with them? It's always good when we talk about Sarah and how she brightened our lives with her beauty and happy nature. She might no longer be with us, but she continues to live on through all our fond memories - and of course, her beautiful paintings are here to remind us of what a wonderful person she was.'

Everybody in the room jumped with a start as Peterson angrily slammed his glass of water onto the table with such force causing water to splatter onto the white linen tablecloth.

'Helena,' he said quietly staring at her intently, his face a deep red, and his hands trembling. 'What is it *you* can tell me of memories? Tell me please, because if my memory serves me well, not once have you met *Auntie* Sylvia, yet here you are speaking as if you've known her all your life!'

Seeing the look of surprise register on Helena's face, her father intervened. 'Come now Ian, I know you're still in shock, but please calm down.'

Oblivious to what was being said, Peterson stood up wiping his face with his napkin angrily. 'You have no right to lecture me on memories of loved ones who have passed away. And as for *Sarah*, there are things that are perhaps best left unsaid.'

He glared accusingly at Helena's parents. 'It seems that some people are unable to accept that when one dies, that is the end and there is no way we can bring them back, no matter what crazy lengths we go to in order to achieve this. Yes Helena, we can speak about our loved ones until we are blue in the face, but nothing changes, because once they are dead they are gone. Forever!' With that he stormed out of the room, slamming the door firmly behind him, leaving the Broadhursts to stare at each other in shocked silence, with just the sound of the clocking ticking on the wall.

◆ ◆ ◆

After passing through the traffic jam on the M25, which turned out to be as the result of a jack-knifed lorry, the remaining part of the journey was fairly smooth running for Kelly and Lee. Having made a stop at one of the motorway services to freshen up and have coffee, they soon reached The New Forest. Kelly was totally enchanted by the horses and ponies, and even a few cows, which had roamed freely along some of the roads. 'This is totally amazing - I've never seen anything quite like this before. Just look at that cute donkey, I don't think he wants to budge from the road!'

Lee waited patiently until the donkey decided to move from the road into the nearby woodland, feeling relieved as a queue of traffic was beginning to form behind him. 'Apparently, all these animals are owned by the commoners of the New Forest,' he informed her.

Kelly watched on in fascination as they drove through heathlands and woodlands, so different from the built-up areas she was accustomed to in Hertfordshire. As they were travelling along a long straight road cutting through the countryside, Lee's mobile rang. Seeing there was no traffic behind him, he pulled up to the side of the road to take the call. 'It's that Katherine calling,' he muttered looking at display screen on his mobile. 'I just hope now that we've come all this way, that she's not decided to cancel.'

Kelly watched intently as Lee answered the call, oblivious to the two Shetland ponies in the distance that were watching on inquisitively. Lee listened with a grim expression on his face and Kelly feared the worst that Katherine Jolley was unable to see them, and they had come all this way for nothing.

'Could you give me a moment while I speak to my partner?' he asked.

'Mrs Jolley-Herbert is unable to see us today as a family emergency has arisen and was wondering because we are here for the weekend, if she could see us tomorrow morning instead.'

Totally unprepared for this, Kelly shrugged. 'Well, I guess so. Yes, ok - we might as well, if you're ok with that as well.'

Lee gave her a nod before continuing his conversation with Helena's friend.

'Yes, I've just discussed it with Kelly, and it's absolutely fine by her. Oh, not at all, we didn't have anything specific planned until this evening. No, no we're not sure at the moment, but might pop into Bournemouth and see what's going on there. It's absolutely fine - these things happen. We look forward to seeing you at 11 O'clock at The Half Moon Pub tomorrow morning.'

After the conversation had ended, they looked at each

other, both realising the implications of staying over in Dorset and not going home that evening.

'I'd best give Bob and Carol a call, and let them know that I can't make Legoland tomorrow,' she remarked as she took her mobile from her handbag.

'Are you sure you're ok with cancelling your plans? I know how much Amy and Josh mean to you.'

She gave a smile. 'I'm not coming all this way without coming back with some answers. I might not have known Helena and the Broadhursts for very long, but I've got to admit, the more, I learn the more I become intrigued by the whole business - besides, I'm sure the kids are not going to miss me on just this one occasion, and there will be plenty of other outings to take them on.'

Lee took a brief look at his watch. 'Well I guess we should go about booking somewhere to stay for the night.' Reading Kelly's thoughts, he gently cupped her chin looking directly into those violet eyes. 'Remember, you don't have to do anything you feel you're not ready for.'

She blinked shyly, then smiling she took hold of his hand gently kissing it. 'Thanks for being so understanding. Now, shall we go and book into somewhere and get something to eat, because I think I'm about to faint with hunger.'

◆ ◆ ◆

Helena returned to the house with Rupert after having taken him for his walk. Her mother, who was in the kitchen busily preparing some ingredients to bake a cake, greeted her with a smile which didn't quite reach her eyes. She couldn't help noticing that her face appeared very drawn and her eyes sunken, clearly not having slept well these past few days. Clarissa had prepared a mug ready for her to make tea.

Helena flicked on the switch of the kettle. 'How's Uncle Ian?' she enquired. 'Has he calmed down?'

Clarissa grimaced. 'He's not very happy. Oh, he's calmed down but he's not very talkative. He's in the living room and really he's best left alone at the moment - so please, no more discussions with him about Sylvia or Sarah.' She gave her daughter a frosty stare. 'Heaven knows, there's been enough tragedy in this family.'

Helena walked slowly through to the living room to find her father sitting opposite Uncle Ian, both in silence, something that was so out of character for them to do be doing during the morning. Normally, at this time of the day they would be busy in the lab, working on some project, discussing ideas with herself or her mother about things that would clearly excite and challenge them. And here they were, their expressions grim with a chat show on the TV that neither of them was paying attention to. Her father sat slumped in his chair suddenly looking every year of his age. Both appeared lost in their own thoughts and seemed oblivious to Helena as she entered the room. She gave her father a kiss on the cheek but not wishing to exclude her Uncle Ian, much to her dismay he flinched and the look of hostility he gave her was unmistakable.

'Would anybody like a cup of tea?' she offered. Both shook their heads.

Professor Broadhurst looked towards her with his frown set firmly across his forehead. 'Helena, we know your intentions are good and you mean well, but the best thing you can do at this moment in time is to let us be. The past week or so has been very traumatic for all of us and we just need a little time to adjust before we get back into our routines.'

'I'm sorry Daddy. It's just that I hate to see you all so sad - is there *anything* I can do to help?'

'I have an idea!' her father announced gruffly. 'Why don't you get Hugo to help you wash the Range Rover - you know how muddy it gets along these country lanes.'

After a few minutes, Helena had reversed the vehicle out of the double garage as Hugo stood there carrying two large buckets of hot soapy water. As always, when he was around, the gates to the entrance were kept firmly locked; not even Mrs Cowley, who came to clean three times a week, was aware of his existence.

She soaked her sponge in the water as Hugo did the same, before hitting it angrily against the vehicle. Not so long ago she was happy to have the company of her robot friend who'd always been an important part of her life. Daddy and Uncle Ian were always creating programmes to make him extra clever, and to become an even more interesting companion. Soon his painting efforts would be better than hers, she thought glumly. But since Lee and Kelly had entered her life, somehow Hugo's friendship wasn't enough; their company and friendship had brought home to her all the many things that were missing from her dull and empty life.

Often, she looked at the photos taken with her parents during her childhood, and could see the way they would hold her in their arms as they posed for the camera. Regardless of how busy they were in their careers, they always made time for her and their unconditional love and pride for her in those photos was unmistakable.

As she soaked the bonnet of the vehicle, she realised her parents never displayed any real affection towards her anymore. Oh yes, she was very much cared for, and didn't want for anything in a material sense, but there was never any *real* love shown towards her. What kind of a life did she really have? One that was restricted and lonely, she now realised, a life where she wasn't allowed to meet Katherine nor to venture out on her own, apart from the occasional trip to the village convenience store. To meet with Lee and Kelly who opened up a whole new world to her, proved to be a constant challenge. What had she done so wrong to receive such hostility from her parents and Uncle Ian, now more prevalent since the death of Auntie Sylvia, who she now realised for the first time had never met? Exactly *why* was she being prevented from living her life in the way she deserved? Perhaps she *did* have some incurable illness, and that would perhaps explain why she was unable to paint any more, and all those problems with memory loss. Maybe one day she would be joining her sister Sarah. If that was the case, she was entitled to enjoy the rest of her life the way she chose to!

Hugo suddenly interrupted her thoughts. 'What is the matter, Helena? Are you feeling sad? Would you like to play a game of chess?'

She looked up to the tall white robotic creature as if seeing him for the very first time. Although she enjoyed his companionship and even felt a sisterly love for him, through fresh eyes was finally seeing him for what he truly was - just a highly intelligent robot created by her father and Uncle Ian. 'No Hugo, it's ok. I'm not really in the mood for a game of chess. I have a better idea instead. Could you go back into the house and fetch me a glass of orange juice and some biscuits. I'm beginning to feel a little peckish.'

Hugo placed his sponge into his bucket giving her bow. 'Yes of course, Helena, some orange juice and biscuits coming right up. Would you care for your favourite custard creams?'

Helena couldn't help but smile. 'Custard creams would be perfect, Hugo. Thank you.'

As he walked slowly towards the house, he turned his large head towards her. 'But I want to play a game of chess later and I will win as usual.'

She placed her hand on her hip giving him a wry smile. 'Yes, we will definitely play chess later, but I'm not so sure about allowing you to win this time!'

Satisfied that Hugo was back in the house, she took the keys to the vehicle from her skirt pocket and quickly climbed into the Land Rover. She took a quick glance behind her to make sure that there was nobody around before placing the keys into the ignition and starting up the engine. Quickly, she reversed then drove down the long winding driveway, before remembering that the gate was locked. She quickly descended from the vehicle and could hear her mother's raised anxious voice.

'Ian! Sebastian! She's driving off! Oh, my Goodness! I think she's still on the premises. Hugo, go and fetch her before she drives off!'

Knowing only too well how fast Hugo was capable of moving when instructed, Helena fumbled, frantically pressing the combination number to the gate. Hearing Hugo's loud footsteps getting closer, she breathed a sigh of relief as the gate opened. Quickly, she climbed back into the vehicle, slamming the door hard as she put her foot down on the accelerator, driving quickly from the exit, narrowly missing an oncoming car that bibbed angrily.

◆ ◆ ◆

Lee and Kelly booked into a small hotel, just at the edge of the New Forest. The decision was taken out of Kelly's hands when they discovered there was only the one room left, which was a double.

'Are you sure you're ok with this?' he quietly asked her.

She nodded shyly.

The receptionist looked puzzled at their lack of luggage with only the toiletries they had bought at the local Spa shop, before giving them the keys to their room.

She smiled cheerfully at them. 'Your room is on the first floor, second door along on your right. Breakfast is served from 7.00 until 10 O'clock. The restaurant is now open for dinner. I hope you have a very happy stay!'

Kelly felt herself blush to the roots of her hair, knowing that the receptionist presumed they had come here for a dirty weekend. But she guessed in her profession she was used to witnessing that kind of activity!

They quietly entered the room, which was fairly basic but clean, and both very much aware of the large king-sized double bed that they would soon be sleeping in. Kelly bit her lip nervously, not sure what was supposed to happen next.

Lee smiled at her reassuringly. 'Well, it might not be the Hilton but it looks nice and very comfortable. He took a quick look at the bathroom, which contained a bath and shower. Stroking her hair, he gave her a gentle kiss on her head. 'I don't know about you, but I'm starving. Shall we get down to the restaurant and grab us a bite to eat?'

She gave him a smile, feeling a mixture of both relief and disappointment. 'I wouldn't argue with you there, I feel hungry enough to eat one of those Shetland ponies!'

◆ ◆ ◆

Helena smiled as she drove confidently along into town, enjoying her new-found freedom; feeling pleased, that apart from the near miss as she escaped from home, was driving very well. She switched off her mobile before tossing it back onto the passenger seat. Yes, *escape* was the perfect word to describe how she was feeling, and that was because she like felt a prisoner in her own home. Why her parents didn't allow her some independence she just couldn't understand. As regards to driving, her parents were the first to admit that as they were getting older their concentration was not as it used to be. Surely between her and Uncle Ian they could take it in turns to drive the family here and there?

A troubled frown spread creased her forehead. When she drove off, she never had any clear ideas of where she was driving to, but found herself heading towards the area where Lee lived. She had been here only once but fortunately was gifted with a very good memory when it came to navigation. It would be nice to spend some time with Lee, and she was sure that Kelly wouldn't mind. She was so fortunate to have made friends with two of the loveliest of people, which was more than could be said of Katherine who never bothered to keep in touch these days!

She pulled up into a parking space outside of the maisonettes where Lee resided and rang the doorbell. After trying about three times she realised that he was out, and possibly still at work or maybe even with Kelly. Her shoulders slumped in disappointment. Hearing the sound of a police siren, she nervously looked around. Surely her parents wouldn't have alerted the police of her disappearance? That notion seemed a bit extreme; but hearing the siren fading away, knew she had been over-reacting.

She took a glance at her watch, seeing that it was lunchtime. Although she didn't particularly want to eat, was in no hurry to return home either. She peered over to the Adam and Eve pub in the distance, which Kelly had once mentioned to her, and thought that might be somewhere she could spend some time. Disappointment swept over her when she realised she hadn't brought any money with her, with this being an on the spur of the moment act. Then she remembered her parents kept some change in the glove compartment for parking and there might just be enough to buy a drink. Returning to the vehicle she switched on the phone, which sprang to life with a voicemail coming through. Reluctantly she answered this and heard a frantic message from her father.

'Helena will you *please* return home immediately, your mother is beside herself with worry. Please can you call home when you get this message then be on your way back!'

With the mood that her father sounded in, she was in no hurry to drive home at this moment. At first, she called Lee, where there wasn't any reply, going immediately onto voicemail, then decided to call Kelly. After a few rings, Kelly responded.

'Oh, Hi Helena how's things?'

She noticed an element of surprise in Kelly's tone. 'I'm sorry, have I called at a bad time? I just realised that you must be at work?'

There was a few moments of silence and Helena thought for a second that the connection had been lost.'

'Oh, no, no, I'm not working today, I've gone away for the weekend.'

'How lovely. Have you gone somewhere nice?'

'I've gone to the coast. To…to Norfolk.'

'Norfolk is a lovely place,' remarked Helena. 'Have you gone away with family?'

Helena detected a moment's hesitation before Kelly replied. 'I guess I might as well tell you the truth. I'm with Lee.'

'Wow! That's fantastic - that will explain why when I drove to Lee's place found he wasn't there. In fact, I'm just outside there this very moment.'

'Helena.' She recognised Lee's voice immediately. 'Is everything ok? Kelly's just told me you've driven all the way to my place!'

'I'm absolutely fine. I know you're worrying because I'm not meant to be driving according to Mummy and Daddy, but I had no problems and got here in one piece.'

'Do your parents know where you are?'

Feeling a moment of shame, she felt she owed it to her

friend to tell the truth. 'Not exactly, but I was beginning to feel trapped as if I was a prisoner in my own home - I just needed to get away.'

She heard Lee sigh heavily. 'I'm not saying I blame you, I do understand, really - but I'm sure your parents are going out of their minds with worry. I'm sorry we couldn't be there but something cropped up - -but nothing to worry about.'

Helena gave a long sigh. 'Really, it's my fault entirely for being silly and impulsive. I should have at least given some notice that I was visiting. That will teach me a lesson for acting on impulse and having a wasted journey!'

'Well, promise me you'll let your parents know where you are and put their minds at rest. When Kelly and me get back, we'll have to arrange another get-together, ok?'

After finishing the call, she felt an overwhelming sense of disappointment. Her moment of triumph at finally leaving the house proved to be short-lived, only to find her two closest friends were not around. She searched for change in the glove compartment and to her surprise discovered a few pound coins and fifty pence pieces, along with a folded twenty-pound note. She looked towards the Adam And Eve pub and a smile suddenly spread across her face.

◆ ◆ ◆

Kelly and Lee were in the hotel dining room when they received the call from Helena. After hanging up, he passed the mobile back to Kelly, shaking his head in disbelief. 'Well, I have to tell you, I wasn't expecting that.'

Kelly toyed around with the seabass on her plate. 'Me neither, but I felt I had to take the call after you ignored her on your phone - it would have looked a bit suspect.'

He took a sip of his white wine. 'Hmm, I guess you're right. Heaven knows what was going through her head to make her drive over to my place the way she did - but I guess she's just feeling lonely.'

Kelly gave a wry smile. 'It couldn't be much fun, knowing the only thing you have to look forward to is the company of a male robot. I've got to admit I still have trouble getting my head around all this.'

'I don't think we would have a chance of getting anyone to believe us, so let's not even try to go there!'

Kelly took a sip of her wine. 'I just wonder what we're going to find out from this Katherine, if anything. She's not going to be too happy, when she realises our true motive for wanting to meet her - but I think this is the only real hope of finding out what's really going on with Helena.'

'Hmm and it'll be interesting to hear her version of events about why they drifted apart.'

After the meal, they relaxed on one of the leather sofas in the bar, each drinking a tumbler of brandy. The atmosphere was relaxing and quiet as there were only a few guests around. Lee gently placed his arm around Kelly and she responded by placing her head on his shoulder.

'This is the most relaxing evening I've had for some time,' he admitted. 'To not have to worry about going to work the next morning'

Kelly took a sip of her brandy, which left a hot trail running down her throat. 'Mm, I've got to admit it's rather nice not having to cook the evening meal and to just chill out.'

He gently stroked her hair. 'This is definitely the perfect place for a weekend away or even longer.' The moment was broken by the sound of Lee's mobile ringing. His expression became grim. 'Who can this be?'

Kelly sat up. 'I hope that's not Helena having another impulsive moment!'

Lee looked at the display of his mobile with surprise. 'It's Roger Morgan - I hope he's not expecting me to come into work tomorrow. He knows I'm away, and I've worked every Saturday, as far back as I can remember!'

'You'd best answer it - Roger's a good boss and I'm sure he's got his reasons for calling.'

'I guess you're right.' With that, he answered the call.

Kelly watched anxiously, but from Lee's serious expression couldn't guess what the call could be about. Roger seemed to be doing most of the talking but couldn't hear what was being said. Now and then he would stare at her intently.

She feared the worst as he finished the call solemnly. 'Thank you for letting me know Roger and really don't mind you calling me about this. I'll see you on Monday. Bye.'

He hasn't got the job, she realised. Roger called him on his break to inform him. Why couldn't he have waited to deliver that news to him on Monday, and not spoil his weekend?

She looked at him with pity, knowing how much he'd wanted that job, and to try and undo all the damage that Miranda's lies had caused. Maybe she was biased, but she knew without a doubt Lee was clever and bright and being a delivery driver was way below his capabilities.

Taking gently hold of her hand, shaking his head he looked at her with, his expression solemn. 'Well Kelly, I don't know how to tell you this. I put everything I could into getting that job - wanted this one chance to prove myself that I could stand in Roger's shoes and improve further.' Then a knowing grin spread across his face and his dark brown eyes sparkling. 'Well, it looks like I've been given that chance - I've got the job!'

'Oh, wow Lee, that's fantastic! I'm so proud of you!' Feeling completely overcome with emotion she wrapped her arms around him, hugging him closely. 'You're such a tease and you really got me going for a moment!'

He kissed her gently on her cheek. 'Roger did apologise for calling me on my break, but felt I would prefer to know the good news sooner rather than later. On Monday, we're going to talk through the finer details, but I officially start in two weeks.'

Kelly wiped the tear that was running down her cheek. 'It's just so well deserved - I knew you were more than capable, after all you achieved at FPS. I bet Mike Stanton's not going to be too happy as he always believed himself to be second in command.'

Lee gave a smile. 'From what I gather, Stanton was pretty much hated by everyone - Roger included. He can either go along with me or not at all. I know how to deal with his kind - we had his equivalent at FPS and they're pretty much there at most companies.'

She leaned her head on his shoulder. 'I'm so glad you didn't listen to that Miranda and decide to take up her offer to return to her daddy's empire.'

He gently lifted up her chin, so he could look her squarely into her eyes. 'Miranda never stood a chance - that ended the day she did the dirty on me by going with Ashley behind my back, and all the lies she told her father. I was livid that I was forced to leave a job that I enjoyed and did well, and paid more than a decent salary. But more than anything, I was furious that the woman I thought I loved, betrayed and hurt me in ways I couldn't possibly imagine.'

After being lost in his thoughts, Lee gently held her face, looking deeply into her eyes. 'Then the beautiful Kelly Phillips came into my life on that day I joined Fast Link, and made me realise that all that love I believe I felt for Miranda was just an infatuation which quickly died after she had shown her true colours. Kelly is the most beautiful woman, both inside and out, and added a much-needed burst of happiness and purpose to my life. I think I loved her from the very day I met her but being the idiot I am, didn't want to admit this to myself.'

His expression became serious as he gently stroked her face. 'I know I've messed up big time and seriously let down the one woman who means everything to me – for that I'm truly sorry. With all that's happened, I know this is a big ask, but can you to give me one more chance?'

A frown spread creased her forehead. 'Lee, could you do me one big favour? Please shut up!' With that she placed her hands around his head and gave him a long, lingering kiss to which he responded in kind but more urgent and lingering as he held her closely in his arms.

Her heart racing, she reluctantly pulled away from him

as she looked into his dark brown eyes sparkling and questioning, appearing equally as breathless as she was feeling. Gently tracing her finger along his lips swollen from their urgent kisses, she watched him intently. 'Consider yourself completely forgiven.'

He took hold of her hand, which he gently kissed. 'Shall we go upstairs to celebrate my promotion - and us? If you fancy, we can toast with a bottle of champagne.'

She smiled at him lovingly, placing a gentle kiss on his lips. 'I would love to celebrate upstairs - but who says we need champagne?' With that they both laughed as they headed to their room.

◆ ◆ ◆

Helena sat in The Adam And Eve pub eating a toasted cheese sandwich accompanied with her second glass of *Spritzer*. She would have much preferred the *Babycham*, which she drank during her university days with Katherine; but much to her bemusement the barmaid informed her they no longer stocked her favourite alcoholic drink because there was no longer much call for it. Although it had risen in popularity recently, it seemed that demand hadn't quite reached Old Church yet.

While she sat with her drink, lost in her thoughts, she

noticed a young man standing at the bar, possibly in his early twenties, who kept looking her way and wasn't sure why. He gave her a small wave, which she returned. She tried hard to recall, if this was someone she'd met before when she was out wish Kelly and Lee. But try as she might, was unable to remember becoming acquainted him, but it was also possible that it was mistaken identity on his part. He turned briefly to the friend he stood with, before coming over to her table.

'Hi darlin', do you fancy a refill?' She noticed with disgust, his breath reeked of alcohol and stale tobacco. Judging by the stubble on his face, he hadn't been near a razor for a few days.

'No thank you.' Looking down to at his sweatshirt with a stain down the front, noticed he couldn't have been very particular about his hygiene.'

He grinned, revealing that he was missing a couple of front teeth. 'It's just that me and my mate noticed you sitting there looking a little lonely - thought maybe you could do with some company. A pretty girl like you shouldn't be sittin' here all alone.'

She took a sip of her drink, glaring at the man in disapproval. 'I can reassure you that I'm not any need of company, thank you very much - I'm quite self-contained.'

With that remark, he burst out laughing, stroking a hand down her face. 'I'm sure you *are* self-contained, babe. My, you do sound a very classy chick with that posh voice. I bet your daddy has got a quid or two!'

To the man's great surprise, Helena firmly took hold of the hand he touched across her face in a vice-like grip, causing him to yell out in pain.

'Don't *ever* touch me like that again!' she warned in a dangerously quiet voice, oblivious to the attention attracted from the other punters now firmly focused on the scene before them. 'For your information my father's financial position or whether or not I'm sitting here feeling lonely is of no relevance to you. So *please* go back to where you came from and leave me alone!'

'Is everything all right, love?' She turned around to see the landlord standing close by. With that she let go of the man's hand, which he held in pain.

'Stupid little bitch nearly broke my hand,' he spat angrily. 'Can't a guy pass a compliment to a woman these days, without it being classed as sexual harassment?'

The landlord stood to Helena's defence. 'I'd been watching for some time and could see you were paying this young lady some unwelcome attention. Could I please ask you to leave?'

Holding his hand still throbbing with pain, he looked at Helena with disgust. 'I'm getting out of this dump. Reckon the beer's watered down here anyway.' He left with his friend muttering, 'The toffee-nosed bitch!'

The middle-aged landlord watched Helena with concern. 'Are you ok, love?'

She gave a nod, appreciating his concern. 'I'm fine thanks - really.'

'I've had these jokers in here a few times causing problems and I really don't want them coming back - I can certainly do without their custom. But fair play to you, I don't think he bargained on you gripping his hand like that - you're obviously a lot stronger than you look!'

People sitting on nearby tables, watched her in admiration, with a woman possibly the same age as her calling out, 'Well done love, standing up to that sleaze bag!'

Taking a look at her watch saw that time was moving on and felt it was only fair that she should call home to let everyone know she would be on her way. For a while at least, she had enjoyed some freedom, just a pity that her two new friends couldn't have joined her.

Within half an hour she was parked outside The Woodlands, lit up everywhere by security lights with her parents and Uncle Ian rushing immediately from the big house. Helena wasn't sure what kind of reception she could expect and immediately felt guilty when she saw Clarissa's face looking drawn and pale in the artificial light. Her father studied her, his pallor similar to his wife's but didn't show any anger, just relief.

'Helena, what on earth possessed you to do what you did? Do you realise how worried your mother and I have been about you? You are aware I'm sure, that neither of us are as young as we used to be and all this stress isn't doing us any good.'

She looked at them both apologetically, with Uncle Ian standing in the distance watching on, with his arms folded.

'I'm so sorry Mummy...Daddy, but I just needed to get away for a while. Please could you tell me truthfully *why* I'm not allowed to do all the things that young people my age can do and take for granted? Do I have some terrible illness, something you're withholding from me, because if that's the case I have a right to know'?

Her father swallowed, with Clarissa watching on with tears in her eyes. 'Helena dear, there's nothing for you to be concerned about. But you must realise we are your parents and we sometimes have to do things you might not particularly like, but please believe me, we act in your best interests.'

Helena felt overwhelmed with frustration. If only she could shed tears the way her mother could do with such ease; perhaps if she were able to weep, she would feel a whole lot better. 'I'm so sorry I've let you all down. It's just that there's a lot of things in my life at the moment that aren't making any sense, the way I'm unable to lead a normal life. *Why* do I have these fits and lapses in my memory? *Why* can't I paint anymore? *Why* doesn't Katherine keep in touch? *What is wrong with me?*'

Professor Broadhurst looked over to Peterson briefly before turning his attention back to her. 'My dear, I can assure you there's nothing wrong with you. It's just that we're a little more than surprised at these traits you are showing of wanting all this independence. Up until recently, you were quite content with just our company, and of course Hugo's.' He smiled at her affectionately. 'So where did your travels take you to?'

She peered over to Clarissa who seemed anxious to know. 'Well, I decided to go over to where Lee lives, but sadly he wasn't there so I went to the nearby pub for a drink. Would you believe they didn't even have any *Babycham*?'

Clarissa raised her eyebrow in surprise. 'That's incredible! I remember how you and Katherine would enjoy a *Babycham*, and that was the only alcohol you would drink. I hope you didn't drink too much today.'

'No of course not Mummy - just one small *Spritzer*,' she lied. 'But you know alcohol doesn't seem to have any effect on me!' Helena felt it was in her parents' best interests if she withheld most of the details of her adventure, including the drunken man at the Adam And Eve.

Broadhurst studied his daughter carefully, letting out a deep sigh. 'Well I have to admit your actions today nearly caused us all to have a coronary, but I don't think any lasting damage has been done. I think you've got this yearning for independence out of your system for a while, so why don't you go indoors. I believe Hugo is waiting to have a game of chess with you. He hasn't stopped mentioning it since you went away.'

She gave a small smile. 'Of course, I did promise him a game. I guess I'd best allow him to win since I went off and left him today - I have to admit, I did miss Hugo.'

As Helena entered the house, her parents and Peterson followed not far behind. Broadhurst quickly passed the car keys to him. 'Please make sure these stay in a safe place - don't want another repeat of this else she'll be the death of us!'

CHAPTER EIGHTEEN

Kelly and Lee were up bright and early the following morning, enjoying their full English breakfasts in the hotel restaurant. Both couldn't stop smiling, as they thought back to the night before. Kelly silently thanked Katherine for not being able to see them yesterday, as the happiest moment of her life wouldn't have taken place - at least not quite so soon.

As tucked into her generous portion of bacon and eggs to satisfy her ravenous appetite, Kelly couldn't recall when she had last felt as happy as she was feeling at this moment in time.

During the early days of her relationship with Eric, she believed herself to be madly in love with him, certain that he was The One. But looking back with hindsight realised that she had just been deluding herself; after the first flush of romance she soon came to the realisation that he wasn't the person she believed him to be. After those first few months, where they couldn't keep their hands from each other, she began to see that really, they had nothing in common. Once they'd moved in together, things changed and Eric chose to lead his own separate social life. Kelly had never once had any issues with him seeing his friends - after all she enjoyed nights out with her closest girlfriends. But the times became all too frequent when Eric would see his best friend Andy, often returning home during the early hours or more worryingly, not at all. According to Eric, there had always been a good reason for being delayed, from job interviews or courses, or even being a consoler for Andy's relationship problems.

Then things came to a head with her suspicions having been confirmed about Eric seeing other women. Bob's wife Carol had seen him on one occasion walking with his arm around a woman, coming out of a nightclub. At first, she was in denial believing there had been some misunderstanding; probably Eric had bumped into an old friend, tending to be a touchy-feely person who thought nothing of displaying affection. But along came further sightings from other friends and acquaintances, claiming to have seen him with different women, and then of course, the rest was history at that fateful day at the restaurant when she confronted Andy.

She turned to Lee who was staring at her intently. 'A penny for them, you were miles away then.'

Seeing his concern, she gave him her warmest smile. 'Nothing for you to worry about, Mr Fisher. I was just thinking about how happy I'm feeling - I can't remember feeling this way for quite some time.'

Taking hold of her hand, he placed a gentle kiss. 'Me neither, Miss Phillips. I know it took Helena's friend delaying the meeting to knock some sense into my head, but I kind of feel another moment would have come along to make this happen.' He took a quick look at his watch. 'Hmm, looks like time's pressing on. If you've eaten as much as you can, shall we start making tracks, to meet the mysterious Katherine Jolley-Herbert?'

Before vacating their room, Kelly gave a small smile of contentment. Although nothing in this life came with a guarantee, she felt with Lee she had met her perfect partner. No matter what life may throw at them, he would always care for her and treat her with respect. It had taken them both a while to realise they were meant to be, but better late than never at all!

The morning began cloudy and overcast but with the occasional glimmer of sunshine breaking through, showing the promise of a brighter day. Regardless of the weather, Kelly felt she couldn't be happier. Enjoying the rugged beauty of the Dorset countryside as they approached Christchurch castle, glanced to at the ruins of the 12th century building. She already knew that the town was a popular area for retirees, but not one for being too crazy about wild nights out any more, felt this was the perfect place for quiet weekend breaks.

The Satnav directed them to Christchurch Priory, the destination where Katherine had arranged to meet them. Earlier, she had sent a text just to confirm the meeting time of 11 o'clock; to help them recognise her, she informed them she wore her hair in ponytail and would be wearing a red dress with a cream coloured jacket.

Apprehension gripped Kelly as they approached the parish, knowing the waiting would soon be over and hopefully some questions would be answered regarding this rift between Helena and her friend. Perhaps some good would come out of all this and the two girls would at least resume contact once again.

They approached the River Stour looking blue in the morning sunshine, with a few boats moored along the edge. In the background stood Priory Church, the tall grey building dominating the parish which took its name.

'Now where's The Half Moon?' Lee frowned, looking around trying to find the pub they had arranged to meet. Although it wasn't a particularly built up area, was populated with a few houses and shops.

'I think this is what we might be looking for,' Kelly suggested, pointing in the direction of a small Georgian style building.'

'Hmm you're right, I can see the sign - well spotted!' Within a couple of minutes, they pulled up inside of the car park. Kelly looked towards him biting her bottom lip. 'Are you feeling nervous? I know I've got more than a few butterflies in my stomach.'

Lee eye narrowed thoughtfully. 'I wouldn't say feeling nervous exactly, but just feel a bit of a fraud getting her here on the pretext of putting some business her way, when we're just here to make enquiries about her friend.'

'She doesn't need to know our true reason - we can just slip Helena into the conversation in a roundabout way. At the end of the day as far as she's concerned, we're just making enquiries, not making a commitment.'

'Yeah, I know what you mean,' he grinned. 'But I guess we're both just too honest for our own good and not used to deceit.' Gently he cupped her chin his lips meeting hers and she responded with their kisses becoming more urgent. Reluctantly he pulled himself away giving her a seductive smile that melted her heart. 'I suppose we'd better go inside as I know I'll never be able tear myself away from you.'

Kelly brushed her lips lightly against his. 'Come, let's go before we change our minds.'

Inside, The Half Moon held all the hidden treasures that Kelly embraced about a country pub, with its white walls and low-beamed ceilings; pictures of boats from various eras hanging on the walls, added a distinctly nautical charm to the pub. They sat at one of the mahogany tables near to the entrance; although a few people were either sitting down or standing at the bar, couldn't see anybody matching Katherine's description.

'What do you fancy to drink?' Lee asked.

She gave a shrug. 'Normally I wouldn't drink anything stronger than a fruit juice at this time of the day, but I think today, the occasion calls for a vodka and coke to steady my nerves!'

Lee was served fairly promptly and soon returned with the drink Kelly asked for and half a pint of lager for himself. As Kelly was studying a model of a sailing ship from the 19th century which stood on a windowsill, noticed a middle-aged woman, carrying a briefcase, walk through the entrance immediately glancing their way. She turned to Lee. 'I should think Katherine will be here soon, though she's a few minutes late.'

The woman, who came in the few moments earlier, looked around vacantly then once again towards the couple. Both looked at each other feeling puzzled as she came over to Lee. 'Excuse me, but are you Lee Fisher?'

Confused, Lee confirmed this. What had happened to

Katherine? After all this, it looked as if she couldn't make it and had sent somebody else, possibly a member of her family, her mother or an aunt. Even more confused, he noticed that the woman was wearing the red dress and cream jacket that Katherine promised she would be wearing to help identify her.

Mistaking their confusion for surprise, the woman looked to them apologetically. 'I'm terribly sorry for arriving late but I was having problems with my washing machine, but thankfully my son managed to prevent the kitchen from getting flooded! Please let me introduce myself! I'm Katherine Jolley-Herbert. She shook Lee's hand firmly and did likewise to Kelly.'

Kelly began to realise there must have been a huge mistake, because no way could this be Helena's friend from university. From the start she had been strongly under the impression that the girls were of similar age, certain Katherine hadn't been a mature student – by all accounts according to Helena, they had grown up together going to the same school. The Katherine standing before her looked to be at least in her early sixties; her dyed ash blonde hair pulled back in a ponytail with greying roots at the sides, a tanned face marked with deep laughter lines around her light blue eyes, and hands peppered with age spots told another story. But Kelly also remembered Katherine previously confirming her acquaintance with the Broadhursts.

As Lee went to the bar to buy the pineapple juice Katherine asked for, the woman opened her briefcase to take out some brochures. She peered over to Kelly with concern as she put on her reading glasses. 'Are you feeling all right my dear?' I'm aware I don't know you, but you're looking a little shaken.'

Kelly smiled apologetically. 'I'm sorry, it's just that I didn't sleep very well last night and I feel a bit out of sorts.'

Katherine looked at her sympathetically. 'I know how you must be feeling, my husband Robert went through a spell of insomnia, and just one bad night's sleep alone is enough to ruin the whole day. I must admit I've having a few problems myself after our return from Miami where we stay every summer -the jetlag can be such a killer!'

When Lee returned, Katherine laid out the brochures onto the table. 'Well, this is just a small portfolio of some of the work we do. As you probably saw on our website are a small family run business, established almost 35 years ago, so we certainly know our craft well! In fact, our workmanship is one of the finest in this area of Dorset; we pride ourselves in our creations of stained-glass windows for churches and various commercial buildings, as well as for the home. Robert and myself also hold classes to teach the art in the creation of stained-glass windows and has proven very popular!

Kelly studied the beautiful designs appreciatively, and in normal circumstances, would have enjoyed doing this. Her feeling of guilt at bringing this woman here on false pretences, was so overwhelming and was difficult to concentrate. She remembered back to the conversation with Helena, that the Katherine she knew had a serious boyfriend called Rob - but none of this was making sense.

Peering over her reading glasses she looked towards the couple. 'Was there a particular area of the house you had in mind?'

Kelly looked over to Lee who appeared to have an answer already prepared. 'Initially we are interested in looking for designs for both our front and back doors.'

Katherine gave him a knowing smile. 'I have a few pictures in my brief case of designs that just might well be of interest to you. There are a couple which seem to be particularly popular of an apple tree with blossom and another of a woodpecker in a tree.'

As the older woman opened up her briefcase once again, Kelly decided to strike while the iron was hot. 'Lee mentioned to me that we have some mutual friends - the Broadhursts?'

For a moment Katherine seemed to almost freeze on the spot. 'Of course, I know the Broadhursts - we go back a very long way. Goodness me!'

Kelly took a long sip of her vodka and coke to try and give her the courage to continue with the questions. 'There is one particular member of the family who remembers you with fondness - Helena. She's always mentioning you and I think to be honest, she's feeling a little lonely at the moment and keeps wondering when she's going to hear from you.'

As she finished speaking, Katherine just stared at her with her mouth slightly open. Despite the tan from her recent holiday, her face paled and she sat completely dumbstruck with the paperwork gripped firmly in her hand.

'Are you sure we speaking about the same Broadhursts?' she asked faintly.

Seeing that Kelly was beginning to look nervous about the reaction from Katherine, Lee decided to take over. 'Helena's parents are Clarissa Broadhurst who's an artist and worked creating special effects on films and her father is a scientist, Sebastian Broadhurst.'

Katherine nodded, her pale blue eyes open widely in shock as if she'd just seen a ghost. 'That, that is definitely the Broadhursts I know of. But I really don't understand. Are you having some kind of joke with me, because if you are this really isn't very funny at all!' The fear in her voice was beginning to turn to anger.

Seeing that Kelly was looking as confused as he was

beginning to feel, decided this needed to be resolved before an unpleasant scene developed.

'I'm very sorry Mrs Jolley-Herbert, but we have only known Helena for a fairly short time, but she speaks about you often, and seems to be in some kind of distress. She claims, she went to university with you studying Art and said that you were once her best friend - she even made some mention about you wanting to learn the art of creating stained-glass windows and said that you had met somebody very special person called Rob.

The woman looked on with bemusement. 'That's definitely true, the Rob Helena knew I married and have been with ever since.'

Kelly mustered up the courage to speak. 'It's just although we haven't known Helena for very long we have become rather fond of her, and we're feeling a little concerned about her wellbeing. I'm not sure how much you know about what she's been up to lately, but she's currently living with her parents and uncle in a village in Hertfordshire, and living bit of a sheltered life.'

Lee continued with the explanation. 'I guess what concerns us is that her parents don't seem to allow her to continue with a life that most girls her age take for granted. They don't allow her to drive anywhere apart from the grounds inside of their property. She's lost her ability to paint but we've seen from many of her earlier paintings that she was a pretty accomplished artist. I know she suffers from these fits as well, because I've witnessed a couple of those myself. But I think what upsets us both most of all is that she's always asking about you, and doesn't understand why you're no longer in touch. We can both see you have a pretty full on life with a family and your business and that must take up a great deal of your time.'

Kelly looked at the woman appealingly to try to help her understand their concern for the wellbeing of their mutual friend. 'I think a lot of the problems occurred when her elder sister Sarah was killed in that car crash. Losing a child must be the worst thing a parent could possibly go through. Understandably, it had a terrible impact on their lives, especially Helena and I guess made her mother and father extra protective.'

To their astonishment Katherine looked at Kelly as if she was completely insane. '*Sarah*? Who on earth is Sarah? There never was any sister - Helena was an only child! I remembered Helena once telling me that Clarissa fell pregnant two years after she was born but miscarried and was unable to have any more children.'

Kelly and Lee looked at each other at this new revelation.

It seemed, the more they were learning the further this mystery deepened.

'But there was a death,' Katherine informed them. 'It was Helena.'

Her face turning a deathly white, Kelly couldn't have felt more shocked if she'd tried. Feeling equally as surprised, Lee gently put his arm around the woman he loved, to make sure she was ok

'Yes, Helena Broadhurst is dead and that is the reason I've not stayed in touch with her - in fact, she was killed almost forty years ago in a car crash. I would never have deliberately ignored Helena - I couldn't have loved her more had she been my sister!' They saw the tears well up in her eyes and knew she was speaking from the heart.'

'Oh my God,' murmured Kelly. 'I'm just not understanding any of this.'

Katherine wiped away a tear that ran down her cheek. 'Helena was my dearest friend. We knew each other since childhood, going to the same schools, both having a passion for art, attending the same university to study art and design. She really had it all and was about to embark on a promising career to become an illustrator.' Taking a swallow of her pineapple juice she continued. 'She met a male student at Oxford where we studied, a serious and studious type, some might say a little on the square side. The university held a dance and that's where their relationship began. With Helena bright and vivacious, you could say they were like chalk and cheese. But somehow it worked and they fell madly in love with each other and got the firm seal of approval of her parents - in fact he first got to know of Helena through her father, who was his lecturer. A few weeks later after Helena met the love of her life, I met Rob who also went to Oxford and the four of us were pretty much inseparable. Well, within a year they become engaged to be married.'

For a moment she glanced out of the window, her lips trembling as tears came to her eyes. 'Just three weeks before the wedding was to take place we had been invited to a dance. Originally, we planned to all go together, but Rob had a minor family crisis, so we decided to take a taxi to avoid delaying Helena and her fiancé, who decided to drive there.'

Katherine looked lost in her thoughts as she thought back to that time, so long ago but firmly etched in her mind as if was only yesterday. 'She looked so incredibly beautiful that evening in her long dress in midnight blue with that beautiful blonde hair hanging down loose to her waist. Nobody could take their eyes off her that evening, and *he* looked so incredibly proud of her - the love just simply shone from his eyes.' She paused for a moment to wipe her tears, but Kelly and Lee remained silent knowing there was more to come.

'Then came the time to leave. We'd all had a marvellous time, with both me, Helena and Rob a little merry from the champagne that flowed during the evening. Only Helena's fiancé remained sober as he was driving. He was never one for drinking, preferring just the occasional glass of wine or whiskey.'

Accepting the tissue that Kelly offered her and wiping her face, Katherine continued. 'She was *so* happy before leaving. On the following Monday, we were to go to London with Clarissa to collect the dresses and make a day of it, going around the shops - I was to be her bridesmaid. I had already seen Helena in the dress and she looked so incredibly beautiful. We were so looking forward to spending the day together, and although Clarissa could sometimes be quite firm, was a great mother who Helena could speak to about anything.'

Fresh tears came to her eyes. 'I will never forget that Sunday morning, during the early hours, when we received that phone call - my mother came running up the stairs crying and as white as a sheet. Sebastian had called to say there had been a car crash and Helena was killed. I don't remember terribly much at the time but only found out later, that I went completely hysterical and the doctor had to sedate me. A few days after I'd calmed down slightly, I learned as they were driving home that evening, a car was coming in the opposite direction, at speed, around a windy country road, driving on the wrong side.'

Katherine closed her eyes as she thought back to that terrible moment. 'There was nothing they could do, no real warning. Helena was killed instantly taking the full impact. Sadly, she wasn't wearing a seatbelt as in those days it wasn't the law. But he blamed himself, said he should have made sure she was belted up. But nobody was blaming him. The driver in the other car was also killed. It was later discovered that the alcohol in his blood was four times over the legal limit. Should he have survived the crash he would have gone to prison, that's for sure!'

'What happened to her finance?' Lee asked gently.

'He was seriously injured and for a while it was touch and go as to whether he would make it. Fortunately, he did, but suffered some quite horrific scars to his face. Clarissa and Sebastian were absolutely devastated at losing their only child, and being a mother of three children myself, I just don't know how I would cope if something happened to one of them. I have one son and two daughters - two are in the family business, the youngest is a junior solicitor.'

'Do you ever hear from the Broadhursts?' Kelly asked.

Katherine sadly shook her head. At one time we were in

frequent contact and I think that somehow gave her parents some comfort and helped to keep Helena's memory alive.' She frowned with a confused expression. 'As time went on, I felt that my attention was no longer welcome, and every time I wanted to come to visit, Clarissa and Sebastian came up with a variety of excuses why it was never a good time. At first, I felt hurt by the rebuff, then thought perhaps it was their way of coming to terms with her death, and was a way for them to move on. I believe the last I heard from Clarissa was around fifteen years ago.' She looked to both of her companions sitting opposite. 'I do make sure when I'm in the Northumbria district that I go to visit her grave. I can see it's tended to and good to know her parents are still alive because I lost mine some years ago. Helena might have died over thirty-seven years ago, but she's still very special to me. Yes, I have other friends, but nobody as special as the girl I practically grew up with. When she died, a part of me died with her, and I miss her so much.' She blinked as she thought back to what got them to this conversation.'

'But how could you both possibly know the same Helena as I do, because both of you look relatively young, and if my guess is correct then neither of you would even have been born when Helena was killed - yet you seem to describe her perfectly.'

Lee frowned, not being able to understand any of this. 'I must admit, the more I learn the more confusing this is becoming. Unless the Helena we know is not their daughter, as we believe but perhaps a relative. Because if I'm being truthful Clarissa and Sebastian look old enough to be her grandparents.' Even older than we first guessed, thought Lee.

Katherine waved her hand dismissively. 'I've known the family for most of my life and I can assure you there were no close relatives.'

Kelly suddenly remembered, 'I have some pictures and video on my phone of Helena, or at least who we believe is Helena!' She wondered how could she possibly forget the camcorder footage she'd taken, when Helena was dancing with Hugo? Thank goodness for smartphones!

She took the device from her handbag and tried to explain. 'There is somebody or perhaps should I say *something* else on this footage Helena wanted us to keep secret, but I think that things have gone far beyond the need for this.'

As soon as she presented Katherine with the photos and her expression told them all they needed to know. With her eyes wide and the blood drained away from her face making her look almost as white as a sheet, she yelled 'Oh my Goodness!' causing a few customers to turn their way.

With her hands shaking she proceeded to show her the

video footage of Helena and Hugo dancing the Tango in the Broadhurst's living room. But neither of them was prepared for what Katherine was about to say.

'I see that Hugo is still very much around.' Her look of total shock suddenly turned to one of sudden realisation. Looking at the couple, she wiped away the tears running down her cheeks.

'Lee, Kelly, I can see you are two very nice people and I can see you mean well, but the best advice I can give you is to get out of the Broadhursts' lives, forget you ever met them. I realise you have the best of intentions, and that you were probably never interested in stained glass windows, but I want you to forget about me too because none of this will do you any good and will only cause harm - mostly to yourselves. Do you understand me?' She smiled at them kindly. 'I'm not sure of your relationship, but I can see you are both very much in love. Walk away from this situation which you will never be able to resolve - focus on your lives and whatever future you may have together. That's the best advice I can give you.'

Reluctantly they all stood up and shook hands with the woman. 'In other circumstances, I would have said it was nice to meet you, but please don't take this personally.' A thought suddenly came to her. 'You said there was an uncle who lives with them although they didn't have any close relatives. Could you tell me his name?'

Placing her mobile into her handbag, Kelly explained. 'His name is Ian Peterson and he's not actually a relative but a close family friend - somebody who does work with Professor Broadhurst.'

Lee saw the woman physically flinch at Peterson's name but she made no comment. 'All I can advise is to enjoy the rest of your weekend in Dorset and try to forget this conversation, and the fact you ever met those people.'

As they made their way back to the hotel, Kelly and Lee drove in silence, not sure what to make of what had just taken place.

CHAPTER NINETEEN

They decided to spend the remainder of the weekend at the hotel, and to try their best at putting the shocking revelations behind them, as much as possible. Fortunately, the room they had checked out of was still available. Once they made the decision to stay on, they ventured into Bournemouth for a few essentials. Hand in hand they walked along the pier, the crisp sea air feeling invigorating against their skin. Despite the day being overcast with a blustery wind, the coastal town was quite lively with visitors and holidaymakers. The strong aroma of caramelised onion brought back memories to Kelly of her childhood, when she would go down to Yarmouth with her brother Bob and their parents, treating themselves to some hotdogs. She peered over to the choppy grey sea, watching as a large jet ski skimmed across the water, giving her an involuntary shiver, glad that her feet were firmly on land.

'Fancy some candy floss Miss Phillips?' he asked with a wicked grin.

'Don't mind if I do, Mr Fisher!'

Within a few minutes, they were nibbling at the sweet

sugary confection.

'Loved this as a kid,' revealed Lee. 'Every time I went to the fair with my mum, I would always have a bag of this. That's after I'd polished off a couple of hotdogs and a toffee apple!'

Kelly licked the sticky sugar off her fingers. 'Such a pig - some things never change! Actually, I never got to try this until I was about ten, because I was convinced it was made out of cotton wool and it would choke me!'

'Well you've certainly made up for it since.'

She giggled. 'Ouch - touché!'

He pulled her close to him. 'Now you realise just how sweet and delicious it is, but nowhere near as sweet as you.'

Their lips gently kissing, she gazed into his sparkling brown eyes, which at that moment appeared to be a shade darker. 'Mr Fisher, flattery will get you *everywhere*.'

'Hmm, well that's the plan. Hey, you're feeling cold - you're shivering, or maybe it's just my male magnetism sending shivers down your spine. Shall we go somewhere to eat? I don't think all this sweet stuff quite fills the gap.'

Soon the couple were sitting at a table in an open-air restaurant overlooking prime views of the coast.

'What are you grinning at?' Kelly asked smiling, as she cut into the cod she had ordered along with a large portion of chips and mushy peas.

'You. Here was I, worried about you getting cold, and out of all the restaurants we could have chosen, you go for one that is open to all the elements.'

She winked. 'There is a method to my madness. I just want to make the most of today - it's not too often these days that I get to go to the coast. Apart from that works outing, when we went to South End a couple of years ago, I've not taken a real-life look at the sea since - besides I'm really not that cold.'

He took a sip of his lager. 'The same goes for me - I haven't been within a hundred miles since then. Look, I know this trip was a bit unconventional, to say the least, and we only planned to go for the day.' He gently took hold of her hand. 'Well, what I'm trying to say is, I'm so glad it turned out the way it did.'

Kelly smiled at him warmly, savouring the feel of his touch. 'Me too.'

'I promise, once I've settled into my job, there will be plenty more trips here, or wherever in the world we may choose to visit.'

'I received a text from Sue this morning, when you were taking a shower,' she revealed. 'hoping we were having a nice time.'

Sprinkling some salt on his meal, grinned at her sheepishly. 'I hope you didn't go into *too* much detail there, because I don't think I'll be able to look her in the face, as I introduce myself as the new manager. Have you actually told Sue about me getting the job, because I really don't mind you sharing with her?'

'Actually, I did mention to her and she's over the moon - but I know she won't let on to anybody else until it's officially announced.' She dug the fork into one of her chips, looking at it thoughtfully. 'I know we agreed not to talk about what happened earlier, but what are your theories on this business with Helena - because at the very least it's pretty weird. You know all this business with Broadhurst and Peterson being scientists, do you think they've somehow cloned her?'

Lee shrugged his shoulders. 'I'm not sure, though I guess it's possible. I know a lot of stuff goes on behind the scenes that most of us have no idea about, with top-secret experiments, cover-ups with the government and all these conspiracy theories that come out from time to time. Personally, I don't go along with the concept that the Helena we know, is some human clone.'

'But I can see from the look on your face that you have some idea?'

He gave her a warm smile. 'There's no pulling the wool over your eyes - but this can wait until we return home. I want both of us to enjoy what's left of the weekend, and worry about the rest later. Ok?'

With that they clinked their glasses of lager and diet coke together to make a toast to this.

The couple enjoyed the remainder of the day by venturing around the many shops in the Boscombe area of Bournemouth, where Lee treated Kelly to a beautiful silver necklace, with matching earrings. The evening was rounded off by spectacular ice-skating show, starring some minor celebrities they had bought tickets for at the last minute.

On their return to their hotel at the New Forest, sitting in the lounge, sharing a bottle of white wine, Kelly couldn't remember when she had last enjoyed an evening as much as she was enjoying right now.

Gently, he kissed the top of her head, as they sat comfortably on the leather sofa. 'I don't know about you, but I think this wine is making me drowsy - shall we make it an early night?'

She gave a knowing smile. 'Hmm, I have to agree with you there - white wine does tend to make me feel a little tired.'

'But I hope not *too* much?' With that, he bought another bottle for them to take up to their room.

They went down to breakfast early the following morning, before checking out. As much as Lee had cherished this time with Kelly, felt he needed to return home as early as possible to prepare for his new position. Fortunately, knowing only too well what the job entailed, she was understanding and supportive of his need to do this.

This time Kelly was behind the wheel to give him some time to relax. As they travelled along, he revealed his various plans to move Fast Link into the next league, knowing her well enough to be sure that she wouldn't discuss this further with anybody else. Lee filled her in about a number of clients, he'd heard of through the grapevine, that were getting more than a little fed up of FPS's increasingly poor service and the fact they'd made a rapid price increase for how much they charged for each parcel to be delivered. It was a fact that many of these clients used at least two or three different carriers, but was satisfied he could make a small reduction in the price as well as providing a quality service that would encourage them to turn away from FPS.

Kelly turned to him, biting her bottom lip thoughtfully. 'I can see it all makes sense and I can see it working out brilliantly - but you do realise it's going to increase the work for Sue and me, you know, with phone calls and the query systems.'

He was quick to reassure her. 'Don't worry Kelly, I have thought it all through very carefully, and I can see more than anybody that you girls are really overworked - I learned that quickly by going through the figures that were shared by Roger. I totally get he did have to pull back the purse strings for a while, but there has been enough of an improvement to take on a part-timer to begin with. Initially, it could be somebody we employ from the Job Centre or employment agency on a fixed term contract, say, for a three-month period. If that person turns out to be satisfactory, then could potentially lead on to a permanent basis. Once the first part of the phase of my plan is in place, then that's the to consider taking on another full-timer. Regardless of everything we do, we need to take on a couple of temps during the Christmas period, one to work with you girls upstairs and another to help with the booking in down in the warehouse.'

'It really would be beneficial,' agreed Kelly. 'Quite often Sue and me are so snowed under, that it's very easy to make a mistake with the pressure. And you know what it's like when one of us is on holiday or goes off sick, it just doesn't bear thinking about. Mike Stanton does give us a hand but he usually ends up making matters worse.'

He gave a nod. 'Well, although it seems we are always aware of being short on drivers, sorters and warehouse staff, then why is it that the administration side always gets neglected? Having been a manager myself before, I know this is one area that is absolutely vital in the efficient running of a company.'

As they were halfway towards Old Church, Kelly's mobile rang loudly. Not being in a position to take the call passed it to Lee.

Peering at the display, he groaned. 'It's Helena. Do you want me to speak to her?'

She glanced at. Him briefly. 'It might be best if we don't take the call - because the truth is we don't even know who she is any more. According to Katherine, she's been dead for nearly forty years and I just don't know what the heck's going on. I'm beginning to wonder if this Katherine's a bit crazy and that's why Helena's parents don't want her having anything to do with her.'

After a few more rings the phone went silent. Sighing deeply Lee said, 'I'll keep hold of this, because if I know her well, she'll leave a message. Before yesterday I knew next to nothing about Katherine Jolley, but she doesn't strike me as a woman with psychological problems - in fact, she seems quite a strong-minded person and clearly capable of running a successful, well-established business with her husband. She was obviously very close to the Broadhursts at one time - close enough even to know about Hugo.'

Unsurprisingly, the phone sprang into life once again, interrupting their thoughts. Lee listened intently to the voicemail from Helena.

Kelly looked over curiously. 'What did she say?'

With his expression grim, Lee updated her. 'Well, sometimes it was difficult to make out what she was trying to say because as usual, when she calls, the reception is never good. But she was literally pleading for us to get back to her as soon as possible as she needs to see us - she feels that her parents are keeping her there against her will.'

Kelly was feeling more than slightly worried. 'I'm beginning to have regrets about getting involved in all this business with the Broadhursts. It looks like we've opened a can of worms and there's a whole lot more to all this than we first realised.'

Lee gave a wry smile. 'But I know you well, Kelly Phillips and I can tell by the look on your face that despite all your reservations, you want to see this through, because you're a caring person. I was going to leave things a week or two, until I'd got settled in the job, but since getting that call I don't feel things can be left any longer. This needs to be sorted one way or another.'

'In what way?'

'There's a motorway services about five miles ahead. This might be a good time for us to stop off for a coffee and a bite to eat - there's also something I need to discuss with you about all this business, because I believe I know the truth about what's going on here. You're going to need to brace yourself for what I have to tell you, because you're going to find it very hard to believe - but you'll need to trust me on this. When we start out again after our break, I would prefer to do the driving because I want to drive straight to the Broadhursts and because I have a little more experience on the roads, I feel it's best that I'm the one to drive us there a little faster - if that's ok with you?'

'Isn't that just a little bit chauvinist?' Kelly suggested with a grin, secretly glad that Lee was back in the driving seat.

CHAPTER TWENTY

Helena was sitting on her bed at the time she tried to call Kelly, feeling a stab of disappointment when she hadn't responded to neither the call nor the message she'd left. With a sigh she picked up the book she had been reading earlier, but was unable to concentrate on the plot. Normally she would be able to enjoy any novel by Danielle Steele, but found her mind was focused on the uneasy atmosphere she was sensing between her parents and Uncle Ian, with a certainty the hostility she was receiving from them all was not in her imagination.

She thought back to yesterday, when she played chess with Hugo and allowed him to win. He felt so pleased with himself that he danced with her in the large living room. This time they did the Jive with Hugo spinning her with ease across the floor. For a while, her parents watched on smiling and just for a brief moment she felt that they loved her in the way they used to, when they posed proudly with her for all those photographs taken in happier times. Only Uncle Ian had walked off in a huff, saying he had things to do. She guessed he was still in a state of grief over his sister, and only time could heal the hurt he was feeling. Helena thought back with sadness, how the closeness she'd once shared with him, had slipped away with Sylvia's passing. Within an instant, things had completely changed, as if he was somehow blaming her personally for his sister's death.

Slowly getting up from the bed, she walked to the window, peering towards the front garden and the fields in the distance. As if realising for the first time that there was a whole world outside waiting to be rediscovered, she sincerely hoped that Kelly would be in touch soon. It appeared since their graduation, she and Katherine had drifted apart - but in Kelly she knew she had found a friend. With their newly formed friendship, came the hope that she might be able to change her life for the better; maybe she could find a job and perhaps even get her own place to live and finally re-join the human race!

◆ ◆ ◆

After their break at the *Moto* service station that had been longer than planned, Kelly and Lee returned to the car in silence. Kelly sat in the passenger seat, whilst Lee took over the driving. With her face looking considerably paler after Lee had spoken to her of his thoughts, felt she wouldn't have been in the right frame of mind to concentrate on driving.

'Are you feeling ok?' he asked, as he negotiated his way

back onto the motorway.

'I think so,' she replied numbly. 'But if I'm being honest, I really feel what you told me, just sounds too far-fetched. I don't mean to be unkind, but I think your imagination has got the better of you from watching too many movies.' In fact, her first reaction when Lee told her of his theory, much to her shame, had been to burst out laughing, causing other diners to turn their way.

'But does it sound any crazier than what Katherine told us about Helena or for that matter what we learned about Hugo?'

She vacantly watched out of the window at the passing vehicles as they travelled along the motorway, giving a shrug. 'Well, I guess we've learned some pretty extraordinary things over the past few weeks - but if you turn out to be right about what you told me, this will be by far the most spectacular thing I've learned in my entire life!'

Lee concentrated on the road ahead. 'If I turn out to be completely wrong about all this, I know in your eyes I will look the biggest idiot walking the planet - but I always hold my hand up and admit when I'm wrong about something. Right, let's hit the fast lane because the sooner we get to the bottom of what's happening here, the sooner we can lay things to rest.'

It was mid-afternoon by the time they reached Hertfordshire, with Kelly feeling increasingly anxious.

'Do you think it's wise go there unannounced?' she asked as they approached The Woodlands.

'I think this has gone way beyond arriving by invitation only - this the only way, because that doesn't give the Broadhursts the chance to think things through and come up with answers which might not necessarily be the truth.'

Kelly loved Lee with all her heart and knew she could trust him with her very life, but with this, she feared he was completely wrong and at risk of ruining his reputation with the Broadhursts - not to mention risking their friendship with Helena.'

As they approached the entrance to The Woodlands, much to their dismay found the gate to the driveway was firmly closed.

'What do we do now?' asked Kelly.

'I somehow doubt that they're out. I'm sure Helena at least, will be in the house - I'll give her a call.'

Kelly watched apprehensively as Lee got through to her. 'Hi Helena, it's Lee. I'm good, thanks. Just to let you know we received your message and just thought we would drop by on our way back from the coast. Yes, we're outside the entrance to your drive but we see the gate's locked. Is it ok for us to come in or have we called at a bad time?'

Helena's parents looked on in horror as she spoke to the

couple. Her mother stood up from the chair where earlier she had been reading the Daily Telegraph.
She took off her reading glasses, wearily rubbing her eyes.

'What on earth are those two doing here? Helena, *please* don't tell us you invited them here after all we've been through lately - you know only too well we're not in the right frame of mind to receive visitors.'

'I didn't invite Kelly and Lee over they've just dropped by after a returning from a weekend trip.'

It was her father's turn to express his displeasure. 'You will have to turn them away Helena, your mother's right - those people have caused us enough problems.'

Helena looked at each of her parents as if they were both completely crazy. 'In what way have they caused us problems? Just because I've finally been allowed a taste of freedom and dared to venture away from this *prison*, because that's what it's beginning to feel like! I love you both very much, but on this I'm afraid I'm going to have to disagree with you and they *will* be allowed to see me.'

With Kelly and Lee hearing the frantic conversation between Helena and her parents, listened carefully to the security number she gave them to unlock the gate. Lee quickly tapped this in before he forgot the combination. As the gate swung open, they quickly climbed into the vehicle, driving along the winding driveway. Kelly was beginning to feel very nervous. 'What are we letting ourselves in for? Her parents were going ballistic at us turning up here - I just hope whatever's going on we're not about to make matters worse.'

Lee looked briefly to Kelly, his expression grim. 'But as far as Helena's concerned, could things really get any worse? She clearly doesn't understand what's going on here. I'm pretty sure I have the answers, and if I'm right about all this, as crazy as it all sounds, then everybody involved has been finding it hard to cope.'

As they pulled up to the house, they saw the door opening with Helena standing there, dressed in her faded blue jeans and pale pink tee shirt, looking so happy to see them. Kelly looked at the young woman with pity, looking so pretty and innocent and felt that Lee must surely have made a terrible mistake regarding his theory. But if that was the case, then who was this person before them who was supposedly the deceased daughter of Clarissa and Sebastian Broadhurst?

As they climbed out of the vehicle, she hugged each of them desperately as if reuniting with long-lost friends. Rupert walked from the house wagging his tail excitedly as Kelly and Lee gave him a stroke.

'Sorry we weren't around on your surprise visit and had a wasted trip,' Lee apologised, trying his best not to look at her with the curiosity he was now feeling.

He peered through the open doorway, not being able to hear the other occupants making the commotion heard just a few moments ago, now being replaced with an ominous silence. 'Have we called at a bad time? We couldn't help hearing what was being said by your parents.'

She smiled reassuringly. 'Mummy and Daddy are just feeling a little unsettled because of Uncle Ian. At the moment he's completely inconsolable. It seems, the more I try to cheer him up, the worse I seem to make matters. Anyway, you're not to worry about him as he's been shut away in his room for the past couple of hours!'

'And you should be respecting his privacy at this difficult time!' barked an angry voice. The three of them looked towards the house seeing Professor Broadhurst standing there, his normally tall slim frame looking slightly stooped, as if he was carrying all the troubles of the world on his shoulders. Kelly couldn't help but feel that the man had visibly aged since she had last seen him.

Helena glared at her father indignantly. 'Daddy, please don't be so rude to my friends! It's all very sad with Auntie Sylvia dying, but that's no reason to take any of this out on anybody! Come along, let's go inside.'

Reluctantly, biting her bottom lip nervously, Kelly

followed the others as they entered the large house. Helena led them to the living room where Clarissa stood, wearing a crisp white blouse with a floral skirt, holding on to her open spectacles.

Helena looked to each of her parents, her disappointment unmistakable. 'I'm very sorry that Mummy and Daddy are being so rude, but they don't seem to realise that at some point we have to put our grief aside and continue with our lives.'

Clarissa stared at her daughter with her frosty blue eyes appearing frostier than ever. 'Don't you realise that Ian has just lost the only remaining member of his immediate family? How do you *expect* him to feel!'

'But I'm not talking about Auntie Sylvia! I'm talking about Sarah! It seems that this recent death has brought back all the memories of my older sister - for as long as I can remember, you have never shown me any love.'

Professor Broadhurst's face paled at the revelation. 'Helena, you know that's utter nonsense.'

'Please don't lie to me Daddy. I know you both care for me and I know before Sarah passed away you loved me a great deal - that's clear to see from those earlier photos in the front room. But I know after she died that your love seemed to die for me as well, so please don't try to deny this.'

Kelly and Lee looked to each other, remembering their

conversation with Katherine, who claimed to know the Broadhursts for most of her life, swearing blindly there had never been a family member called Sarah.

Helena looked pleadingly to her parents who stared at her as if she was a stranger, the silence only broken by the clock ticking loudly on the wall. 'Please tell me *why* I'm not allowed to live the life I should be living? Tell me what is wrong with me, why I am forbidden to drive any further than inside the grounds of this *ivory tower*! I was fine when I drove into Old Church, for heaven's sake! Why is it that not so long ago I was about to become an illustrator, and now I paint no better than Hugo?'

With that remark both Kelly and Lee cringed.

Clarissa glared at Helena with a look of pure rage. 'I thought we'd agreed not to discuss Hugo with others.' A thought suddenly came to her. '*Please* don't tell me they've been introduced!'

Before giving Helena a chance to reply to her mother, Lee quickly stepped in. 'Helena, I've got to be honest with you, and tell you that me and Kelly didn't go to Norfolk as we mentioned earlier. Actually, we went to Dorset and met with Katherine Jolley.'

At the mention of the name, her parents stared as if they had seen a ghost, with Helena looking as equally as surprised.

'Our meeting wasn't by chance. From what you mentioned about Katherine living in the Dorset area and wanting to go into the stained-glass business, we managed to track her down through the internet.'

'Oh, wow!' exclaimed Helena excitedly. 'Now I can understand why you've dropped by to give me the good news! How is Katherine and is she still seeing Rob?'

Looking at her with a mixture of concern and pity, wondered how best to approach this. Lee chose his words carefully, 'Oh, she's doing very well. I know you've not seen her in a while, but what are your memories of her? I remember you saying you practically grew up together and went to the same university. Is Katherine slightly older than you?'

Professor Broadhurst starred at Lee with a look of fury, his face turning a deep shade of red. 'What kind of absurd question is this? I want you both to leave our house immediately!'

Helena turned to her father. 'Daddy, will you please stop being so rude to my friends.' Her attention focused back to Lee. 'That is a rather strange question to ask, but now you're asking I'm actually six months older than Katherine. She will turn 25 in September!'

Kelly turned to Lee, briefly raising an eyebrow, remembering only too well that the woman looked older than her own mother.

Deciding not to mention about the age of her friend, Lee gave her some updates. 'Well Katherine is still very much with Rob and they have a very successful business.'

'Did she ask about me?'

Before having the chance to answer, a voice came through from the hallway. 'I doubt very much that Katherine would have been asking about you.'

Everybody turned around in surprise to see Ian Peterson standing there, dressed casually in some chinos and a navy pullover. With his grey hair slightly dishevelled and his normally trimmed beard overgrown, Kelly could see the man was clearly very depressed.

'*Helena,*' he spat the name almost spitefully. 'You're always so fond of reminiscing with us, all about the happy memories of your childhood and your days at university with Katherine - but tell us truthfully, what *exactly* do you remember of all those happier days?'

Sebastian Broadhurst's face appeared to turn as white as a sheet, as he turned towards the man he'd considered a part of his family for many years but now looked at him as if he was a complete stranger. 'Ian, this isn't going to achieve anything...'

Peterson waved his hand dismissively, causing the elderly man to retreat next to his wife. 'Tell me Helena, what *exactly* are your memories of Katherine?'

Helena stood nervously, her eyes open wide as she looked to those around her, before focusing her attention back to Peterson. 'Why, Katherine was my dearest friend - we practically grew up together, went to the same schools then on to Oxford.'

Peterson laughed mirthlessly. 'You've told that to us countless times, but tell me what exactly can you tell us about Katherine? Describe to us what she looks like - how long ago was it you left Oxford?'

This time Clarissa intervened. 'Ian, this is totally futile - ll you're managing to achieve is to distress Helena.'

'It's ok Mummy, Uncle Ian is simply feeling upset.' She turned her attention again to Peterson. 'You asked me to describe Katherine. Well, she has long blonde hair, a few shades lighter than mine. She's very pretty as I remember - we both left Oxford three years ago.'

Kelly and Lee looked at each other grimly, knowing that Katherine was considerably older than Helena described and that their university days had long finished.

Peterson thought for a moment. 'Ok, this *should* be an easy question. What's Katherine's favourite colour?'

'Oh, this is absurd!' Despite his angry tone, Broadhurst was looking clearly worried.

All eyes were focused on Helena who looked to each person in the room in turn. 'I...I can't remember - it's a long time ago.'

A look of triumph spread across Peterson's face. 'But that's something that Katherine's best friend should remember. Tell me what you remember about those paintings of yours, hanging around the living room? He turned to one of the watercolours that Helena once proudly showed to Lee. 'What are your memories of when you were painting this picture?"

Helena held her hands to her face, looking with dismay to her parents. 'I'm sorry Uncle Ian, but I really can't remember.'

Then he pointed to the painting of a much younger Ian Peterson, wearing thick dark framed spectacles and darker hair but without the scar and beard. 'Can you tell me *who* painted my portrait - it's been around for as long as you can remember, but can you tell me about the artist?'

She stared at the painting, then closing her eyes in concentration before shaking her head in defeat. 'I'm sorry but I really don't know. Uncle Ian, why are you asking me all these strange questions?'

Clarissa stared at Peterson angrily. '*Why* are you doing this Ian? Why *now*?'

He looked to Helena, with a cruel smile spreading across his face. 'I *knew* you wouldn't be able to tell me about the artist, my dear but I can. The painting was done by Helena Broadhurst!'

Helena looked in horror as she took a step back, staring at Peterson as if he was insane. 'But...but I don't have any memory at all of painting your portrait!'

'No, of course you don't, and I know if you think hard, you won't have any memories attached to any of those paintings that are hanging there, just the countless awful attempts you've made in recent times. In fact, you won't ever remember painting anything amazing because those are not *your* memories.'

Helena, clearly distressed, rubbed her hands through her long hair, giving it a slightly ruffled appearance. 'Mummy, Daddy, what's Uncle Ian trying to say? Has he gone crazy?'

But her parents just stood there looking completely distraught, with a tear running down her mother's cheek.

But Ian hadn't finished. 'Helena, in fact do you have any memories at all of your childhood? *Do you*? Can you remember anything about your older sister Sarah, what she looked like? Is there *anything* that you can share with us?'

She closed her eyes and thought hard. All she could think of was all the photos hanging on the wall of earlier happier times, in the front room, but try as she may, couldn't remember a single thing about her childhood nor any of her experiences.

It pained Kelly and Lee, to watch the young woman trying to cry but seemingly unable to shed tears.

Peterson stood there with a cruel smile on his face. 'See Helena, you can try to weep but the tears never come, do they? You see, you're simply not capable of emotions, as we know them, no more than Hugo is able to cry.'

Lee took hold of Kelly's hand for support and found her trembling as the realisation began to unfold.

Helena fell silent staring at the man she thought she loved. 'What are you trying to say?'

'*Think* Helena, why do you think it is that you have no early memories? Why is that you never see photos of Sarah? But *I* can tell you why? She never existed! The only memories you have are the ones we gave to you from our own experiences.'

Broadhurst held his wife as she sobbed uncontrollably, with Kelly looking on in horror at the way Peterson seemed to take great delight in upsetting the people whom he'd shared his life with.

Peterson rubbed his hands through his hair, his eyes looking bloodshot through his spectacles. 'Oh, it's perfectly true there was a death - she was the love of my life, beautiful, kind and loving and a ray of sunshine in my dull world. We met at Oxford where I was studying algorithms under the watchful eye of Professor Broadhurst. I used to see her walking through the corridors, going to lectures with her friend. I would see her look my way and smile. In the canteen our eyes would meet, and she would smile at me shyly and I wanted to speak to her and ask her for a date but seemed to lose my courage.' He walked slowly to the window, looking vacantly at the garden ahead. 'Then came the University Ball, an event which took place every year. It really wasn't my scene, but my fellow students knew how keen I was on her and encouraged me to tag along, telling me this was my one chance to get to know her. I took their advice and watched as she danced with her friend, but I'm afraid I've always had two left feet and knew I would make a complete fool of myself. But then the music slowed down and I mustered up all my courage and asked her to dance.' A smile spread across his face as he remembered back to a time long ago that was still as vivid in his memory as if it was only yesterday. 'I remember that song very well, Close to You, by the Carpenters. I didn't have a clue how to dance, but somehow, together we glided across that floor as one. From that day onwards, we were inseparable.'

Helena listened carefully, her eyes wide with curiosity, her attempts at weeping forgotten for the moment as she listened to the man she had considered her uncle, speak of a love she was never aware of.

'The next two years were the best of my life, with every moment precious. We become engaged, with our wedding date set. I'll never forget her face when I presented her with that diamond ring with sapphires that matched those amazing blue eyes. The ring fitted her finger perfectly with no alterations needed and together we planned our wedding. The church organised, with her best friend as the bridesmaid, and Neil, my friend from University as Best Man - all the arrangements went flawlessly.'

The smile that had warmed his features for a moment faded, his expression turning grim. 'Just three weeks before our wedding day, we went along to the Ball where we met with our friends. I have to admit it really wasn't my thing but I knew how much my fiancé had looked forward to this, and her happiness was always the most important thing to me. At the end of the evening, we said our goodbyes to our friends and left. I drove that evening, deciding not to take a taxi and made sure I abstained from any alcohol. We were about three miles from her home - she looked so happy and was a little merry from the champagne she drank that evening.' He stopped speaking for a moment as a tear came to his eye. 'We were driving along the country lane and I could see bright headlights coming from the opposite direction, but as I drove along the bend saw a car coming along on our side of the road at great speed. I tried to stop in time, and then, and then...'

Professor Broadhurst spoke with the emotion tight in his voice. 'Ian, please, you're just tormenting yourself.'

Oblivious to the elderly man pleading with him, Peterson continued. 'I really don't have any recollection after that. I woke up in hospital and learned I'd been in a coma for eight days. I was told the driver in the other car was killed as he collided with us and later discovered he was four times over the legal limit. It was touch and go, whether or not I would survive. I suffered serious internal injuries and my face disfigured from the impact, but after many operations I was patched up. But my darling fiancé was not so fortunate as she was killed instantly. She wasn't wearing her seatbelt and was catapulted through the windscreen.'

He turned his attention away from the window, his face deathly pale. 'My darling Helena was no more, and it was *my* fault, as I should have made sure she was belted up.' With that Peterson's shoulder shuddered violently as he broke down in tears, reliving the moment he received the terrible news. Kelly and Lee appearing shocked, turned to Helena who stood transfixed to the spot, with Sebastian holding a clearly shaken Clarissa in his arms.

Helena stared at Peterson as if he was quite insane,

looking at the large scar running across his face, as if for the very first time. They had been there as far back as she could remember but never had she considered the cause of them.

She turned to her friends. Their faces were pale, and their looks of pity were unmistakable. Kelly shrugged nervously, not being able to give an answer, before taking hold of Lee's hand.

Looking at her parents pleadingly, with her eyes wide, was desperate for answers. 'Mummy, daddy, what's Uncle Ian trying to tell me? If Helena, your daughter was to marry him and Sarah never existed, then who am I? Please tell me who I am because I have never known any other life. This is all I have known!' With fear written on her pretty face, looked appealingly at Clarissa and Sebastian. 'It's true, all I know is what you've told me about Sarah, but no matter how I try, I'm unable to *remember* her. But I have no memories of anybody else called Helena. Please, Mummy, Daddy if I'm not Helena Broadhurst, *then who am I?*'

Lost for words, her parents looked on in silence, with Clarissa weeping bitterly, wiping her face with her handkerchief.

Peterson broke the silence with a deep sigh. 'I think the time for truth has come - I've become wholeheartedly sick of living this ridiculous lie. And the truth is, although I was sad that Sylvia passed away, we weren't particularly close. But when she died it simply brought home all the memories of losing Helena all those years ago. I wish with all my heart, that when she left me that I could have joined her because what I have lived since is not a life, just an existence. Well *Helena,* you are asking me who you are but it would be more to the point if you asked *what* you, are because the truth is, you're no more real than your companion, Hugo!'

Helena took a step back, looking stunned as if Peterson had slapped her across the face. 'What are you trying to say Uncle Ian, that I'm a robot just like Hugo? That's the most absurd thing I've ever heard!' She looked at her parents, then to Kelly and Lee and burst out laughing. 'Uncle Ian, you're *so* funny!' But nobody else in the room appeared amused.

Peterson sighed wearily. 'I'm sure our goods friends here have been introduced to the amazing Hugo. I've had my suspicions that something was amiss when we were away for the funeral, with those empty food dishes in the dustbin, when Helena was meant to be asleep. Well, Hugo has been a part of the family for many years, in fact several years before the real Helena died. I won't go into all the details, but Sebastian and I were doing robotic research at Oxford, along with some scientists from Ontario in Canada, and over a number of years we created Hugo. As time went by, he became more sophisticated as we developed programmes to improve his various skills. At the time, he was pretty amazing, and Helena loved him.

Lee's eyes narrowed suspiciously. 'Yes, it's true we've seen Hugo for ourselves and he's a pretty special. But how come you've been allowed to keep him at home, because he must be quite valuable.'

'Far more than you realise, but after much persuasion and paying the right people, we managed to convince those that mattered that he was no longer of interest, as other countries such as the US and Japan had developed more sophisticated robots.'

Their thoughts were disturbed as Helena began to laugh again. 'But how can you possibly say I'm a robot, Uncle Ian? Look at me, I'm flesh and blood - I look nothing like Hugo! Uncle Ian, I know you're upset, but that's no reason to tease me in this way!'

Peterson smiled at her cruelly. 'I can assure you I'm not *teasing* as you put it. Think about it, Helena, why is it that you have to be asleep by midnight and always wake up promptly at 8'oclock without fail?'

Helena gave him a look of triumph. 'But the other day I woke up after 11.30!'

'That can easily be explained. You won't have any memory

of this, but before we left for the funeral, I deactivated you. You were put into a sleep mode before we left for Newcastle, and put you to bed. The plan was that you would wake once we returned, but clearly something went wrong and you woke, probably when our dear friends here came to visit you.'

Kelly remembered only too well the confused state that Helena appeared to be in that day, and feared that she was suffering from either a serious physical or mental illness.

Ian Peterson walked slowly around the living room, his face pale against his navy pullover. 'Why is it that you can't draw anymore Helena? Tried as we might, despite all the best programmes, we've never been able to get you to draw and paint as well as the real Helena - she was absolutely brilliant, even better than Clarissa, as I'm sure she would be the first to agree! Now, can't you see why we haven't allowed you to drive outside of these grounds? Oh yes, you can drive perfectly, even better than the original Helena, who was always a little nervous behind the steering wheel. But could you imagine what would've happened if you'd been stopped by the police or involved in an accident even if it wasn't your fault? The consequences don't bear thinking about!'

'This is crazy Uncle Ian! I'm real! I eat and drink just like everybody else in this room. Hugo doesn't!'

'That's perfectly true - you were designed to do most

humanly things. But think hard Helena - do you use the toilet like us? That's all taken care of while you *sleep*. Do you take a shower or bath? When do you remember being in a swimming pool? Helena used to love swimming!'

She blinked, thinking hard and shaking her head. 'This is absurd I can't remember anything because you're confusing me and turning my head upside down!'

'Let her be.' Professor Broadhurst warned gently.

Helena looked pleadingly at her father. 'Daddy, why is Uncle Ian being so cruel? Why? Please tell me that he's making all this up because he's upset over Auntie Sylvia dying. Mummy? Daddy?

Professor Broadhurst sighed deeply, feeling every year of his age. He led a very distraught Clarissa to the sofa, where they both sat down, with the others remaining standing. He looked blankly towards the ceiling, lost in his thoughts.

'Our whole world ended on the day we lost Helena in that car crash. I remember Clarissa and I had gone to bed knowing that Helena would be able to let herself in once Ian had driven her home. When we heard the knock at the door, I grumbled thinking that she'd forgotten to take her key. Her mother got out of the bed to let her in, and the next thing I remember is hearing that cry of horror and calling me to come down the stairs quickly. I feared the worse once I saw the police officers standing there, a male and female, and those looks of sympathy written on their faces. I remember hearing a voice yelling out in disbelief, not realising it was my own.'

Kelly could see the tears welling up in the older man's eyes, as his thoughts turned back to that terrible moment of almost forty years ago. 'The day our beautiful daughter died our whole world just seemed to collapse - Helena was our only child. Clarissa miscarried two years after Helena was born, and was told she would never be able to have any more children. We didn't have the luxury of fertility treatment in those days. It was very touch and go, whether Ian would survive, and thank God he did - he was the son we never had.'

The professor removed his spectacles, wearily rubbing his face. 'Three months after leaving hospital, he came to live with us, and somehow that made us feel closer to our daughter and gave us the strength to continue with our lives, after a fashion - there is no worse feeling in the world than losing your child. You expect them to grow up and live on, to have their own children, things that Helena very much wanted. Instead, we had to face identifying her body, lying cold on the slab in the morgue - her life cruelly snuffed out by a drunken driver.'

He smiled sadly, as his mind shifted to happier times. 'Hugo had practically become a member of our family and Helena adored him - Katherine, Helena's best friend was the only person, outside of the family, to know of his existence. An idea came to Ian and I to create an even more sophisticated robot, something we had been working on with a team of scientists in Canada, in a project we named *Devotion*. But due to other projects taking priority by the powers that be, it was deemed to be too expensive, and was shelved.' A cunning gleam twinkled in his eye. 'But *we* continued independently, with the robot project forgotten by those from the outside. Funding wasn't a problem for us thankfully and over ten years of hard work, which involved much trial and error, with our technical knowhow and Clarissa's immense talent with special effects, we created a robot in Helena's image. In almost every way, she's very much like the daughter we lost - of course, with Ian, she could only regard him as nothing more than an uncle. Until now she has given us five years of happiness and somehow helped to fill the void that our beloved daughter's death had left behind.'

Between them, Peterson and Broadhurst had confirmed all of Lee's suspicions, with Kelly looking at him apologetically as well as disbelief. Lee gazed at the image of the young woman, who appeared so human in every way. All her mannerisms were so normal despite all the strange things, like the time she collapsed in his car, and the moment in the woods when she went into a fit. He thought back to the time when she cut her hand with the knife, appearing to miraculously heal within a short space of time, and to the electricity from the thunderstorm must have had some kind of effect on her and might have explained why her voice always sounded strange when calling him from a mobile.

Helena looked to her parents in horror. 'Mummy, Daddy have you both lost your minds? Why are you telling me all these things? There's no robot that exists yet that appears and behaves a hundred percent human! I know more than anybody the work Daddy an Uncle Ian have done regarding robotics, is truly amazing and Hugo is proof of that.

Peterson walked over to Lee, his expression stern. 'Until you came along, that day with the delivery, Helena was completely content with her life. Ironically, those heavy parcels you delivered were from a company in Japan, that manufactures special long-life batteries that are used to help Helena function. Why she changed, we're not sure - something could have happened when she fell over. But all we know is, from that day onwards, she began to question her life and to tell lies, traits that she had never shown before.'

'Enough!' All eyes turned to Helena who stared at Peterson with fury. 'Will you please stop blaming my friends that I wanted to change my life - that decision was purely mine, without any prompting from anybody else. The only part that

Kelly and Lee played in this, was to show me there was more to life than being trapped within these four walls, with my only contact from the outside world being from Mrs Cowley and Ed the gardener, who comes once a fortnight!'

'But what about Hugo?' demanded Clarissa as she wiped her face with her handkerchief. 'Until recently, you were more than content with his company, and I know he loves you.'

Helena laughed mirthlessly. 'How can a robot possibly feel love? Tell me Mummy? Because I know that's what I feel for everybody in this room despite all this nonsense you're coming out with.'

With his temples throbbing with tension, Sebastian Broadhurst held his hands to his head. 'My God, what have we done? Now I look back, was it really worth all the pain this has caused?'

A look of triumph spread across Helena's face as an idea came to her. 'I've made a decision - I'm going to leave home and find somewhere in Old Church to stay. I'm sure Kelly or Lee will help me find somewhere.' She glared at her parents indignantly. 'You have no right to try and stop me, after all, I'm twenty-five and not a child - finally, I can have my life back and hopefully reunite with Katherine at some point.'

It was Peterson's turn to laugh. 'My dear, you're going to find it difficult to find a place to live when you have no money of your own. How could a savings account be possibly be set up for somebody that no longer exists?'

For Helena, that was the last straw, and much to the shock of everybody, she picked up the heavy crystal vase in the corner, near to the door leading to the patio, and threw this onto the laminate floor, smashing it into thousands of pieces. 'How dare you speak to me this way Uncle Ian? *I hate you!* Mummy, Daddy - why do you allow him to speak to me in this way?'

Her parents looked on with horror, as they both stood up from the sofa. Never before had Helena displayed any kind of aggression and this was very alarming to them.

She looked at Lee and Helena pleadingly. 'Now you can finally see what I'm up against! Please tell me how wrong they are to treat me this way. Please take me away, so I can have my life back. Kelly, Lee tell them how wrong they are. *Please!*'

Her friends stood there, their look of helplessness was unmistakable. Lee was barely able to look her in the eyes, with a mixture of both pity and anger written on his face. Kelly looked at her with tears in her eyes and her bottom lip trembling, as Lee held her in his arms; their body language told her all she needed to know.

She stared at them as if they were strangers, her eyes wide with fear as realisation had suddenly flooded over her. 'My

God!' she cried. 'My dear God!'

With that, she ran across the floor, as her shoes crunched across the fragments of broken vase, running quickly up the stairs before they heard the door to her bedroom slamming loudly.

Lee was furious. 'What have you all done? Didn't you ever step back to think of the consequences that something like this might happen further down the line?'

Broadhurst looked at him with anger. 'Unless you lose a child, you will never understand the unbearable pain it causes, because when it happens your life might as well be over too and we did what we felt was right at the time. We had the capability, and for a while we felt that we had our daughter back. Oh yes, we know that she has gone, but this Helena has brought us all a great deal of comfort.'

'What are we going to do?' demanded Clarissa. 'She's locked herself away in her room - heaven knows what she's capable of. I'd best go up and see if I can coax her out.'

Lee stared at Peterson with disgust, feeling he could have handled things much better, despite all his years of suppressed grief, and hurting all those closest to him in the process.

Locked safely in the sanctuary of her bedroom, Helena leaned against the door with her eyes firmly closed, trying to digest all that she had learned. What did she remember of her life with her parents? They had often spoken to her about places they had all travelled together mainly to do with their careers. Mummy had discussed with her the various movie stars that they'd had the privilege to meet and the private schools she attended for a while in Ontario, Canada, because her father's work meant him staying there for a period of time. She frowned, trying her best to remember the trips all around the world, meeting those famous people and attending the exclusive school in Ontario. But try, as she might, she couldn't remember a single thing.

Oblivious to her mother shouting frantically from the other side of the door, she opened the bottom drawer to her dressing table, taking out a photo album she had looked at many times. Inside the album were photographs taken over the years. She smiled with fondness at a black and white photo of her mother when she was much younger, holding her in her arms, when she was just three years old. She turned over pages to others, with her parents at the seaside. Mummy was so pretty in those days she thought, before a troubled frown creased her forehead. Why had she not realised until now that these pictures had been taken much further back than twenty years ago? The earliest ones were black and white, which was fairly rare these days. Mummy also looked very young almost the age she herself was now, but surely that couldn't be the case, had that been just twenty years ago. Why was it that after all that had been said, that only now had she realised that her parents were really quite elderly? Quickly she turned to photographs taken with Katherine, sitting together whilst having a picnic in the garden with their dolls for company, probably when they were about five years old. She looked at the photographs as they grew older and one where they had gone horse-riding, sitting proudly in their riding outfits and hats.

Again, she turned over the page to pictures, when she and Katherine were probably both in their early twenties and looking adult in their long dresses, with their hair long and loose. Both were wearing make-up, with long false eyelashes, and looked as if they were on their way to a party. Just before she was about to turn the page again, she gave a troubled frown, as if realising something for the very first time. On the photo she noticed she was wearing a ring on the wedding finger of her left hand and noticed a glimmer of light reflected from the jewel setting.

She closed the album as she stared into space before it slipped out of her hands, hitting the floor. The album was full of happy memories, but now she realised none of them belonged to her; she had no recollection of the photos taken with her parents, nor any of them on their travels around the world. Helena had been the greatest of friends with Katherine and together had shared all their experiences as they grew up together. But now she realised that none of these moments had anything to do with her. What could she remember about her dearest friend Katherine? After looking through those pictures, came the realisation that she had never known her, nor this Helena, as she grew up from a child to a young woman, engaged to be married.

Vacantly, she peered at Lucifer, the old teddy bear that sat on her bed. Slowly she picked up the worn and tatty toy that had been her bedtime companion for as far back as she could remember. Now reality had bitten that the much cherished teddy bear had also belonged to the Helena who her parents had loved so dearly and who Uncle Ian had loved with all his heart. Slowly she dropped the cuddly toy onto the bed, oblivious to Clarissa frantically knocking on the door, demanding her to leave her bedroom.

Slowly, she made her towards the large bedroom window and opened it, allowing a cool blast of air to flow through. She looked ahead of her, to the distant woodlands and fields, with the sound of a car driving along the road nearby. As she looked further ahead she noticed a cluster of homes and one of the local farms. Out there, as far as her eyes could see, was a whole world, full of people living their lives in many different ways. Some of them led a happy and comfortable existence, a few perhaps finding it difficult to make ends meet. There were many people in that big wide world, who were yet to experience romance or maybe, like Kelly and Lee, were falling in love with the promise of a happy future ahead of them. Yes, maybe they would have their challenges, but together they would tackle whatever troubles might lie ahead. Feeling liberated for the first time she could remember, smiled as she climbed out of the window, sitting on the ledge.

'Oh my God,' cried Kelly as she rushed from the house into the garden, 'She's sitting on the window ledge!' Hearing Kelly's alarming announcement Clarissa rushed down the stairs as fast as her aching bones would allow her and followed the others into the garden.

All eyes were focused on Helena who sat calmly, looking ahead with her long fair hair blowing gently in the wind. A dark cloud drifted across the grey sky, shielding the sun that shone brightly only moments before with the threat of rain now looming.

Professor Broadhurst looked up to her in desperation. 'Helena dear, you sitting out there isn't going to achieve a thing. Please get back inside before you slip and have a nasty accident!'

She looked down to the small crowd gathered below as if

only being aware of them for the first time. 'What does it matter, Daddy? It's not as if there's going to be any serious consequences if I do - remember I'm not flesh and blood, so not as if I could die!'

'Helena for goodness sake!' Clarissa called out in frustration. Kelly could see that although the older woman sounded angry, the look of fear on her face was unmistakable. 'Can't you see how much you've become an important member of the family? Yes, our biological daughter died many years ago and we still miss her terribly, but you have brought us so much happiness and given us all a reason to carry on with our lives. Please Helena, get back inside and try to forget this unfortunate episode!'

Helena looked at her mother with disgust. 'So, when your beloved daughter died, your answer was to make somebody in her image and likeness. I may look like her and act like her, but I know you could never love me in the way that you loved *her*. Can't you see, that although I might look more human than Hugo, I can never be any more real and lead a normal life like other people? Why couldn't you have been like most people who've lost somebody special and receive counselling, taking up an interest or getting a dog?'

She looked down to Peterson, who stood away, some distance from the rest of the small gathering. 'How must it feel for Uncle Ian seeing the image of somebody he loved dearly, who he was about to marry, and can now only look upon her as his niece?'

Peterson looked ahead vacantly, staring into space, lost in his memories of the beautiful woman who he loved more than life itself and was so cruelly torn away from him. Yes, he might have lost her forever, but at least all their wonderful memories of times together could never be taken away from him.

'Just let me be,' she begged. 'I would be doing you all a favour if I was out of the equation. Mummy, you and Daddy there is still time to enjoy the rest of your lives, maybe going on some cruises. I remember, you telling me that you went on some fabulous trips around the Caribbean.'

Her mother looked at her indignantly. 'Oh, don't be silly Helena - your father and I are far too old now to go flitting off around the world. We did all those things years ago - our days of travelling are long gone!'

'Well, I think Uncle Ian has been grieving for far too long! He should have come to terms with Helena's death long ago and found somebody else.'

Peterson looked up to her laughing mirthlessly. 'Don't you see, there could *never* have been anybody else for me? She was the love of my life, my reason for living, but all I'm doing now is simply existing!'

'There's still time, Uncle Ian - it's never too late to find somebody to make you happy again. You're a kind and decent person and I know if you search hard, there will be a wonderful woman out there who'll appreciate all your good qualities.'

As she finished speaking, the sky darkened, with which began at first a few droplets of rain, quickly turned into a downpour.

'Please get back inside,' pleaded Professor Broadhurst. 'We're all about to get drenched and you're in real danger of slipping over!'

'Goodbye Daddy,' Helena called out, oblivious to the rain soaking her hair and clothes. 'Goodbye Mummy and Uncle Ian, thank you for all your kindness. Kelly, Lee, thank you so much for all the friendship you have given me - it has meant so much, to be given a brief taste of what it's like to lead a normal life. I hope you'll be very happy together and have the happy ever after, that Helena and Ian never had!'

Lee looked grimly, his face pale as he looked to the others. 'I think perhaps I should go up there and try to coax her...'

Before he could finish his sentence, everybody cried out in horror, as they looked towards the house. Helena had leapt from the bedroom window falling far to the ground below, landing on the stone slabs with a sickening thud. Everybody ran back making way for her body as it broke up into pieces on the rain-sodden ground.

Everybody stared in shock, oblivious to the pouring rain, which soaked through their clothing, as they stared at dismembered limbs, split open, exposing various wires. Helena's head had completely fragmented, with her long fair hair still partly in place, showing more wires with integrated circuit boards and processors. A chill ran down Kelly's spine as most of Helena's face had come apart, but with her large blue eyes still in place, staring up to the sky.

She noticed a pale red substance, which soaked her pink top and jeans and the pebbled ground realising this couldn't have been blood as she could detect a type of alcoholic aroma which steamed as it blended with the cooler air.

Everybody stood in silence, numbed with shock, as they watched over what was Helena's body, now almost like a skeleton with the exposed wires still moving on their own accord with an arm that had broken away from the body, writhing independently. Kelly and Lee couldn't believe, that only a day or so ago, assumed this beautiful young woman to be an unfortunate individual with health issues, due to the bereavement of an elder sister, whom they now realised had never existed.

Lee thought sadly, that he came here with the intention of revealing what Katherine Jolley-Herbert had told him about the late Helena, but Peterson had done the job instead.

He knew without a doubt that Katherine had realised what the new Helena was all about, having seen the pictures and video footage of Hugo dancing with the replica of her deceased friend.

Kelly looked at him apologetically, with tears in her eyes, for doubting his theories which had been proven about Helena being the robotic creation of these highly intelligent but crazy individuals, standing before him. But who could blame her for all the doubts, because even to him, it sounded crazy and far-fetched because as far as most people believed, humanlike robots were not that yet advanced. It just went to prove, that there were a lot of things that the higher powers of this world withheld from the general public, because surely there must be governments that were aware of this highly advance technology and using it for, heaven knows what!

Everybody stood in grim silence, staring at what was left of the robotic Helena, created out of love and heartache, in the image of a beautiful and special young woman, so cruelly torn away from them when she had the best of her life still ahead of her. This Helena might not have been a real human, thought Kelly sadly, but in a sense, she had also died like the original daughter had. She knew that despite all these wires and chips she saw before her eyes, this Helena somehow displayed emotions and feelings, experiencing both happiness and sadness and so wanted to live the life she'd had a taste of. Kelly knew she would miss the Helena she had come to know, with her kind and quirky nature. If the original Helena had been half as special as this one, she must have been a truly amazing person.

Lee, placing his arm gently around Kelly's waist, looked at the remains of Helena before turning to the others. 'We're so very, very sorry, truly we are. Is there *anything* we can do?'

Professor Broadhurst shook his head, his face deathly pale as he looked at what was left of Helena. 'No. No - you have done enough,' he added with a twist of bitterness. 'There's nothing more to be done - the best thing you can do is to leave us alone and never come back.'

Peterson looked over to them, removing his spectacles as he wiped a tear from the corner of his eye. 'Don't even consider reporting this to anybody as you would never be taken seriously telling this to anybody, they would deem you insane.'

Lee shook his head. 'I've no intentions of mentioning this to a soul. I think enough hurt has been caused here, not least to you. We will continue with our lives and try our best to put this whole sorry episode behind us.'

They climbed into their vehicle, driving down the long winding driveway, leaving the Broadhursts and Peterson standing numbed with shock, getting soaked in the heavy downpour of rain. As they left the property, Kelly gave a shudder as she suddenly broke down in a flood of tears. Lee found a safe place to pull up before taking her in his arms, gently kissing her on the head, trying his best to give her some comfort.

EPILOGUE

Four years later, Kelly and Lee were sitting in the garden of the cottage, which they had rented at the New Forest, for their summer break. They came to this area at least twice a year, as despite some of the grim memories still firmly etched on their minds from their first visit, was also the place where they had sealed their relationship. But this vacation was particularly special, as they were celebrating their third wedding anniversary. So far, they had been lucky with the weather, with no rain forecast and the sun shining brightly as they sat on their loungers.

'Ah, this is the life,' sighed Kelly, as she removed her sunglasses and put down her paperback onto the dry lawn.

'I wouldn't argue with you there,' agreed Lee, as he flicked through his car magazine. 'It's always good to have a break from work and take a well-earned rest.'

Lee had been managing Fast Link for the past four years, and the business had gone from strength to strength. It's true, it hadn't been an easy task, but after much hard work and patience, Lee had reaped the success from all the efforts that both himself and the dedicated employees had put in.

Much to his relief, Mike Stanton had resigned at the time he'd learned of Lee's posting, and was happy to see this unpleasant man leave with immediate effect rather than work his months' notice. After some investigating, it turned out that Stanton was involved, along with a few drivers, in the theft of those Notebooks that went missing at the time and was swiftly arrested. In his place, Lee had employed his friend and colleague, Stuart from FPS and was confident with his vast wealth of experience and excellent track record, his friend would help to take company to even greater successes.

He thought back to Frederick Porter-Stevens, his former boss and the father of his former fiancée Miranda, who had passed away two years previously, from a fatal heart attack. The business had been doing badly for some time, due to some bad decisions, and was already in the process of going into liquidation. Although the success of Fast Link had been instrumental in the downfall of the delivery company, its demise had already been much on the cards.

Lee gave a wry smile as he thought back to when he learned that Miranda had gone off to the States to shack up with the boss of some big American car plant, thirty years her senior. Trust her to put her own needs first and to continue to lead the life of luxury she was accustomed to.

He looked over to his beautiful wife, with the sun turning

her soft, smooth skin a golden brown. Thank goodness he'd seen sense, before allowing the love of his life to slip through his fingers. Without her love, support and devotion through all the challenging times that came with his management role, knew life without her would have been an even greater challenge. Barry and Sue had got wed six months before they themselves had tied the knot, and were now the proud parents of a son they named Gavin.

Lee placed his magazine carefully on the small table beside him. 'How's madam over there, is she behaving herself?' Together they looked to their two-year old daughter, Amelia, sitting happily as she played with her toys. She smiled at them happily, with dark brown eyes so similar to Lee's, and with short brown hair, which curled just like her mother's, now protected by a small white sun hat. Kelly gently lifted her from the playpen, sitting her on her lap. Her dad gave her a gentle kiss on her head. 'How's my little munchkin?' he asked.

'She's been as good as gold,' remarked her mother, looking at her with love in her eyes. 'I can't believe, since we've been here, she's been sleeping through the night without any trouble - mind you, I guess we're going to have to make the most of it,' she added peering towards her swollen belly.

'You're not wrong there,' grinned Lee. 'In just eight more weeks, our new son will be born - but I'm sure Sandra and Lisa will cope just fine while you're on maternity leave.'

After Sue left to have her son, she had made the decision not to return to work, but remained close friends with Kelly and they often met up socially. A young lady called Lisa joined the company to replace Sue and proved to be very efficient at her job. Since the birth of Amelia, Kelly had worked part-time for the delivery company and along with her parents and Lee's mother, took it in turns to look after their daughter.

Kelly had enjoyed working for Fast Link, as had been a large part of her life for many years, but realised that once their son was born, she would need to focus most of her energies on caring for the children, and wanting to be there for them as much as possible. It looked as if Sandra, who originally came as a temp to cover for Kelly, would be working there for some time to come; the older woman, who was widowed with three grown up children, was very hard working and reliable, and with a cheerful nature. Both Kelly and Lee agreed that she was a great asset to the company.

Lee poured out some orange squash into two tall glasses and pouring some in Amelia's plastic beaker as well. Kelly sighed contentedly. 'I love this place,' she remarked wistfully. The New Forest will always remind me that this is the place our relationship truly started - but I guess it'll also be a reminder of when we met Katherine and what finally happened to poor

Helena.'

Lee took a sip of his cool drink. 'I'm the same as you – I have mixed feelings. Even after four years, I still have trouble taking it all in. I personally don't have a problem keeping all this robot stuff to ourselves because no matter how we'd try, nobody would believe us in a thousand years - we'd be deemed crazy. But at least we've saved that footage of Helena and Hugo, on a memory stick, safely locked away and that will just stay our secret.'

Kelly agreed. 'Some things are definitely best kept to ourselves. I'll never forget, when we drove back to Little Green, just a few days after you took over as manager, and we met Jess Cowley at the shop. I know my jaw must have nearly dropped to the ground, when she told us that the Broadhursts had moved away without leaving a forwarding address. I remember, she was quite indignant about it, because she'd lost her cleaning job - but if only she knew the truth.'

Lee tickled Amelia under the chin and she rewarded her dad with a sweet toothy smile. 'I wonder where that family moved to. I know we looked on the internet from time to time for clues, but I never see anything mentioned that we haven't seen before - I guess we'll never find the answers we're seeking. I know that Helena was nothing more than a robot, but she was very a sophisticated and a very realistic one and even had us fooled.

I guess in their own way, those three must miss her, because one way or another, she played a big part in their lives. Heaven knows how much time and money it must have cost them to create her. I know in the true sense, she was never real as such, but in a way, I still feel on that day, the Helena we knew had died.

Kelly thought back with sadness. 'That's the way I feel, and the reason I cried buckets after we left The Woodlands on that day.' A smile suddenly spread across her face as she looked at Amelia sitting contentedly on her lap, drinking from her beaker. 'Hey, let's not get morbid any more - think we'd best make up our minds fast for a name for Amelia's new-brother-to-be.'

Lee grinned. 'Now what was it to be, Hector or Jasper?'

Kelly stuck out her tongue playfully. 'In your dreams, Mr Fisher!'

◆ ◆ ◆

At about the same time Kelly and Lee were pondering over the name of their new son, about six hundred miles away, on a remote Scottish island, a young woman was waking up in her bedroom.

As she opened her eyes, she saw the sunshine peering

through an opening in the closed curtains, dazzling her for a moment, until she noticed a man and woman anxiously looking over her. Once her eyes adjusted to the light, she smiled in recognition to the couple. 'Mummy…Daddy,' she smiled cheerfully.

Her parents returned the smile with a look of relief crossing their faces. 'Good morning darling,' her father greeted her cheerfully.

She looked over to the clock on her bedside table, which was showing 8'o'clock. Rubbing her eyes, she gratefully received the mug of tea that her mother handed to her. 'Thanks Mummy, I could do with this. Goodness, I slept well - I feel as if I've slept for a hundred years!'

Her parents briefly glanced briefly at each other, her mother raising an eyebrow. 'You're our very own Sleeping Beauty!'

She looked to her Teddy Bear lying forlornly on the carpeted floor. 'Poor Lucifer, got thrown out of bed again whilst I slept - no wonder he looks so tattered and torn!'

Her father smiled at her affectionately. 'Well, I definitely believe it's true what they say about having your beauty sleep - you're certainly looking as good as new!'

She grinned at her father affectionately. 'No wonder Mummy fell in love with you, with all your charming words.'

'Well it didn't have anything to do with his cooking,' added her mother with a wry smile as he's not even capable of boiling an egg!'

Her father looked at his wife indignantly. 'What an insult! I will have you know, I can poach an egg to perfection!' He glanced at his watch. 'Well, time is pressing on, I must go back to the Lab and let Uncle Ian know our latest project is coming along very well - I know he will be delighted.'

'And what project is that?' the young woman asked.

'Oh, just a little something we've been working on for the past four years or so. A lot of hard work was involved, and it was touch and go as to whether we would get this one off the ground - but it looks like we've achieved the desired results.'

She gave a smile. 'That's wonderful - I'm so proud of you and Uncle Ian. You're both so very clever. I know that Sarah would have been very proud.'

Her mother stroked her long fair hair affectionately. 'I'm sure you're absolutely right. But I would take care about discussing Sarah too much in front of Uncle Ian as he does tend to get upset about death since his sister passed.'

She nodded in sympathy. 'Of course, and I guess after Auntie Sylvia dying just a few weeks ago, his grief is still very raw - she was such a lovely person. But I promise I won't mention her, unless of course, Uncle Ian does first.'

Her parents glanced briefly at each other, and gave a smile of approval. 'Good girl', said her father. 'I must be getting on - we'll leave you to change and perhaps you could give your mother a hand with breakfast. We thought with the success of our latest project, we'd celebrate by having a Full English - even if we are living in Scotland.'

The young woman smiled brightly. 'That sounds super. I look forward to doing that, because I feel as if I haven't cooked in ages - I'm sure Hugo will take great pleasure in helping to wait on us, after I've done the cooking!'

Her mother followed her husband out of the door, giving her daughter a cheerful wave. 'I'm sure Hugo will be delighted! I'll see you when you've got dressed. I've got to say you're looking well my darling - I know before you weren't feeling your best, but it's good to have you back.'

As her daughter climbed out of bed, Clarissa returned briefly to the room and gave her a hug. 'You know, it's lovely to have you around, but you know Daddy and I are not getting any younger, and won't be around forever. But Uncle Ian also loves you very much and will always be here for you.'

Her daughter returned the hug. 'I know Mummy and that's very good to know.'

After her parents left the bedroom, she looked out of her bedroom window. Not too far in the distance, was a remote beach, and could see a small fishing boat rocking on the choppy sea. The landscape here was quite barren, with barely a tree in sight, but Mummy loved her garden and was full of bushes and pots of brightly coloured flowers and plants.

Below, she could see Rupert lying down on the patio, taking a snooze. Yes, perhaps the views ahead were rather barren, but here, she was happy in her very own small oasis of tranquillity, with all the people she loved and cared for. She had everything she needed – they knew what was best for her, and life was good.

Printed in Great Britain
by Amazon